The

Hopeful
Romantic

By Susan Colleen Browne

The Village of Ballydara Series

It Only Takes Once
Mother Love
The Hopeful Romantic
The Secret Well, short story ebook
A Christmas Visitor, short story ebook

The Hopeful Romantic

A Village of Ballydara Novel, Book 3

SUSAN COLLEEN BROWNE

WHITETHORN PRESS

The Hopeful Romantic

Print ISBN: 978-0-9967408-0-7
Ebook ISBN: 978-0-9816077-9-5

Library of Congress Control Number: 2015952487

Published by Whitethorn Press

www.susancolleenbrowne.com
www.littlefarminthefoothills.blogspot.com

Cover Design: E-book Formatting Fairies
Interior Design: Author E.M.S.

Published in the United States of America.

For John

A little help with the Irish...

Ailish—pronounced "Ay-lish"

Craic—sounds like "crack," which generally means fun, a good time. *Craic* and crack often used interchangeably.

Do—party or event

Oul'—colloquialism for "old," like ol' or ole

Slainté—an Irish toast, pronounced "slan-cha"

Spit image—spitting image

County Galway, Ireland

Every fix I've gotten myself into, every eejit thing I've ever done, is because of my fatal flaw—I'm a hopeless romantic. And just look where it's taken me.

I gazed at the snowy pasture from the kitchen window, huddled in Stephen's old work coat, the one item of his I'd taken with me when I'd left Dublin three days ago. Okay, there was the ring too—the new gem-studded wedding band Stephen had surprised me with last month. He'd given it to me over the holiday we'd spent with our friend Will, when everything had changed. Well, more like...imploded. But I couldn't quite go there.

Not today. Not on Christmas Eve.

I rubbed my bare ring finger with my thumb. Why I thought of the ring as Stephen's...I'd never felt such a flashy piece of jewelry belonged to me, even though he'd had *Kerry, Forever,* engraved on the inside—such a sentimental gesture for such a prosaic guy. Out of respect, I'd kept wearing the ring, even after he left. But I'd not worn it since arriving here at the farm. I'd put the ring into a saucer next to the kitchen sink and there it had stayed. I would try not to look at it, but invariably, my eyes would be drawn to the flash of sparkle against the countertop. Whether my ring was mocking me or guilt-tripping me, I wasn't sure.

You may ask, why wear a posh wedding band anyway, after your husband says "we need a break?" *Exactly.* But the bigger question was, what had possessed me to come to the farm at all? On the spur of the moment, I'd decided that staying here for a few days would be like a...well, a mini-retreat. On my own, without distractions, I'd find the answers to all my problems.

1

Instead, I'd done a rash, madzer thing and gotten myself completely stranded. Which is where my fatal flaw comes in.

So I've really done it this time. As the rich, buttery sweetness of the shortbread I'd baked still lingered in the kitchen, I stared bleakly at the mounds of sparkling white surrounding the farmhouse. You'd think I would've been grateful for a white Christmas, such a rare thing in Ireland, but I gave the snow a baleful look. I'd so hoped to hash things out with Stephen on his short Christmas holiday in Dublin. Find a way to get past our troubles...

Well. That *was* optimistic. Now, stuck on the other side of Ireland after it had snowed for two days straight, I was completely isolated. And with no working phone, I'd no way to talk to him at all, even to wish him—and our son Jamie—a Happy Christmas.

I turned toward the front room, my eye caught by the small, bedraggled Christmas tree sitting in the corner. I'd cut it down myself, in the fir grove next to the pasture. I'd tried to make the place festive, but the tree seemed a sad little article, weighed down with fairy lights and cheap glass bulbs. Just hours ago, thinking positive, I'd made the shortbread, hoping for a sudden thaw. Then I could head back to Dublin, see Stephen, Jamie, Mam and all my family. A vain hope, as it turned out—because the snow was just as deep as it had been the last time I looked.

I suddenly strode to the back door, pulled on my wellies and flung the door open. Stepping into the snow, I was desperate to think of something else besides all the wrong turns I'd taken, or how I would be utterly, completely alone for the holiday. After all the solitude since I'd arrived at the farm, you'd think spending another day or two on my own would be no bother. Only I was still reeling after what I'd found in the fir grove two days before. And so here it was, nearly Christmas, and I was in shreds. Along with my marriage.

And I'd no one to blame but myself...

Dublin

1

Two Months Before

You'd think I would've been ready for Jamie's question. Or at least wondered why he hadn't asked it sooner.

"Jamie?" I called as the front door closed with a *thunk*. I certainly didn't expect Stephen this early. "You had a good time at Con's?"

Hearing my son's subdued "Yeah," I fastened my flowered skirt. Tempted to kick the tailored gray trousers I'd just removed into the closet, I tossed them over a hanger instead. *You are not your job*, I repeated my usual after-work mantra, and headed downstairs. I found Jamie in his usual spot in the kitchen, standing in front of the opened fridge. "And the pair of you finished your schoolwork?" I aimed a kiss at his cheek.

"I did." Jamie didn't duck away from me like he'd been doing the last few months. Which should have been my first clue that something was up. (I'd yet to see him dodge his dad's kisses, a fact that secretly drove me a bit mad.)

Conversations with Jamie felt a bit like pulling teeth these days, so I resisted quizzing him about how his friend was, details about what they'd done after school or any other tidbits he wouldn't want to share anyway. "You'll have a quick bite before we head over to Granny and Granddad's house?"

As he nodded, I gave him a covert look. My mam always said my son was the spit image of me, with my dark eyes, the dimple in my right cheek, and wavy brown hair. Although when I was small, my great-aunt Rose claimed my hair wasn't brown at all, but the color of blackberry honey—*vastly* better, I'd thought, than plain brown. Jamie's hair hadn't changed, but the rest of him had, so quickly that every time I saw him I'd have to stop for a second and think, *right, this is Jamie*. Cheekbones and a squarish chin were emerging from his boyish features, his eyebrows had thickened, and he'd started wearing glasses this past summer.

Tonight he looked even less like the child I'd raised. His face seemed pinched, the new spots on his face more prominent than usual. Maybe he'd gotten over-hungry, growing as fast as he was. Though how that could be I don't know, since he spent most of this free time eating.

"Will Dad be at Granny's?" Jamie asked, still staring into the fridge. Bulky as a Mini, the polished steel appliance was far too large for the three of us (and the way things were going, our family was likely to stay that size). Jamie was studying the sparse contents with the same intensity he applied to his maths equations.

"He's promised to stop by," I said. That wasn't *quite* true. Stephen had texted me as soon as I arrived at work this morning.

CFO flying in for big meeting 2nite, sorry can't make it to your mam's.

He used to leave me notes on the kitchen table.

In the early years of our marriage: *Last night was...! Love, Stephen.*

After Jamie had learned to read, he'd brought one of the notes to Stephen while we were fixing tea. "What happened last night, Daddy?"

Stephen had met my eyes, his crinkling in a smile. After that, the notes were more...sedate: *Did you sleep well? I'll pick up milk on the way home. Love, Stephen.*

Having taken a stand against texting—call me old-fashioned—I rang Stephen at work for the first time in weeks. I got his voice mail. "You can get away for an hour, can't you? It's our first family do in a long time. And Jamie hasn't seen you in three days." I restrained myself from saying, *Besides, I've had*

it up to here *with the way you've become the invisible man.*
Ringing off, I didn't want to think how things you can't see are
still entirely...well, *real.* A few minutes later, another text
popped up.

OK, will try—but can't stay long.

Mam had invited us to call round this evening, though it
wouldn't be for one of her table-groaning dinners, the ones she'd
once put on for the whole family at least once a week. "I'm just
not into cooking these days," she'd said when she rang
yesterday, sounding apologetic. "Of course we'll have a dessert,
even if it's from the shop."

Into cooking? Was this Mam's latest attempt to sound hip?
She must mean *up for.* "We don't love you for your puddings," I
teased her, "though they do help." She laughed gaily, sounding
like her old self again. "So...what's up?" I was careful to sound
casual. "Did the prodigal ring you and Dad and say he's coming
home for Christmas?"

"Liam?" Mam chuckled again. "When has your brother ever
made his plans two months before the holiday?"

"We can always hope," I said. "Shall we start thinking about
Christmas anyway? You always say it's never too soon to get
organized."

Mam *adored* Christmas. In the past, she'd always started her
marathon Christmas baking by All Saint's Day, and had the
house decorated before the first Sunday of Advent. Besides,
focusing on the future would be good for her. And for me. "It's a
surprise," she said, sounding mysterious. She ended the call
before I could say, *So what's going on then?*

Now, seeing Jamie still staring into the open fridge, I
wondered if I should ask him the same question. Instead I said,
"Surely you've memorized everything in there by now?" I'd
meant to tease him but it came out a bit sharpish.

"Almost," said Jamie.

You're not being sarcastic, young man? I nearly did snap. I
stopped myself just in time. Because the last time Jamie had
gazed interminably into the opened fridge, Stephen had only
said, *Your mam and I might want a go at the fridge ourselves,*

don't you think? Jamie had closed the door without comment. I'd looked at Stephen, wondering, how do you do that? And why can't I? But maybe I should stop overthinking this...

"What's the other father called?" Jamie said abruptly.

"The other father?" I echoed, puzzled. An odd question, from a boy who'd never mentioned church or going to Mass except to complain every Sunday morning, "Why do I have to go? Con doesn't have to."

Stephen never said, "Because I'm your dad and I say so!" Or, "You don't want to grow up into a heathen like your friend, do you?" He'd always say mildly, "It won't hurt you to practice being on your knees, before life brings you to them."

Actually, now that I thought of it, he hadn't said that for a while. These days he said, "Because I'd like you to come with us." While I admired Stephen's instinct for the best way to handle Jamie's on-the-cusp-of-teen rebellion, I wish I could do it as effortlessly as he did.

"Mam?" Jamie prompted, an edge in his voice. He finally closed the fridge.

"You mean...the new assistant priest at the parish?" I thought quickly. He's called Father McQua—"

"Not him." Jamie turned around. "The other dad—the dad who made me."

The shock was like a clout on the head. I clutched the edge of the granite countertop for support. "Why..." I began, my mouth so stiff I had trouble forming the words. "Why do you ask?"

"I just want to know," Jamie said, still not meeting my eyes. "I'm old enough. And Con thinks I've a..." His voice cracked.

I could almost see the thought bubble hovering over his head: *I've a right.*

"James McCormack, how could you—" *How could you mention your biological father to your friend before you'd talked to me?* Everything in me wanted to shut this down. Like *immediately.* Still, I knew I'd have to tell Jamie that naturally he'd a right to know the man's name, and more. When he was four years of age, Stephen and I had told Jamie about how he had another daddy. He hadn't seemed that interested. "I guess that other daddy is invisible," he'd only said. I'd breathed a sigh of relief. *It's grand then.*

But suddenly it wasn't. I gazed at Jamie's face, tears behind my eyes. *What'll your dad think, that you asked after this man? And do you realize how hurtful this could be for you? For all I know "your other father" wouldn't care two pins that you exist.*

"Mam," Jamie prompted again. His brown eyes finally met mine, two bright spots of color on his cheeks. "Is his name a secret or something?"

I blinked hard. In a way, it *was* a secret. Stephen didn't know the man's name. He'd never asked. I forced myself to speak normally. "He's called Mike," I said, my face burning. "Mike McElligott." *Stephen will need to know that Jamie asked after his father. Only how will I tell him?*

"Okay," Jamie said.

"Do you...want to write down the name?" I asked. Talking seemed to ease the shock-induced ache at my temple. "So you'll remember it?"

"I'll remember," he said simply. In one of his lightning fast subject changes he added, "We've ham and four kinds of cheese in the fridge—I'm going to make a sandwich. You'll have one too?"

"That's it?" I rubbed my forehead. "Aren't you going to ask me about him?"

"Um...no."

Oh God, he was doing his no-drama Stephen thing. "Why not?"

"I'm after making sandwiches," he said patiently.

"Jamie..." *Never mind,* I wanted to babble, *I'll tell you what I know, he's Irish, he used to work in London, but when I met him he was temping in Dublin, and I don't know his family, or where he lives now...* "A sandwich would be great," I said instead, though I was sure I couldn't eat a thing.

Funny, you'd think talking about his missing father would've affected Jamie's appetite, but these days, nothing did. Not like when he was a baby—he'd had a delicate stomach, and for the first months of his life, he'd the colic something terrible. I watched him assemble the two sandwiches with his dad's precision—mustard spread all the way to the bread crust, ham and evenly sliced cheese placed carefully on the bread, and cutting the sandwich on the diagonal, no ragged edges. All that practice, I suppose. Since Stephen got his promotion earlier this year, Jamie and I had sandwiches for our tea several times a week, since most nights Stephen wasn't home until ten or even later.

Suddenly I remembered the odd looks he'd been giving me lately after Jamie had turned in. Like he wanted to ask me something. My stomach suddenly clenched. Had Jamie already mentioned his father to Stephen, before tonight?

And Stephen had been keeping it from me?

Sitting across from Jamie, I forced myself to take a bite of the sandwich he'd made. As I tried to sort out how to handle this Mike thing, Jamie announced, "Con and I were on the 'net today reading about string theory—you know about dimensions, don't you, that there's four of them?"

"Four?" I asked blankly. I gave Jamie another furtive look, trying to see traces of Mike in my son's face, but to be truthful, I couldn't quite remember what the man looked like.

"You have to have heard of 3-D," said Jamie, taking another big bite. "Three-dimensional?"

"Oh—like in some films?" I asked, like I was really into it. Having Jamie initiate a conversation was a right treat. "When you wear the 3-D glasses, right?"

"Yeah. Where you see not just height and width, but depth too," Jamie said around a mouthful of sandwich. "Well, the fourth dimension is time."

"Time," I echoed, and was silent for a moment. "There's a mystery."

Well, it was—with all the years that had passed, I still couldn't forget how naïve I'd been at nineteen—a naiveté that even now, made me flush with mortification. Handsome and flirty, Mike was one of those mistakes I suppose every girl's entitled to, but at the time, I felt like the heroine of a star-crossed couple in a novel. When he came along, I was still living at home—one of those late bloomers, too shy to talk much to blokes. And having a terminal addiction to love stories, I'd always found reading about hunks much less threatening than dealing with them in person.

"A mystery—that's what I think!" Jamie set down his sandwich. "Maybe we've got it all wrong, that there's no such thing as time after all, there's no past and present, because they're the same thing! Like, when you have déjà vu, it's the past and present happening like...like spontaneously!"

"Never!" I wished Stephen was here. We would've exchanged a smile, shaking our heads over the way Jamie loved to natter on about his theories. Or we *would* have done, up until a few months ago. As Jamie burbled on about string theory, and additional dimensions, I lost the whole thread, my mind still on Mike.

When he kept asking me out, I was a bit of a sitting duck, but the relationship didn't last long. Nothing new for a girl's first relationship to end badly, but I'd been so humiliated to discover I'd fallen in love, and Mike had only wanted to fall into bed. The problem was, I'd gone all swoony and romantic over him, and wasn't as careful about birth control as I should have been.

Had I unconsciously wanted a way to get Mike to commit? Since I just *knew* we were meant for each other, if a baby turned up we'd manage somehow? I never got a chance to find out— he'd split with me just before I'd found out I was pregnant. "It's been fun but you're getting too serious," he'd said. A week later, in a fit of hormones run amok, I'd typed out a furious, tearful email to him:

> You know what, you gobshite, you've got me up the pole, that's what. But it won't be any bother for you, because the thought of asking you for money or if you want visitation rights makes me as nauseated as the smell of cooked cabbage.

Of *course* I hadn't sent the email, but writing it did make me feel better. For about three minutes.

"Mam, listen!" Jamie was leaning forward eagerly. "What if time is actually folded into the space dimensions we haven't sorted out yet? Because string theory says there could be lots more of them—like…six or even seven!"

Where had my son gotten the capacity for all this deep thinking? Not from his biological father, that's for sure, who'd gone straight back to London. "Amazing," I said. "But I think we'd better be on our way to Templeogue, to enter the Granny and Granddad dimension."

"You're going to finish that?" Jamie asked, pointing at my plate.

I looked at the sandwich I'd hardly touched. "Let's wrap it up—you can take it with us."

As Jamie neatly folded plastic wrap round the sandwich, all I could think was, *he's so like Stephen.* It was yet another mystery how I'd sort out this father issue without Jamie getting hurt, or causing ripples in my placid marriage—well, *mostly* placid. Since I wanted to keep it that way… "Em…Jamie," I ventured, "Do I understand you've not discussed this 'other father' business to your dad?"

He shook his head.

"Can we keep this just between ourselves, then? For now?"

Jamie's brows drew together. "Not tell Dad? But he…he'd be sa…I mean, disappointed if I kept something from him—"

"I know, I know," I broke in. "But I need a bit of a think before I talk to him about it. At least a day or two. Besides, even though we'll see him at Granny's, he'll be working late tonight. So…all right?"

He waited a beat, then shrugged. "I guess."

Rising from the table, I had to bite back an emphatic, *Promise me!* It would hardly do, though, to make a big deal out of not telling Stephen immediately.

Moments later, on the way out the door, I passed the black messenger bag leaning against the foot of the stairs, next to Jamie's schoolbag. "You remembered to bring my laptop home."

"I only left it at Con's the one time." Jamie's reproving tone sounded just like Stephen's. Sometimes it was like having two dads in the house. And with this Mike complication, unless I handled it right, there'd be a third lurking about. At least I'd see Mam soon—I'd pull her aside, tell her what happened. She'd know the right thing to do.

Not that I always *did* the right thing. But still.

2

Sitting in Mam's homey kitchen, I bounced my sister's baby Ailish in the crook of my arm, feeling more peaceful than I had in weeks. "The string theory people think there could be like, *eleven* dimensions," Jamie was saying. Dad and I exchanged a rueful look as my son crammed another crisp into his mouth. "Wrapped one inside the other like a ball of string…"

A nostalgic glow filled me. I'd spent most of my childhood in this room—so like the old-fashioned kitchen in the little flat Stephen, Jamie and I had left last summer, and so different from the bright shiny one where we lived now.

I gave the bronze-colored cooker a fond look—brand-new when I was little, but after thirty odd years, it was somewhere between vintage and junk. Standing beside Mam, I'd learned to make colcannon and soda bread and rhubarb cake and a hundred more of Aunt Rose's recipes. Mam and Dad still had the beige linoleum patterned with blue fleur-de-lis, on which I'd once spilled a bowl of cake batter. Horror-stricken, I'd stared at the mess and started to cry. Mam had only laughed. "Nothing will hurt this old floor," she'd said gaily, then fetched a cloth and helped me clean it up. "Didn't Aunt Rose always say old-fashioned things are best?"

I pressed my cheek against Ailish's downy head. At this same kitchen table, eating my morning egg or my after-school toast and tea as Mam bustled about, I'd buried my nose in the books my great-Aunt Rose had brought back from America.

Then I'd tell Mam about the good parts.

"Meeting a new book boyfriend?" She'd teased me gently the day I opened *Mrs. Mike*. "Who's your favorite now?"

"I haven't decided." I tried not to blush. I mean, I'd so many fellows to choose from! I'd gotten an instant fancy for dashing Sergeant Mike Flannigan from the novel I'd just started. Rhett Butler from *Gone with the Wind* was lovely too, even if he was a proper rascal. I tried the Brontë novels, but Healthcliff and Rochester were just too *tormented*. "You should read *Sense and Sensibility*," Mam suggested.

After I did, I told her, "It wasn't very romantic, if you ask me. I think Willoughby should have ended up with Marianne."

In the end, it was *Little Women* that really captured my imagination. Mostly because of Jo March's soulmate—Laurie, he of the black curls and dancing eyes, had been my total dream guy. Still, there'd been one sticky point: how could he actually marry her sister? (Her *sister*, I ask you!) I'd said to Mam, "Why would Jo throw Laurie over when he's so mad for her?"

She hadn't answered for a moment. "Maybe she thought he was too moody and..." she hesitated a moment. "Passionate."

Hearing Mam say "passionate," I did blush then. "Why wouldn't she go for that?"

"Could be," Mam said, "she wanted a...steadier fellow."

"Like Professor Bhaer?" I said, pulling a face. He wasn't romantic at *all*—more like somebody's dad.

"Jo probably knew he'd be a better husband than Laurie," Mam said. "Someone she could count on, through thick and thin." I'd only rolled my eyes.

I watched Mam now, reaching up for the dessert plates, Dad at her side. After her surgery for early-stage breast cancer last June, she'd been pale and lacked her usual energy all summer. Finally she seemed to be bouncing back. Her brown eyes held their former sparkle, her salt and pepper bob was freshly curled, and she'd regained a lot of her old stamina.

Her cheeks went pink when my dad smoothed his hand across her back. He seemed in good form as well—his hazel eyes warm behind his glasses, and he'd lost that haggard look he'd worn for months. Firmly taking the plates from her hands, he set them on the table, and I saw them exchange a look. As in, a *look*.

"Didn't you say there would be pudding, Granny?" Jamie asked.

"Oh!" She glanced over her shoulder. "Your aunt Suz should be back any minute." Mam still seemed a bit flustered. "With the pie."

I pretended not to notice, thumbing the plain gold band on my left hand. I couldn't remember when Stephen and I had last exchanged any significant glances—which made me conclude I'd ended up with someone a lot like Jo March's Professor. "Good job Suz went to the shop," I said quickly. "So I could have little Ailish all to myself." I pressed a kiss to the baby's soft cheek, and for a moment I was overcome with emotion. To hide it, I said, "You don't mind if Auntie Kerry's all over you?"

Ailish squealed and flapped her hands.

"Not a bit, you say?" I nuzzled her again. "What a relief! Because Jamie won't sit on my lap anymore."

"Aw, Mam," Jamie said predictably, hunching his shoulders as if to ward off a hug from me. Although that would be a trick with my arms full of a squirmy six-month old.

I glanced at the wall behind Jamie, where Mam had hung a snap she'd had enlarged. It was of Jamie, Stephen and myself before Stephen had asked me to marry him. I was holding Jamie, who'd been about Ailish's age, laughing up at Stephen. His usually calm expression looked a bit...stunned. I never could remember what had surprised him.

There was a rattle at the front door. "Must be Suz, back with our sweet," Dad began.

Jamie cocked one ear toward the sound. "No, it's Dad!" He raced from the room.

Moments later, Jamie was back, Stephen just behind him. "Hallo, Tom, Anne." I aimed a grateful smile at him for showing up, but his eyes had already dropped to the baby. His face went still for a moment. "And look who's here!" he said, his tone hearty. Too hearty. "Ailish!"

"You made it after all." I shouldn't have doubted him—Stephen's forte was doing what was expected. Though he rather dropped the ball by not kissing me hello. (If only for my family's benefit, even if we no longer bothered with it at home.) *And what's stopping you from going over and kissing him yourself?* I thought, but stayed where I was.

Jamie's eyes were on Stephen, a crease between his brows. "You'll have some crisps, Dad?"

Stephen ruffled his hair. "I'll be eating at the meeting."

Mam gave Stephen a searching look too, reaching for his hand. "Sit down, love. We haven't seen much of you lately."

Stephen kissed her cheek and took a seat. "It's this job—the hours are mad."

"You're not working too hard?" Mam asked him. "Kerry's told us you've been putting in some terribly long days, especially with all the traveling." Since Stephen had taken the promotion, he'd become a proper globetrotter—off to London, San Francisco, or Toronto every other fortnight.

"I understand you've a meeting with some bigwigs tonight too," Dad put in.

"That's right," said Stephen. "It'll be another late night." He actually sounded rather...cheerful about it. Generally, he wasn't at all keen on wining and dining the clients. "Luckily, the work's interesting," he went on. "The days just fly by."

I often envied Stephen's passion for his work, in IT marketing. My job bored me silly—clerical work at the same engineering firm where I'd met Mike. I could do it with my eyes closed. And sometimes I did.

"Fair play to you, Stephen," Mam was saying. "But you'll want to take time off here and there—don't let your work make you old before your time."

Funny, that Mam was worried about him working too hard— his own mother felt he couldn't work hard enough. I glanced at the photo of the three of us again. So much for the clichés about the worn-out workaholic. Stephen had changed very little from the twenty-something young man I saw just a few feet away. The same close-cropped, mouse-colored hair, the same unremarkable features and earnest, long-lashed grey eyes.

Those eyes rested with real affection on Mam. Stephen's fondness for my mother far exceeded mine for his. Which wasn't entirely my fault—Mary McCormack's heart was as closed as her purse strings, except where Stephen was concerned. So naturally, no girl would be good enough for her only child.

Stephen seemed to hesitate, then said, "Things are going...well, Anne?"

Jamie stopped chewing. He, along with all the rest of us, knew what Stephen was talking about.

"We've actually some news." Mam glanced at my dad.

"Put down your crisp, son," Stephen said quietly. Jamie complied, not even sneaking in another fast bite to sustain him until he could get back to eating.

"We already told Suz and Liam," Mam said. Dad rested his hand on her shoulder. "We were at Dr. O'Leary's today, and she said all the tests came back looking good."

"'Panels,' the doctor called them," said Dad. He was a great one for the proper terminology. "They were clean as a whistle!"

"That's fabulous, Mam!" Tears sprang to my eyes. I rested my cheek against Ailish head, sniffing hard. As soon as I had control of myself, I reached across the table for Mam's hand with my free one and squeezed it. "It's like an early Christmas present—the loveliest one ever!"

Mam laughed as the front door banged. "The doctor actually seemed perplexed that things looked so good—"

My sister breezed in, brandishing a large box. "Sorry, long line at the shop. Here you go." Suz set the pie box on the table. "Hey, Ker, still going for that country vibe, I see."

Shifting Ailish, I laughed, looking downy at my swishy skirt and the denim jacket covering my camisole. My outfits were a standing joke between my sister and me. "Okay, so I dress like a county-and-western singer." I stretched out my feet, clad in ballet flats. "All I need is a pair of cowboy boots."

"That's it," Suz said, and held out her hands. "Where's Mammy's little love?"

I curled my hand round Ailish's tummy. "Aw, do I have to give her back?"

"Sorry," said Suz comfortably. "If you're so keen on little ones, go have another one of your own."

I winced. *Must you say that every time I hold your baby?* Reluctantly lifting Ailish up to her, I met Stephen's eyes. He was the first to look away.

"We were just telling Kerry and Stephen how surprised the doctor was with the test results, even if the cancer was such a small one," said my dad, picking up the story as Suz sat down, Ailish on her lap. "Though I'd say she looked a bit disappointed—"

"—That everything cleared up without the chemo," Mam broke in, with a satisfied air. "Sometimes the doctors don't know everything."

"That's grand," Stephen and Jamie said at the same time. They looked at each other and laughed. Jamie added hopefully, "So...the pie?"

"In a minute, love," I said. *Why doesn't Jamie laugh like that with me?* Then to Mam, "Whether Liam makes it home or not, we'll want to make the holidays extra special this year, don't you think?"

"Extra special?" said Suz, giggling. She tickled Ailish's cheek. "When are your Granny Anne's Christmases not over-the-top?" The baby grabbed a lock of Suz's light brown hair. "No, no, that's Mammy's," said Suz, gently extricating it. "You'll have some hair of your own someday, I promise."

Mam watched them fondly, looking up when Dad squeezed her shoulder. "Girls, speaking of the holidays...that's just what I want to talk to you about."

"Hang on, Mam," Suz said as the baby pushed her head against her mammy's breasts. "I think Ailish wants a snack." She shifted the baby into the crook of her elbow.

"There's our signal, lads," Stephen said easily. "Tom, Jamie—let's find something on telly."

"Huh?" said Jamie. Then seeing his Aunt Suz undoing her top shirt button, he blushed scarlet. Leaving the remains of his sandwich, he scurried from the kitchen, Stephen and Dad not far behind.

"Stephen's like, the only guy I know who doesn't pull a freaker about breastfeeding," Suz remarked, unfastening her nursing bra.

"Nursing is actually the reason he and our Kerry started going out," Mam said. "Isn't that right?"

"More like a nursing…mishap," I clarified.

"Whatever you call it, Stephen was a proper white knight," said Mam.

"Sounds sooo romantic, Kerry," said Suz. Ailish rooted around Suz's breast, then latched on. "Why didn't you ever tell me about it?"

Stephen hasn't a romantic bone in his body. "Well, it was embarrassing."

"Come on." Suz giggled. "Embarrassment goes with the territory of having a baby."

"Starting with childbirth, I suppose." I twisted a lock of my hair in my fingers, thinking back. "I had such a bad case of new-mammy brain fog I couldn't keep a thought in my head, which could be one reason. Or maybe it was because you were fourteen years of age at the time. If Dad had caught me telling you about such earthy stuff, he would've killed me." I exchanged an amused glance with Mam. "He already had his hands full with Liam thinking of girls 24/7."

Mam said, "Your dad used to be a bit…"

"Puritanical?" I put in.

"Conservative," she amended.

"Whatever," said Suz. "I'm not fourteen now, so give over, Kerry," Suz stroked the baby's cheek. "Tell her, Ailish!"

Ailish stopped sucking for a moment, giving me the eye, then resumed feeding. I had to laugh. "I'd just gone back to work, and I hadn't really sorted out a new nursing schedule for Jamie." At the time, I'd been sleep-deprived and hormonal, not quite thinking straight, and I'd worn a pretty summer frock I'd finally been able to fit into. Barely. "There was a big staff meeting one afternoon, and just as the stragglers were going into the conference room, I got this massive ache in my breasts. You know what I'm talking about."

"Do I ever," said Suz. "You poor thing."

I'd looked down to see two wet circles rapidly spreading outward. "I wish I could say just my bra got a bit damp," I said.

"But it was a full-on Niagara Falls. In about three seconds the whole front of my dress was drenched, and I'd no sweater to cover myself up."

"Jaysus, that's awful." Suz grimaced.

I still hadn't been used to the size of my breasts—like aliens, they were, attached to my chest. "My friends Gwen and Sharon were already in the meeting, so there was no one I could grab on the sly and borrow some kind of wrap from."

"So…let me guess," said Suz. "You started to cry."

"Bang on," I said. I'd already been having trouble settling in at work. Everyone had known my story, about Mike getting me pregnant. While the whispers and the pitying glances weren't as bad as when I'd a big pregnant belly, I still felt terribly self-conscious. Plus the night before, Dad had handed me the "flats to let" section of *The Irish Times*, with an apologetic kiss. Maybe he thought I'd be a corrupting influence on Suz and Liam, but he probably couldn't take living with a screaming baby anymore, and what would I do without Mam? This disaster with my dress was the final straw. "So I'm alone in reception, huddled at my desk sobbing, my arms crossed over my chest, and haven't the faintest clue what to do."

"Then the door opens, and in comes a fellow." Mam was grinning. "Of course, it's—"

"Hush, Mam," said Suz. "Let Kerry tell it."

I'd looked up, tears streaming down my face, and saw this vaguely familiar guy. "He says, 'I'm from Power Construction, I've come for the blueprints.' Anyone with two eyes could see the state of me, and I expected him to take off running. Instead, he asked if I was all right."

I'd shaken my head, too at a loss to speak. When he'd said, "Can I help you, then?" I was ready with a teary, "No," but I knew I'd run out of options. Swiping at my nose, I straightened up. As I dropped my arms I recognized the nondescript young man who'd been in the office several times before.

His eyes fell to my breasts. Of course, where else would you look when someone's bosoms—and huge ones at that—are wringing wet? I was suddenly beyond embarrassment with him—easier than you'd think, when you're so *not* attracted to a guy. "Could I borrow your jacket?" I'd asked him, taking a steadying breath. "I need something to...well, so I can get on the bus. I promise I'll return it."

"He was taking off his jacket before the words were out of her mouth," Mam piped up as Suz switched Ailish to the other breast. "And offered her a ride home."

I could still see Stephen quickly shifting his gaze to my face. He didn't look uncomfortable as he handed me his jacket and introduced himself. As I slipped it on, he smiled, a restrained, yet endearing smile, and I was suddenly reminded of the sweet old bachelor farmer who'd lived up the road from Aunt Rose. "Where are you from, anyway?" I asked. "Not Dublin?"

"County Wicklow," he said promptly.

Aunt Rose's county! I smiled up at him and said, "If you can't trust a guy from Wicklow, you can't trust anyone." I'd dashed off a note for Gwen to give to the boss and away I went. Stephen's respectful demeanor was almost a relief after Mike, a guy with the flirt button always on...

Now Mam said, "I was there when Stephen brought her home. He took to Jamie instantly, and the rest is history."

"Actually," I wanted to set the record straight, "it was Jamie who—"

"Great story," Suz said. "It sounds like a romantic comedy film."

"Yeah, but without the comedy," I said. *Or the love at first sight.*

"Ah, go on," said Suz. "Your Stephen is such a lovely man. And I don't care if he overhears." She raised her voice so he could hear her in the front room over the telly. "Stephen, you're lovely!"

"Thanks!" he called back, as Mam giggled. "Kerry's a lucky girl," she shouted. "Did you hear that too, Stephen?"

"We're trying to watch the football!" Jamie complained.

"Oh, stop, the pair of you!" I got up to slice the pie. "You'll give my husband a big head." Actually, that was unlikely—this was Stephen we were talking about. What I could say was that I wasn't as lucky as Mam and Suz seemed to think. I *got* that you had to make your own luck, like everyone said. And since conventional wisdom also said you were meant to work at your marriage, shouldn't I be working harder?

Someone had to.

3

*E*ating a second slice of pie took my mind off Stephen, Mike, and everything else that I just wasn't ready to…deal with. "Mam, you were going to discuss Christmas?" I licked the last bits from my fork. "Have you any new pudding recipes planned?"

Mam's face turned sober. "The thing is, Kerry," she said slowly, "your dad's been thinking we need a holiday. Now that we're done with all this business." She gestured toward her chest.

"A holiday?" I echoed. "But—"

"A cruise, actually," said Mam. "We're leaving in a fortnight—ten days in the Virgin Islands. Then in December, we're going to visit Liam. Lovely, don't you think?"

Utterly shocked, I couldn't speak for a moment.

"Sounds super, Mam," Suz said. "Just think, mai tais in the tropics, and the Texas sunshine in winter! I'm jealous already."

"Mammy, wait." Feeling like a little girl, I reached across the table and grabbed my mother's hand, as if that would keep her from leaving. "You just had surgery—you mustn't overdo—"

"It was five months ago," Mam said. "I feel fine."

"But…but your immune system mightn't be up for taking trips," I argued. "Just think of all those viruses on airplanes!" I was scrambling around for any and all reasons why she shouldn't go. "And cruise ships! They're bloody germ factories! Suz, tell her!"

"I think she should go," said my sister, the traitor. "Just think, Kerry—she can bring back those cowboy boots you're wanting."

"How can you joke? The cancer could come back," I said, near tears again. "Mam, you didn't get proper treat—"

"If you say I didn't get proper treatment one more time," Mam interrupted, "I'll do something desperate! You know as well as I do all those horrible—what did the doctor call them?"

"Protocols," Suz said. "Chemo and radiation. The standard cure."

"Cure, my eye!" Mam snorted. "Filling you with poisonous chemicals till you're the color of mustard, then burning your insides until you're feeling half dead. Or wishing you were. So I don't want to hear another word about it."

Last summer, despite Dad's and my entreaties, Mam had refused any treatment other than surgery for what the oncologist called ductal carcinoma in situ. *I'd like you to reconsider,* the doctor said. *It'll give you the best chance of a full recovery.*

"My mind's made up," Mam had said to us, adamant.

"But Mam." I began to weep. "What if the cancer grows? You know, shows up somewhere else, and then it'll be more surgeries, and then you'll have to—"

"Kerry," Mam said firmly. "You're catastrophizing again. The doctor made it clear the cancer's very small. It's really a 'pre-cancer.'" When Dad left the room, too upset to try persuading her any further, she said to me more gently, "Aunt Rose would have never gone for all those treatments, and neither will I. If I don't…make it, well, it's just meant to be."

How can you be so fatalistic! I wanted to shout. Accepting when it's your time is all very well, but that's for other people. You're only fifty-six years of age! You've decades in front of you!

Instead of throwing a strop, I'd gone home and cried my eyes out. Now, after five anxiety-filled months, I'd no clue how I could bear to have an ocean between my mother and me.

I looked up to see Mam gazing at me with something akin to sympathy. "Kerry, love…" she reached across the table and laced her fingers through mine. "The cruise is all set. And about Liam—we're planning to visit him at Christmas."

"You'll be gone for *Christmas*?" I asked unbelievingly. The holiday had always been *huge* in our family, the decorating, the homemade treats, the big family gatherings—everything I loved about it—with Mam the maestro of her month-long festival. And after I'd been feeling so off-kilter lately, I wanted everything to be just as it always had been. In fact, longing for a break from all Mam's medical stuff, and my...well, Stephen's and my setback, I'd been looking forward to Christmas since the end of summer. What would the holiday be without my mother?

"Your dad wants me to just lounge about. Have a low-key holiday," Mam said. "He told me, 'That way, you won't be tempted to do all those mad weeks of shopping and cooking and the family parties.' And I think he's right."

"I...I..." I simply couldn't take it in. Being without Mam Christmas Day seemed almost as bad as her refusing cancer treatments! My eyes stung. "Be right back," I said, practically leaping from my chair. I raced up the stairs and ducked into my old bedroom.

As a teenager, I would've thrown myself across the bed with high drama, like my favorite fictional heroines, but at this moment I didn't have the energy. I sat carefully on my twin bed and smoothed my shaking hand over my old lilac-colored duvet. Feeling as if I'd shatter any moment, I kicked off my shoes and curled onto my side. I pressed my cheek against the worn coverlet draped over the pillow that Aunt Rose had made for Mam when she was little. Jamie's remark at tea about past and present being entwined came back to me. Sometimes I could swear this little cover still smelled of my aunt's lily-of-the-valley cologne.

I bit my lip hard, to keep myself from sobbing outright, though a few more tears wouldn't hurt this old coverlet. It had soaked up the tears of my childhood, plus the ones I'd shed when Mike left me. And again, when I found out I was pregnant. And...other times.

I dabbed my eyes with the soft cotton, and stared at the bookshelf on the opposite wall without seeing it. Didn't Mam love me enough to stay home and be safe, close to the doctor? But that was my whole problem. I loved people more than they loved me. I mean, think about it: Mike, Jamie…even Ailish.

Of course, I knew I was the apple of my mother's eye, she loved me to pieces. Hadn't she let me wail "I'm such a complete eejit," into her shoulder when I'd gotten a positive pregnancy test? And rubbed my back and helped me breathe when I gave birth? *And* had taken care of Jamie after I went back to work? But clearly, if Mam was determined to go on the cruise and being away for Christmas, she was a prime candidate for the list of "loves me less."

Ah, stop it, I told myself sternly. What are you, eight years of age? Feeling another sob coming, I managed to choke it back as a soft knock sounded on the door.

Mam came in, clutching a handful of tissues. "Darling, I know this Christmas won't be the sort of holiday you've always loved." I shook my head as she sat next to me, handing me the tissues. "I hate disappointing you…but I wish you wouldn't take it so hard." She smoothed her hand on my hair, the way she used to do when I was small.

I sniffed. "Sorry to make such a fuss. I don't know what's the matter with me." Actually I did.

"You've always been sensitive," Mam said carefully.

"I was a right pain, I'm sure." I sat up, blotting my eyes. "Crying over every little thing. And here I am, still doing it."

Mam was silent a moment. "You shouldn't be so hard on yourself, love. Aunt Rose said to care so deeply was a blessing…a gift."

I stared at the chair across the room, where an old doll that Aunt Rose had given me sat upright. "She always saw the good in everything." I blew my nose. "But I have to tell you, Mam, that most of the time being so terribly *emotional* doesn't feel like a gift at all. More like a curse."

She patted my shoulder, in an *ah, what can you do* sort of way, then rose from the bed. "Auntie always had a wise word, didn't she? I don't know what would have become of me without her."

"We'd have both lost out." I sniffed again. After Mam's mother Noreen had died when Mam was a toddler, Noreen's sister Rose had returned from America to look after her sister's motherless child. So Rose had been Mam's mother and my granny in all but name. "Sometimes I can't believe she's gone."

"I feel the same," said Mam from the doorway. "Ready to come downstairs now?"

"In a minute," I said. Mam often treated me like a little girl, yet I couldn't blame her—I often acted like one. All the same, I shouldn't want her to feel any guiltier about Christmas than she already did. I'd always confided in Mam, but I'd never told her how I'd often smelled Rose's cologne in here, even though the cover had been washed dozens of times. Or that when I was troubled I could almost feel her arms round me, her cheek against mine... But Mam might put it down to me being overly sensitive about that *too*.

As she left, my gazed drifted to the bookshelf, filled with the novels that Aunt Rose had passed down to me. When I was small, I'd sat on her lap as she read me *Little House in the Big Woods*. "I want to live in the country when I grow up, just like Laura Ingalls," I must have told her a dozen times.

That first *Little House* story had only been the beginning. Once I learned to read, I'd barreled through the rest of the series, loving every page: Laura helping her dad with the haying. Sneaking her corset off so she could jump on the haystacks. Going on country walks with her sister. And most romantic of all, marrying the handsome neighbor farmer.

After I'd finished Laura's last book, *These Happy Golden Years*, I just *knew* I'd have a farm someday. I could see my future, working all day in the sunshine—not that we had so many sunny days in Ireland, but a girl's entitled to her fantasies—then cooking huge, made-from-scratch dinners for a crew of farmhands in an old-fashioned farmhouse...

Okay, talk about *ridiculous*. The closest I'd gotten to a farm was the fruit and vegetable garden I'd nurtured behind our little flat, thanks to an indulgent landlord. Since we'd moved house, though, I didn't even have that.

I made myself roll off the bed. Slipping into the bathroom, I dashed cold water on my eyes. After I dried my face, I stared into the mirror. *Isn't it time to just...accept what you've got? And quit mooning over what you haven't?*

I'd missed out on so many chances. If Aunt Rose had lived until I'd gotten through school, maybe I'd have had the guts to follow my dreams. Not that I could have taken over her farm, but I could have gotten some sort of nursery or agricultural job. Or at least gone for a horticultural course.

Instead, I'd taken the path of least resistance. Office work. Living in the city.

And doing the sensible thing...

When I returned to the kitchen. Suz had Ailish on her shoulder, perusing some colorful brochures. The cruise, no doubt. As I entered, Mam gathered them up into a neat stack.

"Stephen had to go," Suz volunteered.

"He didn't have time to go up and say goodbye, I guess," Mam said to me, a question in her eyes. She'd probably noticed that Stephen and I hadn't said a word to each other all evening.

"He'd that big meeting tonight, remember?" I certainly couldn't say, *Stephen hasn't the energy to deal with a weeping wife.* "The um...what's it called, CFO came to Dublin, all the way from Canada."

"I was just telling Mam," said Suz, "that if she and Dad are gone at Christmas I can put on the holiday dinner at our house. Anthony's got at least a hundred cousins he wants to invite." Suz's husband's family was old school Irish—ten aunts and uncles who seemed to have eight kids apiece.

"There's tons more room at our place," I said, still hardly able to take in that Mam wouldn't be part of Christmas dinner. "Though I've still no clue what Stephen was thinking, finding us such a massive article."

Days after Mam had gone to the doctor last summer, the owner of our flat had sold the building where we three had lived since Stephen and I married. We'd had to move house in a hurry.

Reeling from my mother's diagnosis, I wasn't up for house-hunting. I'd said to Stephen, "Please, just go find us someplace—I don't care what it looks like or where it is."

He'd taken me at my word. Maybe his latest rise in salary had gone to his head a bit, since he'd brought me to a gleaming new house in Rathfarnham, squished between two houses that looked just like it. As soon as I could tear my eyes from its grandness, I'd stared at Stephen. "I can't live here."

"But you haven't seen the inside," said Stephen. "You'll love it, I promise."

The first promise he'd had to break. Now I said, "The size of the place still embarrasses me."

"I'm sure Stephen did the best he could." Mam frowned at me.

"Your kitchen's like in a magazine," Suz said dreamily. "And your ensuite bathroom is to die for. If Anthony made the sort of money Stephen does, I'd have a house just like it."

"I hope not in our crescent," I said. "All the neighbors coat their lawns with weed killer. You daren't let kids onto the grass. And after it gets dark, there are so many streetlamps the entire neighborhood is lit up like a medium security gaol."

Mam began stacking plates. "Well, you don't have any break-ins, do you?"

"Not so far." Although I wouldn't mind one—a bit of petty crime would give us an excuse to leave. "What I'd really like is a place like Aunt Rose's." I could see her cottage in my mind's eye, the stone walls glowing gold in the sunshine, the climbing roses next to the front stoop, the gnarled apple trees in the back garden. And you could go outside at night and see a sky filled with stars, so many of them it was like staring into eternity. "With a huge garden—oh, and a pasture. Or at least room for some hens."

"Stephen certainly wouldn't have been able to find a house like that in Dublin," Mam said tartly.

She probably thought I wasn't a proper wife—and maybe I wasn't. "Really, Suz," I said, trying to show my mother I wasn't a complete ingrate, "Stephen and I would be happy to play host, have your lot round." Though how I'd cook a big Christmas dinner, I wasn't sure, the way I was out of practice.

"Hmmm," said Suz, shifting Ailish to her shoulder. "I don't know..."

"You girls work it out," Mam said, staring into the middle distance. She was probably already on her cruise ship in her mind, feeling the tropical breeze in her hair. "I'll make sure to do a big Christmas pudding before I leave, though, for all of you. Girls, you'll come round for a baking day, and give me a hand?"

She always included Suz in her invitation, who'd actually just sort of hang about while Mam and I did the real work. Though now that my sister had Ailish, she got a free pass.

"I hate to tell you, Mam," Suz said, patting the baby's back, "that nobody really likes Christmas pudding." Since becoming a mother, Suz had gotten surprisingly candid.

"What are you talking about?" Mam reached for a brochure. "It's Aunt Rose's recipe—we've made it every Christmas, ever since Kerry was small."

"It's a family tradition," I put in.

"We always take a piece to be polite," said Suz, "but then everyone pushes it around their plates until they can sneak it into the bin."

"You're wrong there." Mam set down the glossy paper and smiled reminiscently. "You remember your old friend, Kerry, who came along for some holiday dinners, years ago? What was he called? He couldn't get enough of my pudding."

4

As if, I was still thinking as I pulled my Ford Fiesta into our driveway, a drowsy Jamie sprawled in the back seat. *As if I could ever forget Will.*

Back in Mam's kitchen, I'd gone still, a flush creeping into my cheeks. Glad that Stephen had already left for his meeting, I pretended to study one of Mam's brochures. Instead of blue skies and waves curling on beaches, all I saw was Will sitting across from me at Mam's table, twinkling at me as he'd tried manfully to finish the slab of pudding she'd served him.

"Oooh, I remember him," said Suz. "Who cares what he was called? He was a *ride.*"

"Suz!" Mam admonished. "Your dad will hear you! And Jamie!"

"Well, he was," Suz said, unrepentant. "Those muscly shoulders! I couldn't take my eyes off him." She giggled and poked me in the arm. "But it was obvious that looking at Kerry was what he couldn't get enough of."

I finally mustered up a light laugh. "I thought *I* was the romance addict in this family." I willed my blush to subside. "But back to a baking day, Mam..." As she gave me a penetrating look, I'd jumped up from the table and grabbed a slip of paper and a pen. "Let's make a shopping list, shall we?"

Now I glanced at a dozing Jamie in the rearview mirror. When he rode anywhere with his dad, he'd sit in the front. With me, however, he insisted on riding in the back seat. *What am I, your chauffeur?* I was tempted to ask him. But if I couldn't be a proper wife, at least I could be a proper mother. "We're home, love," I said.

As I let us into the house, Jamie's yawn practically split his face in two. "Up to bed with you," I told him. "I'll come say goodnight as soon as you clean your teeth."

As Jamie went upstairs, I lingered in the entryway. Although we'd lived here nearly half a year, the place refused to grow on me. Or maybe I'd refused to let it, but I still didn't care for the parquet floors, the cheerless, modern furniture that had come with the house, or that there was so much track lighting in the kitchen it could have illuminated the stage at the Dublin Theatre.

When I first walked in last June, I'd stared around the open plan downstairs for a long time. "You know what your mam will say about this house," I said to Stephen at last. "After she has her heart attack."

"That I'm making a show of myself? I don't let it bother me—you know how she is about money." He smiled wryly. "She still doesn't believe we can afford a place like this."

I didn't smile back. "*I* still don't believe we can afford a place like this." The truth was, I knew we could. When I wasn't coping so well with Mam's illness, I'd asked Stephen to take over the household bookkeeping. Given all the years of the careful budgeting we'd done together, I knew he wouldn't have gotten us in over our heads. I said to him, "Did you *have* to sign a year's lease?"

"It was the only way to get the place," Stephen said patiently. "But let's parse out why you don't like it."

Can't you see, the house has no soul? "It's just terribly...ostentatious," I said.

"It's a big step up from the flat," Stephen agreed, "but it'll be perfect with this new position of mine." He showed me around the downstairs. "I expect to be entertaining clients in a few months."

"So why didn't we wait until then to live in such a fancy place?" I walked toward the French doors at the back of the house."

"And move house twice?"

Peering through the doors, I couldn't answer. My throat tight, I stared at the big stone patio covering the width of the house.

There was no room for a row of vegetables, or box of strawberries, much less a proper garden.

I looked back at Stephen. *This is the kind of house you like? Who are you, anyway?*

A week later, I'd learned the entire cul-de-sac had been sprayed with weedkiller—the reason the lawns were as scarily flawless as a putting green. I said to Stephen, "Poisoning the neighborhood is just the limit! I'm choosing our next place myself." *Whether you like it or not.*

I'd expected Stephen's indulgent smile, but he'd only given me a distracted look, then pulled out his laptop.

The story of my life since his promotion, I thought now as I went up the stairs. Trailing my hand up the carved wood bannister, I suddenly saw Will in my mind's eye again. *What would you make of the house?* I wanted to ask him. *You and I always thought alike—would you find it as pretentious as I do?*

I stopped in Jamie's doorway, my favorite room in the house. Despite its general tidiness, I liked the way the poster-covered walls created a riot of color, almost pulsing with planets, nebulas, and other heavenly bodies I couldn't name. Jamie could, though. He was lying on his side, reading a graphic novel. "Just a few more pages, okay?" he said, then looked up. "By the way, Mam—your laptop really wants cleaning."

"Nice try, son, but time to sleep." I came inside. Picking up a stray t-shirt on the foot of the bed, I draped it over the dusty telescope in the corner. "If it makes you feel better, I'll run a cloth over the lid."

"I meant the inside of the computer," he said patiently. "The memory is nearly maxed out."

"Come on," I said. "A bunch of family financial records can't take up that much space."

"It's full of Internet cookies. And you've that old email program too."

"What's wrong with it?" I asked. "It still works."

"Mam." He rolled his eyes. "It's not web-based, so everything's on your hard drive. There must be a million emails you've never deleted."

Emails. I grew warm. I'd forgotten about them. Well, almost. "I didn't do *that* much email."

"Doesn't matter. One of these days, Mam, the laptop'll crash from all that data clogging the works."

"Oh…right," I said slowly. "I suppose I should go through the folders, see if there are a few things I'd want to save." Actually, there was plenty.

Jamie set his book down, pushing his covers aside. "I've a memory stick, we can clean it up and—"

"Tomorrow," I said firmly.

Jamie sighed, and pulled his covers back to his chin. "Can I take your laptop to Con's again? Dad needs his, like, every minute of every day."

I thought quickly. "I might…take the laptop to work myself."

"What for? You've one in your office, why do you—"

"Jamie, I *am* allowed to use my computer when the mood strikes me." I'd actually nailed Stephen's easygoing tone.

It worked. "Okay, okay." Jamie took off his glasses, rectangular frames just like Stephen's, and allowed me to kiss the top of his head. "'Night, Mam."

From the doorway, I glanced back at Jamie. This biological-father shock had me completely off balance. By the time Stephen was home, it would be far too late to talk to him.

Once downstairs, I went through my usual weeknight routine, packing lunches for Jamie and me, and grabbing a sticky note from the jumble drawer to make a shopping list. I stared down at the yellow slip of paper. I could leave a note for Stephen. I could write, *You can wake me up when you get home, if you know what I mean.*

Or even, *Don't forget you're meant to take Jamie to Con's Halloween party this weekend.*

Instead I wrote *apples eggs soup* and slipped the note into my handbag. Setting it near the front door, I crossed the entryway to sit on the bottom step, and looked down at my messenger bag. Stephen would be late—I could take the laptop out right now. Revisit happier days, when Will was part of our lives. I hadn't any photos of him, but I could still see Will as clearly as if he was right in front of me.

"I'm Will Power," he'd said the first time Stephen had brought him round to our flat, when Jamie was a baby. Will's green eyes smiled into mine. "And you might as well know, I don't have any."

"Willpower?" *I'm not sure I have any at the moment myself.* I was so dazzled it took me a moment to gather my wits. "I'll bet you say that to all the girls," I finally managed, smiling back. "And they eat it up like candy." *And I'm no exception.* But then, what woman could resist his cheek, the way he looked like an oversized Christopher Robin with his fair curls and ruddy complexion. There was nothing school-boyish about the rest of him though. And he was just so full of *life*—he'd kept me in stitches all evening with his stories and jokes.

Stephen had been quieter than usual that night. Finally he said, "It's getting late—we've all got work in the morning."

Loath to see the last of Will, I said impulsively, "You'll come to my mam's lunch Sunday next?"

"Only if you'll be there too," said Will, making me giggle again. I pretended not to notice Stephen's frown.

After Will left, I couldn't stop thinking of him, the way he made me feel like a brighter, more exciting version of myself. The feeling hadn't lasted though. In bed that night, when Stephen reached for me, for the first time in a year of marriage I'd turned away…

These days, it wasn't quite clear who was doing the turning.

And now there was the Mike thing. Still sitting on the step, I decided not to open up the laptop. After I'd forgotten to mention my dilemma to Mam, not knowing what I'd say to Stephen was like a cloud over my head. Besides, I'd had plenty of practice pushing away thoughts of Will (full disclosure: except when I was alone). So I set the messenger bag next to my handbag and went back upstairs. The past could wait until tomorrow.

5

Smythe Engineering

MEMO:
Thursday, 9 am, 29 October
To: All staff

A new engineer is scheduled to join us Monday next.
This person comes with the highest qualifications. I ask
everyone on staff to roll out the welcome mat.

Theodore Smythe, CEng

"*Y*ou've timed things just right," I said to my friend Gwen the
next day. Joining the throngs of people in Stephen's Green,
Gwen and I had managed to snag a park bench for our lunch
break to enjoy the rare November sunshine. "Leaving before Mr.
S. gets his knickers in a proper twist."

"He does get into a right tizzy with new hires coming in,
doesn't he?" Gwen wrapped up the remains of her sandwich and
shifted on the hard bench.

I watched her smooth her hand over her tummy. Pregnancy
definitely agreed with her. Her dark hair was shiny, her skin
dewy. Six months on, Gwen was taking her maternity leave
early—likely why she looked so radiant.

"I thought I'd be working here until the end of days," she said
last month, when she announced her departure to me and Sharon,
the other clerical staff. "But with Jonathan's rise in pay, and the
doctor saying he'd like me to take it a bit easier, we thought,
let's seize the day!" Later, she'd whispered to me, "And I've no
plans to come back after the baby."

I never thought I'd be at Smythe Engineering this long myself. It had been my first job, taken as a stopgap. I'd been thinking I was almost ready for a real boyfriend, so a place full of blokes couldn't be all bad. Once I was hired, I decided I'd go for a real job in a year or so, after I got my act together. Whatever that means.

Then Jamie came along, I married Stephen, and we needed my income so he could finish university. At the time, job security seemed more important than fulfilling work. But after fourteen years of wrestling with billing spreadsheets and database management, I was impatient for...well, my *real* career to start. A shame the farm job I'd long dreamed of would always be a fantasy.

"We've been through a lot all these years, haven't we?' Gwen said in a reflective tone.

I lifted my face to the light trickling through the empty tree branches above us. "The redundancies, you mean." Gwen and I had weathered the worst of the recession—when a chunk of the staff was let go, and there was so much work for the rest of us we'd had to eat lunch at our desks. The job market had been

so desperate no one dared leave because nobody we knew was finding employment. "I often wish I'd gotten the ax too," I admitted. At the end of every day, I felt like a prisoner breaking out of gaol.

"I can't believe Stephen would've had *that*!" Gwen said.

"He could hardly blame me for Mr. S.'s decisions," I said. Not that Stephen would actually *blame,* but he would be *concerned.* He would redo our budget, recalculate our savings schedule. His mother would be the one with the anxiety attack.

So I'd told myself for years that as far as earning my crust, this office situation was as good as any. And Stephen and I had lived pretty simply—well, up until he'd leased the new house— so we'd been able to sock away a fair chunk of my paychecks. My problem was, every workday was like that film *Groundhog Day*, where the character relives the same day over and over again. My daily routine involved an overflowing inbox, and data entry tasks backed up like cars in a Dublin traffic jam. Like Gwen's did. But after Friday, she'd be free.

"I feel terribly guilty, leaving you," Gwen said, "since your workload's sure to double. And we both know Mr. S. won't be hiring more clerical staff."

"You're not to worry about that," I told her, my glance caught by a tall man stride along the footpath. The breeze flapped his opened overcoat and ruffled his hair. *Will used to walk like that. Like he owned the world.*

"I do feel better, though," said Gwen, "that now you'll have our cubicle to yourself."

"Think of it!" I looked back at her, grinning. "The luxury of not bumping bums with you every time I turn around. Anyway, what'll you do with yourself until the...baby comes?"

"Oh, I've big plans," said Gwen. "I'll sleep late, and binge-watch *Downton Abbey* and *Call the Midwife* for a few days."

"Might as well do it while you have the time." Wouldn't it be lovely, I thought wistfully, to be at home, free to garden, with a little one in a pushchair parked nearby...

"Then I'll start on what's going to be the nursery—a fresh coat of paint, and new curtains should work wonders."

"Will you do it up in pink?" I couldn't forget Stephen's pained look from last night as I held Ailish. "Even if it's terribly old-fashioned, going with the traditional colors."

"I considered sort of a pinky-apricot." Gwen's ultrasound last month had confirmed she'd have a girl. "Then Jonathan's mother said, 'You can't trust those fancy tests.' You know how Jonathan is—he pretends to agree with her, then all of a sudden he believes it himself. Anyway, since we want more kids," she clasped her hands, resting them on her baby bump, "the room will be greens and yellows."

My gaze went unerringly to Gwen's tummy again. She was a good enough friend not to ask, *So when will you and Stephen go for it, and have a baby yourselves?* Everyone else had. Mam, Suz, even Will.

Stephen and I had actually talked about a baby. For *years*. I'd lost count of the times he'd said, "It's a lonesome life for Jamie, being an only child," longing in his voice. "We'll get to giving him a brother or sister, as soon as we have clear sailing."

There was always some choppy water rocking our little boat,

though. We'd start a baby as soon as he finished university. Or when he wasn't so knackered from work. Or when I wasn't. Or when the Irish economy got out of the pits. By the time we moved into the new house, our talking about babies became more and more rare, like kissing hello, or eating supper together. Or even going to bed at the same time. Then, after our...well, *setback* a couple of months ago, the word *baby* hadn't crossed Stephen's lips. Nor mine...

But I shouldn't want to dampen Gwen's pleasure in her future. "Are you heading straight back to the office?" I asked.

"You know," said Gwen, hefting herself off the bench with difficulty, "I think I'll pop into Mothercare. If I'm late from the shops, what's Mr. Smythe going to do—sack me?"

I made myself laugh. But as I watched her walk away, buttoning her cardigan over her round tummy, emotion clogged my throat.

It's nothing, I told myself. Gwen leaving, Mam's travel plans, and Jamie asking about his other father—it's making me a bit blue. Maybe I deserved a treat. I could go back to the office and turn on the laptop...

As soon as I walked into Reception, though, my workmate Sharon handed me a sheet of paper, a sympathetic look on her face. "Sorry about this, Kerry." She dropped her voice. "You'd think the boss could've just told you to your face."

I felt a jolt of energy. Had all my wishing to be sacked actually manifested itself? Then I started reading.

MEMO:

Thursday, 1 pm, 29 October
To: Kerry McCormack

We are shifting around office spaces to accommodate our staff changes. Please vacate the cubicle you've been sharing with Gwen so that the new engineer can settle in straightaway Monday morning. Veronica will provide technical support setting up a new workspace for you in the file room.

Theodore Smythe, CEng

6

The file room! That night, after Jamie had turned in, I was still gripped with fury. *I give Smythe Engineering fourteen years of my life and what do I get? The file room!*

After Sharon had handed me the memo, I'd barely managed a "Thanks," and clumped down the hall to stare at my new digs. The room was windowless, crammed with beige metal file cabinets and wide gray metal drawers holding topo maps, every bit as depressing as it had been every other time I'd entered. The rickety metal table in the corner would no doubt be my desk. I'd instantly forgotten about getting out my laptop.

Tonight, though, I not only deserved to indulge myself, I *needed* to. And with Stephen away in London, there was no better time. Setting up my laptop up in its usual spot, the nook off the kitchen, I switched on the machine and brought up the old email program. Without hesitating, I clicked on the Inbox. Scrolling back through ten years' worth of emails, I found what I was looking for.

Subject: Stateside

Hi Stephen and Kerry,
  It's been awhile...what, eight months since I saw you, at New Year's. Had some time on my hands so I went out to America to visit my parents. Uncle Casey came too—Stephen, he's never gotten over you deserting all the great opportunities to work your arse off (Kerry, excuse my French) at Power Construction for a little thing like university! When I got here to Minnesota, the family pressured me to stay and what do you know, I gave in. Summers are beastly hot here, and I told everyone, Jaysus,

I can't wait for the weather to cool off. They said just wait, the winters are absolutely brutal!

On the upside, I've lots of family connections here, and my mother is over the moon that the whole family is together—and I don't mind a bit she and my sisters are back to spoiling me rotten! Right now, I'm looking for a job. Not too hard, though—you know me. Cheers, Will.

Reading the email with Stephen all those years ago, I'd closed it quickly, hurt rising in my throat. "I don't understand why Will would leave Ireland." He'd been our close friend for more than a year—how could he just go, without calling round one last time?

"You read it." Stephen didn't seem surprised. "His family wanted him to—"

"He's certainly old enough to tell his parents no when they snap their fingers!"

Stephen gave me a level look. "Kerry, Will's been playing about long enough, don't you think?"

"What do you mean?"

In a voice that sounded a lot like his mother's, Stephen went on about Will leaving his uncle high and dry at the construction firm the last year to play with that rugby club, and that he spent all his free time in the pubs. Trying not to cry, I'd hardly listened. Until he said, "Those rugger guys...well, they get jarred six nights out of seven, with a different girl every night."

"So what?" I snapped as a pang of jealousy hit me. "He's single, why shouldn't he? And I don't get how you can slag him—he was your best mate."

"Sure, he's a great bloke, a great friend." Was that a shadow on Stephen's face? "But he's no saint, whatever you think."

For all his criticizing Will, Stephen had ended up sending back a friendly email.

Now, I clicked on another folder. I found my own reply, inspired by the gazillion romantic novels I'd loved all my life. I'd written the email the night we'd heard from Will. After Stephen had gone to bed.

Dear Will,

I hope you're keeping well—how exciting, that you've relocated to America! It must be fantastic to be with your family after being so long apart.

Speaking of family, you certainly charmed mine from the moment you came to my parents' door, for that first Sunday lunch. I can just hear you saying, "Oh, I'll bet the flowers and O'Mara's I brought had a lot to do with it," but really, everyone was mad about you.

Do you remember how you helped me with the washing up, while everyone else was in a post-lunch stupor in the front room? "Now that you've made yourself indispensable," I told you, "we'll expect you every Sunday."

"Glad to help," you said, so gallantly, but you looked terribly comical, soap suds up to your elbows.

You smiled down at me as you lifted Mam's heavy meat platter out of the water. Suddenly it slipped, but in one smooth move you caught the plate before it fell onto the counter. You said something about my mam not wanting you here if you broke her dishes, but I had to laugh—I wouldn't have cared if you had broken the platter! (Or a dozen dishes besides.) Although the noise probably would have woken up Jamie. And Stephen. And I wanted them to stay asleep, at least a while longer. With that thought, watching you rinse more plates, I couldn't think of anything to say.

"Kerry? You've gone awfully quiet," you said. "What are you thinking?"

I looked up and met your eyes. Stephen's never said "penny for your thoughts" or anything like it. As you know, he's not a talkative sort. In fact, he's told me he likes that I don't mind it—that he isn't a big talker. Sometimes I do mind, though. Especially since the longer we've been married, the more he keeps himself to himself.

But you were such a carefree sort, how could I share my worries about my relationship? I grabbed another plate in the water, and my wedding band scraped against the china. I pulled my hands out of the water and said, "I forgot to take this off for the washing up." Slipping off my ring, I set it in the saucer Mam kept nearby.

You didn't say anything for a moment. Then, "No wonder you forgot—you're the sort of girl who wears her wedding ring all the time."

I felt my face warm. "Doesn't everyone?"

You said something about knowing a lot of girls at the pub who took off their rings as soon as a bloke bought them a drink. Then you told me, "Stephen's one lucky bloke."

I blushed beet-red at that! Curious about you, after Stephen and I got home and tucked up Jamie, I asked him if you had a lot of mates.

"Loads," Stephen said, and went on about you being the life of the party, and that you played rugby with a crew of lads every Saturday.

I couldn't help asking, "Has Will any...girlfriends?"

I remember exactly what Stephen said. "He has— knows—lots of girls, and I suppose they're his friends. But that doesn't make them girlfriends. Why?"

"Well...if he had a girlfriend," I said, "he would've spent Sunday afternoon with her."

"Maybe," said Stephen, but as far as I know, none of his girlfriends are the sort he'd spend his daytime hours with."

All right. So you liked girls. There are worse things! I confess, I was relieved you didn't have a special girl in your life. On the other hand, I didn't want to know how many you had that weren't.

Anyway, good luck with everything...I'll miss you.

Always, Kerry

I'd read over my email, wondering if I should keep the *I miss you* bit. *Well, it's true.* Then I'd moved the email into the Drafts folder.

Of course, I'd never sent it.

Now, I shut off the laptop, my thoughts full of Will, and went upstairs.

In the bedroom, the streetlamps penetrated through the blinds, making it seem like twilight all night long. With all that light in the room, I'd become an expert at looking like I was sleeping when I wasn't.

I ran my hand over the lacquered wood jewelry box I kept on top of my bureau. I hadn't much jewelry—I wasn't a great one for bling. But the box was my favorite place to stash keepsakes. I still had Stephen's little notes, and underneath was a cache of letters my great-uncle Seamus had written to Aunt Rose. Now he'd been *romantic*. He always began the letters, *Dear Anam cara*. Soul friend.

I'd never had a soul friend—a connection with someone so deep you knew that you'd be friends beyond the grave—unless I counted Aunt Rose. But at this moment, Will, and the closeness we'd shared, made me feel like he could have been that kind of friend too. *Do you ever think of me?* I wanted ask Will. *Do you ever wish for a different life?*

Really, I couldn't regret mine—or I shouldn't. Suddenly, I wished Stephen was home, that he'd find me here and wrap his arms round me from behind, like he used to, and press his face into my neck. Then I could stop thinking of my job or Jamie's *other father* question or my silly fancies from the past. And we could have wondered together about what might have been.

7

"I can't believe Mr. Smythe isn't giving you our cubicle," said Gwen as we packed up her desk the next morning. "With your seniority too!"

"The file room is terribly...uninspiring," I said glumly. "Not like in here." The cubicle Gwen and I shared had grown quite comfy over the years. The high walls made the engineers' buzz of conversation and activity more companionable than intrusive. I stared out the window to the Dublin streetscape below. "You've been a darling, to let me have the window spot all this time." As much as I wanted to give out royally over the ignominy of being kicked to the curb, on Gwen's last day I could at least keep my complaining to a minimum.

"Giving up the window was no bother," said Gwen. "You're far more of an outdoor girl than I am." She set a framed photo of her husband in a box then held out the spindly potted philodendron she'd had on her desk. "Maybe a bit of green will cheer up your new—well, new to you—desk."

"A plant will probably die from lack of light," I said. "It'll be happier at your house anyway." With house plants, I'd a complete black thumb, but in the garden, I could coax a half-dead tomato plant back to life in three days. A shame, that reviving a job that was near dying on the vine was a different story. Just like a marriage...

"I should write up my own memo," I said suddenly, keeping my voice down. "Before I pack up my desk! Let the boss know shifting a valued employee around like a sack of potatoes isn't on."

"Wow, you'd do that?" Gwen looked at me admiringly. We

staff mostly regarded Mr. Smythe with an unpleasant sort of awe, like how you'd treat a very distant father figure—although his usual chilly, authoritarian demeanor hardly encouraged communication.

"Yes, I will!" I sat in front of my computer and opened a document. "Register an official protest to this…insult."

"'Insult's a bit strong," advised Gwen.

"Demotion then." I typed:

MEMO:

Friday, 11:10 am, 30 October.
To: Mr. Theodore Smythe, CEng

My fingers poised on the keyboard, I thought, *forget this!* I jumped up from the chair so fast it spun sideways. "Memos are for cowards. I'm going to man up—woman up—and talk to him! He's in his office this morning, isn't he?"

"Still reading the morning paper," Gwen said nervously. "You sure you want to do this now? He'll be in a better mood after lunch."

"Positive," I said grandly. "It's time I created my own…well, destiny—face the lion in his den." Actually, I needed to get the confrontation over with before I lost my nerve.

"You'll have your office space settled before our girls' lunch," Gwen said encouragingly.

"Unless the boss gobbles me up first," I muttered. Still, I strode purposefully out of the cubicle.

"You girls are great for picking up my share of the fare," said Sharon, as we piled out of the taxi on Anglesea Street in Temple Bar. "I'm terribly skint these days."

"I wouldn't have minded walking," I said, enjoying the cool air against my face. My cheeks still felt warm after the facedown with the boss.

"I'd have been happy to walk too," said Gwen, wobbling a bit as we ventured onto the cobblestone pavement to walk the short distance to Crown Alley. "But since I've just about hit the waddling stage, the taxi gives us more pub time. By the way, you're all jolly sports about going all the way to O'Fagan's for lunch."

O'Fagan's was generally deader than Jacob Marley—a girl couldn't get hit on by a bloke if her life depended on it. It was the one pub Gwen's husband Jonathan didn't mind her visiting without him. "Though why he thinks I or any other pregnant girl is pick-up material is a mystery."

Before we left the office, our other friend Veronica suggested that we have Gwen's celebratory lunch at one of the lovely cafés on Grafton Street. "I'm all for that," I told the other girls. "I can go to the shops and find a baby gift." Sharon, however, had lobbied for the more reasonably priced O'Fagan's.

Now as we entered the pub Sharon confessed, "I just spent half a week's salary on a new outfit at Brown Thomas." She looked a bit shamefaced. "After my husband found the credit card bill and gave out at me, I had to promise no more shopping."

The downside of lunch with the girls, I thought, following Gwen to a table. Husband bashing.

"With Christmas coming, that'll be a challenge," said Veronica in a tart voice.

"There's that," Sharon said morosely. She looked round O'Fagan's. "I swear this place gets drearier every time I come in here."

I gazed round the pub—the place would put anyone in poor form, with the brown, smoke-stained walls, and Guinness flags, limp with age, dangling from the ceiling. "Still, it's a step up from the file room," said Gwen, which earned me sympathetic glances from Sharon and Veronica.

In the taxi, I'd told the girls about confronting Mr. Smythe over my new office assignment. "I said straight out that the file room isn't an appropriate workspace." I'd thrown in some ergonomic drawbacks too. "And the room is hardly conducive to efficient workflow." We all knew Mr. Smythe valued efficiency more than his own mother. "And since the file room is where the staff hangs out, all that chatting about the GAA scores and what they did all weekend is terribly distracting."

"Never!" said Sharon, wide-eyed. "He didn't like…order you out of his office?"

"Well, he harrumphed a few times," I said. "Then I sort of got him to admit that I'd a point. 'I'll do some calculations about how we might reconfigure the offices, then,' he says. I said, 'And you'll get back to me when?'"

"Don't tell me," said Veronica. "He said he'd need at least a month to think it over."

"He tried," I said, "but I told him, 'I'll want your answer first thing Monday.' He harrumphed some more but he said he'd get to it. Monday it is." I'd been quite proud of myself, the way I'd handled it.

Now that we were in the pub, Gwen wiggled in her chair, clearly trying to find a comfortable position. "It's about time one of us put Himself in his place."

"There's that," Veronica said, "but we all know he's not going to lay out any money for a larger office space, the tight-fisted old—"

"What'll it be, girls?" called Eamonn the barman. The place was so quiet you'd no need to go up to the bar to order.

"Our usual?" Gwen asked us. "Four ploughman's sandwiches," she called back. "And two pints."

Veronica and Sharon liked stout, but I didn't much care for it myself. (Another full disclosure: I'd liked it well enough when Will had taken us to his favorite pub, years ago.)

"Working for a Scrooge is bad enough, but being married to one is the pits," Sharon put in. She rarely wasted an opportunity to bemoan her financial situation. "So I'll do without a pint today—save a few euros that way."

"Oh, Jaysus, I'll stand you one," Veronica said. "But you think your husband is mean? Ed gave me a houseplant for my birthday."

"Which, don't forget, you regifted to me for my birthday," Gwen teased her. "The one on my desk."

"It would be easier if Ed was only a cheapskate, though,"

Veronica said. "He's such a bloody neatnik he drives me round the bend."

"I wish Jonathan wasn't such a slob," Gwen said. "But that's the least of my worries. He admitted the other day there's a girl at work whose been seriously chatting him up—she knows he has a pregnant wife. He's got one of those super friendly, sociable offices, so he says he can't ignore her." Gwen didn't look seriously concerned, however. The whole idea of sharing was to participate in the lunch tradition.

"Tell him to bloody well try," said Veronica, "or he'll be getting the cold shoulder at home."

The three girls looked at me expectantly. Clearly, I was meant to dish some dirt, but I hadn't much to contribute. Stephen didn't ogle girls, adored Jamie, and while he could be terribly tidy, he didn't expect the same from me. Nor would I win any points with the girls to say that Stephen not only made a great salary, but he was generous—we'd worked out a budget so I could use a lot of my pay to build my own savings, instead of putting it all in the family kitty. "My mother always said wives should have their own money," he'd said firmly when we were first married. As if he wasn't already like, the "perfect" husband, Stephen was good-natured too. He'd gotten angry with me— truly, blazingly angry—only once.

Not that I wanted to revisit *that*. I suppose I could've said to the girls, *Stephen never shares his deepest feelings*, only Veronica would be sure to say something like, *And if you're lucky he'll keep it that way*. I finally settled on, "With this new job, it seems like he's never home." I suppose that could even be a plus—we didn't see each other enough to get on each other's nerves.

"I'd like it fine if Ed traveled," said Veronica. "I could keep our house in whatever state I liked. I swear, Kerry, you've all the luck." She went up to the bar to collect our sandwiches.

Suz had said the same—that I was one lucky girl. Feeling myself flushing, I dug into my bag for some euro for my lunch. There was something I could say that would make the girls feel lots better about their husbands, but it was too embarrassing to mention. That Stephen and I hadn't made love for months.

We weren't in a bad patch or anything, I told myself as I ambled through Temple Bar Square after the get-together. Stephen and I were only in one of those marital lulls, that once you've been married a dozen years or so, are *perfectly* normal.

Threading my way through the noisy, late afternoon crowds, I couldn't help thinking that Stephen was beginning to feel as much a stranger as the people I passed. So I still hadn't a clue how to bring up Jamie's biological father, especially since I hadn't given Mam the chance to weigh in on my dilemma. I didn't tell Mam a lot of Stephen's and my private business, but she, well…understood my marriage in ways no one else did.

I suppose I could have confided in Gwen or my sister Suz, but neither of them had been married long, and they were still in that crazy in love stage. They probably wouldn't get the sort of long-term marital issues that can make…trouble.

I quickened my stride, past O'Donnell's gift shop, where Mam and I often shopped for Christmas clobber. She and I had gone there one day, when Jamie was much younger—it was soon after Stephen and I told him the truth about his father. There in the shop, amongst the fairy figurines, I'd admitted to her that I'd never really talked to my husband about the guy who'd fathered my son.

Mam set down a figurine, looking horrified. "Not talked about it?" She lowered her voice. "Whyever not? Stephen's human, he has a past too."

Actually, I don't think he does, I'd wanted to say but didn't. Even if Mam on some level *got* Stephen and me, really, talking about sex with her was So. Not. On.

Then *and* now. I was sure that if I *had* brought the Mike problem up with her last night—once Suz had left, that is—she would've told me to just sit Stephen down and get on with it. Good point, but he had to be home to talk to.

Once I left Temple Bar, I took the long way to the Grafton

Street shops. Slowing, I passed the bronze statue of Molly Malone and her impressively upright bosom. Maybe I should pop into a lingerie shop? Get a push-up bra to help me—help us—get back on track? But with a few more steps I forgot all about bosoms and brassieres. Because there it was. Lynch's. Will's favorite pub. Through the window I saw that the place was still filled to the rafters with twentysomethings—blokes in crisp trousers and loosened ties, pretty girls with their styled hair and trendy high heels. I could almost see Will in the middle of them, his fair hair shining under the light. I grasped the doorknob, then looked down at my khaki skirt and practical anorak. Wouldn't I just stick out like a nettle in a rose garden? I quickly turned away, and started walking again, the chilly autumn air clearing my head.

I didn't need to go inside to remember visiting the pub with Will.

8

Stephen and I almost hadn't gone out with him.

When Will, his face eager, proposed going to Lynch's the Saturday after Mam's gathering, Stephen had said immediately, "It's a bit far to go."

I was tempted to roll my eyes. Trying to sound loyal, I said, "Jamie's a restless sleeper—we'd hate for Mam to be up late with him."

"And we're saving for my university fees," Stephen said. "Pub visits aren't in the budget."

He sounded like such a wet blanket I felt we needed a better excuse. "Actually, Stephen and I—we're not much for drink."

"Is that a fact?" Will said, laughing into my eyes. "I remember ol' Stephen here really tying one on, right before he brought me round to meet you."

I wanted to tell Will "you're exaggerating," but Stephen had given me a right shock that night, a fortnight ago. In a very un-Stephenlike way, he'd burst in the door hours late with his hair on end and a big tear in his new work coat, only to tell me he wanted me to meet a mate of his. A mate who was actually waiting outside in the hall! Still, I wanted Will to think I could take a misbehaving husband in stride, so I laughed instead. "God only knows what the pair of you had been up to—"

"You want me to tell you?" Will's grin was wicked.

"Will," Stephen broke in, "I—"

"I don't want to know," I said, still teasing. "If Stephen was scuttered, it was a one-off then. Really, we don't drink."

"Then you'll be cheap dates," Will said. "Because I'll be standing every round. The taxi too."

Taxi? I met Stephen's eyes, both of us thinking, *Now that's extravagant.* But I'd given Stephen a pleading glance. We never went out, it would be just this once…

Now, I booted up my laptop. Since I was facing another Friday night alone, why not indulge myself? What harm could it be, to revisit some good times with an old friend?

I clicked on Will's second email.

Hi Kerry and Stephen,
   Thought I should check in before you thought I'd disappeared entirely. Been playing rugby with a crew from the local college. Round here, they call it Paul Bunyan State after this logging legend of the north woods, a bloke the size of an elephant. You'd think a college town would have lots going on but it's pretty quiet round here. Not a decent pub for miles around—not like Lynch's. Didn't we have some great craic there? Anyway, don't be strangers.
Cheers, Will

He sounded homesick, I'd thought, the first time I'd read it. Feeling a bit misty-eyed, I'd quickly written back.

Dear Will,
   As if I'd forget our times at the pub! Even if talking Stephen into Lynch's was an uphill climb—he wouldn't know fun if it hit him on the head, right? But what a fun lark it turned out to be. For one thing, you were just the guy to give a girl a break from being a mammy. And I had to laugh after you had a couple of pints, then practically flirted the knickers off every girl under forty. Do you remember? They were fawning over you something desperate. Looking like a naughty schoolboy, you grinned at me, as if to say, Aren't they all eejits, falling for a line like mine?
   That next two visits, it was great craic, like you said—especially for you, I imagine, the way those girls were at you all night! But Stephen and I didn't feel right, you paying our way. Having you round for Sunday lunch at our place seemed like a fair trade. And well…I know I shouldn't say this, but I rather liked not sharing you with the Lynch's crowd! Anyway, who knew that inviting you to Sunday

lunch at our place would turn into dozens of long, lazy afternoons?

You'll never read this. So I may as well say I loved every one.

Cheers, Kerry

I jumped guiltily as the front door opened. I quickly shut the computer down and practically leaped from my chair. Heart thumping, I'd just opened the fridge as Stephen entered the kitchen. "I didn't expect you until later," I said over my shoulder. Did it sound like an accusation? "I mean, with you coming from London." I closed the fridge without taking anything out.

Stephen set down his briefcase. "This series of meetings was more...intensive than I thought it would be." He pulled out a kitchen chair, one of the stark, Danish set that matched the shiny modern kitchen, and sat down heavily.

I glanced at the Italian leather briefcase I'd got him for his last birthday. "This article's far too posh for me," he'd said when he pulled it out of its wrappings, frowning as he turned the case in his hands.

"I thought you'd want to look the part, now that you're upper management." I wondered if he was cross with me for spending so much.

"You're right, I probably should." Stephen began shifting all the papers out of his old one, and took the new case to work the next day. And came home with two new suits.

Now I said, "Are you hungry? I was just laying out a few things for breakfast, and I could make up a—"

"No thanks—had a quick bite at the airport," he said, the recessed kitchen lights casting harsh shadows on his face. "I've been eating on the run since that big dinner with Doug the night before last."

"The CFO? The one you met with the night we were at Mam's?" It was often hard to keep track of Stephen's comings and goings. Mostly goings. "I'll be the meeting was at another fancy restaurant." I used to question Stephen eagerly about the gourmet meals he'd eat when the company entertained their clients. I'd try to replicate this or that dish that was all the go—when was the last time I'd done that?

"Yeah, the Siobhan Hotel—one of those five-course yokes. Jaysus, what a packet it cost. But the boss thought we should really put on the ritz for our man, coming all the way from Canada."

"How did it go?" I'd forgotten to ask him when he came home late Wednesday night. Wait...I couldn't. Because I'd been feigning sleep.

"Not bad, considering." A tired, wry smile crossed his face.

"Considering?" I repeated.

"Right in the middle of my presentation my laptop went all wonky on me. I had to finish my talk on the fly. But Doug thought it was great."

"That's fantastic." I envied Stephen's ability to wing it—whenever my plans went awry, I tended to drop the entire deal. "Sorry about your laptop."

"Isn't it funny how that old dinosaur of yours keeps ticking along?" Stephen said. He looked at his briefcase, then back at me. "Actually, there's something I should probably—" He broke off, and rubbed his eyes.

"You look knackered." I was suddenly flooded with guilt as I remembered the Mike thing with Jamie. The situation could turn into a proper mess. And the longer I waited to tell Stephen about it, the harder it was becoming to broach the subject.

But really, the way he spent all his evenings at work, when did I get a chance? "These meetings till all hours—do they really accomplish anything?" *That came out all wrong,* I thought immediately. *You're meant to sound interested, not sharp.*

Stephen lifted his briefcase to his lap and opened it. "Often they don't, but for this meeting—there were a number of initiatives on the table..." His voice trailed away.

We sound so stilted, like strangers. As if we were two people sharing a bus seat. "Did something big happen—" A big yawn caught me unawares.

"I...I'm thinking you'll want to go up to bed." He rifled through some papers. "We can talk over the weekend. All right?"

"Aren't you coming up?" I don't know why I'd said it, since I knew what his answer would be. *No.*

Stephen glanced up at me, an unreadable look on his face. "I've a few items to add to this report—I've nearly nailed it, but it needs one more pass. I won't be long."

"You haven't forgotten your Halloween date with Jamie tomorrow?" Stephen only shook his head without looking up. "'Night then," I said and turned away. Clearly, Stephen would rather please the boss than be with me. So I was back at square one. Padding upstairs, I knew I had to have it out with Stephen. Yet I didn't know how to initiate a heart-to-heart with my husband, any more than I knew how to rekindle our love life.

No wonder I couldn't stop re-reading those old emails.

I lay next to Stephen, listening to his slow, even breathing. He'd actually come up soon after I did and fallen asleep without saying anything. He was probably used to finding me asleep—or appearing to be—before he climbed into bed.

I liked to blame this house for our lack of sex. I felt like a guest here—you know how it is, when you're staying at someone else's house. You wouldn't *dream* of having sex. Unless you were in that first, passionate stage of a relationship, when you can't keep your hands off each other. Which Stephen and I certainly were *not*. It was already proven we *could* keep our hands off each other.

We used to fall asleep spooned up together. Now, I wondered if the next step for us was swapping our queen-sized bed for a pair of twins, like in hotels. We wouldn't be missing anything.

Because we hadn't made love since June.

After Mam and Dad told us about her cancer, I'd gone home and crawled into bed, unable to stop crying. Stephen had found me there. I'd needed comfort, so badly, and he'd given it to me. Now, I looked at him, the streetlamps penetrating through the blinds outlining the back of his head and his sturdy torso under the covers. How hard would it be, to turn toward him and run my finger down his spine? Curve my hand over his hip? Whisper, *Do you want me as much as I want you?*

But the inches between us might as well have been miles.

I stared at the ceiling. It wasn't all Stephen's fault we hadn't made love all this time. After that night, I'd been too heartsick for anything sexual. Then we'd moved house, and Mam had her surgery. Soon after, Suz gave birth to Ailish, leaving only myself to help our parents. Then, with Stephen's new position, he and I seemed to be living on different planets.

I thought of that photo back at Mam's, of Stephen, Jamie and me. Maybe our problem had started a long time ago. When we'd first gotten together, we hadn't had the big, grand passion like in all my favorite romantic novels. I'd always enjoyed Stephen's lovemaking. But he hadn't been the sort to get all soppy over me, even at the beginning. I had to wonder, how far can fondness and practicality take you?

That weekend, I found out exactly how far it'll take you. Nowhere. Because Stephen didn't bring up his big meeting again. And I didn't bring up Mike.

9

*M*onday, there was no Gwen at the office to cheer me up when the spreadsheet program we used for billing went haywire. Or vent to after Mr. Smythe lowered the boom.

When I'd popped into his office to check on my new workspace, he told me the office reconfiguration would have to wait. I was to settle into the file room straightaway.

I gathered all my courage. "Mr. Smythe, I've been here for fourteen years. Given my seniority I'll expect you to have my new workspace sorted before Christmas." As Mr. Smythe began glowering at me, I got a bit nauseated. But I was determined to see this through. "Or I'll be forced to…to reconsider my future here."

Mr. Smythe's frown deepened. "We'll have no threats round this office, Kerry," he said, like I was a recalcitrant teenager, then looked back down at the papers in front of him.

I left without answering. All afternoon in the file room— between stewing over the injustice of it all, and the boss treating me like a kid—I'd nearly driven myself mad trying to solve the computer glitch. When I got to our house, I let myself in and burst into tears.

Stephen was actually home. He rushed to the entryway, alarm on his face. "What's happened? Are you sick?"

"No!" I sobbed harder. "It's my job, Mr. Smythe has—"

"You haven't been sacked?"

I flung my bag onto the floor. "I wish! I just wish he'd sack me! He can get some other dogsbody to do his billing sheets—"

"Come on now." Stephen's face relaxed. "You don't mean that." He retrieved some tissues from the downstairs loo and handed them to me. "Not after your last rise in pay," he said calmly.

"What does a good salary matter?" I blew my nose. "When my boss pisses me about?"

"Kerry," Stephen said in reproof. "Jamie's upstairs. What'll he think, if he overhears you slagging your boss?"

"Oh, love of God! So I'm not perfect!" I hissed. "You act like not working would be the worst thing that could ever happen! And don't say it—just don't say it, that with this economy, it's still hard to find a new job. Or that all these years I've been lucky to have one at all!"

He only stood there, not answering.

I tore off my damp anorak and threw it on top of my bag, then stomped past him to the French doors. It was after dark, but I could see the patio clearly, the starkness of the back garden. If we still lived at the flat, I'd have spent my weekend raking leaves and mulching the small space the landlord had let me use in the back garden. Then dreaming of what I'd plant next spring. Would I ever have a garden again?

I thought of Aunt Rose's farm. The climbing roses against the golden stone. The gnarled apple trees. The green, rolling pasture, with golden woodbine and pink wild fuschia in the hedgerows, her small herd of cows grazing peacefully. The farm no longer existed, except in my memory. And knowing what had happened to the place soon after Rose had died, I felt a wail of pain and frustration building in my chest.

"Kerry." Stephen had followed me. "Now that your mam's better, maybe we could think about—"

"Do you ever think about just chucking it all?" I whirled to face him, trying to keep my voice low. "Job, bills, responsibilities, just find a cliff and hoick the whole lot over the edge?"

Stephen's gaze shifted for an instant. "How would we live?" he asked reasonably. "Who'd pay the rent then?"

"No one!" My voice shook with passion. "We could chuck this place too! Life's so short—you hear about people making every second count, sailing round the world, going on a safari,

God help us, I don't know. They're just not living like *this*. Every day the same. Nothing but computers and…and concrete."

"Maybe you—we—need a holiday, Kerry." Stephen reached for my hand. "We could ask your mam to look after Jamie sometime soon—take a weekend, go on a trip—"

I pulled away. "When you work all the time? When was the last time we went anywhere?"

"I realize it's been a while…" Stephen flushed.

I wondered if he was thinking of more than holidays. "It's been forever! But then, you don't need a break, you're so keen on your work! You don't know what it feels like to have a dead end job—that you dread going to every day." I shredded the tissue between my fingers.

"Actually I do," he said slowly. "Those years as a construction laborer—"

"At least you had some great times, working alongside your friends," I flung at him.

"You mean Will?" he asked. "But I didn't. It was just a job."

A job he'd kept so he could afford to get married. And be my son's father. Because Jamie's *other father* was a gobshite. Shame curled through me, overwhelming my anger. "I'm sorry—throwing things on the floor, taking my frustration out on you," I said finally. "I know, I can hardly *not* go out to work." It had never felt right to even consider letting Stephen support Jamie and me. And didn't feel any more right now.

"The way you're saving, you're growing an impressive nest egg," Stephen said in an encouraging tone. "You'll be set for retirement—which is more than a lot of people can say."

Retirement? Waiting thirty years to start a life I loved? "I just wish I'd a different sort of job." I said, overcome with that all-too-familiar feeling, that the walls of my daily life were closing in on me. But after all the years Stephen had put our family first, how could it have been right for me to have my head in the clouds?

"Why don't you sit down, relax for a bit," Stephen said. "Jamie and I will put together something for our tea."

I stood motionless as he patted my arm and returned to the

kitchen. Then I knelt and picked up the bits of tissue I'd dropped. If we couldn't have a place in the country...well, could we at least *start* talking about babies again?

You shouldn't have a child because you want to quit your job. I bowed my head, the grief I pushed down every day rising up in me. *Or to fill the empty spaces in your heart.* But what if another five years go by without us deciding, and suddenly my fertility has disappeared and it's too late to even try?

I got to my feet slowly and stared out at the dark patio again. Tomorrow I'd be riding the bus, and I'd look at the crowded streets, my ears assaulted by the dull roar of the traffic. As usual, I'd be thinking, *Is this all there is?*

After my outburst, I couldn't think of one thing to talk about with Stephen at supper. As Jamie ate silently, I stared at my little nook on the far wall behind Stephen, my laptop out of sight but not out of mind...thinking of Will at our little flat, and the lively meals we'd shared. I nearly jumped when Stephen spoke.

"I forgot to tell you—your dad filled me in about their cruise. And that they'll very likely be away in America for Christmas."

"Yeah," Jamie said glumly. "Christmas is going to suck without Granny's dinner."

"Jamie, you're an imaginative young man, you can find a better word than 'suck,' can't you?" Stephen said calmly. "Since there'll be no saying it at the dinner table. Or in front of your mother."

"Okay," Jamie said. "I'll think of something else, then."

I took a careful sip of the tinned potato soup Jamie had heated up. If his dad hadn't been here, and I'd reprimanded Jamie, he'd have protested, and maybe tried another word. Like *blow*. "I forgot to mention it myself." I reached for my water glass. "I still can't take in not being at Mam and Dad's for the holidays."

"Speaking of parents..." Stephen looked at me. "We haven't been to County Wicklow since the summer."

I nearly choked on my water. Oh, yay. A visit to Stephen's parents.

Jamie looked thoughtful. "Granny McCormack...she's not much like Granny Anne, is she?"

Pretending to study my plate, I shot Stephen a sidelong glance.

He looked wry, as he usually did when his mother's name came up. "I suppose not."

"Her dinners aren't very good." Jamie wrinkled his nose. "Not like the Sunday lunches you used to make, Mam."

And I'd thought he hadn't noticed that I hadn't cooked for ages. Not so long ago, I wouldn't have been caught dead having tinned soup on our table, but look at me now.

"And Granny McCormack always acts funny when Mam kisses her," Jamie added. "It's like déjà vu—the same look every time."

Stephen didn't answer for a moment. "It's just her way," he finally said.

That's what he'd always said about his mother's idiosyncrasies. Since I'd no hope of getting out of the visit, I said, "How about Sunday next? I'll bring a pie."

"I'll put it on my calendar," Stephen said. These days, even his Sundays were full.

I pushed my plate away. Indulging every quirk of Mary's—among them her excess worrying, and that her tightness with a euro made Ebenezer Scrooge look like a big spender—drove me mad sometimes. And if my day hadn't been...well, *sucky* enough, I had the depressing prospect of a Sunday at the McCormack's ahead of me.

Not to mention my big talk with Stephen I'd been postponing. I knew I couldn't keep him in the dark much longer about Mike McElligott. I glanced at my husband, resting his elbows on the table, staring into the middle distance. Clearly somewhere else entirely. I couldn't blame him, after the words we'd had earlier. Still, I dropped the impulse to speak to Stephen. I'd have to be in great form to take that on.

Which I definitely was not.

10

$\mathscr{E}$very woman has a guilty pleasure—gourmet chocolates, celebrity magazines, expensive manicures. If mine is revisiting some old emails, what's the harm?

Still shaky and wrung out after the meltdown I'd had before our insipid tea, I really needed a distraction from my workday tomorrow. After Stephen turned in early, and Jamie disappeared into his room for his nighttime web surfing fix, I ducked into my office. I turned on the laptop, my fingers drumming on the desk—finally, I pulled up Will's third email. *Anyway. It's not like I'll ever see Will again.*

> Hi Kerry and Stephen,
> Those brilliant Sunday lunches of yours! I'll bet the pair of you really busted the budget with those meals you put on. I still dream about them—Kerry, I probably would have wasted away to skin and bones without your roasts and puddings! Now that my mother's given up on Sunday cooking, I've gone to the dark side—eating cheap burgers on the go! Cheers, W.

The email was far too short—Will had given me only crumbs of his life, when I wanted a banquet. When I'd first opened this note, I tried to read between the lines. Did he miss me, or just my cooking? But as far as I could see, the betweens were blank. Then I reminded myself—*what are you complaining about? He's just a friend*—a friend.

I did feel sorry for Will—he was probably skint, not having a job yet in Minnesota. Trying to formulate a reply, I'd suddenly gotten a brilliant idea: my email could be like...like a diary. I could share my *real* feelings.

Dear Will,

I may as well admit straight out I invited you for Sunday lunch—despite Stephen being less than keen—to distract you from all the girls and the pints at Lynch's! But didn't we have some lovely meals? With my job being such a drag and some worries I was having about Jamie, Sundays turned into the highlight of my week. I'd get up at dawn, and cook all morning, hardly able to wait until you walked through the door.

There's one epic lunch we had in springtime that I'll always remember. I can't quite recall everything I made, only that I'd just picked my rhubarb patch and every other dish had rhubarb in it! Is it coming back to you? I was rather full of myself that day, putting out—if I may brag a bit—such an impressive spread. Stephen settled Jamie in his highchair and said something about everything looking so great, but the way your eyes shone as you pulled up a chair made me really glow inside.

When I served the pudding I was still preening a bit. "I'll have some homegrown strawberries in a few weeks," I told you. "Count on a few jars of homemade jam."

Naturally, Stephen had to remind me that I'd promised some jam to the landlord. I put my hand up to hide my expression from him, then pulled a face at you. Stephen the killjoy, right? "Oh, our man'll get his share," I said, watching you tuck into dessert.

Then out of the blue, you said it was a shame we didn't live closer to your granddad's farm, in the West. I nearly choked. A farm!

You'd gone on about the place, like you were doing a proper travelogue, and how your old granddad could barely keep up with the apple trees and berry bushes. I was as green as your eyes with envy. "I'd be happy to take some of that fruit off his hands," I said, laughing. Although I didn't mean to hint exactly, you invited us to come up and visit the place sometime! I was ready to say, "I'd love it, more than anything," then Stephen chimed in, a frown on his face. "If Kerry wants to see a farm, there are plenty of them near Dublin."

After you left, Stephen was quieter than usual. I asked him if something was wrong and he said the big meals were starting to add up. I was certain he didn't begrudge the food you ate (not like his mam probably would) because he wasn't like that. But you know Stephen—careful with money, careful with...everything.

I told him the lunches were our only splurge. And that maybe having a mate round was good for him. I couldn't help saying, "Sometimes you're just so serious, Stephen!" I kept thinking that having you round would help Stephen lighten up. So far, though, it's been a wash!

Anyway, given our tight budget, I knew there'd be no trip up to the West. But what wouldn't I give to see your farm, and have you show me round the place yourself. On the upside, having you for lunch was like cooking for the crew of farmhands I used to imagine when I was young! I miss you.

Cheers, Kerry

Now, I stared at the screen. I hadn't hesitated with the *I miss you*. But then, in a diary you can say whatever you please.

Picturing the farm Will had described so vividly, I suddenly couldn't bear the thought of facing the file room again. If only I could live the life my aunt Rose had, spending my days working outdoors...growing vegetables, picking fruit to bottle or even sell—

"Mam!"

Quickly closing the email, I turned as Jamie clattered through the kitchen—everything he did was noisy these days. I gestured at the tablet computer he held. "Time to wind things down, I think."

"It's only half-nine," he said. "I'm old enough to stay up till—"

"Teens need their sleep," I said firmly, standing up for a stretch. "Every bit as much as younger kids. The latest research says so."

"Well..." Jamie had great respect for scientific research. "Whatev—"

"I think your dad and I agreed," I said, "that you don't get to say 'whatever' to either of us. Despite how the kids talk on American telly."

"Okay," said Jamie, and held out his tablet. "Anyway, I wanted to show you this particle collider they've got in Switzerland—it's massive, they're trying to sort out the origins of the universe."

"Very interesting." I peered at the photo, an undefinable mass of metal and tubes and lights straight out of a James Bond film. "It doesn't look like much of anything to me, but if you say it's a particle collider I'll take your word for it."

"Well, it is." Jamie swiped the screen and the photo disappeared. "Couldn't we go on holiday in Switzerland sometime? Wouldn't it be great to go and see the collider?"

"I doubt the facility would be open to the public, love—"

"But we never go anywhere. Con's family takes a holiday practically every weekend."

Con, again? There's no end to the trouble he causes. "Lucky Con," I said.

"What about that holiday we planned last spring?" Jamie pressed. "Can't we do it now? Please?"

Just after Stephen was promoted, we'd talked about all of us taking a proper holiday abroad. I'd even obtained a passport for Jamie and myself. But then Mam had gotten her diagnosis, and I'd put our lives on hold.

I could see Jamie was getting a bit worked up about his holiday idea. Ever since he was small, he'd been funny that way—when he got something in his head he'd be like a dog with a bone. While it seemed unlikely that he would have buried the Mike bone, he hadn't mentioned it since he brought it up days ago. "We'll talk to your dad, okay? Now go clean your teeth."

"Aw, Mam, that's what you always say—"

"We should get you an app for your tablet," I told him, "that's programmed to announce, 'now go clean your teeth.' Just think of all the breath I could save not telling you twice a day."

"Not funny, Mam," Jamie said, tucking his tablet under his arm. When I aimed a kiss at him, he backed away so fast he crashed into chair. "Can't we go on *some* kind of holiday?"

So kissing him was verboten. "Who says we never go

anywhere? In just a few days, we've got our fun trip to Wicklow."

"Aw, Mam!" Jamie headed back upstairs. If Stephen were here, he probably would have given me a chiding look that said, *Sarcasm doesn't become you.* But the prospect of an afternoon with Mary McCormack's dour face made my days at Smythe's seem like a lark.

Alone downstairs, I was more restless than ever, *really* trying to keep to a strict diet of one Will email at a time. A country scene rose in my mind, inspired by the faint memory of my aunt's farm and what I imagined of Will's. Suddenly, I felt an overpowering desire for something *else* hum though me.

There had to be something that could help me get rid of this strange jitteriness. In a sudden impulse, I plopped back into my desk chair and went online. I keyed in the search words I'd never had the nerve to before.

Farms for sale.

11

If Jamie wanted more déjà vu experiences, I thought as Stephen drove the familiar country lanes, he couldn't do much better than visit his McCormack grandparents.

Despite my lack of enthusiasm for the visit, I loved the trip from Dublin to the south end of County Wicklow. As we passed through the bog and moorland, I admired the mountains curving up to the sky on both sides. The sight of the wide open spaces was bittersweet, though. The site where Aunt Rose had had a farm wasn't far away—but a place I'd no wish to see in its present form.

Stephen's parents' home, near Arklow, was a nondescript bungalow that hadn't changed in all the years I'd visited. As I got out of the Toyota, waving at Stephen's dad Brian on the stoop, I looked at my father-in-law more keenly than I had for a while. He'd aged the last few years...his hair had thinned, and his shoulders stooped a bit now. But as Mary joined him, I thought, *Jamie was bang-on about his Granny McCormack.* Like their house, she seemed exactly as she had the day I'd met her after Stephen and I got engaged—iron-gray hair, not a shred of makeup, wearing a flowered polyester dress that had to date from 1977.

Her guarded look was identical to the one she'd had years ago, when Stephen had brought Jamie and me to meet them. I'd said, "Lovely to meet you both," passing the baby to Stephen so I could give his mam and dad a kiss. Before I could get too close, his mam extended her hand. "Kerry," she said stiffly. "The same to you, I'm sure." Her gaze skittered off Jamie like he wasn't there. All I could think was, *Just what am I in for?*

To my further shock, Mary didn't kiss Stephen, only looked at my bare left hand. "I see the pair of you aren't fussing with the expense and fol-der-ol of an engagement ring."

"I didn't want one," I said quickly. It was true. What would I do with fancy jewelry anyway?

"We're saving all we can, Mam," said Stephen, shaking his dad's hand. "Kerry understands that."

"Does she," said Mary, and I could swear the woman was assessing the likely cost of my skirt and jumper.

Brian McCormack still hadn't said a word, and I was sure he didn't like me any more than Mary did. I felt the telltale prickling behind my eyes. *I can't let myself cry now, but God help us, you're not cut from the same iceberg as your wife?*

Then Brian said, "A fine little fella," and tugged playfully on Jamie's bootie. As the baby chuckled, he gave me a wink.

I'd smiled weakly back, releasing the breath I'd been holding. Then Mary had told us, "The stew won't be fit to eat if we stay out here much longer."

She said the same now, as she led us into the house, Jamie's newly coltish energy seeming to disturb the mortuary-like vibe of the place. My in-laws hadn't any knickknacks around—not even a crucifix on the wall. The one adornment was on an end table—a pair of plastic-framed photos of Stephen as a boy.

The furniture was the same as the day I'd first visited, sagging with age. "I'll just pop into the loo to wash my hands," I said. Walking past Stephen's room, I peered in. Nothing had changed in here either. You'd think while dusting the place—it was always clean—Mary might move some item a few centimeters here or there. But no.

After Stephen left home, she seemed to have made the room into a bit of a shrine. The plain beige duvet had Mary written all over it, but the walls were pure Stephen: covered in photos and drawings and school awards, with shelves full of books—*Peter Pan, Robin Hood* and *Treasure Island*. H.G. Wells' *The Time Machine* and *The War of the Worlds* were bookended by a football, alongside some neatly arranged hand tools. The last time we'd visited, Jamie had asked his granddad,

"Can I take *The Time Machine* home? It's like early science fic—"

"Of course you can," said Brian.

"Ah, no...sorry," said Mary with an odd expression. "It'll stay on the shelf."

A rebellious look crossed Jamie's face. He had to be thinking, *But it's Dad's, not yours!* Luckily he was too polite to protest. But I wanted to say, *It's a book, for God sakes. Meant to be read.*

Brian had glanced at his wife as Stephen continued to eat, not looking up. "You're welcome to read a chapter or two every time you call round, lad," Brian said, clearly embarrassed.

"That would be all right," said Mary, setting down her knife and fork across her plate. She'd bisected it in a perfect half. I had to wonder if Mary was just sentimental, or OCD?

Today, eating her stew, whose only seasoning was salt, and lots of it, was rather a chore. Mary favored inexpensive—and invariably gristly—cuts of meat, but nothing new there either.

After the meal, Brian brought in a shop-made cake, covered with white frosting and blue icing roses.

"Wow, Granddad," said Jamie. "I'll take a big piece."

"Kerry, Stephen said you offered to bring a pie," Brian said, "but I wanted to make your visit special."

Mary's face looked tight. "Puddings are nothing but an extravagance, if you ask me. And store puddings? You could buy twenty-five kilos of potatoes for the packet you laid out for that cake."

As usual, Mary was begrudging a few euro for dessert. Although which was worse, I didn't know—a woman so cold she didn't kiss her son, or who was too mean to have pudding every day.

After Brian passed the full plates around, I started in on the overly-sweet cake, which was nowhere near as flavorful as the cakes Mam and I made. At least there was my little ritual with Brian that made the visit worthwhile. As soon as I'd taken my last bite, Brian gave me a shy grin. "I'll get out the old snaps, shall I, Kerry?"

Mary began gathering plates—she never let me help with the washing up. The rest of us trooped into the front room, Jamie taking a detour into his dad's bedroom to retrieve the Wells' book. As Stephen and Jamie took the loveseat next to the couch—the only spot of love in the entire place, if you ask me—Brian and I settled on the couch. I knew enough to sit carefully. The upholstery was some scratchy material I could feel through my jeans. Stephen's dad fetched a photo album from the scuffed wooden dresser on the opposite wall.

"Mam, you look at those photos every time we visit," said Jamie, returning to the front room. He slid into his chair with so much force the picture frames rattled on the nearby end table and opened his book.

"That's because I never get tired of seeing the farm where your granddad grew up," I said, smiling at Brian. I peered at the faded black-and-white photos. "These country scenes bring back lovely memories, visiting my Aunt Rose's farm." I pointed to a close-up. "Her cows looked just like these."

"Jerseys, they were," Brian said. "Gentle as lambs, too."

"Here's the milking shed, right?" I liked giving Brian a chance to natter on about the farm.

"It is," said Brian. Then to Stephen, "And don't I always say, you were a grand help to the old ones, growing up."

At this point, Stephen would always come sit next to us, to look at the snaps. He'd get his dad reminiscing about the old tractor he called "Miss Kitty" (Brian swore it had nine lives), the sheep-shearing process, or how Brian, barely a teenager, had managed to fix the baler just before a rainstorm blew in, narrowly avoiding the loss of the entire hay crop. Stephen leaned forward. "Remember, Dad, when—"

"Did I ever tell you, Kerry," Brian broke in, "that Stephen here took charge of the milking during a school holiday?"

"What?" I stared at Stephen. He'd told me shortly after we met that his mam had her heart set on him getting a degree, having a career in Dublin. "The country hasn't any place for an ambitious sort," he'd said firmly.

"Seriously, you did the milking?" I asked, trying to picture

Stephen in his tailored suits and well-shined shoes wrangling a cow into a milking stall. "I thought you just visited the farm—"

"It was even before he'd his first whiskers," Brian went on, a faraway look in his eyes. "My da was ailing, and Stephen just rolled up his sleeves and pulled on his granddad's old wellies and away he went. Milking fifteen cows by hand, mind."

"It was nothing, really," Stephen said to me, "Just helping out—"

"You'd have made a proper farmer, son," Brian said. "But your mam..." he shook his head. "She was all for—"

"I'll give Mam a hand in the kitchen." Stephen practically leaped up from his seat.

"He's a good lad," said Brian, his eyes on his son as Stephen left the room.

Right. A good lad who kept himself to himself so well he'd never mentioned he knew how to milk a cow! "I know how he got that way," I said to Brian and patted his arm. God only knew what kind of childhood Stephen might have had without him.

He reddened, but looked inordinately pleased. "But if the land's not in your blood, you can't fight nature." Brian shrugged philosophically. "One of my nieces ended up with the place after my mam and da went. Sure, times are changing—I wonder what my old da would have thought, to see women running farms?"

"I think he would've been overjoyed, to see his farm stay in the family." If only I could say the same about Rose's place, I thought mournfully, and pulled the album back onto my lap. "And here's Miss Kitty, right?" I said above the clatter coming from the kitchen. "The old tractor that wouldn't die."

The light from outside was starting to dim when Stephen came in with a fully-laden tea tray, Mary right behind him. As the cups rattled in their saucers, Jamie set down his book. "Granny, can I have another piece of cake?"

"If your mam and...dad says it's all right," said Mary, her face softening a bit. It had taken a few years, but she'd finally come round about Jamie.

"I'll have another one myself," said Brian, actually not

looking at his wife for permission. Stephen poured the tea then passed it round, along with the cake. With teacup in hand, Mary took the straight chair next to the doorway, the seat furthest away from the rest of us. I looked at her, and for a moment, compassion struck me. *It must be terribly lonely, being you...*

Brian took an enthusiastic bite of cake. He'd a cross to bear, all right, having a rogue sweet tooth in this sugar-free house. "Stephen, everything all right with the new place?" he asked.

"That city manor house," Mary said, sounding grumpy again. "The one you're making a show of—"

"Dad, you know it's brand new," Stephen said quickly. "The builders did a good job, nothing shoddy about—"

"I meant the cost," Brian said, looking anxious. "Didn't you tell me it would be a stretch until your bonus came in?"

What was Brian on about? I set down my fork to look at Stephen. He wore an odd expression.

"What have you gotten yourself into, Stephen?" said Mary, the lines in her face deepening "Didn't you tell me you'd have no problem with such a big outlay?"

Stephen was practically squirming in his chair. "It's all right, Mam, I've got it—"

"And here you've spent a packet, a *fortune* on that gift that—"

"Mam!" Stephen interrupted. In a calmer voice, he said, "Really, there's nothing to worry about. I've got our budget all sorted."

"We'll be skint for sure, though," said Jamie, round a mouthful of cake, "if Mam quits her job."

Mary's teacup rattled on her saucer. "Quits!" She set her cup down. "Kerry, you wouldn't!" I thought she'd be furious, but she'd gone pale, like she was going to throw up. "Not in these hard times!"

I tried to laugh. "Leave my job! Jamie, where'd you get an idea like that?" *Don't tell me I detest my job so much you can sense it coming off me.*

Jamie ran a finger over his plate, collecting the icing clinging to it. "I heard you and Dad talking, that you wanted to be sa—"

"Your mother's not going to leave her job, son," Stephen said sternly. Then he sent me a look—like, *will you back me up here?* "Your mother and I have enough savings to…" His face looked tight for a moment. "To make sure we don't have to worry about money."

Jaysus, he could be a chip off the old Mary block. "That's right," I said brightly. Then to Mary, I said, "That's Stephen—he can do it all, manage to get us a big house and a massive car and any number of over-the-top yokes." My fake smiled petered out. *But last spring, he said we couldn't* quite *afford another baby.*

Jamie looked at his dad, then me. "But Mam, you said that—"

"Jamie," Brian broke in. He got up and switched on the telly. "There's a new science program on. I'd like it fine if you'd watch with me."

I sensed Brian looking from me to his son and his wife, and not liking what he saw.

It was dark by the time we drove away from the house. The goodbyes had been a bit terse. Mary had hardly spoken since the "quit your job" thing came up. She and Stephen had disappeared into his room for a moment—presumably to tidy up anything that might have gotten disarrayed from Jamie being there. When she emerged, she'd looked even more anxious than she had when Jamie had uttered the dreaded word, *sack.*

Before we left, Mary surprised me by smoothing her hand on Jamie's hair. Then as if she'd been caught out doing something forbidden, she cleared her throat and handed us the gift she gave us every time we visited. A tin of shop shortbread. Thoughtful of her, I'm sure—given her stance on buying sweets—but really! Shop biscuits?

Before we'd clambered into the car, Stephen said to Mary, "Don't worry about the house, Mam." He kissed her cheek quickly, before she could move. I'd always guessed it was the one way he could have any physical contact with the woman. "Kerry and I have the house and…and everything else covered. I may be getting another rise in pay before long too."

Well, that's the first I'd heard of it. Just like finding out after thirteen years of marriage that Stephen had been a real, if temporary, farmer. And here I'd thought life held no more surprises for me.

As Stephen drove in silence, I looked into the darkness beyond the car window, missing the country sights I'd seen on our way to Arklow in the daylight. The turnoff to Aunt Rose's place would be around here somewhere. I'd never asked Stephen to take a detour, to find the village near the site of her former farm—and I wouldn't ask now.

With Jamie dozing in the back, I let my mind wander to the farms I'd seen online last week. Several nights in a row, I'd pulled up page after page of photos, feasting my eyes on green fields and old-fashioned tractors, cozy cottages, hayfields and cows, each farm more inviting than the last. Longing for a place like in the photos, like my aunt's, I realized with a twinge that if Stephen hadn't given up on farming, I could have had the life I'd dreamed about.

"It's great that your grandparents' old place is still a working farm, and still in the family," I ventured. Maybe getting Stephen to reminisce might help us, well...reconnect. The trouble was, my flirtation skills were as rusty as old Miss Kitty the tractor. "When you were young, weren't you at all tempted to stay on the farm, growing things, being with animals every day?"

Stephen didn't take his eyes from the motorway. "No need to tell you farm pay would never have supported a family. I knew even when I was young that I wanted to get married, have k...." His voice faltered.

Have kids. I wished I'd the courage to say, *then why don't we?*

"And it's a hard way to earn your crust," Stephen went on. "Even with a modern milking system, you're up before dawn to milk, with sixteen, even eighteen-hour days, seven days a week."

"You work plenty of sixteen hour days now," I pointed out.

"And I'm paid well for it." He stopped at a crossroads. "The thing is, Kerry, with farming, there's always something coming at you—you're at the mercy of weather, or sick animals, or equipment breakdowns—or a hundred other things that can go wrong. Not like other jobs, where your success is entirely up to your own efforts. After that summer of milking, I was sure if I never saw another cow again it would be too soon."

As Stephen let the car idle, I crossed my arms and looked out the window. That was a long speech for Stephen these days. "I suppose your mother was happy to hear that." That is, if Stephen had even mentioned his distaste for farming to her. I knew he hadn't told his parents what had happened to us in August. Just like I hadn't mentioned it to my family either. Mam would have felt terribly guilty, and how could I intrude on Suz's happiness?

I thought again of the moment I'd seen Mary's loneliness. How would it be to have only one child who rarely visited? Because her daughter-in-law didn't like her...

And how would *I* feel if Jamie married once he was grown, and his wife didn't like coming round so I never saw him? "Stephen," I said suddenly, "your mother—"

"What about her?" He hunched one shoulder, putting the car into Park. "You're not blaming her, for reacting like she did when Jamie spoke out of turn?"

"I realize how anxious she gets," I said, but I remembered the caress she'd given Jamie. Maybe it was time I learned to get on with her a bit better... "Perhaps we could invite—"

"Knowing how she is, especially with money," Stephen broke in, "Let's watch what we say in front of Jamie—all right?"

His reproach, edgier than the mild tone he used with our son, was like a cold water bath. Stung, I said, "That night I complained about my job wasn't *in front* of him." Suddenly it seemed ridiculous, trying to cultivate my relationship with Mary, when I couldn't get along with her son. "At least I was expressing myself." *Which is more than I can say for you.*

Whenever I got after Stephen for his lack of communication, I felt him shut down, like a change in the atmosphere. Tonight was no different. He said briskly, "By the way, did I tell you? I'm off to Toronto." He put the car back into gear. "First thing tomorrow."

"Toronto," I repeated. "Again? You could have told me sooner." Suddenly, my own lie of omission poked my conscience. *You've carried your Mike secret around for well over a week. When are you going to tell him?*

I glanced at Stephen resentfully. I'd gotten proof today there was plenty he didn't tell me. And if he kept up this traveling schedule, there never *would* be an opportunity to bring up Mike.

Or a chance to break down the wall between us.

12

"You'll never believe what's happened at work," I told Mam on the phone the next evening. "With Gwen on leave, I'm not to have our cubicle all to myself."

"Hmmm," said Mam.

I was in the kitchen, swiping the already-clean counter with a cloth. "No, I've been shuffled off to a spot no better than a broom closet—for the next month too!"

As Mam made more sympathetic noises, I wished I was at her house. Complaining in person was so much more satisfying. "I'm seeing my future, Mam. Every time the firm hires new staff, I'll be treated like the lowliest temp until all the offices get sorted."

"Poor girl," Mam said absently. I could hear background noises—she was probably multi-tasking. Lest one might think Mam didn't care about my problems, I should confess I'd whinged about this before.

"The one upside," I said, wiping down the fridge, "is when I pass by my old cubicle, it seems much more attractive than when I was working in there."

"Right," Mam murmured. "You've been there…how long?"

"Seems like forever," I said glumly, thinking of Jamie's Theory of Time. I was clearly stuck in the myriad folds of the Smythe dimension.

"Sorry, I've got to go, love," Mam said. "I've tons of packing to do."

I considered bringing up Mike McElligott but Jamie was still around. "Talk later, then."

After we rang off, I felt I should do something useful. With

Stephen in Toronto, and Jamie in and out of the kitchen as he played a game, I slipped into my office nook. After the uncomfortable exchange with Mary and Brian the day before, about us being short of money, I knew it was time I got up to speed on our household accounts—especially if Stephen was going to have this mad travel schedule long-term.

I removed the paperwork from the small filing cabinet next to the desk. I was all for paper records, and surprisingly, Stephen, Mr. Techie himself, was too. He kept everything—he was like his mother that way. So it wasn't hard to go through all our living expenses, lease payments, petrol, groceries, and our credit card statement for the last year. Everything looked fine, even if our household balance seemed a bit low last June, when Stephen had signed the lease. While I was at it, I took a look at my own savings. It had a healthy total, thanks to Mary's influence. Well, my Smythe Engineering salary had a lot to do with it too, but I was in no mood to be grateful for my job.

I suddenly remembered the savings account Stephen and I had started when we first married. We'd kept it separate from the other accounts, since it was meant to be our emergency fund. Stephen and I couldn't stop laughing when we'd agreed we'd only use the money in the event of a natural disaster. Or maybe the apocalypse. "Our ten euro will go far, won't it?" I said between giggles. Of course, we'd added to it all these years, but I'd stopped tracking the balance.

As I located the neatly-marked file at the back of the drawer, the phone rang at my elbow. I jumped. Stephen? To apologize for his reproach last night?

It was Suz. "Good—you're still up."

"Yup," I said in my best cowgirl accent. I set the file on the side of my desk. "I seem to be turning into a proper night owl." *Looking for ways to distract myself.*

"We still haven't planned our Christmas dinner," Suz said in between some crunching sounds.

"What's the rush? It's only the first week of November."

"Right, but'll be the first big dinner I've put on since I had Ailish." Suz took another bite of something.

"You're eating this time of night?" I said.

"Oh God, when am I not eating?" Suz said. "This breastfeeding thing—I'm just so *hungry* all the time! Were you like that?"

"Probably," I said. Truthfully, I didn't remember much about it—I was too busy wallowing in my heartbreak over Mike. "Was that why you rang?"

"Certainly not," said Suz in a dignified way. "I don't want any surprises, so I really want to get started on our menu. And I just got this total brainwave. Couldn't you make that fantastic pudding you made years ago? I think it was one of Aunt Rose's recipes. Just thinking about it has driven me to eat an entire package of shop biscuits since I tucked up Ailish."

I opened the bank account file, and began rifling through the pages. "Not sure I know what you're talking about," I said, scanning the row of numbers. "I make lots of puddings."

"You can't have forgotten this one. You brought it to Mam's when I was a teenager, Jamie was a baby. I think it was...hummm, I'm *sure* it was that New Year's your man The Ride joined us for dinner. With that girl."

"Oh," I said slowly. "You mean the orange cake with the whipped cream filling."

"That's it! You still have the recipe?"

"I think so." I shut the savings account file with a snap. If I'd lost the recipe, it would be no bother. I knew it by heart. Because I'd made that cake expressly for—

"Mam!" Jamie was calling for me. "Can you get off the phone?"

I turned to see him opening the fridge, looking uneasy. Angling the phone away from my face, I said, "Just a minute, love." Then to Suz, "Jamie actually wants me. Which may not happen again for another ten years."

"Okay, we'll sort out the menu tomorrow," said Suz. "In the meantime, I'm daydreaming about that cake."

Ringing off, I swiveled my chair round to face Jamie. "What's up? It's nearly time for bed."

"I..." He closed the fridge, and shifted his feet. Those feet that had grown three sizes this year, Stephen had said. "Don't tell me, you need a new pair of trainers?"

"No," Jamie said, reddening. I guess it was all right for his dad to tease him, but not me. "It's that...I've been looking for our Christmas decorations. I can't find them."

Tempted to remind him Christmas was still weeks away, I said instead, "I keep forgetting how fast Christmas can sneak up on us." With all my worries lately, I'd hardly thought about the holidays—except that Mam and Dad wouldn't be part of them. But I hadn't considered Jamie. Far easier to conclude he was getting too old to bother with Christmas.

"I thought Dad might...might like it if we decorated the house early this year." Jamie looked anxious. Had Stephen's long hours been harder on our son than either of us had thought? "D'you think we lost them when we moved house?"

"Of course not," I said, sounding more confident than I felt. I'd been in a daze back in June, with Mam's surgery coming up, and I'd let Stephen manage all the house stuff. Even if he'd been preoccupied by his new job responsibilities, surely he wouldn't have given our Christmas things away? Or put them in the bin? "They've got to be around here somewhere."

Searching this big house was a more extensive project than I'd counted on. We'd enough closets to open a mini-storage business. And I confess, I hadn't kept our decorations very organized. I was always reluctant to take them down, even after Epiphany. Often, it would be mid-January before I'd mustered the willpower to gather up the lights and tree decorations and tabletop ornaments and put them away. I'd be embarrassed to still have decorations around, so I'd be in a big rush, throwing them helter-skelter into boxes and shopping bags.

"We'll need a knife," Jamie decided, grabbing one from the kitchen drawer. "In case we have to cut some packing tape." We started on the downstairs: Front closet, pantry, garage. Then it was up the stairs to the rest of the closets: linen and hall closets, Jamie's, mine in the master bedroom, guest bedroom. Then together, Jamie and I pulled down the folding ladder to the attic, and searched all through boxes and cartons. The decorations were nowhere.

Jamie looked pale—it was way past his bedtime. And I was near tears. How could I lose track of—

"Mam!" Jamie suddenly brightened. "We haven't checked Dad's closet!"

"I...guess not," I said. Jamie immediately clambered down the ladder. I left the attic in a pile of jumble and climbed down slowly. I'd never really looked in Stephen's closet, not in this house. He kept his things tidy and organized, and what would he want with storage items littering his shipshape space? Besides, it would've felt...well, intrusive to rifle through my husband's things. The husband who'd stopped confiding in me long ago. If he ever had.

By the time I was back in our bedroom, Jamie was pulling his dad's shoes out of the closet, followed by some unidentified boxes, all neatly sealed with tape.

"Your stuff's a narky mess compared to Dad's," Jamie said, looking over the boxes he'd just pulled out. "He's actually got a lot of stuff in here." Gleefully cutting into one of the boxes, he lifted the flaps and peered inside. "Baby things," he said.

Looking over his shoulder, I felt a stab. Jamie's baby clothes were folded and stacked neatly. I felt tears in my eyes, picturing Stephen all by himself, handling Jamie's little shirts and rompers, his love for our son in every carefully stowed piece. I bit my lip hard, to keep from crying.

"Why would Dad keep these old yokes in his closet?"

"I...I—" I paused, until I had myself under control. "I guess he's like your Granny McCormack." I smoothed my hand over the soft materials then closed up the box. "Likes to keep things forever."

Jamie selected another box, a big one, and cut it open. "Yessss—a Christmas box!"

Jamie began yarding out strings of lights, which were all wound up to keep from getting tangled (not like I'd have done it, just tossing the strings any old way). Then smaller boxes of all the tree decorations, shiny bulbs and angels and glass icicles, packaged up tidily like you see in "Get Organized" magazine articles. Stephen had done this? Then I remembered. "Do you see a...small white box? With a cellophane lid?"

"Nope," said Jamie. He opened a second box, full of figurines wrapped in tissue paper. Then a third. "Odd and ends," he said, closing the box. "I think that's it." He beamed at me. "We can start decorating now."

"Wait." I slipped past him, to burrow through the box Jamie had just closed. It was full of wrapping paper, ribbons and bows, gift bags and Christmas cards I hadn't gotten around to tossing. Pulling out the clobber every which way, I was close to the bottom when I found it.

A medium-sized white box. I extracted it carefully, and set it on top of the first box we'd opened. Lifting the lid, I pulled out the satin-dressed treetop angel I'd stored for years. The loveliest Christmas decoration I'd ever seen.

"Where'd that come from?" Jamie asked now. "I've never seen it before."

"It was a gift," I said. "From a...friend."

"Looks like it's meant to go on top of the tree." He turned to the first box, and found a pointy object, in tissue of course, and waved it toward me. "We always use this old star, with the light in the middle."

I couldn't take my eyes from the angel I'd kept boxed up for so long. "I guess I've been keeping the angel for...special," I said, almost to myself.

"What's more special than Christmas?" Jamie picked up the biggest box easily. "Let's get started. Downstairs first?"

With the angel in my hands, I gazed around the bedroom Stephen and I shared. It looked familiar, yet didn't really feel like my room at all. Glancing at my bedside clock, I snapped out of my reverie. "Jamie, it's half eleven!" I carefully set the angel on the bed. "You've got school tomorrow!" And I have Smythe's file room.

"Aw, Mam..." He set the box down. "We'll need to put this all away first—won't Dad be cross to find such a mess when he gets home?"

"Bed for you," I said. "I'll take care of it." *Later.*

"But just *look* at all this—it's too much," he said doubtfully. "It'll take hours."

"Now I know you're trying to get round me, to stay up late." I frog-marched Jamie toward his bathroom. "Teeth—now." While he readied for bed, I went back into my bedroom and set my angel back in the white box, then reluctantly replaced the lid.

As I returned to Jamie's room, he was climbing into bed. "I...liked what we did tonight," he said. "It was like a treasure hunt."

"I liked it too," I said from the doorway, and turned to go.

"Aren't you going to...tuck me up?"

My heart caught. *How many times have you told me you're too old for it?* "Of course." I felt tears behind my eyes again. I wouldn't have much more time, being this way with my child. Unless...unless Stephen and I could work things out. I pulled Jamie's covers up to his chin, and kissed his temple. "You're the hero, finding our Christmas things. Won't the house look grand a few weeks from now, when we've got it decorated?"

"Let's put up some lights right away, okay? That angel too. Won't Dad be surprised?"

The tender feeling in me disappeared. *He'll be surprised, all right.*

I turned out Jamie's light. Thinking of the angel, I headed straight downstairs, back to my laptop, and didn't think twice. I clicked on my email program.

13

Kerry and Stephen,

Happy Christmas! Can't believe it's been nearly a year since I spent New Year's Day with all of you. Big news—I finally got a job! I'm the assistant coach for a new athletic program at the college. The place is small, like I told you, so the pay's not great. But I've a chance to rise in the ranks! Or so I hope. Any chance you remember my friend Jennifer? My boss is her dad, can you believe he'd hire a tosser like me? Anyway, I'm keeping well—okay, I do miss home. And though the country's not really my thing, I even miss my granddad's farm, if you can believe that.

Will

Stephen had read the email aloud to me as I'd prepared our tea. "Will's landed on his feet, wouldn't you say?"

"Didn't take long, did it?" I spoke lightly, but all I could think was, Jennifer's *dad* had hired him? After reading the email, I couldn't wait for Stephen to turn in. As soon as he was in bed, I'd sat in front of the screen, my heart swelling with longing. I remembered every moment of the New Year's Eve when Will had come round to our house, the night before the dinner at Mam's. I'd never forgotten that kiss either—cheeky, but all in fun.

Now, I read Will's email again. The picture of him in my mind grew sharper, more vivid. Then I opened my reply—the letter where I'd poured out my heart, holding nothing back.

Dear Will,

It's funny, how that New Year's Day at my mam's you were early and we were late—usually it's the other way round. I hadn't been in great form, which is very unlike me at the holidays. You probably remember that I'd had too much to drink the night before, which I'm not used to. And Stephen and I had had a bit of a tiff after you'd left the night before.

When I saw the pretty, fair girl you'd brought, I have to say I was a bit taken aback (because of all the times you'd come round to our place alone). Until you said Jennifer was a family friend, just over from the States. The do at your uncle's had been completely slapdash, so you wanted to bring her to a proper celebration. Which of course completely made Mam's day!

I thought you'd be the life of the party as usual. But you hadn't much to say, and I missed your jokes—the late night at your uncle's, I guessed. Jennifer didn't seem to notice how pale and quiet you were. I'd watched her kind of a lot that day—I was a bit in awe of her, so slim and stylish, with that long streaky blond hair. I felt like quite the frump!

I tried to enjoy the day anyway, but wondering what was wrong with you, I felt the day lose its luster. After dinner, when Mam and I went to the kitchen to bring out all the Christmas puddings, she commented that you were looking a bit off.

I told her about your family party late the night before. Mam raised her brows. "So, our Will has a bit of a head on him."

I suddenly felt like an eejit—your puffy eyes should have clued me in. I said a bit crossly, "I imagine he wanted to show Jennifer a good time."

Mam said she thought you would, even if Jennifer was only a family friend. I didn't like the way she'd emphasized "family friend" but I didn't say anything. But I'll tell you now, I was sure Jennifer saw herself as more than a friend, the way she draped herself over your arm any chance she got, or followed you with her eyes, though you were all but ignoring her.

As I started cutting the cake—I'm a slow learner sometimes—the light went on: You'd probably met her long before last night. And family friend or not, you'd been dating her. So why would you be treating her like extra baggage?

Then Mam said, "Kerry, you're meant to slice the cake, not kill it."

I loosened my grip on the knife. It wasn't like you to treat a girl badly. In fact it made me sad because I'd wanted today to be altogether lovely. Especially after what happened the night before.

The thing is, I didn't want to like Jennifer, but I did. And I even felt a bit sorry for her, with you in such bad form for New Year's. And maybe this sounds like scolding, but if your pub flirting was any sign, you really weren't boyfriend material. Part of me wanted to pull you aside, tell you to be nicer to her, but you suddenly showed up in the kitchen, saying you had to leave.

I couldn't believe you'd leave before pudding. I was a bit crushed too, that you hadn't had even a bite of the orange cake that I'd made especially for you. I'm not sure how it came about, what with Jennifer and the whole family around, but do you remember? We found ourselves alone in the entryway.

The regret was plain on your face when you told me you and your parents were heading to your granddad's farm, to check up on the old fella.

You're incredibly lucky to have a farm, I said, but your face seemed to droop even more than it had all afternoon. You said your granddad was struggling, trying to keep up the place. No wonder you'd been blue, I thought. Then, as you met my eyes for what seemed like the first time all day, I promptly forgot about your granddad and his farm. I still remember every single word you said to me.

"About Jennifer—my parents had pushed me to bring her. But that's not why I did."

I was so flustered I couldn't speak for a moment. Then I finally said that naturally you should spend Christmas with your girlfriend.

Here's what I never saw coming. Suddenly your eyes were so intent I had to look away. You said, "You know why I brought her."

Then you took my left hand and rubbed my wedding ring with your thumb. Feeling the metal press hard into my skin, I found the courage to look at you again, but I couldn't speak. I could see the longing in your eyes, telling me everything you'd never said, could never say. Was the angel you'd given me the night before saying it for you? I was overcome by confusion—happiness and misery mingling in my heart until tears rose to my eyes. You dropped my hand, but I swore I could still feel your heart reaching out to mine. *Are you my anam cara?* I thought wonderingly. *My soul friend?*

You came closer, and I felt delight and panic at the thought of a real kiss between us. Then Jennifer came in and the moment was lost—a moment I sensed would never come again. I felt even more wretched as she gave me a hug, saying she hoped she'd see me again. I mean, I liked her! And it wasn't right, what had just taken place. What was I, what were we thinking?

It was all I could do to stammer, "Good-bye, God bless." I knew from your face, so sober, that this was the end between us. You said, "Good-bye, Kerry." Not cheers, or see you later, or 'til next time like you'd always said before. Goodbye.

Always, Kerry.

All those years ago, I'd been crying as I typed the last of the email. But even through my tears, I thought my letter was lovely. Like a story. Especially how I played up that last bit, my eyes meeting Will's with longing between us, the *anam cara* thing. My tears dried as I decided I had rather a talent for romantic stories. Just look at what I'd come up with! My hero and heroine expressing all the emotions they'd been holding in *forever*.

Not that I'd quite shared *all* my feelings. I'd written, "Stephen and I had a bit of a tiff." I mean, I could hardly tell Will *everything.*

14

Time to quit all the email business, I told myself briskly the next evening as Jamie and I carried a box of Christmas lights downstairs. The night before, I'd done all the sentimental wallowing any girl should allow herself. Anyway, all this living in the past was getting me nowhere—time to get back to the real world. Be productive for a change.

As Jamie unwound a set of fairy lights, he looked distastefully at the sellotape he'd brought in. "I wish Dad was here—he'd rig up some proper fasteners."

I looked at Jamie's face, wondering if he'd talked to his dad. About his "other father." I quickly decided he hadn't. The way Jamie went on about his theories and his this's and that's, I was sure he wouldn't have been able to hold in any big stuff. And while Stephen was good at keeping things to himself, even he couldn't be *that* good. I suppose I should have said, *I wish your dad was here too.* But to tell the truth, I didn't. Because if Stephen *was* home, I could no longer postpone the Mike thing. My problem was, it seemed too intimate, really, to bring up your former lover with the husband you didn't know how to talk to anymore.

As Jamie taped the lights round our big front window, I returned to my bedroom to tidy up the other two boxes. First, I surreptitiously pulled out my angel for a good long look. Then I pulled all the items out of the larger box so I could put the angel carton at the bottom, just as Stephen had packed it.

Piling the miscellaneous yokes on top, I spied a fat red envelope with an American stamp. And here I'd thought the card was long gone! As I reached for it, I suddenly thought, *No.* Not after my email binge last night. Instead, I put the envelope on top of everything else, and resolutely closed the box.

I'd been feeling guilty all day—not only for visiting the old emails, but how I was letting the past occupy my thoughts, even getting all swoony over that angel. Like I was regressing to my teenage years. Or something.

After I got Jamie to bed, I decided telly next. Then I realized I hadn't finished looking through our finances. So I dutifully sat down at my desk, where I'd left the mess of papers the night before. I glanced at our old emergency fund account, which seemed a lot lower than I would have expected. I made a note to myself to ask Stephen about it.

Half-heartedly stacking the file folders, all I could think was, *I am so not into this.* I put all the files back in the bottom drawers and drummed my fingers on the newly cleared desk. Trying to summon the energy to go into the front room, I turned on my laptop instead and went online. Studiously avoiding the email program, I clicked on the farm site I'd bookmarked.

I lost track of time, gazing at cottages and cows, sheep and pastures, and lingering at the sight of one old barn with the sun slanting on it, casting the whitewashed building in a rosy glow. I viewed more Web pages, more photos, until the prompt at the back of my mind grew too strong to ignore: *you'll be useless at work tomorrow if you keep this up.*

The next day at work, it was all I could do to focus on the tasks at hand, daydreaming about having a lovely country place with a whitewashed barn. Mooning over farms seemed harmless enough, I decided. There were worse things for a married woman to fantasize about.

"We can't stay long," I said to Mam and Dad the following evening.

Dad had brought home Chinese takeaway for the goodbye dinner. He and Mam were leaving for their cruise Saturday, in two days. Mam's brochures were strewn all over the table, "to build the anticipation," she said as she swept them aside to make way for the cartons.

Jamie was scooping the last of the fried rice onto his plate. "Aw, come on Mam, we can stay, if Granny has a sweet."

"And what about your science project?" I asked him. "Didn't you say you'd miles more work on it?"

I wasn't really so invested in Jamie's schoolwork. I actually wanted to get back to doing all the farm web surfing I liked before Stephen came home tomorrow. Although I might not have as much time online as I wanted, since Jamie needed to use my laptop to type up his report.

Some daughter you are, I told myself. *Some mother.* I seemed to have exchanged my email addiction for a farm one. My problem was, lost in all those farms online, I was starting to feel like they were my real life.

"It only takes a minute to eat a few biscuits." Dad smiled fondly at Jamie and set out a plateful. I couldn't argue with that. Not as fast as he could eat.

Jamie said, "Granny, could I take home one of those thingummies?"

"Brochures?" Mam passed him one. "Don't tell me, you want to take a holiday where you sit round a deck with a crew of middle-aged people and look at the scenery?"

"Well, no," said Jamie. "But I would like to travel." He bent his head to his plate. "Dad gets to go to Europe, America, all over the place, and Mam and I just sit at home."

"You know Dad's working," I told him. "And you've school. Your education would be a right mess if you were jetting around with your dad."

"I don't want to jet around," said Jamie. "I just want to go somewhere...cool."

"Where would that be?" Dad shot me a grin over Jamie's head. "We don't know the trendy places."

"Switzerland," Jamie said promptly. "There's this particle collider near Geneva, under the mountains or something—it's massive, you wouldn't *believe* the size of it! They're trying to sort out the origins of the universe."

"That does sound...cool," my dad said. "I don't suppose they'd let you down there?"

"Highly doubtful," I told him, then to Jamie, "If your dad gets assigned a trip to Switzerland, let's ask him if we can come along." *The worst he could say is no.* "Now it's time to get going."

He dawdled over another biscuit, then said, "I have to use the loo."

I rolled my eyes at Mam. Postponing his schoolwork, more like. As Dad got up to collect the cartons, Mam took my hand. "Dear...isn't it time you took a holiday?"

I made a helpless gesture. "You know Stephen's travel schedule."

"His 'schedule' doesn't have to run your life," Mam said tartly. "Why don't you and Stephen take a holiday, a proper one?" Then her voice softened, and I remembered the concerned look she'd given us at this same table just weeks ago. "Every couple needs time away. When was the last time you did that?"

She knew as well as I did we rarely had. Our life together had marched along, parenting and jobs taking priority. In the early days, Stephen and I hadn't had any money to spare. Later, our extra money went to savings and I'd grown so keen of my garden I found it hard to leave in the growing season. Then in the summer Stephen had gotten this promotion and soon after, we'd hit a snag. Had our setback. I didn't know why I called it that, *setback*, but maybe the word made what happened seem like not a big deal. Something entirely ordinary and commonplace...

Mam touched my hand. "Dad and I will look after Jamie."

"You heard him," I said, trying to smile. "He'll want to come with us."

"You can take Jamie next time," Mam said. She gathered up the glossy cruise brochures and handed them to me. "For inspiration," she said. "Say you'll consider it?"

I stared down at the colorful scenes. Sparkling blue sea, lush, tropical hillsides, people sipping drinks in open air cocktail lounges. It all left me cold, because of course I'd something entirely different in mind—old barns, cool, misty pastures, tramping up hillsides. The sudden impulse hit me, to jump up and push Jamie out the door, so I could get back home and online. I looked back at Mam, at her dear face, and Dad, bustling round tidying up, the pair of them just happy being together, and I wondered all over again—*what's wrong with me?*

Daydreaming of Will, re-reading my letters to him, well, it wasn't entirely on the up and up, but really, who was it hurting? The farm thing, however—suddenly it felt worse than if I'd been flirting with another man. *Because what I'm doing is flirting with another life. That doesn't, and can never, include Stephen.*

Hours later, I was still at it. Sitting at my desk, I gazed at photos—more pastures, more farmhouses, more high green hills and wide open spaces—that had me wanting to run away from home.

Finally, I tore my eyes from the screen. Okay, this was no way to cope. Not only because it was nearly midnight. If my marriage—and I—were in the doldrums, I knew the best way to get over the blues was to do something. Like Mam said. I glanced at the brochures under my elbow. Take a holiday. Or a night class. See more of Suz and Gwen...

I opened my email and quickly typed:

> Suz, are you up for a girls' day in the next week or two, if Anthony's mam can watch Ailish? I'll see if Gwen's free too. Lunch is on me—Love, Kerry

I pressed Send. Feeling like I was making progress, I got another brainwave. What if Stephen, Jamie and I planned a B&B weekend in Wicklow next month? Have a pre-Christmas mini-break in the country! Surely Stephen would be up for it, if we worked in an extra visit with Brian and Mary. Feeling virtuous, I opened my browser back up and keyed *Wicklow B&Bs* into the search bar. But even before the page loaded, I couldn't help myself. I clicked back on the farm site.

More cows, more haystacks, more picturesque tumble-down barns. Then I started to yawn, and couldn't stop. Soon, with each yawn bigger than the last, my eyes were blurring so much I could barely make out the screen images. Ready to force myself to shut down the laptop, I clicked one more link. In an instant, I was wide awake.

15

$\mathcal{S}$pellbound, I gazed at the photo.

It was a farmhouse. Of golden stone. With climbing roses next to the stoop.

It was Aunt Rose's cottage, come to life. I cupped my cheeks, my eyes filling. Of course, it wasn't *really* Rose's place—it was long gone, I knew that. But this house was the closest thing I'd seen to everything I'd dreamed about.

I leaned close to read the caption: *Farm property, County Galway.*

So the farm was all the way across Ireland—not that it mattered, a dream could be anywhere! But the estate agency's Web page was woefully short on basic information. I grabbed the mouse again, clicking madly at links. Wouldn't there be more photos, like a barn or outbuildings? Pastures and cows? Snaps of the farmhouse interior? Surely a list of the property's amenities—

The front door rattled. "It's me," Stephen called. "Caught an earlier flight."

"Oh!" I shut down the laptop without bookmarking the page. "I didn't think you'd be home until after midnight." I heard that accusing tone in my voice again. Trying to look busy, I straightened the brochures back into a neat stack, then casually slipped into the kitchen just as Stephen came in.

His face was drawn. "What, am I interrupting something?"

"Of course not," I said hastily. "I was just doing some...research." Stephen raised his brows. "Jamie's got a huge assignment coming due." *Both true.*

"Surely you're not doing it for him—"

"We were at Mam's tonight," I said. "He's been working hard, but he didn't have as much time as he needed."

"Jamie emailed me about his project." Stephen ran a hand over his hair. "He's good at keeping in touch when I'm away."

Daily contact was one more thing Stephen and I had dropped the ball on. "Maybe on your next trip," I ventured, "we could ring each oth—"

"God, I'm jet-lagged," Stephen said, rubbing his temple. "Feels like I've been living in airports."

"You rather have, lately." Stung that Stephen hadn't even heard me, I wondered why I even had to *ask*. If he wanted to connect with me when he was gone he'd just ring.

"Before I crash," he went on, looking rueful, "I should tell you Jamie's been playing hooky with his schoolwork a bit, reading."

At least we still had Jamie to talk about. I tried on a smile. "The apple doesn't fall far from the tree."

"That's right," said Stephen, smiling back, "weren't we both a pair of bookworms!"

"Hopeless," I said. "Your dad told me you read under the covers with a torch. Like I did. But what's this about Jamie?"

"It's not that he's reading, it's *what* he's reading," Stephen said. "I told him that even if he was thirteen years of age, his mam still had something to say about his reading material. But he said he hadn't the nerve to tell you."

Suddenly alarmed, I said, "Jamie hasn't gotten hold of some books with…with adult content?"

Stephen's smile widened. "I'm afraid so—he's deep into *The Mists of Avalon*."

Relieved, I had to laugh. "I suppose I should tell him, 'Hold on, that story's too racy for someone your age,' only it's funny how sex and violence in a fantasy is less threatening than in the real world."

"My thoughts exactly," said Stephen. "I actually read the book three times."

"Never!" Despite his fatigue, Stephen hadn't been this jokey in *ages*. "You didn't stick to the G-rated stuff?"

"No—but I kept my, ah...improper books in the closet so Mam wouldn't see. Our Jamie, though..." Stephen's face grew serious. "He's growing up terribly fast, isn't he?"

My own smile faded. "Too fast." The neatly folded baby things Stephen had stashed in his closet seemed even more poignant now. "Doesn't it seem like yesterday that he was small?"

He frowned, his expression even more somber. I looked at Stephen like I was seeing him for the first time in months. With the stubble on his chin, his rumpled hair—he hadn't taken the time to get a haircut for a while—he wasn't the familiar husband I'd known all these years. Suddenly, I wanted so badly to share my dreams with him.

Wouldn't it be great to have a country place of our own? Spend more time together? It wouldn't have to be a proper farm, not exactly, but we'd want a big vegetable bed, and some chickens wouldn't we? And a bigger family in the middle of it?

I pictured myself running to him—but it wasn't only my dreams I wanted to share. I wanted *him*, his arms round me, his body next to mine. I wanted to whisper against his neck, *It's not the end of the world, what happened—we can get past it, there's hope for us...*

Stephen wore a blank look. Like his body was here but no one was at home. Finally he said, "I'm asleep on my feet." His eyes drooped. "I'd better turn in."

"Can't you take tomorrow off?" I asked, concerned. My hopes that our lovemaking drought would break anytime soon had been *so* premature. "Or at least go into work late? For pity's sake, you're on Toronto time..."

Stephen shook his head. "My colleagues will be expecting my report in person." Before I could move, he stumbled to his feet and headed upstairs.

I watched him go. We'd had a moment of connection...only we'd need far more than moments if we were to start fresh.

And that empty look on his face suddenly scared me. I could believe all I wanted, that couples got over setbacks all the time, that we could get past ours. Our miscarriage.

But if we didn't, what hope did we have?

I flew into the house after work the next day. I didn't want to think about what was happening to Stephen and myself, or the distance that seemed to be turning into a gulf. Or that when we'd had that moment of connection the night before, maybe it wouldn't have been so hard to bring up Mike McElligott. Only I'd lost the opportunity, dwelling on our lost baby instead. Something that could never, ever be helped.

Now, I knew the sight of that golden-stone farmhouse I'd seen online would be a comfort. I ran upstairs to greet Jamie, finding him reading a graphic novel. "Hey," was all he said.

He really *was* turning into a teenager. "I'll start our tea in a few minutes, okay?" I scooted back down to nip into my office computer nook, for another quick look at that farm. My desk was covered with the brochures again, so clearly Jamie had been looking at them before I got home. Shoving them aside as the old laptop booted up, I pulled up the site I'd been on when Stephen came home.

The farmhouse wasn't listed. I clicked on this and that link, then typed in *Farmhouses-Co. Galway,* but no luck. I tried another site—I'd been awfully knackered last night, had I got the site name wrong? I searched the page, then more of the site. Still nothing. I broke out in a sweat. I *couldn't* have lost track of this lovely place, so like Aunt Rose's—it was my dream! I tried more sites, more searches, but the place wasn't to be found.

I pushed away from my desk. I could grab my car keys, lasso Jamie into the car, and hit the motorway right this minute. Stephen would be sure to be working, so I'd have the whole weekend to drive round County Galway until I found it! Ready to leap into action, I made myself clutch the arms of my chair. *Don't be such an eejit!* There had to be hundreds of farms in County Galway. I could hardly search the entire county.

The alternatives didn't bear thinking about—but really, I had to. This golden farmhouse had been perfect, exactly what I'd imagined. Was the farm exactly that? Imaginary? Had I been so tired last night I'd nodded off in the chair, and dreamed up the place? Or worse, gotten so lost in my fantasies I was starting to go round the bend?

Trying to calm myself down, I remembered the fat red Christmas card I'd found in our Christmas stuff that I'd set aside two nights ago. I fetched it quickly from the box in the front room. Returning to my desk, I turned the envelope over in my hands. I didn't need to open it to know what was inside...

I jumped as the landline phone rang, buried beneath the brochures. I reached over and pushed the papers aside, looking resentfully at the ringing phone and the unfamiliar number on the ID display. It was probably one of those marketing robocalls. After four rings I picked up, just to have the pleasure of ringing off the annoying telemarketer—

"Kerry, is that you?" said a familiar voice.

16

*W*ill.

Oh, my God, Will was ringing! After all these years! "Yes, it's me," I said, my voice shaking. I sank back in my chair, joy filling me at the sound of his voice. "It's been *ages*—how are you?"

"I'm great—we're all great," he said. "You?"

"The...same." Then caught by my girlhood shyness, and remembering my silly emails, I couldn't think of anything else to say. *You'd think after all these years we'd be talking each other's ear off.* I certainly wouldn't dump my worries onto Will—Mam traveling after her cancer, my marriage going sideways and the empty nest blues that had me Web surfing, daydreaming mad things, that I couldn't shake off.

Until now... *Are your eyes still as green?* I wanted to ask. *Does your smile still light up your whole face?* "You wouldn't believe how tall Jamie's grown," I said instead. "Mam and Dad are well—they're actually off to the tropics." Then I was tongue-tied again.

"Good!" After a pause, he said, "The reason I'm ringing—it's rather a long story, but d'you remember me mentioning years ago, that my granddad that had a farm in County Galway?"

"Of course I remember," I said. *I remember everything you told me.*

"Well, he died nearly two years ago. And the bloke renting the farm had a stroke a few months ago, and—"

"I'm so very sorry," I said. "I mean, that your granddad died. Not about the renter."

"Thanks," Will said. "Granddad was a good old fella. Right

fond of me too. Anyway, now that the renter's giving up the place, we're finally getting round to sorting out the property. Apparently," and he laughed, an odd sort of chuckle, "my granddad wanted me to have it."

A farm. Will owned a farm! A strange, wild longing ripped through me. Finally, I managed, "Are you going to take up farming?" *And come back to Ireland?*

"Me? Hell no." He laughed again, sounding more like his old self. "The athletic programs at Paul Bunyan State keep my nose to the grindstone. At least, as much as anything can."

My stomach dropped. Will wouldn't be coming home. He hadn't changed in yet another way, though—he was still good for turning the laugh onto himself. "So what'll you do with this farm?" All I heard was silence. Had the line disconnected? "Will?"

"We...haven't decided," Will said. "The property manager bloke says the farm needs some work but there's a lot we could do with it."

"That's...lovely," I said, wondering why, after all this time, he was ringing from America to tell me this.

"I haven't been to the farm since I left Ireland years ago," Will went on, "but as far as I remember, it was a great little place. If you like the country, that is."

"You know I do," I said wistfully. "What it's like?"

"Well, let's see..." Will paused. "It's in the hills above a little village, near...Lough Corrib? That's it. There are orchard trees, I think. And some, uh, fields."

My yearning surged even stronger, imagining a farm nestled in green rolling hills—a lot like the farms I'd been staring at online. "Sounds gorgeous."

"It's all right," said Will. "Back to why I'm ringing—the family's after me to look things over, sort out what's needed, especially if the place has gotten a bit run down." He was silent again. "And my dad says every kid should spend some time on a farm."

I heard that same odd note in his voice. Was it...resentment? "Anyway," he went on, "I'll have to miss all the football parties—the Thanksgiving holiday here is football heaven. But we're heading to the farm in a few days for a short visit."

"You mean, to Ireland? You're coming to Ireland?" I felt my world expand again.

"That's it, back to the oul' sod. You'll join us?"

For a second, I thought he meant just myself. Then he said, "Can you stay with us, you three? For a few days?"

A holiday. With Will. On a *farm*! Excitement spiraled inside me, zipping along to my fingertips and toes. "What day would you like us to arrive?"

"How about Monday the twenty-third? It'll be like a...a pre-Christmas holiday. No deluxe getaway, but there's a decent-sized farmhouse. It's terribly short notice—"

"I'd love to!" I finally found my voice. "Count us in." *I'll worry about us getting the time off later.*

"Fantastic!" Will said. "We're all keen to...to see you."

"We are too." My eyes fell to the red envelope on my desk. *This could get complicated*, I thought, but a farm holiday! Like I'd ever turn that down! "I'm sure Stephen will be as thrilled as I am," I said, crossing my fingers. "Jamie too. It'll be a brilliant holiday, us all together!"

There was some banging in the background, then Will said, "That's it, brilliant! I'd better run, so I'll email the direction."

"Great! See you then!" I rang off, elation filling me like air in a balloon, until I felt like I could float away. I'd soon see Will again! But what really had my heart beating faster was my dream coming to life.

It was too good to be true...A holiday on a farm!

I was too excited to think about tea or anything else. I turned the red envelope in my hands, and pulled out the card. Surely it wouldn't be so bad, ten years later, to read it again...

Stephen and I had gotten the card in the post the year following the New Year's Day we'd spent with Will—when he'd been so glum at Mam's. Stephen handed the envelope to me as I came in from work. "Will sent a Christmas card?" I hadn't been able to keep the excitement from my voice. "Instead of emailing?"

"Sort of," said Stephen, showing me the front of the envelope. It was in Jennifer's handwriting.

The envelope contained more than a Christmas card. Inside it was a note—and a wedding announcement. A fortnight ago, Will and Jennifer had gotten married.

I'd stared at Jennifer's flowery script. *I didn't want a long engagement, not after the way Will proposed. It was so romantic—it was at Homecoming, at halftime, and the football stadium was packed. My dad was giving a little speech from the field, like he always did at Homecoming, with the rest of his staff flanking him on either side. Then Will stepped up to the microphone, meeting my eyes from all that distance, and said, "Jennifer, will you marry me?" In front of everyone! It was like a fairy tale...*

There was more, but I'd read enough. "Not much of a surprise, is it?" I finally said to Stephen, keeping my voice even with an effort. "And would you look at this." I pulled two photos out of the envelope. "A Christmas wedding."

One featured Jennifer surrounded by the wedding party, attendants in holiday red, poinsettias and greenery all over the place. The second photo was one of those artful yokes, with the bride's left hand draped over her prayer book, diamond engagement ring twinkling in the candlelight. With no sign of Will in the photo. It was like Jennifer had married...herself. "Lovely ring," I said, just for something to say, and handed the card and photos to Stephen.

I felt his eyes on my face before he looked back at the photos. He finally said, "That's some rock he's put on her finger."

I'd touched Stephen's hand. *I've got to sound normal when Will's name comes up.* "Can you believe it? Will, *married*?" I tried on a careless laugh. "He really must've changed."

But the phone call just now told me Will was still the same! Buoyed by the upcoming holiday, I suddenly craved a hearty supper, like I hadn't wanted for months. I jumped up from my desk, and in the kitchen, I pulled a big frying pan off the hanging rack. Jamie clattered in, book in one hand and tablet computer in the other. "It isn't sandwiches again, it is?" he asked.

"I'm making us a proper meal!" I almost sang the words. Setting the pan down, I threw my arms around Jamie. "You'll never guess what great news I have! We're going to—"

"Aw, Mam." As Jamie squirmed, the house phone rang again. "C'mon, let go of me, I'll get the phone."

"I'll get it," I said, and squeezed him one more time before reaching for the handset. Maybe it's more good news, we've won the lottery, but we don't need it, life is grand!

"It's me again."

"Will?" I froze. "You haven't..." *Changed your mind?* "I haven't had a chance to ask Stephen, but the visit's still a go?"

"You bet it's on!" said Will. "But...I've a bit of a confession." He chuckled, then went silent.

"A confession?" I repeated. When Will wasn't forthcoming, I finally said, "Well, come on then."

"I...ah, tracked down Stephen's new email address, and contacted him yesterday to invite you all for the holiday," Will said. "So no need to ask him twice, right?" I sensed a forced jolliness in his voice.

"Right," I agreed. "With Stephen on board, we can make our plans straightaway."

"The thing is," Will said slowly, "Stephen emailed me right back."

It wasn't like Will to hang back. "To say yes?"

"Not...exactly. Actually, he didn't seem keen. In fact—"

"In fact, what?" Was it *possible* that Stephen didn't want this holiday?

"He said, 'not this year.'" Will paused, then said quickly, "'But thanks for thinking of us.'"

I felt a hard knot of anger in my chest. The nerve of Stephen, turning Will down—and without a word to me! "So," I sputtered, "he said no, straight out, before he—" I remembered that Jamie was right there in the kitchen. And it wouldn't do to throw a strop with Will on the line either. I drew a deep breath. "Thanks for letting me know." I tried to sound blithe. "I'm sure I can..." *Talk Stephen into it?* "Make this holiday happen. You can still count us in."

"You'll not go after Stephen?" Will asked, in the old coaxing tone I remembered. "I'd never want to...cause trouble."

"Of course I wouldn't!" I forced a laugh. "Anyway, who are you kidding? Trouble is your middle name."

"Not anymore," Will said, chuckling. "Wife, kids, a mortgage—who's got time?"

I pictured his grin. *If anyone could wink over the phone, it's you.* "I'm sure Stephen had his reasons for saying the visit wasn't on, but don't worry, he'll change his mind." *After I've set him straight.*

"You'll not be upset with me either, in case there's a little dust-up with Stephen?" Will's voice sounded even more caressing.

I felt a little shiver go up my back. "Absolutely not—really, I'm over the moon that you asked us! We'll look for your email, and see you the twenty-third."

"Cheers, then," Will said. "I knew you'd come through. You always have."

As soon as I rang off, that lump of anger toward Stephen grew. Who did he think he was anyway, making this decision on his own? Barely restraining myself from stomping into the kitchen, I glanced at Jamie. What had he heard? But he was huddled over his tablet, clearly lost in some game. "I'm *starving*, Mam," he said without looking up. "Aren't you going to start the tea?"

Ready to froth at the mouth, I took a deep breath. "In a moment." With my joy at Will's invitation all but buried under the fury expanding inside me, the last thing I could think about was food. "But it'll be sandwiches after all."

I found my handbag, pulled out my mobile, then slipped into the downstairs bathroom. Here I was, breaking my vow not to ring Stephen at work. Pressing his number, I clenched the phone when only his messaging came up. With a terse, "You're wanted home, *now*," I rang off. See what he thought of that!

As I turned to open the door, my mobile rang. Stephen. "What's happened? It's not your mam?"

"It's nothing to do with Mam," I said dangerously. "But if you know what's good for you, you'll come home. Straightaway."

17

"I suppose you'll not want to get into it now," Stephen said. When I didn't answer, he added, "I'll be out of here in a few minutes."

Leaving my mobile on the bathroom counter, I returned to the kitchen. Stephen probably knew exactly why he was needed home, I thought with satisfaction. He had to have worked out that Will contacted me, and I wouldn't have to explain a thing. I was almost looking forward to arguing with him.

I seethed all the way through getting the meal on the table. Shifting my food round my plate, I pretended to listen to Jamie rattle on about some scientist researching the God particle, whatever that was. Stephen's commute was often three quarters of an hour—only how I'd wait that long to give him the bollacking he deserved I didn't know.

After an interminable meal, Jamie took his last bite of food. "Back to your studies, love." I wanted him out of the room before Stephen came home.

Jamie grabbed his tablet from the counter and slouched back into his chair. "Okay, I'll just play another level—"

"Then do it upstairs." I banged the plates into the sink.

Jamie pushed up his glasses with a hangdog look, then left the kitchen, tablet in one hand. Too jumpy to go online—even if I'd every intention of finding that farmhouse or die trying—I paced from the kitchen to the entryway until I heard Stephen's key in the lock.

I crossed my arms as he came in. He looked wearier than he had last night. Too bad! "Well?"

Stephen set down his briefcase with a snap. "You heard from Will. Why am I not surprised?"

"*I* am," I hissed, feeling my insides clench. "*I'm* surprised that you took it upon yourself to make family decisions all on your own!" Stephen opened his mouth, then closed it. "*I'm* surprised you'd turn down the invitation without one word to me!"

"I see Will hasn't changed," Stephen said slowly, hanging up his coat. "Still likes to make wav—"

"Forget Will!" I tried to keep my voice down. "How could you say no, when you know how it's been with..." Us... "Been with Mam all these months, how much I want to get away?"

"I didn't get a chance to tell you—"

"You could've mentioned it last night! So if Will hadn't rung here to invite us, you were just going to keep it to yourself? Even if your job is the center of your universe, I can't believe you'd stoop to that!"

Stephen's shoulders sagged. "I—" He looked like he hadn't sorted it out in his own mind. "Look, I can see you're thrilled to bits about this invita—"

"Yes, I am! A holiday in the country, it's what I've always—"

"Kerry, please listen—I wish I didn't have to tell you this. But I can't do it. There's some big things going on at work, it's being sorted over the next few weeks—"

"You can't be serious!" My voice rose. Your job, again—" I bit my lip. Knowing how sounds in the stone entryway could echo up the stairs, I headed toward the kitchen. "I wish, for one minute, you'd put us first!" I ground out over my shoulder.

Stephen followed me. "I'd go if I could," he said, low. "But I really can't take any sort of holiday until Christmas."

Angry tears choked my throat. "Anyone in a top position can get away for a few days."

Stephen sighed. "You know these stateside outfits, management runs things like they're back in the U.S. If you're not willing to put in 24/7, don't bother."

Leaning against the counter, I swallowed hard. "Don't give me that—Will implied Thanksgiving is a really big holiday in the

States!" When Stephen touched my arm I shook him off. "The bloody firm can just do without you for a few days." Stephen's mouth went tight. "Well, they can!" I added childishly, and then I couldn't help it, my tears spilled over. "I could let go of my worries with Mam off on her cruise, and it'd be a dream come true for me to be in the country! And Will really wants us to come!" Stephen's face darkened, but I couldn't hold my emotions in. "I'll...I'll just go...go *mad* if I can't do this!"

"Or if you can't see—" Stephen broke off.

But I couldn't listen to him, so lost in wanting something...different. "And if I'm to spend another moment in Dublin, when I've a chance to see a farm, I can't bear it!" I swiped at my nose.

"Kerry, you're being dramatic, getting so worked up—"

"I'm not!" I hated it when he got all sensible. "If you won't go, I'll go by myself!"

Stephen waited a beat, then he said levelly, "Stop this. You can't go on your own and you know it."

I dropped my eyes. He wouldn't be alluding to... No, he had to know it was the farm that drew me! But there was that shiver I felt, talking to Will, and for the space of a moment, I wondered if this visit was a good idea after all...

Only Stephen was being so...bullheaded! "How can you say no? Haven't I always gone along with what *you* wanted? Always!"

"I wouldn't quite say always—"

"What about putting off a—" I couldn't say it. *A baby*. "And you'd said only last week that we could take a holiday! Here you've known Will for nearly a dozen years—what kind of a friend *are* you?"

Stephen seemed to look right through me. Then he turned away. "Right, then."

"Right...what?"

"You win," he said tiredly. "We'll go to Galway." Before I could answer, he strode out of the room. Through the doorway, I saw him stop in the entryway for a moment, staring down at his briefcase. Then he snatched it and marched up the stairs.

Hearing him open a door and say hallo to Jamie, I collapsed into a kitchen chair, the tears I'd suppressed spilling onto my cheeks. So I'd have a country holiday after all—shouldn't I feel joyful?

Somehow, though, my hollow victory felt...wrong. Once Stephen went to bed, I knew exactly what I needed to cheer myself up. Back to revisiting another email—the one I'd composed after the wedding announcement...

Dear Will, and of course, Jennifer too!

Congratulations on your marriage! How exciting, a holiday wedding. I loved the photos too—Jennifer, you looked absolutely breathtaking!

Will's proposal—well, it sounds as romantic as what you see in a film. When Stephen asked me to marry him, it was anything but romantic. It's rather funny too, that he did it before we became a number. After Jamie took a shine to him, Stephen became rather a fixture at my mam and dad's. Stephen would play with Jamie, or watch the GAA with Dad, the baby on his lap. He and I were friends, I thought, until one day when everyone was out. Stephen and I were romping on the floor with the baby, and out of the blue he proposed—in a really roundabout way.

I'd stopped writing at that point. It didn't feel right, to share such a private moment—even if Will nor anyone else would ever read it. I'd saved the email and closed it.

Now, feeling guilty with the row with Stephen a few minutes ago—quite rotten really, that perhaps I'd behaved like a spoiled child—I stared at the screen. Stephen had actually been more...tender than I'd let on.

He'd said suddenly, "You know, Jamie'll be talking soon."

"He will, won't he?" I was thinking it was getting close to tea time, and since Stephen usually stayed, even if Dad wasn't here, shouldn't I invite him to have tea with us?

"He'll be calling me something. A name."

"Right." Give Stephen sandwiches, or a proper meal?

"Jamie could either call me 'Stephen'..." I looked up, seeing a strange look on Stephen's face. "Or...Daddy."

"Oh!" I'd gone completely speechless. Stephen and I weren't that close—I mean, not that way at *all*. We'd kissed for the first time only the week before. "But..." I was casting round in my mind all the reasons us marrying was really just...*mad*. "We hardly *know* each other." I blushed. I hadn't meant to emphasize *know*.

"That can change," said Stephen, and he touched my hand. Even if I'd been out of circulation a really long time, I didn't have to be hit over the head to know what he was talking about.

I started babbling, "Have you really considered what you're in for? I'm terribly emotional, crying at the drop of a hat." It was only right that I confess all my faults to him!

"I don't mind," Stephen said. "My mother probably hasn't shed a tear since November of 1963."

"When the President was killed?" I said in a mock-scold. "How can you joke about that?"

"I'm not joking." His face was serious. "She really never cries."

"So you think you can handle a few tears," I allowed, "but...but you'll be taking on a wife *and* a baby. It's a lot of baggage—"

"Don't call Jamie baggage," Stephen told me, and took Jamie on his lap. "He's going to be my son." I thought that was so sweet I couldn't speak. I leaned over Jamie and quickly kissed Stephen. Somehow that became my assent.

"But I haven't a ring for you," he'd added quickly. "You know how it is for me, saving every penny for university fees and all that." Practical even at the most tender moments, was Stephen.

Now, I clicked on the next email I'd written, when I'd finished up the message I'd written about Stephen and me getting together.

Jennifer, you may feel it's strange that Stephen didn't get me an engagement ring. I told him straightaway I didn't need a fancy ring, but before I could make my point he promised that one day he'd give me a grand ring I'd be proud of. Well, if he wanted to dream, I thought, no harm.

When I told my parents, Mam was really surprised. She even tried to talk me out of it, can you believe it? Which is quite comical, since she absolutely dotes on Stephen. Not like the way his mother feels about me—she can take me or leave me. Mostly leave! Anyway, so there we were, engaged. It seems rather ironic that after Stephen and I decided to get married, I stopped reading all my aunt's romantic novels. When I realized I hadn't picked up a love story for weeks, I had to wonder, was the romance over for me already? Had I said yes to Stephen, when I should have said maybe?

But that's ridiculous, isn't it? I have to admit that Stephen's and my wedding was a much simpler affair than yours. There's one moment, though, that I'll never forget—when the priest blessed Stephen and me and presented us to the wedding guests. I caught a glimpse of Stephen's mother—her eyes were cold and stern, mouth pinched tight. Here it was, what's meant to be the most romantic time of a girl's life, and all I could think was, Love of God, I hope Stephen never looks at me like that.

Always, Kerry

18

$\mathcal{I}$ awakened early the next morning, with Stephen sleeping deeply beside me. Rare, even for a Saturday. I looked at his face, remembering what I'd left out of the emails I'd re-read last night.

That after I said yes to Stephen, he'd taken my hand and kissed it, a very un-Stephen-like gesture, and said, "I'm going to give us a good life, you and Jamie and I." Knowing Stephen would never take my heart and stomp on it, like Jamie's father had, I'd been convinced I'd done the right thing.

Unlike last night, when I'd argued with Stephen over the Powers' invitation. Not that he was off the hook for his high-handed refusal. You'd think he'd have realized how much it meant to me, to get away. It was like he didn't know me at *all*. I glanced at Stephen's still face. Whatever the distance between us, Stephen and I couldn't join Will's family in the middle of giving each other the silent treatment.

I crept out of bed, and after fixing myself up—arranging a few curls round my face, a bit of mascara to hide the lingering traces of tears—I went straight into the kitchen. By the time Stephen came down, I'd a fresh-baked loaf of soda bread on the counter, and a pan of eggs on the cooker. "Hungry?" I pinned on a smile.

Stephen didn't return it. "It looks great."

I swallowed. Was he holding a grudge? It wasn't like him. "Slice the bread for us, will you?"

"Sure," he said stiffly, reaching into a drawer.

Since Stephen had consented to the holiday, it was up to me to smooth things over. With Jamie still in bed, I might not have a better chance. "About last night...I was also thinking getting away will help us all regroup. After Mam's cancer scare."

Stephen only nodded, carving the bread with quick, sure strokes.

"And...the hours you've been working are—" Stephen looked up at me, so I quickly added, "Right, I know that's part of your job. But I recently read that people who don't take holidays have a higher incidence of heart attacks."

"So," he said, his head bending to his task again, "you're concerned with the state of my heart?"

What was that about? "And there's Jamie. He studies so hard, he never gets much fresh air, or time in nature—" I broke off as Jamie bounced into the kitchen. I hadn't even heard him come down the stairs.

"I'll take a plate of eggs, Mam." Jamie nipped two slices of bread from beneath Stephen's flashing knife, and not for the first time.

"Good Lord, Jamie," I said, "Will you be more caref—"

"Son, someday you'll run out of luck and lose a finger or two," Stephen said at the same time.

"Whatev," said Jamie, unabashed. When Stephen gave him a look, he said, "Well, I didn't say *whatever*!"

Stephen set the knife down. "Just don't push your luck."

Jamie said, "What's that you were saying, Mam, about fresh air?"

"Well," and I turned off the cooker, "We're going on a holiday!"

"Where?" Jamie asked. "Con's family is going to London over Christmas—I'd be totally keen for that."

"Actually," and I didn't look at Stephen, "it's not for Christmas. We'll be in Galway next week, visiting our friend Will Power and his family. You remember Will, don't you?"

"No," Jamie said.

"You haven't even a dim memory?" I asked, impatient. "He called round at our house dozens of times when you were small. Tall, fair—"

"Talked a lot," said Stephen, his voice laconic. "A *lot*."

"Well, maybe I remember him a bit," Jamie allowed, taking a huge bite of egg.

"Right, then," I said. "So we'll be visiting the Powers in the country—I understand their place is near Lough Corrib—a bit off the beaten path, but just lovely, Will said." Actually he hadn't.

Jamie brought his laden plate to the table. "I don't think that'll work, Mam. There's sure to be no proper broadband."

I gave him an exasperated look. "That may be, but we're going anyway. We'll be celebrating an American Thanksgiving. Won't that be great?"

"Sorry, Mam, I don't want to go." He stretched out one long leg. "It'd be completely boring."

"Jamie." I was unprepared for his resistance. "That's enough. It's already decided, you'll just have to go along with—"

"But I don't want to," he interrupted, his face flushing. "I'm old enough to stay home by mys—"

"You most certainly are not, mister!" I scooped up some eggs, banging the spoon onto my plate. Jamie had picked a time to decide he'd a mind of his own! "You'll do as you're tol—"

"I'll go to Aunt Suz's then," he interrupted. "It's grand there, no one tells me what to do—"

"Son, you could bring your telescope on holiday," Stephen put in.

I froze in surprise, the spoon in midair. I would've never expected Stephen to back me up. Especially after last night. Hardly breathing, I made myself stay silent.

"Why would I want that?" Jamie's tone was mulish.

"Well," Stephen said, dishing up eggs for himself, "you'll recall we bought you that telescope because you said you wanted one more than anything, only to discover it's useless here at our new house. That the whole neighborhood's too bright to see anything. In the country, the sky's dark as pitch. Best stargazing around. All we need is a clear night while we're there."

Jamie stared into the middle distance, chewing. Then his face cleared. "Okay."

"Okay?" I said, still tense.

"Okay, I'd be up for that," Jamie said carelessly.

I released the breath I'd been holding. "Our trip's a go then," I said carefully.

"Right." Jamie stuffed half a piece of bread in his mouth. "When do we leave?"

After Jamie had breezed out of the kitchen, I gave Stephen a rueful smile. "I should have known doing the authoritarian thing with a teenager is hardly effective."

Stephen shrugged. "When you're negotiating, it helps to approach things sideways. Let the other party see some advantages to your position. Soon they'll think it was their idea all along."

"Well, it worked," I told him. "I often forget that I need to treat him a bit differently now.

Stephen seemed to relax. "Me too."

Was all forgiven then? "Have you any free time today?" I ventured. "I was thinking we could do some kind of outing, all of us." I could feel Stephen out about the Wicklow idea I had. "I can't remember the last time we had one."

"I'd like that," Stephen rose from the table. "But Jamie asked me to take him to Phoenix Park. Apparently he wants to go to the zoo."

"The zoo," I repeated, perplexed. "Since when does Jamie like the zoo?"

"He was keen on driving up to Armagh, to go the the Planetarium there," Stephen said quickly, "but I told him that's a bit of a trek for an afternoon outing."

"The zoo sounds...lovely," I said, even if I'd prefer to walk the grounds. "I can pack us some treats to bring along—"

"Kerry," Stephen said, sounding awkward. "Jamie asked if this could be just himself and myself. A father-son thing."

"I see." Feeling wounded, I was determined not to show it. "No problem, I've plenty to do here. In fact, I've got to ring Suz—I made plans with her but now I've got to cancel...My voice trailed away as Stephen's expression grew uneasy.

"Kerry, before we put this whole issue behind us..."

I didn't have to ask what he was talking about. "Yes?"

He leaned against the counter. "I don't want to start another row over this visit to the West, but...how d'you think I feel, Will going behind my back?"

"Oh," I said involuntarily. Will rather had.

"I can't help but think there's something else to the invitation," Stephen said slowly. "That Will wants us to come badly enough that he'd ring you after I told him it wasn't on."

This was the most...open Stephen had been for months. Still, I felt my goodwill toward him evaporate. "Must you look for an ulterior motive?"

"I'd rather not," Stephen said. "I'd rather take his invitation at face value, but—"

"No, you'd rather be suspicious, wouldn't you?" Will hadn't a devious bone in his body. "We're likely some of his oldest friends," I said. "Why wouldn't he want to see us?"

Stephen sighed. "Forget I mentioned it, will you?"

"Right." I didn't bother hiding my sarcasm. "I'll forget it. Easy-peasy."

He didn't appear to notice. "I've got to sort things with the boss right away for the time off, but no question, while we're in Galway I'll have to stay in contact with the office."

"I'd expect nothing less."

"Okay, then?" Stephen stood there, like he'd something else to say.

Whatever it was, I didn't want to hear it. "I've the washing up to do." I slipped past him and banged a pair of pots so he'd leave.

Predictably, he said, "I'll catch up on email before Jamie and I nip out."

I didn't watch Stephen leave. Resenting him, I still couldn't help wondering why Will had invited us, after all these years. Surely it couldn't be that he wanted to see me? Had Will sensed my unhappiness, despite the time and distance between us? It was as if he truly *knew* me, heart and soul...

"Oh, don't be cracked," I muttered, laughing at myself. Enough of the romantic fancies! Still, this holiday would be good for us, for Stephen and me. It had to be.

I rang Suz to tell her the girls' lunch we'd fixed wasn't on. "We're leaving Dublin, to stay with some old friends," I said.

"Anyone I know?" Suz inquired.

"You've...met them," I said carefully. "Years ago. Our friend Will and Jennifer, his wi—"

"Not the hot guy from way back?" Suz squealed, sounding a lot like Ailish. "Lucky girl! Give him a kiss for us, will you?"

I got a bit warm at the thought. "As if—he's got three kids. And he's probably bald and pot-bellied by now."

"Guys like him don't go bald," Suz said decidedly. "They stay ridey forever."

I was inclined to agree, but Suz wasn't to know that. "*Anyway*," I said, "How about we try for a day away the following week."

"I suppose." Suz sighed theatrically. "Have a grand time with Mr. Hunk."

"Suz, really—"

"But not too good, right?" She laughed. "Cheers."

I rang Sharon next to apologize for taking a week's holiday with so little notice. "I know I'm leaving you with more work than one person can handle."

"Ah, don't worry about it," said Sharon, sounding philosophical. "I'm not going to. Since Gwen left, I've rather gotten used to the work piling up."

"Thanks, you're grand!" I said fervently. "Maybe Mr. Smythe will bring in his missus to help out, like she did last time we were short-staffed."

"Just don't concern yourself," said Sharon. "Have a fantastic holiday!"

As we ended the call, Stephen and Jamie were ready to take off. "Have a lovely time, you two." I felt too awkward kissing my son and not my husband, so I didn't kiss either of them. They hadn't been gone a minute when my mobile rang. It was Mam.

I picked up straightaway. "Is everything all right?" I asked anxiously. "I thought you'd be leaving for the airport any minute now."

"I just heard from Suz." Mam sounded odd. "She said you're going to Galway next week. To see your old...friend."

"I was going to ring you," I said, not very convincingly. "We're taking that advice you gave me the other night—having a holiday."

"And Stephen's...keen to go?"

"Oh sure," I lied. *You're a terrible daughter, lying to your mam.* "We're both looking forward to seeing Will's wife and kids," I added. Well, I was! Okay, at least I wanted to meet the girls.

"Well..." Mam all but *harrumphed*, "I suppose Jamie will have some playmates."

Playmates? Mam must still think of her grandson as a little boy. "That's it," I said, even if Jamie was more likely to go hang gliding than hang out with three little girls. I rushed to get off the phone. "Have a wonderful cruise, Mam."

After ringing off, I looked round the empty kitchen, my gaze going unerringly toward my office nook. *If I'm not wanted on the family outing, I know exactly how I can amuse myself.*

19

Getting back on my laptop, I opened up my email folder, and clicked on the one from Will a year after his Christmas wedding. Although technically, Will hadn't written it.

Hi Kerry and Stephen,

Our little girl, Mackenzie, was born in October! Everyone teases us, the way she came 10 months after we got married, but I was so ready to be a mom. And I love it! I told Will I want a houseful of kids. My dad's promised Will a promotion down the road, but I don't want to wait that long for another baby. Merry Christmas to you all, Jennifer

Will had added a few words—but not to moon over his new daughter.

P.S. The in-laws are mad about me, now that I've given them a grandchild. And the pressure's on already for more kids, can you believe it? By the way, when are the pair of you going to take the plunge and give Jamie a sib?

That's it then, I'd thought. Will was *really* committed now. All grown up and responsible. Suddenly this email-diary thing I was doing seemed so...so silly and childish. But I hadn't been quite ready to give it up. One more go then, I'd decided. I'll give this email my all.

Hi Will and Jennifer,

What fabulous news—a baby girl! I can hardly believe it, Will—you, a father! Jennifer, I can practically see the stars in your eyes. You must love babies if you're already thinking of more when you're in the midst of night feedings and dirty nappies and baby sick!

Naturally, Stephen and I are terribly envious. "Looks like they beat us to the baby punch," I told him as we read your email. "Aren't they lucky?"

Stephen took the practical view. "Having a family before they can afford it?" he said. "Sounds a bit mad to me."

Okay, sometimes I've want to ask him, Do you always have to be so sensible? Can't we ever do anything mad, ourselves? But you know Stephen. Yes, Stephen does always have to be sensible. And no, we can't.

But then, I'm no stranger to doing the prudent thing...At least once, anyway!

That's marrying Stephen. The morning after Stephen's proposal—or shall I put it, "proposal," I couldn't help thinking I'd been awfully clear-eyed and practical about a decision most girls would be all starry-eyed over. But at least Mam and Dad would be happy. Or so I thought.

My mam actually tried to talk me out of marrying Stephen. But when it was clear I wasn't to be persuaded, she put her hand on my shoulder. "Just be certain it's Stephen's face you want to see across the breakfast table for the rest of your life—the man you want to have more babies with."

I was sure. Still, after we'd been married a few years, I'd felt a niggling doubt. In fact, I'll confess something straight out that I've never told a living soul: I wondered if it would be right to have Stephen's baby. If I was to have another child, shouldn't it be with...like, a soulmate? Stephen and I...well, we get along fine, but he isn't like an anam cara—a soul friend, who's always in perfect sync with me, who can see into my heart...But you know, I always tell myself, What an eejit romantic notion! Stephen's so good to me. If that's not being your soul friend, what is?

Cheers, Kerry

The email had joined all the others. In the Drafts folder.

I pushed my chair away from my desk. I must have been off my head a bit to write such drivel, about babies and soulmates and all that—to veer from diary to fairy tale. I found it easier to think back to Mam's concerned look the morning after Stephen proposed. "Stephen's lovely," she'd said slowly, "But he won't be too quiet a sort for you?"

I thought you liked him was on the tip of my tongue. Dad, however, gave me an approving look. "Fair play to you, love— Stephen's already part of the family." Then he kissed me on the way to fetch his morning paper.

"Stephen'll be a great daddy," I told Mam. "That's enough for me."

"You've said it yourself, you're the romantic sort." Mam sounded exasperated. "You'll want to marry someone you're absolutely mad for, someone you can be passionate about in every way—"

"If you must know, we've plenty of passion." I blushed. *If the way Stephen had made me feel after he proposed is anything to go by.*

Mam waved her hand. "God love you, I'm not talking about *that*. I mean, having a passion for your life together—not marrying for practical reasons."

Than Dad came in, newspaper in hand, and sat down. "Now Anne, no need to go off on one of your fancies. Our Kerry's got her head on straight. Stephen's a good fella." He'd smiled at me again, then opened his paper with a satisfied snap.

Now, I left my nook, shrugged on a jacket and let myself out the front door for a walk. After all these years with Stephen, I had to ask myself—was a soulmate just a romantic fantasy? Or simply the man you loved and held in your arms every night the whole of your married life?

I strode along the footpath, past all the carbon-copy houses and gardens. It was a question I couldn't answer, since our holding was a thing of the past. How many nights had Stephen and I lain side-by-side in bed, me staring up at the ceiling? The worst of it was, so many times I hadn't had the nerve to look at my husband, because I'd been afraid his eyes were open, and doing the same.

20

MEMO:

Monday, 9 am, 16 November
To: Mr. Theodore Smythe, CEng

I am taking a week off starting Monday next, 23 November, for a family matter. I regret the short notice but the situation demands my presence. I trust you will understand. Perhaps in my absence you might have an opportunity to consider my workspace issue. In any event, I apologize for any inconvenience.

Kerry McCormack

"How many more kilometers?" Jamie asked as we left Galway City.

Admiring a particularly sweet little stone barn not far from the country lane we were traveling, I turned to smile at him. "Here I thought you'd taken a vow of silence." Immersed in a game on his tablet, Jamie had hardly spoken a word all the way across Ireland.

"Aw, Mam, you and Dad weren't talking either."

I glanced at Stephen, but his eyes were on the road. Turns out, an uneasy truce is really no truce at all. Especially if your teenager notices it. Stephen had seemed pensive after he and Jamie returned from the Planetarium, the day we'd argued over Will *again*. Every word out of him since had a tone that told me he was putting a good face on. For whatever it was. And once we were on our way to Galway, his dialogue had consisted of talking to the office on his mobile when we stopped for breaks. *So be like that*, I thought, determined to enjoy the drive.

Simply being away from the office—and Mr. Smythe glowering at me ever since I'd given him my memo—was a pleasure in itself. But as Gwen had pointed out earlier, if the boss didn't like me taking time off, what could he do to me? Sack me? When he was already short-staffed?

I put him out of my mind to watch the scenery again. After the city gloom of Dublin, the clouds had broken up as we made our way across the Midlands. My senses expanded as I took in the country scenery flanking the motorway—the hills with their patchwork of stone walls, the winter fields, bare of crops, the sheep and cows dotting green pastures. Rolling down the window, I breathed in the fresh air, strangely balmy for November, and tried to calm the nervous energy running through me.

Hearing from Will had been a rather surreal experience—especially after the contacts after the first baby news had been entirely sporadic.

Two nights ago, I'd taken a look at the email Will had sent four or five Christmases ago. I'd read it so many times I knew it by memory.

> We just had daughter #3, how about that? This one is already a little mischief-maker—a right little bruiser too! I suppose one of these days, when we have enough kids for a basketball team, she'll be captain. Lucky for me, I've just gotten another promotion—to assistant head of the athletic department—finally! Jaysus, I'll really have to behave myself—especially now that Jennifer wants a big house, with room in the garden for every kiddie yoke at Toys R Us, a swing set and a playhouse. No sandbox, though—too much dirt!

It was the last email he'd sent. I'd never written a reply. Not even a fake one.

"Well, does *anyone* know if we're getting closer?" Jamie broke into my thoughts.

I put Will's email from my mind. "It won't be long now, I'm sure," I said cheerily. Not that I knew exactly where Ballydara was.

If Stephen did, he wasn't saying anything. Yesterday, he'd spent his Sunday pounding on his keyboard in his office. When I asked him when he was going to get ready for our trip, he said, "Got to get some emails off before we leave."

Jamie was running round upstairs. He'd never packed his own things for a trip before, and kept coming up with this or that to put in his bag. "And Mam, can you bring your laptop? Dad's has been dodgy lately, and I've that school project I'm still working on."

"Right," I said, not that any kid would be doing schoolwork during a holiday. Yesterday, I'd been wondering when I'd get to my own packing when the phone rang. Seeing the familiar number from America, I felt my spirits lift. I held off a moment, to see if Stephen would pick up. But on the fourth ring, wondering if he was avoiding Will, I couldn't wait any longer.

"I'm glad I caught you." It was Jennifer. "We're getting ready to leave for the airport and I just realized my procrastinating husband never got around to emailing you directions to the farm!"

"I wasn't worried," I said quickly, lest she hear the disappointment in my voice. "We can muddle our way to Ballydara, and Stephen has GPS in his car." Stephen, such a planner in every other part of his life, hadn't concerned himself with looking up the route either.

"Will," she called, "they have GPS in the car."

I heard a guffaw, then she said to me, "GPS might not work out in the boonies. Good thing I've got a map app on my phone…" Jennifer rattled off the route, starting in Dublin—as if we couldn't find our way simply pointing the car west—then burbled on about this and that road through Galway City and into the country. By that time, however, I'd completely lost track. Jennifer had a way of rather going on. "Um…wait," she said. "Ballydara's not on the online map." Then she called out again, "Here, Will, you take the phone."

I tensed, anticipating Will's voice… But it was Jennifer again. "He says, just go to Hurley's pub or the shop in the village and ask. Everyone knows where the Power farm is."

I tried not to think that Will couldn't be bothered to get on the line. "Really, I'm sure we can find it," I'd said. "See you tomorrow!"

"I can't wait!" Jennifer said, and we quickly exchanged mobile phone numbers. "I'm *so* happy you can join us. The girls are looking forward to a real Irish vacation and—" I heard a voice in the background, then she said, "Will says this international call will break the bank if I don't get off the phone, so see you then!"

Now, in the car, I told myself I should try harder to warm to Jennifer. Focus on the farm. And mending this rift with Stephen…

I looked over at him as he drew the Toyota to a stop at a crossroads, and a signpost caught my eye. It pointed to about ten different locales, all of them in Irish. "How will we ever find the place?" I asked him.

"With no GPS out here, we could be, like, lost." Jamie sighed dramatically. "Forever."

Stephen's mouth quirked. Without hesitating, he took a right onto a road bordered with low stone walls, patches of woods just beyond. "Have you forgotten I was a country boy once? I'll get us there."

I breathed a sigh of relief. So we weren't lost—and Stephen actually seemed to be getting into the spirit of this visit! My mobile rang.

"I was afraid I'd missed you!" Jennifer again. "I just found out there's no cell reception here at the farm or around Ballydara village. Can you believe that? I mean, it's like the dark ages! I'm calling from the neighbor's landline. Thank *God* they were home."

"Is everything all right?" I asked anxiously.

"Oh, it's fine," Jennifer said breezily. "I was just hoping that when you get to the village, you'll pop into the shop, and…wait—" She called out, "What's it called, Mr. Whelan? The shop?"

"Just the shop," a man said. "Okay," said Jennifer, "it's the shop—if you could pick up a few packages waiting there for me that would be absolutely *wonderful*."

"We'd be happy to—"

"Fabulous!" she broke in. "I went online before we left home and ordered some food for Thanksgiving dinner—I wasn't up for roasting a turkey so I got a really gorgeous ham and two desserts you wouldn't believe! But right now I've got to unpack and the girls are starving and I'm trying to get some dinner started, and I just don't know how I'll find the time to run down to the village, especially since…already bought groceries…Galway City…" The reception began getting a bit garbled.

"I'm losing you," I said, wondering why she couldn't ask Will to go to the shop. "We'll get whatever you need…Jennifer?"

No answer. "We just lost our mobile signal, I guess," I said to Stephen, and turned off my phone. "Jennifer has an errand for us at the village shop."

"Right, no bother, said Stephen, zipping fearlessly along the lane, although the Land Cruiser took up nearly the entire width.

I found myself clutching my armrest a bit too hard, nervously eyeing the curve ahead. "You *have* noticed there's no room for error on this road?" I asked Stephen.

Jamie was less subtle. "You're going awfully fast, Dad. What if we meet another car, or a lorry or something?"

"I often drove my granddad's tractor on lanes like this," Stephen said lightly. "It's like riding a bicycle, don't you know?" He rounded the long curve, then all of a sudden I was blinking in the sunlight. As he slowed the car, we passed three houses, one a charming little cottage with a vivid red door.

A short distance later, Stephen pulled up alongside a small village green. Hurley's Pub was on the other side of it. "What did I tell you? Ballydara!"

21

I looked round the village, completely charmed. The pub had a green sign across the front of the second story, with "Hurley's" written in white letters, and window casements and doors painted the same bright green. There were two empty storefronts on either side of the pub with the same painting scheme, one red, the other in blue. Just across the road, a shop with a beige-pink awning read "Murphy's Shop," with a similarly patterned pink door and window casements. Lit fairy lights were strung round all the storefronts, seeming incongruous in the sunshine.

I looked over the top of Hurley's roof. The hills beyond the village had the same patchwork of stone walls I'd seen all across Ireland, with cows, sheep and piles of stones here and there, houses and farm buildings spread out. The late afternoon sun was low in the sky, bathing the pastures with a golden-pink glow. Misty clouds drifted round the hilltop, giving it a mystical air...

I felt tears behind my eyes and an ache in my heart. The rainbow-hued buildings and green hills reminded me of the village near Aunt Rose's place—and held a welcome I'd never felt anywhere else. Suddenly, I felt pulled into this place, body and soul—like I'd just come *home*.

I opened my door, eager to get our errand at the shop out of the way and up to the farm. Stephen didn't move, staring up at same hillside I'd been gazing at. "I'd nearly forgotten," he said low, as if to himself. "How lovely the country is."

I looked at him quickly, bemused. "It's beautiful here, isn't it?"

"Look at the mist, there." Stephen didn't take his eyes from the hills. "It must be coming in from Lough Corrib to the north, on the other side of those hills." After a long moment, he opened his own door and stepped down from the Land Cruiser, taking a deep breath. "Smell that country air, Jamie?"

Jamie wrinkled his nose as I exited the car. "All I can smell is something sort of...nasty," he said frankly.

"That little hint of manure?" Stephen leaned against the bonnet and pulled his mobile from his pocket. "Since when are you so sensitive, lad?"

Apparently the picturesque scenery drew his attention only so long. He did look up as a heavy-set older fellow with a full head of snowy white hair came out of Hurley's. "Hallo there!" The man gave us a cheery nod.

Waving back to him, I said, "I'm off to the shop. You'll come, Jamie?"

"I'll stay in the car." Jamie bent his head toward his tablet again. "And finish this level."

"I'll only be a moment," I promised Stephen. Heading toward the shop, I heard him exchange a few words with the gent from the pub. As I admired the holiday display in the shop window, the man came to the door just behind me and opened it, the shop bell tinkling. "After you, Missus?" he said with a warm grin, and followed me in.

Stepping aside as the older fellow headed straight for the counter, I watched a dark-haired, fortyish woman with a long plait behind the long counter, arranging a shelf of chocolates in an artful way. An older woman with tightly permed curls was near the cash box. "Bernard!" she said to the man. "I'll get your parcel." She disappeared into a back room for a moment, then emerged carrying a parcel. "You're lucky I could find it, what with all that other clobber taking up my storeroom." She thumped the package on the counter. "You'd think your woman would have wanted to pick up her boxes the minute they arrived—they're stamped 'Perishable' every which way."

"I understand she's ordered an entire banquet from America!" the man chuckled merrily, leaning against the counter. "Who ever heard of such a thing?"

"And what's wrong with good Irish food, I'd like to know?" said the older woman, obviously the shop owner. "Her order must've cost the earth and the moon besides—"

"A lot of folk are doing it these days," said the dark-haired woman, not breaking from her task. "Ordering food online."

"Too busy to put on a proper dinner?" The older woman sniffed.

"Not everyone has a husband at home who loves to cook," the younger woman said lightly.

"Excuse me," I said quickly. They had to be talking about Jennifer. "Could either of you give directions to the Power farm?"

"Ahhh," said the shop owner, exchanging a glance with the man. Then she looked past me, through her window, where our Toyota was parked out front. "You'll take the road uphill—" She broke off. "From the city, are you?"

Did she mean Galway City, or Dublin? Didn't matter. "Yes," I said. "I've never been—"

"You've come to look at the place, then? I do hope you'll buy it." Her voice warmed. "Doesn't seem right, to have it empty, and fall to rack and ruin." She didn't need to say how many ancient, deserted cottages dotted the length and breadth of Ireland. "Especially since it has lots of...of..."

"Potential," said the man.

Where had they got the idea Will's farm was for sale? "I imagine it does." I tried again, "So...the direc—"

"Someone should start farming it again," the man said, smiling at me. "Maybe you're just the one to do it?"

"And if you're going to fix up the place," said the woman, "your man Bernard here can help you."

"I do kitchens, baths, anything you need," said Bernard with a wink.

Did they think I'd come to Ballydara to look at properties for sale? "Actually, all I need is—"

"You'll want to follow the road up the hill," the younger woman said suddenly, glancing over her shoulder, her lips curving in a smile. Her features, that had seemed plain in profile, were transformed. "It'll be two, two-and-a half kilometers—past a dairy farm, that's my dad's place. The Power farm is just up the road. If you get to Ballydara Lodge you've gone too far."

"Thank you," I said gratefully, ready to go. Then, "Oh, I nearly forgot—I'm here to pick up some parcels. For Mrs. Jennifer Power."

The two older folk exchanged glances again as the younger woman resumed her task. "You must be...em, the visitors they're expecting," the permed woman said slowly.

"That's right," I said. Apparently everyone knew everyone else's business here. I rather liked it.

"I'll be right back." She ducked into the back again.

"What do you think of the warm in November?" said Bernard. "And the sunshine? Like September, it is."

"I love it," I said, smiling. "But I hope it doesn't mean this coming winter will be even wetter and colder—"

"Here you go." Perm Woman had returned with two large parcels.

"Thanks, this is grand." I took a parcel in each hand.

"There's more," and she disappeared once again. I heard more boxes being shifted around.

"Need some help back there?" Bernard was still leaning on the counter, like he was just starting to settle in.

"Got it," said the woman, and came out with an even larger package, her face flushed with effort. "I'll take it out for you."

"Thanks again," I said to the younger woman, then headed for the door. Perm Woman said, "I'll meet you at your car in two shakes." Then, "Bernard! Show our visitor some manners!"

"Oh, right!" He pushed away from the counter, then with a courtly little bow, opened the door for me again. "Reasonable rates," he said to me, with another wink. He reminded me of Barry Fitzgerald from *The Quiet Man* at his twinkliest.

"Thanks," I said to him. "Cheers, then."

"Sure, we'll be seeing you around," he said confidently. "By the way, your man Power has a big red hire car. It'll be in the drive, unless he's gone off to Knockferry for a pint."

This Bernard had a strange sense of humor. As if Will wouldn't even be at his farm to greet us!

Stephen wasn't waiting at the car. I set the parcels on the ground. "Where's your dad?" I asked Jamie through the window.

He barely looked up. "Um, I dunno. Looking around maybe?"

On a hunch, I headed for the pub, even if it was hardly likely Stephen was getting a fortifying pint before facing our hosts. Pausing in the doorway to let my eyes adjust from the sunshine, I saw a tall, striking girl with dark hair hurling darts at a board like she was throwing grenades.

"Grainne! Will you take it easy on my darts?" the barman said good-naturedly to the tall girl. "You're going to break them in two!"

"Maybe you'll want to invest in better darts," she said with a cheeky grin, and threw another dart.

Stephen suddenly materialized in front of me, pocketing his mobile. "You're ready then?"

As we crossed the green, he didn't volunteer the reason for visiting the pub, and I didn't ask, not wanting to disturb his good form. By the time Perm Woman emerged from the shop with the third parcel, Stephen had the Toyota's big rear door open, Jamie's telescope box carefully stowed to the side. "Thanks," he said to the woman, smiling as he took the heavy package from her. "You'll be...?"

"Mrs. Murphy," she said, as I picked up the remaining parcels and handed them to Stephen.

"We're the McCormacks," he said, as friendly and outgoing as I'd ever seen him—as if he was in his element, just like he was driving the country lanes. "I'm called Stephen, this is my wife Kerry, and that'll be Jamie, there inside, too busy to say hello."

"Well," said the woman, "I knew some McCormacks, in County Cork. Are they your people?"

"Could be," said Stephen, setting the boxes in the car. He suddenly seemed to have all the time in the world, and before I knew it, he and Mrs. Murphy were going through a list of names and potential relations.

I could feel my nervousness return. "We're expected, so we'd better be off," I broke in. "Perhaps next time Stephen sees his dad, he can ask about the McCormack folk."

"I'll do that," he promised, arranging the parcels neatly around our luggage.

"Cheers," I said to Mrs. Murphy as I opened my car door.

"And to you, Missus," she said, then low, "And please don't mind what was said in there." She nodded toward the inside of the shop. "I get a bit…pressurized, as Christmas comes closer."

"I've already forgotten it," I said smiling. Even if I'd had to twist Stephen's arm to get here, meeting three lovely people already seemed like a good omen for the holiday.

22

Stephen drove up the road as the sun sank behind the hills. We traveled past a working farm, where a herd of cows congregated near a shed. "Yuk." Jamie wrinkled his nose again. "How do people stand it, living next to cows?"

"You get used to it, son," said Stephen, peering at the cows. "In a way, you come not to mind it a bit."

I didn't. Aunt Rose's place had smelled the same. As the road curved, Jamie cried, "Dad, watch out!"

Stephen slammed on the brakes, stopping the car just a few meters from an undersized brown cow in the middle of the lane. After giving us a long, placid look, she ambled to the side.

"Thanks, Jamie. Close call," said Stephen, putting the car back in motion. After a couple of minutes we came upon a drive, a big red car parked crosswise off to one side. "This must be it." As he let the engine idle at the bottom of the drive, I took in the two-story farmhouse, and my heart stopped. I mean, it *stopped*.

Bathed in the light of the setting sun, the house was of golden stone, like Aunt Rose's, with a climbing rose near the stoop that still held some leaves and a few dying blossoms.

What had me utterly spellbound was something else entirely. The house was a twin of the one I'd seen online only days ago, right down to the missing shingles at the apex of the roof. Tears welled in my eyes, and I had to dig in my bag for a tissue.

Stephen touched my arm. "What is it?"

Of *course* I couldn't tell him about the farm web surfing. Besides, it couldn't be the same house—that just wasn't possible. "I'm so happy to be here." I dabbed my eyes, not wanting Will and Jennifer to see me with a puffy red face. "I never thought the place would be so...breathtaking."

"What are you talking about?" Jamie asked from the back seat. "It's like a...a kip!"

"I love it," I told him firmly. The property was a bit run down, but still charming. In front of the house, an area bordered by low stone walls must have once been a cottage garden. Now, it held only clumps of grass and weeds. Outside the walls, a crooked wooden swing dangled from a massive tree. Across a stretch of rumpled grass, a low barn of the same golden stone sat nestled in a small rise, its rusty metal roof taking on a reddish glow in the light of the setting sun. A shed of the same rusty metal was nearby, and another small structure that seemed to list to one side lay just beyond it. A chicken coop?

And encircling the house and outbuildings was single line of brushy trees. "Those must be the apple trees Will mentioned," I said.

Stephen put the car back in gear. He turned into the drive, past a fir grove in a hollow, and slowly went up the small incline. With a quick look around, he parked the car. "The way the trees surround the farm," he remarked, "it looks a bit like an...an island, don't you think?"

As we climbed out of the car, the front door squealed on its hinges. Will appeared, taking the entire stoop in one graceful stride. Under the spell of the farm, I felt I was in a dream. Or that I'd traveled back in time.

Will hadn't changed at all. In his mid-thirties, he still had the look of a larger-than-life Christopher Robin. As trim and broad-shouldered as ever, he was tanned, his ruddy cheeks a marked contrast to Stephen's city pallor.

I hung back as Will reached out a hand to Stephen for a forearm-clasping handshake. "Been a long time," said Will. "Glad you could make it."

"Thanks," Stephen said quietly.

"Welcome to the farm," Will said to Jamie, giving him an equally man-to-man handshake. "Would you look at the size of you!" Then he met my eyes, his handsome face crinkling into that warm grin I remembered.

"I can't believe we're all together again," I said. "After all these years!" I thought it would be odd, if after all these years I didn't give Will a hug. But before I could move he wrapped his arms round me, giving me a squeeze and a big smacky kiss on my ear. "Will!" I laughed as he released me. "You're still full of cheek!"

"Well, full of something!" Will chuckled, and elbowed Stephen. "What d'you say?"

"Full of something, all right," said Stephen. He didn't smile. Then the door banged again and out came Will's wife and daughters.

In the hubbub of greetings—a kiss for Jennifer, Jamie's awkward "Hallo" after which he escaped from the crowd to wander round the yard—my eyes went straight to the three girls. If you'd gone to Perfectchild.com to order three daughters, you couldn't have found any more beautiful. Long-lashed blue eyes, honey-colored hair in ponytails, and tanned coltish legs. The two oldest stayed alongside Jennifer, while the youngest, who must've been around four or five years of age, ran straight to Will. She jumped into his arms with the confidence of a child who knew her father would always catch her.

Jennifer was every bit as attractive as I remembered. Her fresh make-up, highlighted blond hair and form-fitting jeans made me feel my flowered skirt was rather...mumsy. If only I'd put on an extra coat of mascara, or fixed my hair after having the car window open. Jennifer's only defect, if you could call it that, was an anxious air about her, and the crease between her brows that seemed too deep for someone her age.

I smoothed my hair. "It was so generous of you to invite us—"

"Mackenzie and Emerson." Jennifer said proudly, drawing the two older girls forward. She gestured toward youngest, still in Will's arms. "And that's Madeline."

"Maddie," said the little girl, her mouth set stubbornly. "I don't like Madeline."

I stifled a laugh, seeing that the two older girls were actually the "perfect" ones. They wore the kind of trendy outfits I'd seen in magazine adverts, their hair tidily captured in shiny pink slides. Maddie's ponytail drooped, one slide hanging drunkenly over one ear, and she'd a fleck of mustard on her too-small Dora the Explorer fleece top. "It's a stupid name," Maddie added.

"We don't say 'stupid,'" Jennifer told her. "You know that."

Maddie only grinned. She'd her daddy's charm, no doubt about it. His mischief too. As Jennifer reached for the smear on her daughter's shirt, Maddie ducked away, and wiggled out of Will's arms. Racing to the swing, she heaved onto it on her stomach. "Wheeeee," she squealed, and tore her little legs through the grass to set the swing in motion. "I'm flyiiiiing!"

"That child," Jennifer sighed. "I don't know how she got so wild."

I gave Will a surreptitious look. He was watching Maddie, a funny mix of pride and envy in his face.

23

As Jennifer ushered me inside, I was enveloped by the magic of entering my fantasy farmhouse. The front room was papered in faded pink roses, the threadbare lace curtains pushed open, with a squishy-looking chintz couch and three easy chairs surrounding a frayed rug. A dusty, old-fashioned radio sat on a table in the corner.

I followed Jennifer past a closed door and into the kitchen. Despite the cluttered countertops—boxes, groceries and the three parcels Stephen had brought in—I felt like I was back at my Aunt Rose's. The lino floor was cracked in places, like hers had been, the countertops chipped, and the appliances were vintage 70s. *This*, I decided, was a kitchen I could cook in.

"I'm sorry the house is such a pit," Jennifer said.

I set down my handbag. "I think it's rather cozy."

"Really? I wanted us to meet for Thanksgiving in Galway City, at a nice hotel. Then we could have gone out for the holiday dinner." She frowned at the stains around the edge of the sink. "Look at this grime! I don't know why Will insisted on coming here."

Because he knew how much I loved the country? I couldn't wait for tomorrow so I could tour the farm at my leisure.

"And the dust is unbelievable. You sit on the couch and clouds of it pouf into your nose," Jennifer went on. "It's an asthma attack waiting to happen."

"How awful!" I hated to think of her lovely little girls wheezing for breath. "Which of the kids has asthma?"

"Actually, none of them." Jennifer seemed unabashed. "Anyway, Will and I are in the downstairs bedroom, and the bedspread is even dustier than the couch! How all of us will tolerate this gnarly place until the 28th is anyone's guess." Glancing toward the front room, I saw the luggage Stephen and Will had hauled in from the car. Now they were on the couch, sitting in front of a laptop, while Jamie and the girls were gathered on the rug, peering at his tablet. As far as I could tell, nobody was sneezing.

I felt foolish for getting so alarmed. "As far as I'm concerned, a bit of dirt is no bother." The careworn farmhouse was actually a welcome change from our almost pathologically tidy home back in Dublin.

"If staying here isn't bad enough," Jennifer said, "organizing Thanksgiving dinner was a nightmare." She began unboxing the biggest parcel, a pre-baked ham. "Men! They just don't think of these things."

Well, Stephen would. "I suppose not." I helped her wrestle the ham into the fridge.

"Have you ever seen a grimier refrigerator?" Jennifer shoved the ham inside and banged the door shut. "The freezer hasn't been defrosted for so long it hardly works at all. And don't even talk to me about the oven! Must be ten years of baked on crud in there." She looked distastefully round the room. "Will said the farm kitchen was 'a bit old-fashioned,' but I get here and find it's a disaster."

"At least there's the grandfather's kitchen things," I said. The old dresser against one wall was full of dusty chinaware. "Even it they'll have to be washed."

"Like everything else in this house." Jennifer bit her lip. "A neighbor came in and put clean sheets on the beds—by the way, the beds are *tiny*, I don't know how people can sleep a wink here—but I thought I'd cry when I saw the bathrooms. And there's no cleaning services locally."

"I'll clean them," I volunteered. Which should teach me not to get so starry-eyed about a country holiday, I thought ruefully. "Really, I want to help out."

"Would you?" Jennifer smiled gratefully. "I don't want the girls to catch some germ or whatever."

"Anyway, it's a stroke of luck, to have two bathrooms," I said. "Most old houses wouldn't."

"Oh, Will knew he'd *never* have gotten me here if there'd been only one," Jennifer said. "And if all this dirt isn't bad enough, there's no dishwasher, so you can't really sanitize the dishes."

"Sanitize?" I thought she was having me on. But from the look on her face, I saw she was dead serious.

Jennifer pulled her mobile out of her handbag, then just as quickly, shoved it back inside. "I keep forgetting there's no cell reception out here—one more thing to worry about. What if one of the girls should get sick? Or cut themselves on all that rusty junk around the yard? Emerson's already skinned her knee, tripping on that crack on the stoop. And that swing! Maddie's been on it non-stop—I'm just waiting for that old decrepit rope to snap. But Will just says they'll be fine. Everything will be fine. Then he goes back to his sports videos."

I had to wonder how a carefree bloke like Will ended up with a worrywart like Jennifer. Seeing the crease between her well-groomed brows deepen, I said quickly, "Any special plans for your, em, Thanksgiving? I don't know much about the holiday."

"Not much to tell," said Jennifer. "It's four days of food and football. Oh, and shopping."

"Shopping?" I wasn't getting this American tradition at all.

"You know, Christmas shopping. People go crazy, trying to get the best bargains. Not that you can do any shopping in the village."

"Oh...right," I said, and began ferrying the dusty china from the dresser to the sink. I wasn't much for gift-buying—I preferred giving homemade goodies. Besides, even with Stephen's increasing income, we still kept our Christmas presents low-key. Not that I'd any idea what to get for Stephen anymore. If he needed anything, he'd just buy it himself.

Jennifer pulled a face. "Oh, the *worst* thing—there's no TV here. The girls will be bored out of their gourds."

Worst thing? "They could...play outside?" I turned on the taps. "While this lovely weather holds, anyway."

"But Will's the one who'll go absolutely *nuts* without TV," said Jennifer. "He's a total sports fiend—football, soccer, rugby, you name it, he'll watch it."

I thought it better not to point out that sport was his profession. Spying the other two packages from Murphy's shop as the sink filled, I said, "Do the other things go in the fridge?"

"Oh, I almost forgot!" Jennifer pushed some of the countertop stuff to one side. "I like having a TV in the kitchen myself, to watch cooking shows while I heat up dinner," she confided, unwrapping a parcel. "I don't do much cooking or baking from scratch, so I was totally excited to discover two of the most fabulous desserts in a magazine. I couldn't decide which I liked best...so," and she freed a box from its bubble wrap, "I got both of them."

As she lifted the box top I shut off the water and peered inside.

"Blue velvet cake," she said. "It cost a fortune, but totally worth it, don't you think?"

"It's blue all right." I gazed at the resplendent dessert, wondering how much food coloring you'd need to attain that shade of lurid blue.

"And look at this one!" She quickly unwrapped the second package to show me a chartreuse iced cake with a tomato colored bow. "This one is chocolate cake with salted caramel filling, fondant frosting, and a white chocolate ribbon. Isn't it just *amazing*? It'll be a great dessert to get us in the Christmas spirit early."

The yellow-green and dark orangey colors, so very un-Christmasy, sort of hurt my eyes. "Amazing," I agreed. Unable to picture myself eating either cake, I said, "My mam always says, you can't have too many puddings."

"Actually, pie is the traditional dessert for Thanksgiving—any chance you're up for baking? Maybe you could make something that's sort of...Irish," Jennifer said tentatively.

"Be glad to—how about apple pie?" I smiled at the thought of baking again.

"Whatever you make, Will would love something Irishy."

Jennifer turned away to start putting away groceries. "Anyway, with this grungy house, thank *God* this is a short visit—Oh!" Her hand flew to her mouth. "I didn't mean that the way it came out—honestly, it's great to share the holiday with you."

"Oh, no worries—we're so happy to be here." I began collecting dusty china from the dresser to wash.

"My parents were upset enough we didn't spend Thanksgiving with them," Jennifer said. "I had to promise we'd spend a long Christmas weekend at their house."

Settling in at the sink, I gazed out the window, seeing the outline of an abandoned vegetable garden, filled with two-foot tall weeds. Beyond the garden plot were three neat rows of bare shrubs, nearly lost in the tall grass. Blueberries? Craning my neck, I could see a pasture choked with brambles up the slope from the firs.

Jennifer was going on about all the holiday traditions in her own family, but I tuned it out. She'd be sure to work in another complaint somewhere. Anyway. I wouldn't have to share her company all that much, since I was going to spend as much time outdoors as I could, to fully enjoy the farm. That's what I'd come here for.

Well, almost all.

24

*A*t dinner, with Will chatting non-stop, it felt like the old days. Only with bad food. And Jennifer.

The kids had quickly finished the tea of fish fingers and tinned green beans, then escaped to the front room to cluster round Jamie's tablet. Will soon took the floor, telling Stephen and me about his coaching work. As he kept the talk and the drink flowing—lager for him and wine for the three of us—I gazed at him, pretending to pay rapt attention.

Will's stories, more palatable than the food, were all about the hijinks of Paul Bunyan State's sporting activities—the pranks, the parties, the all-around crack, we heard it all. Stephen didn't say much. Hoping I didn't look bored myself, after half an hour I pushed my half-filled plate away. "Sounds like you have too much fun to call this job a *job*."

Will leaned back in his chair, his eyes sparkling. "You know me, *craic* is my middle name."

Laughing, I said, "Wait, I thought it was *trouble*."

"Speaking of trouble," said Jennifer, "Mackenzie had to miss her dance recital for this trip, and the teacher had to re-do all the choreography and then—"

"Did I tell you about two of my football lads?" Will interrupted. "Who got caught posting videos of—"

"Will!" Jennifer hissed. "The kids could hear!" Will only launched into a different story.

Through it all Stephen seemed attentive, but I glanced at him at one point and saw his eyes had glazed over. As for me, I was daydreaming of exploring the entire farm tomorrow. Despite only listening with half an ear, I could still feel the pull of Will's dancing eyes, the way he brought light into a room.

"Did Will tell you about our new house?" Jennifer broke in with a determined expression. I was house-hunting for—"

"Eons!" said Will. "Jaysus, I thought I'd be old and gray before she found a place for us to live."

"Well, I didn't—find something, that is," Jennifer said. "Not something I liked, since I wanted it to be *perfect*. So we decided on new construction. It's taken forever to build, but finally the house was done this last spring! It's really fabulous, isn't it, Will?"

"High-end digs all right." Will took another swig of beer. "A dead-on McMansion."

"I wish you wouldn't call it that," Jennifer said crossly. "Kerry, I have a picture of it on my phone." She jumped up from the table and pulled her mobile off the counter. Turning it on, she practically thrust the phone under my nose. "See?"

"It's really lovely," I said. The house had the same generic quality as ours—an oversized portico, lots of windows and stone accents, though only two stories instead of our three.

"Yeah, we're livin' large, as they say in the States," Will said. "The place is big enough for all the girls' princessy yokes that my wife here buys by the shiteload, excuse my French." He laughed. "No one tells you kids are a straight shot to the poorhouse."

But you're so lucky to have them! Will had obviously had one too many slurps of lager.

"You never apologize when you swear in front of *me*," Jennifer pouted. "And you *know* I want my kids to have the best."

Stephen suddenly pulled his own phone from his trouser pocket. "We moved house ourselves this summer," he said, scrolling for a photo.

Will didn't lean in for a look. "I saw the house when you emailed me a photo."

Stephen, sending round photos of our posh house? I looked at my husband, bewildered.

"You didn't show it to me," Jennifer told Will, peering at Stephen's mobile before he pocketed it.

"Looks like we need another round," said Will without answering her, and fetched more beer from the fridge. "The Yanks have me drinking it cold, do you believe it?" As he opened another bottle, I listened to the kids' chatter coming from the front room. Maddie's piping voice was the loudest, mingling with giggles from her sisters and Jamie's intermittently squeaky baritone.

Jennifer said, "Stephen, the house is *gorgeous*, but we haven't heard about your job. Didn't you get a promotion recently?"

"Yes—it's worked out pretty well." He didn't look at me.

Will grinned. "Didn't Oscar Wilde have it right? 'Work is the curse of the drinking class.'"

"Oh, *Will*." Jennifer rolled her eyes. Then to Stephen, "I hear you take a lot of business trips. It must be a blast, all that world travel!"

"Not as fun as you might think," said Stephen.

"What have you to complain about?" said Will. "From what you must be pulling down, you've the Midas touch, that's for sure."

How Will would know anything about Stephen's income, I wasn't sure. "I—we—do all right," Stephen said evenly.

"Right-o," said Will. "I've seen your house. And your car."

"It's not all roses," said Stephen. "I've got to entertain clients—it's a lot of late nights. Kerry will tell you it puts me in a bit of a fouler."

"Wining and dining, there's another hardship," said Will. He took another long drink. "Shall I open another bottle for you lot?"

Stephen put his hand over his glass. "None for me. I think I'll look in on the kids, then head for bed."

I was weary myself. "I'll do the same, straight after the washing up."

"Will, you could do the dishes for a change," Jennifer said. "Not let our company do them."

"Really, it's fine," I said quickly.

Will flashed me a grateful smile. "Thanks, Kerry—I've a few

plays to study. The old man wants me to hit the ground running as soon as I'm back."

Rising from the table, Stephen began collecting plates. "I suppose you've got to keep the boss impressed."

"Oh, I don't let my dad put too much pressure on him." Jennifer's laugh sounded forced.

Opening another beer, Will didn't answer. I'd wondered how he liked working for his father-in-law—and now I had my answer: not so much.

Before starting the cleanup, I peeked into the front room. I'd thought after about a minute with Will's daughters, Jamie would either shoo them away like flies, or retreat upstairs to the bedroom Jennifer had organized for us. But he was still in the center of the little bevy of girls, showing them the photo of the particle collider he'd downloaded to his tablet. Quite a stretch for a lad who'd always regarded girls as a foreign and not-very-interesting species.

By the time I turned in an hour later, Jamie was already snoring in his sleeping bag on the floor. He had my laptop beside him, the screensaver still running.

Stephen, already in bed, rolled toward me. "Hi," he said drowsily.

He hadn't done that for a while—waited for me before falling asleep. As I knelt in the cramped space to shut down the computer, I nearly fell onto Jamie. When he didn't move, I stifled a giggle. "Does anyone ever sleep as deeply as a teenage boy?"

"Uh uh," said Stephen.

I stretched out next to him, feeling less self-conscious with him than I would've thought in such a narrow bed. But then, there was zero pressure about whether to make love or not when you were sharing your room with your teenager. "Jamie surprised me, working on his report on our holiday."

"Maybe he got inspired—he seems to be having a grand time already, doesn't he?" Stephen whispered back. "I can see why—the girls are lovely." His breath seemed to relax. "Lovely," he repeated. I wondered if he was thinking the same thing I was.

What had Jamie missed, not having any siblings? Under the covers, I let my hand rest against his.

It felt like the old days, Stephen and myself falling asleep at the same time. Maybe he'd even take my hand in his sleep, like he used to. I suddenly felt hopeful, that being away from our Dublin house, away from the unhappy memories, would be good for us...

I wiggled into a more comfortable position on the lumpy mattress, envisioning my jaunt round the farm tomorrow. But Will and Stephen's passive-aggressive dialogue at dinner intruded on my daydreaming. I told myself that was how blokes, old friends talked to each other—still, I'd have thought Stephen was above that sort of thing.

I knew *of course* he hadn't gotten our big house to one-up Will. All the same, I didn't feel the need to hide any strain between Stephen and me—he and Will appeared to have that department covered.

25

"Where's Dad?" asked Jamie, ambling into the kitchen.

The room was bright with morning sunlight. Dragging my gaze from the window view of the barn, I pointed my spatula toward the door. "Front room, I think. Please tell him breakfast is ready." I asked Jennifer and Will, "Wouldn't the girls like some eggs?" I served the omelet I'd made onto five plates. "I'd be happy to make more."

Jennifer shook her head. "They've had plenty of cereal." As Jamie came back from the front room, he helped Jennifer and Will bring the filled plates to the table.

"Looks great, Kerry," Will said, bright-eyed and smiling as he took a seat. He was clearly no worse for wear, despite the lagers the night before. "Just like back in the day, when you cooked up a storm. My wife here doesn't believe in our big Irish breakfasts."

And Stephen rarely has time for them. "It's lovely, cooking for a crowd," I told him. As the others tucked into the meal, there was still no sign of Stephen. Skipping breakfast so he could work? I set the frying pan in the sink and went to the doorway. In the front room, Mackenzie was occupied with Jamie's tablet, while Emerson and Maddie sat on the floor with Stephen around the tea table. I leaned against the doorway, smiling and wanting to cry at the same time.

The table was laid with four china saucers and teacups, and the teapot I'd washed yesterday. Stephen was bringing a cup to his lips.

"Wait, you can't drink your tea yet!" said Maddie. "It's too hot—you have to blow on it first."

Stephen obediently blew into his empty cup, then pretended to sip. "I'll take a scone, if you have it."

"We only have toast," Emerson said. She put some imaginary food onto a saucer and passed it over. Stephen lifted the invisible toast and took a bite of air.

A snort of laughter escaped me. "It looks quite yummy from here."

Stephen looked up, with a soft expression I hadn't seen since Jamie was small. "Actually, it's delicious. The girls are very fine cooks."

"You're probably full by now," I said, "but if you're interested, there's a plate of omelet waiting for you."

"Got to go," Stephen said to the girls, clambering to his feet. "But we can have another tea party soon, right?"

"You forgot something, Stephen," Emerson said.

He appeared to think hard. "I can't think what."

"You forgot to brush your toast crumbs off your front!" Maddie said, laughing.

Stephen glanced down at his crisp blue oxford shirt. "Well, would you look at the state of me—I'm covered!" He brushed his shirt vigorously. "I'll see you girls later."

"Can we watch a movie on your laptop tonight, Stephen?" asked Mackenzie. "With you and Jamie?"

"You bet." Stephen chucked her under the chin then followed me into the kitchen.

"You're so sweet to play with the girls," said Jennifer, then shot a glance at Will.

"I haven't been to a tea party in ages," said Stephen. "Jamie's never invited me—"

"Aw, *Dad*," said Jamie, and soon cleared his plate. "Is there more omelet?" he asked hopefully.

"You can finish mine," said Stephen, and set his plate on top of Jamie's. "I'm going to nip out for a bit."

Was Stephen actually interested enough in the farm to look around with me? "What have you in mind?" I asked, hearing the girls head upstairs.

"I need to do...some shopping," Stephen said. "And...other things."

"You always shop online, Dad." Jamie cleaned his father's

plate. "May I be excused?"

As Stephen nodded, I looked at him, baffled. My husband's off-line shopping was limited to big things. Like cars. Or high-rent houses. He said, "Jennifer, is there anything I could pick up?"

Jennifer pushed her plate away, her omelet only half-eaten. "I think we're covered."

"We picked up all of life's essentials in Galway City." Will rolled his eyes at me. "Cleaning stuff, sanitizer, and loads of disinfectant."

I couldn't help smiling back. "I'll be well-armed, then, when I take on the bathroom."

"Oh, and blue ice," added Will.

"The fridge isn't keeping the food cold enough," Jennifer said defensively. "I don't want the girls to get some food-borne illness."

Will took a big bite off Jennifer's plate, looking at Stephen. "We'll see you back here for lunch, mate?"

"Actually," Stephen rose from the table. "I'll be gone all afternoon."

All afternoon? All the tenderness I'd felt for him, seeing him play with the kids, completely disappeared.

Will narrowed his eyes at Stephen. "Well, do whatever you have to do." He gave a careless laugh. "In fact, have yourself a great ol' time."

Stephen didn't answer him. With a subdued "Cheers," he left the kitchen. I jumped up myself and followed him to the front door. Hearing Jamie upstairs, I whisper-hissed, "What are you about, leaving for the day?"

Stephen paused, his hand on the door. "I have to go to...Galway City."

"Why? We just drove through there yesterday."

"Actually," Stephen turned to face me, "I've a meeting. Three of the firm's top directors are flying in from Canada and want to see me. I couldn't say no."

"What you could say is, you're on holiday!" I struggled to keep my voice down. "So you're going to interrupt the first break we've had in ages, for a meeting you arranged on the sly?"

"It's the sort you can't turn down." Stephen's voice was stubborn.

"But what'll Jennifer and Will think?"

"I hope they'll understand," said Stephen, "that this meeting is important."

"All your meetings are important, aren't they?" I snapped. "God forbid you should put your family and friends first." Turning on my heel, I felt his eyes on my back. Then with a faint snick, the door closed.

Let Stephen go to Galway City, I thought balefully as I cleaned the bathrooms. I won't have him spoil my day.

After I'd doused both rooms with enough disinfectant to snuff every germ five times over, I remembered that Stephen had told me he'd have to stay in touch with the office. So…it looked like I'd been in the wrong, to give out at him over this meeting. I'll apologize later, I told myself, then shrugged on a fleece jacket and escaped outdoors.

The air was as balmy as yesterday, puffy clouds casting shadows on the hillside. Lifting my face to the sunshine, I decided it was too gorgeous to let myself stay in bad form over Stephen. Suddenly smiling, I headed for the barn.

I nearly wrenched my arms off, trying to open the door on its rusty hinges. But once I was inside, I felt I was back at Aunt Rose's place. Nesting in dirty straw inside was loads of old farm stuff—pieces of an ancient tractor, it looked like, a horse harness maybe, a few muck boots strewn about. I breathed deeply of a ripe, sour-sweet smell, one I recognized from the past—old hay and animals. There was no sign of damp in the place, so apparently the rusty roof was sound. As I turned to leave, I spied a rickety-looking one-speed bicycle leaning against one wall, a wire basket attached to the handlebars. Might come in handy, I told myself, though I hadn't ridden a bike in years.

Passing under the big tree, by the swing, I scuffed through the dried oak leaves on the ground. Jennifer needn't worry about her kids swinging on a sturdy tree like this one. I rambled further afield, around the pasture, then down to the small stand of firs. They looked like Noble firs, most of them easily three or four meters high—even a few fives—too tall for Christmas trees. Unless you'd some sort of manor house or castle or something. But there were some young ones too—someone could even sell them for Christmas trees in two or three years. I broke a few needles off one tree and inhaled deeply, the fresh piney scent reminding me that Christmas wasn't far away.

I gazed back toward the farmhouse, the stone golden in the sunshine, and I felt a sharp, sweet pleasure. What if the house actually was the one I'd seen online? That I hadn't imagined it? Whether it was or wasn't the same place—the kind of coincidence you'd experience maybe once in a lifetime—suddenly I felt I was meant to be here.

Walking back to the house, I gazed at a leafless apple tree caught in a beam of sunlight. A few apples still hung on the tree, glowing dark red like Christmas tree ornaments. Upon closer inspection, I could see the apples were decomposing, a few with big divots rendering them completely rotten—birds, I guessed. The fruit was too narky even for applesauce.

I remembered my promise to make a pudding. Dashing into the house, I grabbed some euro from my bag, then rustled though the kitchen drawers to find a slip of paper. After making a list on a tablet I'd found, I ripped the paper free. "Off to buy some apples," I called to anyone who might be listening, and rushed back to the barn.

Taking a chance, I wheeled the bicycle out to the drive. In the light, the bike didn't look too bad. When I pinched the tires, there wasn't too much give either. Maybe the farm renter had kept the bike in working condition. Climbing on the saddle, I reminded myself, *You never forget how.* Taking a deep breath, I pushed on the pedals. Wobbling my way down the drive, I practiced braking, and managed not to tip over. Then wonder of wonders, I found my balance and was on my way.

My spirits lifted even higher, seeing the rooftops of Ballydara village. In Dublin, just to get a few apples, you'd have to fight traffic to go to a crowded supermarket. Here, you'd a quiet lane all to yourself, and a small, friendly shop at the end of it. After I passed the dairy farm, I saw someone walking toward the village. As I drew closer, I saw it was the woman from the shop with the lovely smile.

"Hallo," I called before I got too close, so I wouldn't startle her.

She turned and waved. "Hallo yourself."

Even from a distance, I could see her warm smile. I carefully braked, then dismounted. "Mind if I join you?"

"I'd love the company," she said. As I walked the bike alongside her, we introduced ourselves—she was called Fiona Whelan—and discovered we were both bound for Mrs. Murphy's shop.

"How do you like the Power farm?" Fiona asked. "Everything comfy enough?"

"It's fantastic!" I burbled on about the place, inside and out. "You must be the neighbor who tidied up the house—how absolutely lovely of you."

"It was no bother." Her face turned rueful. "I understand your high opinion mightn't be shared by—" She stopped. "Really, I shouldn't—tell tales, I mean."

"It's all right." I inferred that Jennifer hadn't kept her dismay at the state of the place to herself. "I think Mrs. Jennifer Power prefers..." I laughed. "Let's call them...city lodgings."

"A nice way to put it," Fiona agreed. "After the Missus called round to use Dad's—our—phone yesterday, Dad said he couldn't make head nor tail of what someone like herself would want with a farm." Fiona pressed her lips together for a moment. "Here I am, speaking out of turn again."

Would she be talking about what I heard in the shop yesterday, that Mrs. Murphy and Mr. Twinkly Bernard thought Will's farm was for sale? Trying to be tactful, I turned the conversation to how much I was enjoying the area, and Fiona confided she was working at the shop just temporarily. "I've a job in Galway City, and share a flat there. But I didn't want Dad to spend the winter by himself. Mrs. Murphy, dear soul that she is, told me she could use some help."

As we approached the village, I realized I mightn't have another opportunity to decipher the mystery of the matching farmhouses. "Beg your pardon, Fiona." I stopped walking, leaning the bike against my hip. "I shouldn't want to gossip. But if you don't mind telling me, is the Power farm for sale?"

"Folk around the village seem to think it is," Fiona said. "Bernard Hurley—who has a way of finding out these things—says the farm was actually on the market for maybe a day or two. Then suddenly...it wasn't."

"I saw a house exactly like it online," I told her.

"Maybe the Powers changed their minds?" Fiona said. "Or it could have all been a mistake—who knows?" She smiled a farewell. "I'd better dash—I promised to get the shop's accounts in order today."

So there *was* a chance that Will's farm was the one I'd seen! I stayed outside for a moment, admiring the picturesque village. Setting the bike against the front of the shop, I grinned at the novelty of leaving your bike unattended. Do it in Dublin and it would be gone in thirty seconds.

The bell tinkled a cheery welcome, and Mrs. Murphy looked up from the tins she was arranging. "If it isn't Mrs. McCormack! What can I help you with today?"

"Apples for a pie," I said, nodding to a pair of other customers. One was the tall, dark-haired bosomy girl from the pub, the other was a smaller, plainer girl with light brown hair— the pair of them were almost comically opposite. "What about organic sugar?" the shorter girl was saying.

"No way," said the tall girl firmly. "Mam's off sugar of every sort."

"She wants a sweet, but how can you make a proper pudding without sugar?" the other girl said, sounding exasperated. "Honey doesn't give the right crumb..."

"Well then," said Mrs. Murphy, bustling over. She led me to several baskets of apples. "Granny Smiths—will they do?" She already had a paper bag for me. "If you'd been up at the Power farm just two months ago you'd have had more apples than you know what to do with," she went on. "They've all sorts of varieties, fresh eating and cooking." Her face fell a little. "But now that I think of it, the harvests have been spare the last few years, with no one tending the trees. A shame, to let those trees turn to useless brushy things."

I meandered toward the baking section, to get sugar and some pie spices. "I feel a need for darts," the tall girl was saying to her companion. "Before Mam drives me round the bend." She set a jar of honey back on the shelf, then looked over at me with that cheeky grin I'd seen on her in the pub. "Hey there—do you play?"

"Not yet," I said, smiling back. "But I'd be up for a go sometime."

"Just don't make any bets with this one," the smaller girl said to me, rolling her eyes. "She'll take you for everything you've got." Then the pair turned their attention back to the shelf.

As I paid for the apples, Mrs. Murphy looked behind me, toward the window. "Ah, I see you found old Mr. Power's bicycle. You're a proper country girl now, cycling instead of driving." She chuckled. "Or you will be, if you can cycle back up that hill!"

26

On my way home—to the Power farm, I mean—I was huffing and puffing before I'd gone a half kilometer. I ended up alternately cycling and pushing the bike on foot.

"Guess I'm not a country girl just yet," I grumbled to myself on the last stretch up the hill. But as I walked up the drive, pleasure filled me to be back on the farm again. I came upon Will and the four kids kicking a football in the ragged patch of grass near the barn. Will was in shirtsleeves, muscly arms exposed, his fair hair shining in the light. He was still so handsome and fun to be with, the same guy who had attracted me years ago. Yet I realized—I was rather surprised, actually— that my heart wasn't beating any faster. Nor had it, ever since I'd seen him yesterday.

Maddie was running after the ball, her little feet dancing over the grass. Jamie was actually giving it a go too, his hair windblown and glasses askew as he maneuvered around Maddie. "That's it, lad!" Will called. "Try the scissors move!"

It's the sort of encouragement Stephen should be doing. Seeing Jennifer sitting on the stoop, in a fashionable anorak, I determinedly put his desertion out of my mind. Once I parked the bike back in the barn, I joined her. Jennifer's face was glum.

"Bought some apples for that pie we talked about." I showed her the bag of fruit I'd bought.

"Great," she said absently.

"I've had a good look round the farm," I tried again. "You and Will are so blessed to have this place."

Jennifer gave me a puzzled look. "Actually, it's been nothing but a hassle." Her frown lines deepened.

"What do you mean?"

She pursed her lips for a moment. "I mean, it seemed like a windfall at first, Will inheriting the property." Jennifer's voice grew more animated. "But when we realized what we were getting into..." She shook her head. "We couldn't do anything with the farm while the renter was here—Will said it just wasn't done, to kick some old guy off the place, even if we were getting only a pittance."

"Your Will has always had a good heart," I said.

Jennifer only shrugged. "To tell the truth, I think Will didn't care one way or another what happened to the farm. But after the renter left, his dad got after Will to settle the place. My dad did too—I mean, why own a farm and not try to do anything with it?"

"From what I can tell," I said, "the folk in Ballydara think your farm has potential."

"They're absolutely right," said Jennifer. "I mean, there's some money to be made here! So that's why my dad and I got upset—well, Dad went a little ballistic—when we found out Will had had the farm listed for sale."

"When?" My heart was beating faster *now*. "Recently?"

"Actually yes," said Jennifer. "A couple of weeks ago, I think. He was ready to let it go as is, at a rock-bottom price, can you believe it? I made him get right on the phone and cancel the whole thing. I told him we could come up with" and she looked uneasy for a moment, "a better plan."

I clutched my sack of groceries. This golden-stone farmhouse had to be the *one* I'd seen online—the farm I'd dreamed about! But if it wasn't for sale anymore... "What will you do with the farm if you don't want to sell it now?"

"Well," Jennifer began, her voice eager, "We're looking at some options. One is to do some basic cleanup and repairs, and hope to get a decent price from someone who wants to farm it. Although Will's dad keeps saying there probably isn't enough acreage here for a proper farm."

"What about a hobby farm?" I asked. "There's that big vegetable plot out back, and the apple trees—it shouldn't be too hard to raise a tidy amount of food."

"Well, either way, that kind of price would barely cover taxes and the real estate agent's fees." Jennifer unzipped her coat halfway. "So my dad and I thought, what if we were to sell it as a rental property for even more money? Of course we'd have to *really* fix it up, make it supercute."

"Supercute," I repeated.

"But remodeling would be a financial black hole," said Jennifer. "I mean, it would absolutely *kill* us. With no guarantee we could get back the money we put into it."

"I see your point," I said slowly. I took an apple from my sack and rubbed it with my sleeve.

"What I'd really love to do is subdivide," Jennifer confided. "Or whatever they call it in Ireland. You know, sell it to a company that could turn the place into a housing development!"

I felt a stab, right in the middle of my chest. *You can't mean that!*

"Wouldn't that be great? Back home, if you can sell your farm to developers, you can make a fortune!"

I could see the future here. This lovely farm nestled in the hills—the house and barn leveled, the pastures plowed under, the apple and fir trees bulldozed, to make a housing estate of wall-to-wall...McMansions. Like Aunt Rose's had been. The lump in my throat grew.

"But Will said he didn't think it would work." Jennifer's tone turned sulky. "Who knows how complicated subdividing could get, you know, with Irish regulations, or how long it could take before we'd see any money. So we'll have to look at hiring some consultants, lawyers, to give us an idea of what we can do. Will's against it—he just wants to have the farm off his hands. But *that's* not happening if I have anything to say about it. Not if there's a chance we could make some real money."

I stared at the apple in my hands. I wanted to protest, but really, this was *so* not my business.

"Anyway," Jennifer went on, "Visiting the farm couldn't have come at a worse time. The economy's getting better, but Will's had his salary frozen—no one in his department has gotten a raise for a couple of years."

"I'm sorry to hear it." Raising three kids on one income— how on earth did Will and Jennifer manage it? Especially with that new house of theirs?

"And tuition is due at the girls' school—actually overdue, but with this trip and the holidays…The cost is always a worry, and Will says there's nothing wrong with public school. But I went to St. Brendan's, and I'm just *determined* that our girls will have a high-quality, private school experience."

Jennifer's oversharing was wearing me out. Especially with the talk of hers and Will's disagreements. It seemed clear the storybook romance she'd written about years ago really wasn't all that…well, storybookey. And if they were as short on money as she was implying, why the extravagance of the trip to Ireland? The shipped-in ham and cakes? I couldn't work out what Will and Jennifer were about.

On top of it all, I was getting a bit nauseated, thinking of what she'd in mind for the farm.

"What if you and Will found another renter…and kept the place?" I ventured. "Wouldn't a small rental income be better than nothing? Then you could have…em, family reunions here, and—"

"Are you kidding?" Jennifer looked aghast. "Who in their right mind would want a vacation stuck in the middle of nowhere? Or spending thousands on airfare to stay in this awful dirty house?"

I would. I returned my apple to the sack, no longer hungry. *With all my heart.*

27

*D*usk was falling. I was sitting alone on the stoop, watching the stars emerge, when our Toyota lumbered up the drive. As Stephen got out of the car and walked toward me, his step seemed lighter than it had for weeks. To make up for giving him a hard time this morning, I was ready to say, *How was your day? Was it a good meeting?*

"They're selling the farm," I said instead, my throat going tight again.

Stephen's footsteps slowed. "Oh." Disregarding his nice trousers, he sat next to me. "I'm not surprised."

"I don't know why I am," I said, keeping my voice low. "I mean, what else would Will and Jennifer do with it?" All afternoon, I'd been feverishly thinking of how I could save this place—but all the time knowing I was spitting into the wind. With all the farms I'd viewed online lately, I'd gotten a good idea of the cost of a small one. I'd some savings, but it was only a fraction of what it would take to buy Will and Jennifer's property. Even as is. "But Jennifer wants to sell to..." I could hardly get the word out, "*developers.*"

Stephen nodded. He knew I'd never quite got over what had happened to Aunt Rose's place. "They mightn't be able to work out the planning and legal kinks," he said.

"I know." I swallowed past the lump in my throat. "But if they can, the property could be worth as much as...as Ashford Castle." I sniffed. "Just think, they could buy a new, bigger McMan—" I broke off, aware of a racket from the other side of the door. Still uneasy about Stephen showing off our house last night, I knew I'd said too much already about our hosts behind their backs.

"Kerry, I've something to tell you," he said suddenly. I sensed his suppressed excitement. Wouldn't you know he'd be far more interested in his job than my piddly concerns about a farm getting bulldozed into oblivion. "The meeting today—"

"Dad!" Jamie burst through the front door, the girls right behind him. As I scooted out of the way Stephen jumped to his feet. "The stars are out, did you see? Help us with the telescope?"

"Stephen, *pleeease*," said Mackenzie and Emerson in unison.

Maddie grabbed his hands, dancing round him. "Come on, Stephen, right *now!*"

"Sure, kids." Stephen gave me a helpless look that I pretended not to see.

I watched the girls flutter impatiently round Stephen and Jamie as they set up the telescope, positioning it just so. Jamie soon had all three girls peering through the lens, providing a running commentary.

"...Once you see the Big Dipper, you'll find the Pole Star easy," he was saying. "Draw a line from the upper corner of the dipper to..." As Maddie elbowed Emerson out of the way, he said, "Now Maddie, wait for your turn," in the same mild tone Stephen used.

I felt tears in my throat. After this farm shock, I was feeling too emotional—seeing Jamie chat with the girls as effortlessly as if he'd little sisters of his own.

"November is a great time to view Orion," Jamie continued, and swung the scope to the southern sky.

Mackenzie took her turn. "What about the Milky Way?"

"I want one, I want one," sang Maddie. "I love them!"

"It's not a candy bar, silly," Mackenzie said. "It's a bunch of stars. A gal...gal—"

"Galaxy," said Jamie. "The Milky Way's not so easy to see in the winter, but I read that some Native American cultures call it the 'Road of Souls.'"

"Souls like they talk about at Mass?" asked Mackenzie.

"*I* know what Native Americans are," said Emerson importantly. "We've been studying them for Thanksgiving..."

"Looks like you've everything under control, son." Stephen had a tremor in his voice. "I'll leave you to it."

As he headed toward his car—to fetch his briefcase, probably—I rose and went inside. I didn't want to look at his face, and see the regret and pain there. Because I'd enough of my own.

"Be ready for a tramp tomorrow, mate," Will said to Stephen after another heat-and-eat supper—pre-made frozen lasagna. The girls had been excused, but Jamie was at the countertop, busily scraping the last bits from the pan.

"O-kay," Stephen said slowly. "For...?"

"You're so busy nipping out for your mystery errands," Will jibed, popping the top of another lager, "That you've forgotten it's nearly Christmas?"

Jamie turned round. "Huh?"

"As far as I know, it's a month off, said Stephen, still looking miles away.

"Jen's had a brainwave," said Will. "At home, we put up our tree Thanksgiving weekend. She thinks the girls will really go for having a tree for our vacation here."

"If that's what you want," said Stephen, and I was annoyed with him all over again for taking off for the day. Meeting or not, how rude could you be to your hosts?

"It would give the girls something to do," said Jennifer, turning on the taps.

"We'll pick something out in that little bunch of firs near the road," Will said. "Just us blokes."

"Can I come?" Jamie asked, his voice eager. "I can help carry the tree."

I smiled at him. At least my son was in the holiday mode. "That'll be a big help, won't it, Will?"

"'Course you can, Jimbo," Will said carelessly. "Be ready right after breakfast, rain or shine."

"I saw some spare boots in the barn for you, love," I said to Jamie. "But you lot will have your work cut out for you, finding a tree that'll fit in the house."

"Oh, we'll find something." Will took a long swallow, then glanced at Jennifer. "And it better be perfect."

"I just want a nice tree." Jennifer tossed a handful of flatware into the sink and slammed off the taps. "Is that so wrong?"

"What's for pudding?" asked Will, clearly ignoring her pique.

"No dessert tonight," said Jennifer. "Live with it."

As a beleaguered look came over Will's face, Stephen jumped up and put his plate in the sink. "Thanks for supper," he said. "But Jamie promised the girls we'd watch a film with them before bedtime." He left before Will could corner him with a new set of training videos. Jamie set the scraped-out lasagna pan in the sink and followed.

After Will left the kitchen, I stayed in the kitchen with Jennifer, scrubbing the countertops, the cooker and the sink until everything shone. I didn't want to see Stephen and Jamie surrounded by the little girls.

Jennifer rinsed the last of the plates, then sat at the table, giving me a strained look. "I'm sorry Will and I are...I don't know. Tense. Being away from home—you know, the expenses, the...the expectations."

"It's all right." I slowly draped my dishcloth over the faucet. This holiday wasn't quite turning out as I'd hoped. Had we done the right thing, coming here?

Maybe Stephen and I should have worked out our own conflicts before spending a long weekend with a couple who had as many as we did. If not more. And if I hadn't come, I wouldn't be letting my heart break over yet another Irish farm lost to progress. "I think I'll have another look at the stars before I turn in."

I grabbed my jacket. Outside, I settled back on the front stoop, the sound of the girls' film on Will's laptop audible through the closed windows. A sheen of cloud cover had dimmed the brightness of the stars—Jamie had gotten his telescope out just in time. As the door opened behind me, I braced myself for more of Jennifer's oversharing.

"Kerry," Stephen said low. He sat next to me. "I didn't like having to leave today, but the meeting was worth it."

I didn't answer. If I was going to be a crap wife, might as well go all the way.

Stephen waited another beat, then said, "If you're interested, I may be looking at a promotion. A big one."

So that was what he'd been all excited about. Naturally it would mean more late nights, less time for our family. "It going to be the story of our lives, isn't it?" I said. "You'll always be going for another rise in pay, more travel, more responsibilities." Though it wasn't cold, I crossed my arms over my chest. "Always up, up, up—more, more, more. But tonight, I'm too upset to talk about it."

"The farm, I suppose." Stephen's voice was resigned. "Why drive yourself mad over it? When the future of this place is completely out of your hands?"

"Thanks for that oh-so-sensible advice," I said. "Next you'll tell me we always want what we can't have."

He was silent for a long time. "It's true isn't it?"

Was he talking about the baby we'd lost? Ready to relent, and take his hand, I realized he was more likely referring to his boss' job. "I'm going back inside," I said, and clambered to my feet. Because I'd no reply to either.

28

Jamie spooned up his last bite of corn flakes, then bounced up from the table. "I'll go find those boots Mam saw in the barn," he told Will. The day before Thanksgiving, we'd settled for cold cereal, since the lads were in a rush out the door to fetch us a tree.

His mouth full, Will glanced at Jennifer for a moment, then swallowed. "Em…Jamie, I have to—"

"Time to go?" Stephen drained his tea mug, then folded up yesterday's *Irish Times*. "Guess I'd better get bundled up too. I'll meet you lads outside." He left the kitchen without looking at me.

I suppose I hadn't expressed the right amount of enthusiasm last night for his new job opportunity. Or maybe the Powers' tension was rubbing off on us. Whatever it was, if he wanted to be all peevish with me—which wasn't usual for Stephen at all—who cared?

"What do you need boots for, Jamie?" Maddie demanded.

"I'm going to cut down the Christmas tree," he informed her loftily. "We blokes have a long hike in the rain."

"Can I go? Can you get some boots for me? I wanna jump in some mud puddles!"

"If you're gonna get all dirty you can't wear my leggings," Emerson said. "Take them off right now."

"No, Maddie, you can't go," Jennifer said. "Emerson, she's got wear your leggings, she's running out of clean clothes."

"But I wanna go! Why does Jamie get to go?"

"He's bigger. It's too far for you to walk," Jennifer said. "You're too little."

"I'm not too little!" Maddie's face went red, and she banged her spoon on the table, drops of milk flying. Some hit the newspaper, and a couple wet my cheek. "I'm not! I want to *goooo!*"

Apparently oblivious to Maddie's strop, Will picked up the *Times* and opened it. Jennifer sprang from the table, picked up the child and carried her out of the kitchen. "You need a time out," she said over Maddie's howls.

Emerson and her sister Mackenzie exchanged a look, like they were used to this, and slunk off to the front room. I couldn't help thinking that if I'd had a stroppy wee one like Maddie, I would never have told her she was too little for anything.

"Jamie, about the Christmas tree..." Will set the newspaper on the table, shooting an indecipherable look at me. "Something's come up. It's just going to be your dad and me."

Jamie's face fell, like a soufflé you'd stuck a fork into. "But..."

"Sorry," Will added, his wide mouth turned down at the corners.

He did sound sorry, but how could he disappoint my son like that? "Will, can't you—"

"It s'alright," Jamie mumbled.

"It's not that you're too young, nothing like that," Will said to Jamie in a cajoling tone. "It's just that I got to thinking, your dad and I, we've been mates forever, we've so much to catch up on. We can go on a hike, you and me, ah, a bit later?"

"It s'alright," Jamie muttered again. "I've finished, Mam, can I go?" I nodded. Head hanging, he left the table.

Alone with Will, I wanted to throttle Will, despite the regret on his handsome face. Couldn't he see how much Jamie wanted to be a part of a man's world? Still, if Will really did want to renew his friendship with Stephen... Not knowing what to say, I rose and started clearing the table.

As I set a pile of bowls in the sink with a thump, I felt Will's hand on my shoulder. "C'mon, Kerry, don't be mad at me." His voice was caressing. "I'll make it up to him." He ran a finger down my arm.

Ready to shrug off Will's hand, I looked sideways at him. *Do you need to have everyone like you? And surely you're not flirting with me?* Then meeting his green eyes, I instantly softened. This was *Will*. I waited for that old pull of attraction, the thrill that had once run through me, but somehow all I felt was sympathy. Will did seem to be under a lot of pressure. Jennifer's demands, his father-in-law all over him, getting this farm organized…and their money problems.

How could I be cross with him, anyway? "I know you will."

He looked like he wanted to say something else, but he only gave my shoulder a squeeze and was gone.

"Hallooo, Jimbo! C'mon out here! I need some muscle!"

Jamie vaulted up, leaving his lunch half-eaten.

"It's really wet—you'll want your coat," I began, but he'd already rushed through the front room and outside, leaving the door open.

As all three girls jumped up too, Jennifer said, "Wait a minute! You haven't finished—"

But all three were at the doorway before the words left her mouth. "It's going to be just like home," Mackenzie said. "A Christmas tree at Thanksgiving!"

Maddie squeezed between her sisters and scampered down the driveway in her stocking feet before Jennifer could stop her. "That child," she said, shaking her head as we crowded behind Mackenzie and Emerson for our first glimpse of the tree. "Sometimes I just don't know what to do with her."

She'd taken the three girls down to Murphy's shop to buy some tree decorations. When they returned, she'd said Maddie had run all over the store like she'd never been in one before.

"All that buzzy excitement for kids, it's hard to mind their mammies," I said now, and starting laughing, seeing Will and Jamie in the middle of the driveway tussle with a massive fir. "You look like a pair of crocodile wrestlers," I called out to Will. He looked like a real family man, with his jeans dirty and hair a mess. It came to me then, that somewhere along the line he'd become not the guy I'd mooned over for years, but just an old friend.

Maddie was already clutching a bough near the top. "I'm helping! I'm helping to carry the tree!"

The tree that Will and Jamie were wrestling up to the house had to be one of the firs I'd seen yesterday. They'd obviously chosen the tallest one. "It's too big for the house." Jennifer sounded anxious.

"It's too big for most mansions," I said, still laughing. But that was Will for you. Always larger than life. "By the way, Will," I said to him, "How are you going to get that monster inside?"

"I dunno," Will called back. "Surgery, maybe!"

He and Jamie heaved the tree onto the stoop with a grunt. Straddling the tree, Maddie released her grip on the bough and grinned at her dad. One entire side of her was wet, with mud on her top, her leggings, and a big streak on her cheek, and her socks were soaked. "It's the biggest tree ever!" she crowed.

Jennifer gave her daughter a warning look. "Maddie, in the house. And get those socks off!" Then to Will, "We don't have enough decorations to cover a tree like that!"

I met Jamie's eyes, stifling a giggle. Only Jennifer could make an emergency out of a too-large tree. As I backed out of the doorway, she reached out and grabbed Maddie's arm. "Maddie, I said, in the house!" Pulling the child inside, she said, "Girls, you're letting all the cold in."

"Actually, you are," Jamie said. Always literal, was Jamie. "The tree's big, but we can trim off the top."

I grinned at him and put my finger to my lips as Jennifer went on, "Will! Couldn't you have found a smaller tree? Where are we supposed to put it? Where's the saw?"

"No I couldn't, in the front room, and Stephen's got it," Will said, his eyes merry as he looked from me to Jennifer.

As Jennifer's pout seemed to melt—really, a girl would need a heart like a stone to stay angry with the man—I realized Stephen was nowhere to be seen. "You left my husband in the woods?" I said with mock indignation.

Will shrugged. "Aw, he was wandering round—probably trying to find a signal for his mobile." He looked in the middle distance for a moment, then back at me. "Who's he got to chat with when he's on holiday, anyway? That bloke is sure tied to his phone."

I felt my cheeks burn, all merriment gone. My husband would rather talk business than be with his family. A lump of angry tears crowded my throat. "Did Stephen…" I swallowed. "Did he say how long he'd be?"

"Nope—hope it's soon, though," Will said, and he and Jamie came in, leaving the tree on the stoop. "He's meant to bring the saw. I know it needs at least a meter hacked off, but we can't do anything until he shows up."

"Guys, off with those muddy shoes," Jennifer said, then I felt her eyes on me.

She could probably tell I was furious. Trying to hide it, I headed for the kitchen. Out of the corner of my eye, I saw Will lean toward his wife. "It's all sorted," he said, low. "We're grand."

I was too worked up to wonder what that was all about. Setting out the ingredients for my pie, I was totally primed to smack some pastry around. Stephen and his workaholic habits were positively ruining our holiday.

Shortly before dusk, I heard a thump outside. Stephen.

Any other time, I would have felt pleasure at the sight of my fresh-baked pie on the counter. Yet right now, I was burning to give my husband the sharp side of my tongue. Leaving Jennifer to the dinner prep, I strode past Will and the kids on the couch, ready to burst out, *Where the hell have you been!*

Opening the door, I stopped, pressing my lips together. Stephen was sawing off a chunk of tree trunk in the dim light, his anorak wet and dirty, his face pinched with cold. He looked up at me. "Got…sidetracked," he said, and bent to his task again.

I took a deep breath to keep from exploding in front of everyone. *That's all you have to say?*

"Better late than never, mate," Will put in.

"I was afraid we wouldn't have a tree," said Emerson.

Maddie said, "What if we can't get the tree in the house?"

"We'll get it in," said Jamie, going to the door. "Need some help, Dad?"

"No need for you to get all dirty again, son," Stephen said, breathing hard.

"I don't mind," Jamie said and stepped around me. "I'll hold the tree steady while you cut the top part."

"Oh, right, need a hand there?" Will didn't move from the couch.

"I've got it," Stephen said, starting to hack at the lower boughs. I watched him, forgetting for a moment how angry I was. He wielded the saw skillfully as he trimmed this branch and that, kicking the sawed off pieces out of his way. Jamie gathered up the branches and tossed them off the stoop.

Soon they'd fashioned the tree into a Christmas tree shape. They stood the fir upright, shaking and brushing the loose needles off it, then Jamie said, "What d'you think, Mam?"

Stephen shifted his eyes, the merest glance at me. I could feel it. He wanted me to like it.

"It's beautiful," I told him, trying to keep the edge out of my voice. But it would be a long time before I could forgive Stephen for sneaking away.

29

"The girls always pester us something awful to get a present, the day we put up a tree," Jennifer said as I dumped a package of pasta into a pot of boiling water. "Even though it's Thanksgiving, I get them a little token, just so they can open *something*."

Will was on the couch, his head in the newspaper, while Stephen dozed in a corner chair. It had to be exhausting, I thought tartly, traipsing through the woods all afternoon to catch a mobile signal.

The kids were decorating the tree. Jennifer had actually asked Jamie to supervise the operation. "The girls'll listen to him," she said. "Of course, the ornaments won't be evenly spaced, but after they go to bed I can fix it."

Jennifer was spot on about the girls and presents—as we prepared supper, one of them would pop into the kitchen at regular intervals to ask about them. The last time had been Emerson. "What did I say when your sister came in two minutes ago?" Jennifer asked her.

"Um…after dinner?" Emerson said.

"And is it after dinner yet?"

Emerson rolled her eyes. "Okay, okay!" She retreated back to the tree.

"The pressure gets intense," Jennifer said, though her eyes were sparkling. "The girls don't even care what the gift is!"

Despite my crossness with Stephen, and to be honest, feeling a bit claustrophobic after two days in a small house with eight people, I felt a bit of early holiday spirit myself. There was a lovely fir scent coming off the tree, and the lights the kids had strung on it were reflecting into the kitchen. And the girls' excitement was contagious.

"Daddy, put down your paper," Mackenzie was saying. "We need you to put the lights higher on the tree!"

Once we sat down to supper, the girls were bugging their mother non-stop between bites of pasta. Finally Will cast a stern look at the three of them. "One more word about presents and Santy Claus is going to have serious second thoughts about coming to our house next month."

Emerson dropped her fork, her eyes filling with tears. "Santa won't come?"

"But Daddy, how will he know we're bein' bad?" Maddie didn't look worried. "He's too busy to see with his magic eyes cause he's making toys with the elves at the North Pole!"

"He knows," Jamie said, his eyes dancing. "He knows *everything.*" He deepened his voice for a doom-like effect.

"That's right," Will said as Mackenzie giggled. "So eat your supper."

The warning subdued the girls for only a few minutes. Before long, they were back at such a fever pitch Jennifer jumped up from the table, "Okay, okay, but remember, it's just a small Thanksgiving present." She dug into her large handbag, drawing out three small parcels. Within seconds, the girls had torn the wrapping off. Each had a small princess figurine.

All three girls looked underwhelmed. "We already have all these." Mackenzie shrugged.

"But where's Jamie's present?" Maddie asked.

"He doesn't get one, 'cause he's a grown-up," Mackenzie informed her.

Jamie pushed his glasses to the bridge of his nose and sat up a bit straighter.

"Well, then, Jimbo," said Will, "You'll have to wait until Christmas, like the rest of us."

"He shouldn't have to." Jennifer bit her lip, then she pulled another package out of her bag. "Here you go."

Delight breaking out on his face, Jamie held out his gift—a

self-tracking wristband device. "Wow, this is brilliant." His grin was wide. "I saw these in a magazine. Thanks."

A bit horrified, I didn't know what to say. Those devices were awfully dear—and Jennifer had said they couldn't quite manage their bills. I also guessed she'd bought it for herself. "How...lovely," I stammered. "But you—I mean, it's a month until Christmas—"

"What a great gift," Stephen said, but he was frowning—probably thinking the same thing I was. "Jamie, you'll want to show the girls how it works?"

As the kids left the table, Jamie was already undoing the packaging. "It's massively cool," he was saying on the way to the front room. "You can strap it on and see your heart rate..."

I waited until the kids were out of earshot. "Really, Jennifer, you shouldn't have spent so—"

"Of course we should," Will said. "Jamie's like my godson, isn't he? Worth a bit of a splurge." He went to the fridge and brought out a brown paper sack, which showed the clear outline of a large bottle. "Just like our reunion!" He pulled out a magnum of Champagne.

Jennifer rushed to the cupboard to gather four teacups. "Will and I...well, we wanted something special for us getting together after all these years." She pulled a bottle opener from her handbag.

"I don't think we've had Champagne since our wedding day, have we, Stephen?" Pasting on a smile, I could see he was doing the same. More extravagance with those two.

"Will this opener work?" Jennifer asked as Will ground the screw into the cork.

"There's no bottle that's defeated me yet," Will said, sliding a teasing smile at me. He eased out the cork neatly, with a minimum of liquid escaping, and poured us each a cupful. "Cheers!"

The rest of us echoed, "Cheers," touching the rims of our cups together. Jennifer and I had only had a few sips before Will was on to a second glassful. Stephen watched him for a moment, his face unreadable. Then a resolute look came over his face. He downed his Champagne in one gulp, then poured himself a second cupful, and gulped that down too.

I frowned at him. "What are you—"

"Since we're in a celebratory mood," said Stephen, reaching into his shirt pocket, "I've something for Kerry." He set a small bundle before me, enfolded in pink tissue paper.

"But…tonight's meant to be only little things for the kids," I said, not touching the parcel.

"Looks little to me," Will said.

Stephen wore an expectant look. "I don't want you to wait until Christmas. Come on, then."

More to avoid a fuss than to please Stephen, I unfolded the tissue paper. Even before I'd finished, I could feel the outline of a ring inside. Stephen *knew* that jewelry was so not my thing… I drew away the last layer of tissue.

It was a ring, all right.

Jennifer gasped audibly. I said under my breath, "Holy Mother of God…" Feeling Stephen's eyes on me, I could only stare down at his gift.

It was a wedding band with a large, square-cut emerald set in the middle, a row of smaller diamonds on either side.

"It's about time you got your wife a proper ring." Will laughed, but I caught a bitter note in it. "Even if you really know how to show up a bloke."

"That wasn't my intention," Stephen said quietly.

"Will's getting me a Vita-mix for Christmas this year." Jennifer broke in, glancing at her own ring finger. Her wedding set, that I'd thought so lavish in the photo she'd sent years ago, paled in comparison to this yoke. "The low-end model."

I looked up at Stephen helplessly. Why had he bought such an extravagant gift? And give it to me now? Surely he wouldn't throw his prosperity in Will's face…

"I don't know what to say," I finally got out. *For God's sake, tell him thank you and give him a kiss, don't shame him.* But I couldn't move.

I dimly sensed Jennifer pulling at Will's sleeve, and the pair of them leaving the kitchen. Alone with Stephen, I looked from him to the ring, and mumbled, "I didn't expect—I mean, this must've cost the earth, I've a perfectly good ring..."

"I know you do." Stephen's voice was even. "I put it on your finger the day I married you."

I swallowed. "But really, you needn't have gone all the way to the city for this—did you make it up, having a meeting yesterday?"

Stephen's face settled into hard lines, the kind I'd never seen before. "I've never lied to you."

"I know that." I refused to be flustered. "You only...well, you keep things from me."

Stephen only looked away. "I really did have a meeting—and I didn't get the ring in Galway City." He set his clasped hands on the table. His knuckles were white. "You'd said it yourself, you'd been through...a lot this year," he said. "And I remembered how you looked when you saw Jennifer's wedding ring, in the photo they sent years ago."

But I wasn't envying it! With a shaking hand, I removed my plain wedding band. Putting it in the pocket of my jeans, I slipped on the new ring, the emerald and diamonds catching the light. Then realized I should have asked Stephen to do it. "If you didn't buy it yesterday, when did you?"

"It doesn't matter." He rose from the table, the chair scraping the linoleum, and collected the cups, mine still half full. "Well, that should about do it," he said, as if he was closing a business meeting. "Shall we join the others?"

His face was expressionless, but I knew I'd hurt him. Terribly.

30

$\mathcal{E}$lectronic burps and *pings* filled the front room. I settled into the corner armchair, hearing the occasional lowing of the cows from the Whelan farm. I felt so unsettled and out of place that part of me wished I could be hanging out with them instead of here. I glanced at my gift, the unaccustomed weight of the ring heavy on my hand, then at Stephen. He was sitting on the floor with Jamie, their heads together over the intricacies of the new device.

I tried to feel grateful to him. Instead, all I could feel was resentment about the stunt he'd pulled this afternoon, gone for hours to use his phone. And the part of me that didn't want to be with the cows itched to tear the ring off. Did my own husband know me so little, thinking I'd want an elaborate piece of jewelry that had to have cost thousands of euro?

But this is no way to be on holiday, I scolded myself, focusing on the tree in its oversized grandeur, even if the fairy lights drooped, and shiny ornaments hung higglety-pigglety.

"Kerry!" Maddie came over and tugged on my sleeve. "We've got a new *Barbie* movie."

"Sounds lovely," I said, glad for the distraction. Jennifer and the two girls were settling on the couch with a laptop. Will, in the easy chair closest to the couch, had a bottle of lager in one hand, mobile in the other. As I took a seat next to Emerson, Maddie climbed onto her dad's lap. "No more Temple Run, Daddy," she ordered, and plucked the phone from his hand. "Watch the show with us."

As she stuck the device between the squishy cushions, I glanced at Will. He was staring straight at the screen, but I could tell he was no more watching the previews than I was. He was probably used to a more festive gathering, lots of extended family gathered round the punch bowl while he entertained them with his jokes and stories. Not hunkered down on the couch for a quiet night at home.

I couldn't help thinking of the New Year's dinner when he'd brought Jennifer to Mam's so long ago...and our emotional goodbye. But somehow, the memory didn't bring back all the sentimental yearning it used to. Only the sense that I'd been only a kid then—rather silly and misguided. I was a completely different person now. And so was he.

After the film was over, the girls had to have baths. The taps had been running for five minutes when squeals echoed down the stairway.

Jennifer yelled, "Will, the hot water's run out!"

"Can't do anything about it tonight!" Will called back, hardly looking up from his phone.

"The girls will have to share bathwater!" Jennifer sounded indignant. "Honestly, this old house—how will they get clean?"

As Will sent me a grin, I giggled. "In the old days, you'd wash a dozen kids out of the same washtub."

Stephen paid no attention. He'd moved into an easy chair to work on his laptop, eyes intent on the screen. Once the kids were back downstairs in their jammies, he pulled down the laptop cover. "Everyone ready to say good night?"

"But first I want a bedtime story," said Maddie. "A Christmas one."

"Yeah," said Emerson. "We don't care if it's a month til Christmas."

Jennifer looked helpless. "I forgot to pack any books."

Jamie spoke up. "How about *The Night Before Christmas*?"

Jennifer looked confused. "That would be great, but..."

"Mam and Dad read it to me every Christmas Eve," said Jamie with a shy grin. "I know it by heart."

My own filled with pride as he gathered the girls round him, and recited the tale without missing a word. The story seemed to have a magical effect not just on the kids, but the rest of us. I could feel the tension drain from me. Stephen lost that stiff look on his face, and Will and Jennifer looked more relaxed than they had all evening. For a moment, a sweet hush descended over the room, then the girls going round with a kiss for all of us. I thought Jamie would make a run for it and hide out in the loo, but he accepted the kisses, blushing. Myself, feeling the touch of their soft lips on my cheek, I could forget the conflict with Stephen.

As soon as the girls trailed back upstairs, Jamie waved his new device in the air. "Dad, I think we're ready for a demo."

"Give me a minute," said Stephen, opening the laptop again.

After fiddling with the tracker for a few more seconds, Jamie checked his wristband again, cracking a huge yawn. "Let's do it tomorrow instead."

"I'll just be another moment," Stephen said.

"My body temp has dropped," said Jamie. "So I know I'm meant to go to sleep. Mam, Dad, are you coming?"

"You go up," I told him. "I'm going to unwind for a few more minutes."

Jennifer looked glued to her spot on the couch, her eyes glazed. "God, it's been a long day."

"Come on then, Jennifer, give it up," said Will, and winked at me. He powered down his laptop and collected the three empty lager bottles on the side table with a practiced move, one bottle wedged between each of his fingers. "Stephen, haven't you had enough emailing?"

"Almost," said Stephen without looking up.

I shot him another resentful look. If Stephen had meant for his fancy, gem-dripping gift to have any special meaning, he must have forgotten it. He was only a few meters away, yet I felt a vast, yawning gulf between us.

"See you in the morning," Stephen said a few minutes later, still not looking at me.

"Wait," I said suddenly, keeping my voice low. "What Will was saying, about showing him up with my...my ring. "You didn't buy it for that, did you?"

"I've no need to put Will in his place," Stephen muttered. "He does a great job of it on his own." He headed for the stairs.

Feeling more uneasy than before, I took off the new ring and slipped it into my pocket next to my wedding band. After ten minutes of creaky plumbing noise from the two loos, the house was finally quiet. But I was too restless to go to bed.

I opened the front door and gazed outside. The rainclouds were breaking up. A half moon shone in a patch of clear sky, illuminating the garden. The towering oak with the dangling swing cast a shadow that reached the stoop. And it was so quiet—the absence of sound seemed unearthly. For a moment, I wanted to go get Stephen, and share this lovely scene with him. I could try and forget his preoccupation with work, and apologize for receiving his ring so gracelessly. Even tell him, *you needn't have given me a ring—you could have just given me yourself.* Maybe outside, in the peace and silence, I could find the courage to say it.

I grabbed my anorak. Bundling into it, I let myself out, softly closing the door. I went straight to the oak tree and settled onto the swing, lazily pushing off with one foot to set the swing in motion. Gone were the days when I'd come to bed late, and Stephen would rouse and pull back the covers for me. Then he'd draw me close, spooning me up against him...

Closing my eyes, I felt a longing deep inside me. I tried to tamp it down, but it had been so long since we'd held each other... Then the front door rattled.

31

I jerked my eyes open. Stephen, seeking me out to beg pardon for being gone all afternoon? I fumbled to my pocket to slide the ring back on, ready to say, *Stephen, I'm so sorry...*

"Saw someone on the swing from the window," Will said, jumping off the stoop in one long stride, his teeth flashing in the moonlight. He was brandishing the bottle of Champagne. "I had to make sure it wasn't some crook."

"You've brought a weapon?" I pushed all thoughts of Stephen away, suddenly tired of feeling guilty and resentful unloved and all the rest. I set my foot down to stop the swing, and without thinking, slid my hand to the back of my neck, releasing my hair from my coat collar.

"This?" Will waved the uncorked champagne bottle, and liquid splashed on his hand. "As if I'd ever waste good drink!" He handed me the bottle. "It'll be flat by morning. So why not polish it off tonight?"

"Why not?" I said, though I had my fill of champagne earlier.

Will pulled a flask from the inside pocket of his fleece. "More to my taste," he said, and clicked the flask against the bottle I was holding. "*Slainté.*" I smelled whiskey as he unscrewed the top and lifted the flask to his lips.

"*Slainté*, yourself." I hesitated, then thought, *ah, why not.* I took a careful sip of the champagne right from the bottle. It tasted far better than it had at dinner, in the tense atmosphere with Stephen and Jennifer.

"Got a bit of a shock, seeing you out here," he said. "A pretty girl shouldn't spend a moonlit night by herself."

Will's flirting was as automatic as his breathing, but tonight, I didn't mind. "I wasn't sleepy." I brought the bottle to my lips again.

"Neither was I," he said. Leaning against the tree trunk, he gulped another mouthful of whiskey, then stared at the flask. "Restless, I guess."

It felt like the old days again. Will and me, on the same wavelength. "I think lots of people get that way on holiday," I ventured. "You know, away from the usual routines…"

He still looked like the Will I'd fancied years ago. In the mood I was in, I wanted to feel at least a little desirable again—and a bit of chat with a handsome guy was better than nothing. "And there's all the family around."

He snapped out of his trance. "Don't I know it—a bloke's got to be on his best behavior for days on end." His expression sobered. "And there's too much time on your hands. Too much time to think. And…" his voice trailed away. He took a long swig of whiskey.

"And?" I prompted.

"My problem is, I feel like this all the time," he said, his voice rising. "Like I want to crawl out of—" He stopped. "Ah, hell, forget it. We're on holiday—drink up!"

To please him, maybe help him shake off his bad form, I took a small sip.

"No," he said, his mouth curving back into a grin, "Come on, down the hatch!" He nipped the bottle out of my hand, put it to his lips and took a drink of the Champagne. Handing it back to me, I could see the challenge in his eyes, even in the moonlight. "Finish it off!"

Suddenly, a fizzy sensation rose in me that had nothing to do with the champagne. Feeling daring, I lifted the bottle, setting my mouth where his had been, and took a draught. Just when I was sure I'd cough and ruin the moment, I managed to swallow it all. Then swiped the back of my hand against my mouth, smiling back at him.

Will grabbed the empty bottle, and threw it over his shoulder. As it hit the ground with a thud, he pocketed his flask. Swaying a little, he pivoted behind the swing, and suddenly his big hands were on my back. "You know what we're missing, way out here in the boondocks?" He gave me a push.

"More Champagne?" I teased.

"Music!" Will gave me another push. "How can I give a girl a good time without a tune?" He burst out, "'In the merry month of May from my home I started—'"

"'Rocky Road to Dublin'—that's perfect!" I laughed. "'Left the girls of Tuam nearly broken-hearted,'" I sang along. *What the hell are you about, drinking and flirting with Will, alone?* asked my conscience, but I squashed it ruthlessly. In between giggles, I joined in the chorus, "'One, two, three, four, five...Whack fol-lol-de-ra—'" I stifled a shriek as he gave me another gigantic push. "Not so high!"

But I actually liked it, giddy with laughter and the drink I wasn't accustomed to. I didn't protest as I felt his hands push lower on my back. When his next push was on my hips, I didn't mind that either—I felt young and carefree and desirable in ways I hadn't since I'd had Jamie.

But after another two pushes I could feel the drink slosh round in my stomach, and my head started to spin. "Stop!" I gasped. "No more!"

Will grabbed the swing, grunting with the effort to slow it down. "You're okay?"

"Just a bit dizzy." I clutched the ropes. Feeling steadier when he wrapped his hands round mine, I breathed slowly until my head stopped swimming. "I think I'm all right now." I waited for him to move away. "Really, I am." But he stayed where he was, his hands warm and firm against my skin. To distract myself from his closeness, I said, "Em...a minute ago, you were saying you felt a bit...well, not quite yourself?"

He didn't say anything for a moment, then a bark of laughter erupted from him, as bitter as I'd ever heard. "Yeah—most of the time I feel like I could crawl out of my bloody skin! I'm stuck in a life I didn't choose—that I don't want."

"Oh, Will." My sympathy was roused all over again. Hadn't I felt the same? Like I was suffocating, sitting in my office day after day, plunking away at spreadsheets until I wanted to scream. "I wish I could help." Wanting to look at him properly, I flexed my hands so I could slide off the swing.

He finally released me, stepping round the ropes to face me. "No one can help," he said, then the words poured out of him like a torrent. "No one has any idea what it's like when your father-in-law gets you a job, it's like he fecking owns you, with his beady eyes trained on you like a scope of a rifle."

The drink must've addled my thoughts. Had I heard him right? Most men would be grateful for a secure job. But he was obviously jarred, not thinking straight. To comfort him, I said, "It must be difficult—"

"If being beholden to your wife's old man for the rest of your fecking life isn't bad enough," he interrupted, "I look at the lads I'm coaching, and all I can think, 'you lucky little sods, you've got your whole lives in front of you. You can do what you want, see who you want!' Jaysus, I would kill for that freedom!"

I thought of the three little girls asleep in the house, while here was their father, vibrating with drink and resentment. He'd regret his drunken rant in the morning, but suddenly I'd had enough. "You've been fortunate in other ways," I told him in a chiding voice.

Will didn't seem to hear me. He clenched his fists, his hands working. "And just when you think your life's all bollocks, the whole world's got you by the short hairs, you get saddled with something else! This bloody farm!"

I was completely taken aback. "This place is beautiful, how can you not love it?"

He still wasn't listening. "I told my parents I didn't want it, they could have the will changed, they could donate the place to somebody, I don't give a rat's arse, but they said the farm is mine—and it was time I took responsibility."

Will really hadn't a clue how lucky he was! And I didn't want to hear any more. Still on the swing, I made to clamber off but he suddenly moved behind me again and gave me a push. "Stop it," I said. "It's time I went—"

"Wait!" Will caught the rope. "Don't you see? How everyone wants to tighten the noose round my neck?"

But I don't care! Before I could jump away from him, he wrapped his arms around me from behind. "Everyone except you, Kerry," he said, and pressed his face against the back of my neck. "You've always understood me."

I jerked, sobering up instantly. Years ago, in my secret dreams I'd thought of being in Will's embrace. But the reality felt...horrible. "Will, don't." I tried to shrug away. As pissed as he had to be, I didn't want to make a fuss. "I want to go inside—"

"I've always wanted you, you know that." He pulled me closer so my back was full on against his body. He kissed my neck, chuckling against my skin. "And you've always fancied me, haven't you? We could go in the car, no one would know..."

Frozen in shock, all I could think was, *this couldn't be happening.* "No," I whispered, forcing the word through my frozen lips. "We can't—"

"We could even go up in the barn, have a proper roll in the hay. You should have a bit of fun—Stephen's having his."

I felt like I was in an alternate universe. Will had turned into a stranger, and nothing made sense. "What...what do you mean?"

He nuzzled my neck again, "Come on, you're no eejit, you know exactly what I mean..."

This is so wrong. He is so wrong..."Stop it!" I finally managed to wrench away. Scrambling off the swing, I turned to face him. "You think Stephen's having an *affair*?"

Will stepped around the swing, his teeth flashing. But this time there was no charm in his grin—it was more like the leer of a Jack o' lantern. "Has he said where he's been disappearing to, who he's been with?"

"There was a meeting—"

Will laughed, the sound harsh in the quiet. "That's what they all say. It's obvious he's got some girl in the city. Why d'you think he bought that flash ring for you? It's a guilt present if there ever was one." He tried to seize my hand. "Forget him— you can be with me, get your revenge—"

"Shut up!" Feeling a surge of strength, I gave him a shove.

Will stumbled backward. Tripping over his own feet, he fell down. "What the feck—"

"You're pissed—and you don't know what you're talking about!"

As I stepped around him he said, "I get it." He got clumsily to his feet and shrugged. "It's the money."

"What *are* you on about?" I stared at him. *Who are you? What happened to the boy I'd dreamed about all these years?* "I'm not listening to this—you're a liar and a cheat," I said, breathing hard. Then it hit me, how practiced his embrace had been. "And I'm not the only one you've tried to have a go at, am I? So if you've a shred of decency you'll forget this ever happened. I already have."

As Will's handsome mouth went slack, I turned and ran to the house, letting myself in as quietly as I could. I stood just inside the door, shaking with disgust. Because I knew I was a liar, just like Will.

I'd never forget what had happened just now. When I'd discovered the secret longing and connection between Will and me had been nothing but a sham. And I'd never forget that he'd done me a favor, tearing the blinders from my eyes.

32

In our bedroom, I changed into my nightdress and slipped into bed. Listening to Stephen's and Jamie's quiet breathing, I couldn't stop shivering. Tears leaked out of my eyes, trailing down my temples and into my hair, and the urge to weep was nearly overpowering. But I didn't dare. Didn't dare make a peep and wake Stephen. Not so long ago, I'd have pressed up against him for warmth, and comfort too, but tonight I was too ashamed. Ashamed for flirting with Will, with both of us married. And too angry at myself for all the years I'd wasted fancying him.

It was so clear now. His feelings for me had been a figment of my imagination. How wrong could I be, to think he'd loved me when it was only lust. Or boredom. *And* to think he could have been my *soulmate*, when he was the sort who'd probably cheated on his wife so many times he'd make a play for anyone, even a friend.

Here I'd romanticized him all these years, but for all his charm, his looks, his sense of adventure, he was nothing but...what? An overgrown Peter Pan. And a whiny one at that.

My shivering began to ease. Drying my face with the sleeve of my nightie, I realized I'd wasted the peace and joy I'd felt tonight with the little girls, flirting and drinking with Will.

I turned toward Stephen, to watch him sleep, suddenly regretting I'd taken his ring off. He wasn't a shiny or flashy sort, but he was real. What we'd always felt for each other had been real. And lasting. I could hardly wait until morning to tell him so—and tell him too, that we could feel that way again.

Feeling the sting of Will's betrayal, it didn't feel right to put my arm round Stephen and spoon up against him. Instead, I curved my hand round his bicep, but in his sleep he rolled away from my touch.

I awakened as the bedroom door opened. Stephen slipped into the room. Although it was barely light, he was fully dressed. I struggled to sit up, feeling a bit queasy from the drink I'd had last night, and saw our son's empty sleeping bag. "You and Jamie are up early."

"He's looking after the girls, so Will and Jennifer can sleep a bit longer," Stephen said, his cheeks and ears red. As he closed the door behind him, a fresh, outdoorsy scent came off him. "A Thanksgiving present, Jamie said."

After that awful scene with Will, I'd actually forgotten what day it was. "You've been outside already?" Up at dawn to exercise wasn't Stephen's style at all.

"I had an email to finish—then I went for a walk." He leaned against the door. "I needed to…clear my head."

With all that I wanted to tell Stephen, I smoothed my hair and rubbed the sleep from my eyes, wishing I was washed and dressed. I patted the bed next to me, gathering my courage. "You'll sit down?"

When he didn't move, I drew up my knees and wrapped my arms round them. "Is everything…all right?"

"I see you're not wearing your new ring." His voice was ironic.

"Right!" I looked at my bare left hand as if in surprise. "It's just in my pocket, I was—"

"You don't have to explain—I saw your face when I gave it to you. You don't like it."

"No, the ring is lovely, really," I lied. "It's just that I couldn't see spending—"

"Don't." Stephen's expression hardened. "Just…don't. You've never been all in, have you? Not like I have."

Shocked, I struggled for a reply. "What do you mean? Our…marriage? Of course I—"

"So it's no wonder you don't like it," Stephen said. "Let's face it—you wouldn't want any ring of mine."

"That's not true—" I was utterly blindsided. I wanted to tell him how much he meant to me, and he was arguing about the ring? "Why…why would you think that?"

"Because…" A muscle moved in his jaw. "I saw you outside last night. With Will."

"Oh, God." I felt a hard knot of guilt in my throat. "Stephen—I'm so sorry." This was where my eejit fancy for another man had got me. Had he seen Will put his arms round me? Then turned away before I pushed Will away? "Please believe me, nothing happened—"

"Nothing physical, you mean?" Grief flashed in his eyes. He went to the window and pulled the lace curtain aside. "Physical infidelity has never been the problem with us—"

"But you know I would *never*—" I couldn't say the rest.

He turned to face me. "Never what? Be with Will? Cheat on me with a married man? Maybe there are other ways to be unfaithful."

And I'd done them, years ago. Daydreaming about Will. Even imagining us together. And Stephen had sensed it. I tightened my arms round my knees, hardly able to think about the pain I'd caused him. After a long silence, I said, "Will thinks you're the one having an affair."

Stephen didn't blink. "Yeah, he'd think that, wouldn't he? Bringing every other bloke down to his level."

I wanted to ask, *Well, you haven't been having one, have you?* Just to hear him confirm, *Of course I haven't, you know that.* Before I could get the words out, he said, "There's something you need to know." He took a deep breath. "About the promotion I mentioned."

The one I hadn't asked him about. The guilty knot in my throat spread into my shoulders. "The one you discussed at your meeting?"

"It would be a great career move." If Stephen was pleased about this you wouldn't know it by the grim look on his face. "The CEO offered me a top spot, getting a new team up and running."

"It does sound fantastic," I said faintly. "Is the job in...Dublin?"

"Vancouver, B.C."

I stared at him. A job in Canada. What did that mean for our family?

"It's not a permanent assignment," Stephen said. "Unless I want it to be. I was all set to lay out all the parameters to you— where we could live, a school for Jamie. When I gave you the new ring, though, I realized maybe it wasn't on after all."

I could hardly breathe. "Are you saying you'd give up a grand opportunity like that?" *So we can get our marriage back on track?*

"I would have...before." He shoved his hands into his trouser pockets. "Then I saw you and Will. So I'm taking the job—and going alone."

"Alone?" My head reeled.

"What I'm saying is, we need a break."

33

*T*ears spurted into my eyes. I bit my lip, hard, to keep from weeping. "But Stephen...that won't help us sort out what's happened between us."

Stephen's hands balled in his pockets. "After what I saw last night, I thought you'd feel the same."

"I don't," I whispered. "I told you, it was *nothing*. I don't even like Will anymore."

He didn't say anything for a moment. "The job starts straightaway, so we'll leave tomorrow as we planned. On the way, you can drop me in Galway City so I can hire a car to get to Shannon. Then you and Jamie can head back to Dublin."

I dropped my chin so he wouldn't see the devastation on my face. "What about Jamie? We'll need to explain—"

"We can talk to him this afternoon—he'll understand that going to Vancouver is part of my job."

But he's just a boy, he'll miss you terribly. I determinedly blinked my tears away. "You'll visit him?"

"Of course, but we can sort all that...later." His voice faltered. "I know the timing's rotten, being here, but...but I haven't any choice—"

A knock sounded at the door. Stephen opened it so quickly I knew he was relieved for the interruption. "Look who's here!" Stephen opened the door wider. "Jennifer!" He sounded more hearty and fakey than I'd ever heard. "I guess I should say, Happy Thanksgiving!"

"Good morning," I managed, taking in her glowing face and stylish outfit. I had to look even more desperate in comparison.

"And Happy Thanksgiving to you!" Jennifer's smile could

have lit up the room. "I heard voices, so I figured it was safe to pop in and see you. It's godawful early, but I couldn't wait another moment to—"

"Jennifer—sorry," Stephen broke in, "Jamie's waiting for me. I'll catch you downstairs." He slipped past Jennifer and closed the door behind him before either of us could react.

Rising from the bed, I pasted a smile on my face as best I could. Love of God, what if she'd seen Will and me last night too? But she seemed as happy as I'd ever seen her. "Has something…happened? I hope it's good—"

"I've been holding it in since yesterday—and I just *had* to talk to you." Eyes sparkling, she clasped her hands to her heart. "About what you've done for us—you and Stephen."

Clearly, she was in the dark about Will's behavior. But I'd no clue what she was talking about. "Oh, it was noth—"

"It's *everything*!" Jennifer reached out to hug me. "The best present ever—the loan will totally save us."

Loan? My knees buckled. As she released me I sank to the bed. Will had asked Stephen for *money*?

"We'd already borrowed money from my parents," Jennifer said. "And Will and I thought, well, it never hurts to ask. He's kind of sensitive about not making the kind of money Stephen does, but when they were out getting the Christmas tree, he told me it was just like old times—that it would be okay to approach Stephen just once more."

For money. Yesterday's events began making an awful kind of sense. Why Will had told Jamie he couldn't come to fetch the Christmas tree—he'd wanted Stephen alone. And later, saying to Jennifer, *we're sorted*. Then last night, to me, *I get it, it's the money.*

"What a relief!" Jennifer was still burbling on. "Now we can pay the girls' tuition, hire the people we need to get this farm sale jump-started."

I couldn't take it in. This shock on top of Stephen's was too much. Had Will invited us here with the express purpose of shaking us down for money? When I was actually thinking he wanted to see me again?

I felt ill with the timing of Will's perfidy too—that he'd gotten Stephen's promise for money yesterday, and only hours later, he'd had the utter *nerve* to try it on with me. The wife of the man he'd borrowed from. The disgust I felt for Will—and for me, to have been so easily taken in—nearly overwhelmed me.

Although all I wanted was to curl up on the bed, and shut out of the world, I had to say something. "Stephen..." I could barely move my lips. "He'd want to help out an old friend." Realizing Jennifer had to have been in on this too, I felt gut-punched. Had her friendship been as false as Will's?

I searched her face, and saw only sincerity. And genuine gratitude. I felt better, but not much.

"I just can't thank you enough." Jennifer said. "Stephen was so understanding." Her voice caught as she reached for the knob. "When Will said we wouldn't be able to pay you back until the farm sold—which could be months, or years, even—Stephen said that would be fine. He's a great guy."

I could only nod, dreading the moment I'd have to face Stephen again. Yet as fresh and sharp as my pain was, I could only imagine how Jamie would feel. That his dad, leaving me, would be leaving him too.

Once I was alone, I collapsed back onto the bed, burying my face in the pillow. Will's proposition, and now this money thing—I felt sick, trying to take it all in. As for Stephen's rejection—his leaving me seemed like such an outsize reaction. He'd seemed to have believed me—that I would never had gotten physical with Will. But the fact that he could even suspect me of being unfaithful, and his refusal to talk things out was a hurt I could feel in my bones.

Too bad spending the day in a fetal position just wasn't on. Although I felt like I'd been through a war, and on the losing side, I forced myself upright. And with a short, lukewarm shower and some extra makeup, I managed to pull myself together enough to go downstairs. I didn't know what was worse, facing Stephen and putting on a good face, or pretending to be friends with Will when I despised him. But I had to get on with it. I'd my son to think about. And the little girls.

Gluing on my fake smile again, I entered the kitchen to find Stephen manning the toaster while Jennifer refereed a tableful of squabbling girls, platefuls of scrambled eggs in front of them. No trace of Will, though. Thank *God*. Jennifer was frowning at her youngest. "No one gets to play anything before breakfast!"

"Maddie gets really naughty on an empty stomach," Emerson said to Jamie. "Mom always says so."

As Maddie stuck out her tongue at her sister, Mackenzie crunched a piece of toast like she was in an eating contest and nearly knocked her glass of juice over. "Hey!" Jamie caught it just in time. "Watch it!" He looked like he wanted to be somewhere else.

"Will's still asleep," Jennifer said over the racket. "I can't...blame him for wanting to avoid..." She gestured round the table. "This."

"The natives are definitely restless," I said, hoping my voice sounded normal. I sent Stephen a *we have to talk* look, but he was staring into the toaster.

"You said it," said Jennifer, then was back to scolding the kids.

Sidling toward Stephen, I said low, "I need to speak with you."

He nodded without looking up. "Stephen and I are going out for some fresh air," I told Jennifer, and went to fetch my jacket, Stephen slowly following me.

Jamie appeared in the doorway. "Can I come?" Apparently he'd had his fill of girly energy.

"In a few minutes," Stephen pulled on his own anorak, still dirty from working on the Christmas tree yesterday. "We'll be right back."

We walked in silence down the drive, the drifting mist hovering above the hilltop. As we reached the lane, I couldn't hold my feelings in any longer. "This loan—what in God's name is going on?"

Stephen looked straight ahead. "I know, it's a dodgy situation—"

"Dodgy doesn't begin to cover it! I can't believe you'd promise money to Will and Jennifer without discussing it with me first—even if we are…" I swallowed hard. "Separating."

"You of all people know how persuasive Will can be," Stephen said shortly.

I turned toward Fiona Whelan's farm, guilt nagging at me all over again. But knowing I was in the right about this loan, I straightened my spine. "There's such a thing as a sin of omission," I said, burying my hurt in indignation. "Don't throw this—keeping the loan to yourself—on me! Were you even going to say…"

I slowed my steps, suddenly remembering something. A lot of somethings over the years that hadn't made sense. Our old savings account, "for the apocalypse" with a balance much lower than I'd expected. Stephen assuring me our finances were in good shape, then suddenly telling me they weren't. And Jennifer saying this morning, *it wouldn't hurt to ask just once more…* "This isn't the first loan to Will, is it."

"There have been…several." Stephen's voice was bleak. "Over the years."

I stopped to face him. "Tell me."

Stephen hunched his shoulders. "The first time, it was his plane fare to the States. I was bloody happy to give it to him."

To get Will out of our lives. Out of my life.

"Then there was his wedding." Stephen's jaw was tight. "He said he couldn't let his father-in-law—his boss, remember—think he was a freeloader."

"So he freeloaded off us, instead."

"There were 'little emergencies' here and there—like the hospital bill when Maddie broke her wrist. Then this last spring, he asked me to help him out when he and Jennifer bought that big house."

A house they clearly couldn't afford. "So that's why money was tight, like your dad was talking about, when we left our flat and you lined up our new place." And I'd thought Stephen had kept things from me before? "Now Will and Jennifer need more for the girls' tuition, and to hire consultants so they could make a killing on this farm." Trying to get my head around an amount, I asked, "Including this last request, how much have you loaned Will?"

Stephen waited a beat, then said a figure that made me gasp.

When I could speak again, I said, "He hasn't paid back any of the other loans, has he?" Stephen only shook his head. "After we'd been so thrifty—at your insistence, mind—you throw our money away on him?"

"I thought you'd want me to help Will. Because..." His voice trailed away. "Because I knew you...cared about him."

"That's not good enough, Stephen." I tried to meet his gaze but his eyes were on the Whelan farm. "It makes no sense that you'd risk our finances, our future, on that pair, who spend like they've a money tree in the back garden."

Stephen only shrugged.

"Don't do that!" I wanted to hit him. "Stop shutting me out, for God's sake!" Then it came to me, all the times Stephen had said, *It's not on just yet, to try for*— Suddenly, all these loans added up to an unavoidable conclusion, and the anger choking me shifted into a vast hurt that nearly made me crumple to the ground. "He...he owes us thousands, and now you've promised him even more—is he the reason we put off having a baby?"

Stephen's mouth tightened.

Knowing it was true, I grabbed his arm, swinging him around to face me. "If you're going to leave me, at least for once in our lives tell me what you're really thinking!"

"Because I owe him, all right?" Stephen's face had gone white. "I'll always owe him—because he saved my life."

34

$\mathcal{I}$ stared at my husband, feeling like I'd been punched in the chest. And this was the man I'd thought I knew better than anyone else? "When?" My lips trembled.

"A long time ago. Just before I first brought him round to our flat."

I thought of that night, Will coming through our door, handsome and vital and larger than life. "What happened? Please, have the decency to tell me, now that you've let this out."

He was quiet for a moment. I wondered bitterly if he was sorting out how much to keep from me. "One of those freak things," Stephen finally said. "It was a blustery day. Will and I were four stories up, on the scaffolding. A huge gust of wind hit us and blew me sideways. Will caught my coat, and hauled me from the edge before I could go over."

So that's how Stephen had torn his coat, the one we'd bought him for work when we were first married. It had cost far more than we could afford. The next day I'd reproached him. *How could you be so careless?* "And you didn't...say anything."

"Will kept telling me, 'it was nothing, no bother, let's keep it to ourselves.' He made a real point of it. So I thought the least I could do was keep my mouth shut, stand him a pint and invite him home to supper. Later, I found out he hadn't wanted his uncle to give him a bollacking for not getting us rigged out with a safety harness." His expression turned even bleaker. "You know the rest. I brought him round and life turned upside down."

"Why do you say that?" My voice was tremulous.

Stephen stared fixedly at the Whelan's herd of cows.

195

"Because I could see that you...fancied him. Then with all those times we had him round for Sunday lunch, I could see he felt the same about you."

I felt ice in my veins. So I'd damaged our marriage long before last night, when Will tried it on with me. "But I...I—"

"I knew some part of him regretted he'd saved me," Stephen said slowly. "Then he could've had you."

"But that's...that's rubbish!" *We can get past this. We've got to!* "Will and I...we would never have met."

"Is it? You'd have seen him at my funer—"

"Don't say it." I clenched my fists. "For God's sake, don't say it!"

Stephen finally met my eyes. "If you'd known he saved my life, I'd have to wonder the rest of my days if you'd wished Will hadn't been on that scaffolding with me. Or wished he hadn't been fast enough, or strong enough, or that my new coat had given way."

So Stephen had come home to me, bringing Will with him, and watched me start falling for him.

The "friendship" we'd shared with Will, then, was one more thing that was all in my imagination. I'd sensed Stephen's reluctance to pursue a relationship with Will, but I'd been the one to invite Will to Mam's house, to have him round for dozens of Sunday lunches. "Did you even want to be mates with him?" I asked Stephen. "Ever?"

"No," Stephen said. "But I knew you did. Why else would I keep seeing him? Why else would I go on this holiday? It seemed the least I could do for you, after we lost..." He still couldn't talk about the miscarriage.

And I was too bludgeoned by shock to make him try. The silences, the gulf between Stephen and I had never seemed so wide. I stared at an ancient, rusty tractor sitting in the Whelan's farmyard. Fit only for the junkyard. Like our marriage?

Maybe Stephen and I could salvage one thing out of this disaster... "Hasn't this 'debt' been hanging over our heads long enough?" I turned to walk back to the farmhouse. Stephen waited a moment, then stepped alongside me. "Even if Will saved your life, you don't have to live a Chinese proverb, and pay for it until the day you die."

I began walking back toward the Power's farmhouse. *How different our lives might have been if only Stephen had told me all this,* I kept thinking. Was keeping this secret, about Will saving him, the moment we began to grow apart? And Stephen began closing down? So our marriage had tottered along, balanced on the rickety foundation of my husband believing he was my second choice.

I felt the wind rise, and looked up to see that the sky had darkened. "It'll rain soon," I said, to break the crushing silence between us.

"Like it does most Novembers," Stephen said heavily. As we approached the farmhouse drive, Jamie appeared on the stoop and walked down to meet us. "You said a few minutes, Dad."

Stephen ruffled Jamie's hair, the frozen look on his face easing. "Right, I did." For a moment, he gazed around the farm. I wanted to think the place had grown on him. But he was in sales, after all. He'd be working out how to sell his move to Vancouver to Jamie. "Son," began, "I've had an offer—"

"Dad, you never said where you were yesterday," Jamie interrupted. "When Will was bringing home the tree."

"Didn't I?" said Stephen, looking surprised.

I looked at Stephen. *When did you become so good at prevarication?* "Your dad said he'd gotten sidetracked," I said, keeping the irony out of my voice with effort.

"Will said you were wandering all over," Jamie said, looking straight at his father, "trying to find a mobile signal for your calls to the office."

"Will may be our host, but he doesn't always know what he's talking about," said Stephen. "But what I wanted to tell you is, I've an opportunity for a promotion, starting straightaway."

"You mean, *another* promotion," Jamie said.

"That's it," Stephen said. "The job's abroad, in Canada."

Jamie's face lit up. "You're not serious!"

Stephen said, "You and your mother—you'll be staying in Dublin."

Jamie's eyes dimmed. He was quiet for a long moment. "Why aren't we all going to Vancouver?"

"It would disrupt your school," Stephen said quickly, as if he'd rehearsed the words. "And your mother's work."

"But she doesn't even like her job." Jamie gave Stephen and me one of his assessing, adult looks. They'd been a source of bemusement to me when he was young, but now, I was afraid he was seeing far more than either of us wanted.

"It's a grand opportunity for your dad." I'd put on a united front for our son even if it killed me. "Going alone, he can completely focus on his work. It'll only be a few months, after all."

"Jamie, you can come see me whenever you want," Stephen added. "I'll get a flat with a second bedroom for you. Vancouver's a great place, there's tons of things to do there—"

"You mean, I could visit during school holidays," said Jamie with another level look. "Can Mam come too?"

"Of course she can," said Stephen in his overly hearty tone. "Whenever she can get time off."

I pinned on a bright smile. "You'll have some great holidays, Jamie, and the months without your dad will go by fast."

"But Dad..." Jamie's face suddenly crumpled. "Why do you have to go?"

"I know, it's not much time to get used to the idea." Stephen put a gentle hand on his shoulder. "The...situation is not what I would have...would have wanted. But there's no way round it."

Jamie stared into his father's face. His eyes were shiny with tears, but he nodded, an almost imperceptible dip of his head. "I'm going to walk up the road. Just myself."

"When you're back at the house," Stephen said, still in that hearty voice, "We'll all play Minecraft, you and me and Mackenzie?"

Jamie only shrugged Stephen's hand off.

Stephen glanced at me, then back to Jamie. "Son? One more thing—can you keep this just between ourselves? I haven't mentioned my promotion to the Powers."

Did Stephen not want Will to know he'd be earning even more money? Or that our marriage was on the skids? Did it matter?

Jamie knuckled the tears off his face. "Right."

He was old enough to realize that keeping this a secret meant there was something not quite right going on. I wanted to embrace him, say, *it'll be all right, you'll see,* but it was clear he wouldn't want that. "Off you go, then," I said, my heart aching as our son walked away. Out of the corner of my eye I could see Stephen watching him too. After Jamie moved out of earshot, I said, "There it is—the first casualty of our split."

I wanted so badly for Stephen to say, *we're not splitting up, it's only a short break,* but he only said, "I suppose I'd better get my gear organized, look over my paperwork." He was all business now, like he was ticking off his to-do list. *1) Leave your wife. 2) Blow off your son. 3) Then ask him to keep your secrets.*

"Wait." I reached out to catch Stephen's arm, then drew my hand back. Touching was too loaded now. "This money business with Will—it's got to stop."

Stephen looked at the farmhouse for a moment, then back at me. "You're absolutely right. Before we leave, I'll tell him that—"

"No, *we'll* tell him."

"All right." He thought for a moment. "How about this—if he wants this last loan, he'll need to give us repayment terms. With interest."

"And on paper." So that Stephen and I could be repaid, the farm I stood on would have to be sold. Perhaps leveled. For us, our benefit, when we no longer were an "us." How ironic was that. "Your balance sheets with Will can be cleared. You'll be even."

Stephen's face turned bleak. "I wish we were. But we'll never be even."

My chest clenched in grief. Was he thinking that even after all this, Will still had a place in my heart? "Stephen, please, just let me explain—"

"No." His eyes turned chilly again and he went inside.

As if on cue, I felt the first drops of rain.

35

My first Thanksgiving wasn't the relaxing, joy-filled celebration I'd thought it would be. Only a day to be gotten through.

After helping Jennifer heat up the mail-order food, I did my best to eat the tasteless holiday dinner—though whether the Internet meal was actually bad or that I was so upset everything tasted horrible who knows. The kids' byplay and Jennifer's attempts to keep some order to the proceedings gave me an excuse to say as little as Stephen and Jamie did. As for Will, the man was almost invisible. He didn't bring any drink to the table, not even a beer. Halfway through dinner I realized that without alcohol, Will was no longer the life of the party. In fact, he was rather…boring.

The one bright spot was when Jennifer brought out the cakes. At the sight of their orange/chartreuse and lurid blue splendor, all three girls clapped their hands. "They're princess cakes!" Emerson cried, while Maddie reached out a finger to swipe at the blue icing. "Don't touch the cake with your germy fingers!" Mackenzie warned, and batted her sister's hand away. *Like mother, like daughter*, I thought. Not long ago, I would've sent a teasing look at Stephen to share the joke. But those days were over.

I ate my own piece of cake mechanically. This dinner was one step closer to ending this awful visit—but also to the moment Stephen would be out of my life.

The meal ended abruptly. As the girls pleaded for a third

serving of dessert, Jennifer snapped, "You've had enough sugar!" The kids' faces froze, then they stampeded from the table, the two men right behind them. Jennifer immediately began wrapping up the leftovers, her beautifully shaped brows drawn together. "Thanks for helping, Kerry," she said, her eyes on her task. "Will's still not...feeling well. I'd asked him to say a special Thanksgiving grace, but he must have forgotten."

I could see Will sprawled on the couch through the doorway, thumbing his mobile. Next to him, the girls were watching another film on the laptop, this one about a life-size, pratfall-prone elf. Stephen and Jamie were back to tinkering with the new device. I would've liked to be by myself, to lick my wounds. But you'd need a heart of stone to leave a tired mammy to deal with the clean-up alone, and right now mine was a cracked, bleeding mess.

"Everyone has their bad days," I said, trying on a smile.

"Bad days," she repeated. She scrunched a wad of plastic wrap ferociously between her well-manicured hands, then looked up at me. "Oh, hell, who am I kidding? Of course Will's not sick, he's hungover. How do you like that? He stays up half the night drinking, on our Thanksgiving vacation!"

"Jennifer..." The guilt I'd tried to forget rushed back. "Maybe he was celebrating the...loan, and all that," I said clumsily.

"Celebrating?" The words rushed out of her in a torrent. "Will doesn't need an excuse to drink. It's pints at the bar, it's beer at home, it's whiskey in between. And the last year or so, he's been hitting the bottle a lot more than he used to."

I didn't know what to say. "I'm sorry—"

"We saw a marriage counselor awhile back, but he only went because I threatened to tell my dad about his drinking. Of course, he was all smiles with the therapist, making *me* the one with the problem. To hear Will, he's just frustrated trying to support our family by himself. He thinks I should get a job and the girls can go into daycare, and all my worrying is hard on his nerves—"

She jammed the plastic wad into the bin, then dropped her head, bracing her hands against the sink. Her misery compounded my regret. How many times had I given Will a free pass for his drinking? I touched her shoulder. "I wish there was something I could say."

Jennifer reached up and covered my hand for a moment. "You'll probably think I'm crazy for staying with him. Sometimes I don't even like him." She pushed away from the sink, and met my eyes again. "And this sounds even more nuts, but despite everything, I still…I still love him." She shrugged. "And there are the girls."

You're not the first woman to stay with a man because of the children, I wanted to say, but I was in no position to play counselor. Given Jennifer's challenges, I could see there were worse things than my troubles with Stephen. Feeling grief for both of us, I said, "Your girls are lovely—you've done a great job with them." I'd seen by now that Will had done very little parenting.

Jennifer's mouth crooked, a painful, accepting little smile. "I told Will if he drank today, I'd kick him straight out of the house and he could spend Thanksgiving with the cows down the road. And you saw—he didn't touch a drop. But who knows how long that'll last."

Hours later, Stephen was sleeping as far away from my side of the bed as he could without falling out. Lying next to him, I stayed as stiff as a corpse, listening to the rain pounding on the roof, having discovered yet another Downside of Holiday Visits: If your marriage breaks up when you're at someone else's house, you still have to share a bed—since you've nowhere else to go. After a few hours of fitful sleep and bad dreams, I couldn't bear to lie here a moment longer. Not next to the man who was leaving me. I rolled out of bed, and dressed in the dark, making my movements as tiny and careful as I could.

Craving at least a liter of hot, strong tea, I entered the kitchen and turned on the light. There was Will sitting at the table, his flask in his hand. Unshaven, with bed hair, he wore a rumpled dressing gown, purple half-moons under his eyes.

If Stephen found me here, would he think I'd lied about my changed feelings for Will? But risking staying here would be my only chance to have it out with Will before we left.

"Getting jarred at five in the morning?" I said quietly. "You'll be sleeping with the cows tonight for certain." I turned away to fill the kettle.

"I'm not pissed," he said, his voice low. I looked over my shoulder to see him unscrew the top of the flask and turn it upside down. It was empty. "I finished this off the night before last, after you told me to feck off. In so many words."

"What's wrong with you anyway?" I set the kettle on the cooker. "You've a lovely family—why would you muck that up?"

"Don't you remember?" He refastened the top of the flask. "When I met you, I said I've no willpower." He grinned, but it was only a ghost of his old winning smile.

Hard to believe I'd been so taken by him. I gave him a long, dispassionate look. The kitchen clock ticked in the silence.

Finally he said, "Ah, c'mon, Kerry, I was drunk, I didn't know what I was doing—"

"That's bollocks, Will. And you know it." I got out the packet of tea and a cup. "When are you going to pull yourself together?"

"Maybe today." He made an ironic laugh. "Black Friday, we call it in the States—isn't that a laugh? Me, the black-hearted bletherskite who tries it on with my friend's—"

"Shut up," I said, my voice level. "When did you turn into such a gobshite? My husband lends you pots of money, then you mock him."

"Aw, he's swimming in euro," Will began, sounding aggrieved. "And he probably told you—he owes me."

"Oh, yes, you were the big hero, years ago," I said as calmly as I could when I wanted to spit in his face. "Stephen wouldn't be here at all if it wasn't for you, I suppose."

"Well, yeah. Besides, he's the big executive, the loan is spare change for him. Look at that rock he gave you—"

"You want to talk about money? Why don't we chat about

your spending problem." As the kettle boiled I saw he'd a slight tremor to his hands. "Along with your drink problem." I filled my cup.

Will looked at his hands, then wrapped them tight around the flask. "Okay. Jaysus." He was quiet for a long moment. "I know...I'm full of shite. His wheedling tone was gone. "I was actually hoping for a chance to thank you for not...telling Jennifer."

If I had, I would've had to confess my part in it. And how could I hurt her that way? I didn't answer.

"The thing is," Will said, "I haven't had my head on straight since the day I met you."

I gave him a straightforward look. "I won't have it, Will."

"It's true," he said quietly, "I don't like to say it—fancying a married woman when I'm married myself is more gobshitey than anything else I've done. But I've always wondered, what if I hadn't gotten to Stephen in time? And he'd gone over that ledge?"

Stephen had guessed right. "Don't go there, Will. I told you, I'm not hearing it—"

"I have to say it," he insisted. "You'd have been...you know."

A widow. Free.

I averted my face, my stomach clenching in shame. Once or twice during my marriage, I actually had wondered, what if I'd met Will first? What if I'd married him? I saw the answer now, so clearly, what my life would have been like.

Like Jennifer's. Married to a guy who just wanted to play about, like Stephen had said years ago. He would've never have been a proper father to my son, not like Stephen. Will was nothing but a sports-mad boy who'd rather go to the pub or hang out with other women than be with his family.

But as I looked back at Will, I knew I was no better than he was. We'd each spent too much time wanting what we couldn't have, instead of appreciating what was in front of us. "Forget that," I told him crisply, fetching another teabag and cup. "We've something far more important to talk about."

36

Footfalls sounded on the stairs as I set the steaming cup in front of Will. Stephen came in, checking his step as he saw us. "I'm not interrupting anything?" He was dressed in the jeans and shirt he'd worn yesterday, the shirt buttons done up wrong. Had he rushed to come downstairs?

"Not at all." I wouldn't let Stephen's ironic tone put me at a disadvantage. "I was about to tell Will we'd a certain loan to discuss, and was going to fetch you." I pushed on the nearest chair leg with my foot. "Have a seat."

An uncertain look crossed Stephen's face, then he took the chair I'd moved for him.

Will took a swallow of tea, leaning back in his chair to look at Stephen, sneering. "Don't you mean *loans*?"

"Whatever," I said, matching his insolent tone. "We'll want to be repaid every last euro, starting—"

"We can talk about this later," said Will. It was like Stephen's presence was bringing out the worst in him. "I don't want to disturb my wife—"

"We'll talk about it now," Stephen said in a level voice. "We can always step outside."

Will glanced at the darkened kitchen window. The wind was driving the rain in sheets against the glass.

"Well?" Stephen crossed his arms.

"I told you, I'd pay you back when I've got the money."

"That's shite and you know it," said Stephen. "You've been promising to pay us back for years."

"I want to know exactly when you'll start making payments to us," I said.

"I'll expect one from your next pay packet," Stephen said quietly. "With interest."

"Oh, I get it," Will smirked. "You're turning the screws because I almost shagged your wife the night before last."

Too shocked to defend myself, I turned a pleading look at Stephen but I may as well not have been in the room. "If you're trying to get me to plant my fist in your lying gob," Stephen said almost pleasantly, but his eyes were as hard as agates, "you've failed. Kerry told me what happened."

I sagged in my chair. *So you do lie sometimes...only I never thought I'd be grateful for it.*

"So get this into your thick head," Stephen went on, his voice like steel. "You won't see another penny, not even for this last amount you asked for until I—"

"We—" I put in, my voice shaking.

"Get something in writing," Stephen finished. "Before we leave today."

"I told you, I don't have any money right now." Will sounded like a sulky boy.

I looked at him with distaste. I'd ruined my marriage over this whiny article? "Then find it," I said, feeling stronger knowing Stephen had my back, that we were dealing with this together. "And by the way, we're done being your personal bankers."

"Jaysus." Will's face was sullen. "Some bloody friends the pair of you turned out to be."

"You're running out of time," I pointed out. "Jennifer and the kids will be up any min—"

"Is this blackmail, Kerry?" A sheen of sweat showed on Will's upper lip. "I've got to pay up or you'll tell Jennifer I tried it on with you?"

"I think Jennifer has enough troubles without me adding to them," I said. "But blackmail's starting to sound better and better."

"Especially if we don't see some repayment terms," Stephen said.

"All right!" Will ran his fingers through his flattened curls. "I can't pay you a farthing because I'm completely skint! Is that what you wanted to hear? We've bills coming out of—"

"Tough." I opened a drawer, pulling out the small tablet I'd found. "You'll draft a repayment schedule right now." As I slapped it down on the table in front of Will, Stephen drew a pen from his shirt pocket.

"You're going to get blood out of a turnip?" Will mocked. "Good lu—"

"You can always sell that fancy new house of yours, pay us back with the proceeds," said Stephen.

Will only shoved the tablet away, looking hunted. "Okay, you want blood? Have the fecking farm!"

I blinked. "You mean...as collateral?"

"That won't put money in our pockets now," said Stephen.

"Not collateral—just take it! The farm's worth twice as much as I owe you—"

"You're having us on, right?" I'd a sudden vision of apple trees laden with fruit, a cow grazing in a pasture.. "Jennifer would never give up the chance to—"

"Well, she'll have to, won't she?" Will's lip curled. "I don't want to deal with the bloody farm—you'll be doing me a favor."

"God knows we'd love nothing better than to do you a favor," said Stephen, a bite to his voice. "So we accept."

A look of surprise crossed Will's face. "Right then, it's settled. Are we done here?" He made to rise.

"Hardly." As Stephen shoved the tablet back in front of him, Will sat back abruptly. "Write it down. That you're turning the property over to us."

Will began scratching on the paper, his hands shaking more than they'd been earlier.

"Actually, write up a second copy for us," Stephen said. "You'll have a solicitor look over your copy, change it into legalese. After you've signed off on it, you can post the legal papers to us. Then I'll send you a bank draft for this last amount you asked for."

Will looked up from the paper, his face twisting. "You're

pissing me about, right? I've got to work out telling Jennifer first! And Chrissakes, I need the money now—"

"Then you'd better see your solicitor ASAP, don't you think?" I slammed the door on my bucolic fantasies. Stephen and I would have to sell the farm ourselves, to replace all the money Will had borrowed. "We'll expect your repayment proposal within a couple of hours."

"Before we leave." Stephen rose from the table, his gray eyes wintry. "And one more thing."

Clenching the pen, Will's gaze stayed on the paper. "What?"

"If I never have to look at you again," said Stephen, "it'll be too soon." He turned on his heel and strode out.

Ignoring Will, I rushed upstairs after Stephen, feeling reprieved. *We faced Will together, like a team—a proper married couple. Maybe he'll relent, change his mind about the Vancouver job?*

I made it to our bedroom just a few steps behind him. "Wait, Stephen." I closed the door. I could hear the rain pounding on the roof.

"Look, Kerry," he said, his face averted. "I'm completely knackered, and I've a long flight ahead of me. And I've got to run to the village to ring for a hire car. I don't want to—"

"Please, just hear me out," I said low. *You don't have to be resigned to your lot, like Jennifer,* I told myself. *You can just be straight with your husband and have it out with him.* "I've been so wrong about things—about Will—I hardly know where to start. Everything's been handed to him on a platter, and I was an eejit, years ago, to have romanticized him—"

"Kerry—"

"I was just a kid, and he was like…like a gift wrapped in shiny paper and ribbons. I didn't know that inside there was nothing but an empty box—"

"Don't." Stephen took a clean shirt from his luggage and tossed it on the bed. His face was hard again. "I don't want to hear it. I've had my fill of that blagger."

"But Stephen," I said, desperation filling me, "how can you shut me down like this? For getting flirty with an old friend the other night? Won't you at least let me tell you that—"

"No." The look he turned on me was so forbidding, it was like a chill in the room. "I told you, I'm sick of talking about that gobshite." He began tearing at the buttons on his shirt.

"But we can talk about us—"

"No."

"Love of God, Stephen! You're actually breaking up our marriage, for...for what? Why are you doing this? What's happened?"

"Stop it!"

I stepped backwards, away from the coldness in his face. "But—"

"Stop asking! I can't—I'm done talking. So for bloody's sake, leave it!" As he yanked off his shirt, a button flew off and it hit the floor with a tiny *ping*. "And this is the last time we'll ever row about Will Power."

37

The first row we'd had about Will had also been our worst. And had seemed to come out of nowhere.

"What time will your mam want us round tomorrow?" Stephen asked, checking the stew I'd made for our tea on New Year's Eve.

Stephen and I had been married less than two years. He was still working at Will's uncle's construction outfit, though we'd seen very little of Will the last two or three months.

Playing on the floor with Jamie, I said, "I think Mam would love us to spend the day." I saw we'd forgotten to plug in our Christmas tree lights. Getting to my feet to grab the lead, I added, "So…we'll go as early as we can manage—" I jerked up my head as a sharp rap sounded at the door.

Will poked his head inside, his green eyes twinkling at me. "Am still I welcome? Had to wish you lot a Happy New Year—"

"Will!" I dropped the lead, a glow coming over me as he let himself inside. Shrugging off his wet coat, Will tossed a shop-wrapped package onto the couch, the fancy present seeming out of place in our plain little flat.

Jamie scrambled straight to our visitor, clutching him round the legs. Stephen's subdued "Hallo" as Will came into the front room was nearly lost in our son's excited, "Wiw, Wiw!"

Will gave him a hearty kiss, then tossed him in the air. "Jamie, my boyo!" He seemed taller and broader, his sandy curls shaggy, and clearly, cheekier than ever.

He set Jamie down. Before I knew what he was about, Will grabbed me round the waist and twirled me in a circle. "And Happy New Year to you!"

"Will!" I protested, laughing. "Mind the baby! And the tree!"

Will set me down, and kissed the corner of my mouth. Cheeks flaming, I smelled the stout on his breath, and almost didn't hear Stephen say, "That's enough, Will."

As tension filled the room, Will murmured in my ear, "Oh, it's not nearly" and gave me a big smacky kiss, on the cheek this time.

I backed away, dizzy, as Will turned to Stephen, his hand extended. "Ah, come on, mate, it's New Year's Eve. Every girl needs a bit of a snog on New Year's."

Stephen gave Will a level look, then lifted Jamie off the floor. He took his time, settling our son in one arm before shaking Will's hand. "So. What brings you round?"

Will hadn't been available for Sunday lunch since October. Tonight, I'd resigned myself to a rather dull holiday, but suddenly I felt all lit up inside. "Maybe we should punish you for pulling a disappearing act," I said roguishly. "But we'll put it off until you'll agree to stay for supper."

"I wish I could," Will said. "My Uncle Casey's throwing a big party tonight, and the parents were all over me to go. Some friends of theirs are visiting from America."

"But you'll stay long enough for a little holiday cheer?" I was already heading for the kitchen. Stephen and I couldn't usually afford to have drink in the house. But just for New Year's Day, I'd picked up something special to bring to Mam's. Opening the fridge, I pulled out a bottle. "Sparkling wine?"

"That'll hit the spot." Will was right behind me, pulling the opener out of a drawer. "Else how will I get through a boring family do?"

I handed the bottle to Will to open. As I fetched three glasses out of the cupboard, I caught Stephen's frown. I knew what he was thinking. *Didn't you buy that wine for New Year's dinner?*

I ignored his silent hint. The wine had been expensive, but with Will finally here, I wasn't going to let Stephen kill my holiday mood. I got a cup of juice for Jamie as Stephen set him in his high chair, and defiantly poured out three generous glasses of the wine. "To the New Year!" I raised my glass.

Will clicked his glass on mine. "That's it—to the holiday and grand friends—past, present and future!"

I matched Will sip for sip, the bubbles making me feel a bit giddy. Stephen was a bit slower to join in. He leaned down, and clicked his glass first with Jamie's cup. "To you, my little lad," he said somberly, then lifted it toward Will and me. "And you."

I wanted to chide Stephen for being such a killjoy, but before I could give him the eye, Will said, "Kerry, I see you're still wearing your plain little ring." He chuckled. "You know, if you were to lose it, maybe your man there would get you a new one." Then to Stephen, "The trouble is, how can she lose her ring if she hardly ever takes it off? You know she wears it all the time—"

"Of course I bloody well know that!" Stephen bit out.

Aghast at his tone, I said, "Stephen—"

Stephen ignored me, his eyes boring into Will. "Why are you wasting your time with us anyway? You could be ringing one of those girls you're talking about, the sort who hasn't any problem taking their ring off every time you give them the eye."

Will shrugged. "Whatever, but most girls want a proper wedding ring, don't they? Something big and shiny?"

I don't, was on the tip of my tongue. Then I saw the rare, angry flush creep up Stephen's neck. "Getting *my wife* a better ring isn't on now," he snapped, "but someday, I'll have the money for it."

I was nearly squirming with discomfort—it was so unlike Stephen, to pick a fight like this. And with our best friend!

Will stared at his empty glass. "Yeah, maybe someday we'll all have money." Then he held out his glass, smiling again. "I'll take another splash?"

Stephen only stared at him. "We can spare it," he finally said. "I think." He seized the bottle and gave Will exactly what he'd asked for—a splash and no more.

Will drained his glass, then headed for the front room. "Okay—I'm off."

I followed him. "But you just got here—"

"The family will give me hell if I'm late, especially with their friends around." As Stephen watched from the kitchen doorway, Will picked up the package he'd brought and handed it to me. "But first, I've a little something for you. It was meant to be for Christmas, but..." he shrugged. "I didn't get a chance to come round. So..."

I held the box carefully and met his eyes, shining with boyish expectancy. To draw out the pleasure, I slowly unwrapped the shiny paper and elaborate bow. As I raised the lid, a small *ah* escaped me. Lifting out an angel treetop decoration, I gazed at its little china face, delicately painted in a serene expression. I ran my fingers over the gown, of silver filigree and satin, then the gossamer wings, silver glitter embedded in the fabric. "It's...gorgeous," I finally managed, then looked up at Will. How well he seemed to know me, to get a gift like that. Out of the corner of my eye, I saw that Stephen had gone still. "But you...you..."

"Shouldn't have?" Will had said, smiling. "Oh, but I should! Especially after all those Sunday lunches I freeloaded off the pair of you." He held out his hands. "I'll do the honors, shall I?"

"Oh, you've never freeloaded," I protested as Will set the angel on top of the tree. "But can you come round to my mam's, for New Year's dinner tomorrow?" I tried not to sound plaintive. "Everyone will be thrilled to bits to see you."

"I'll try." Will pulled his coat off the doorknob. "My lot has got their hooks in me, but maybe I can sneak away for a couple of hours." With an offhand wave, in a flurry he was gone, taking all the light in the room with him.

I wasted no time rounding on Stephen. "Well, you really made him feel welcome, didn't you?"

"He crossed a line," Stephen said evenly. He moved to the kitchen and dished up a small bowl of stew for Jamie. "And you know it."

"Oh, for God's sake." Exasperated, I stepped to Jamie's high chair to cut his meat. "You mean that silly kiss? It was only a bit of holiday jolliness. You know how he is after a couple of pints!"

"Sure I do," Stephen said. "If he thinks he can paw my wife,

213

it's a good job he had a family do tonight. Or I would've kicked him out myself."

Feeling angry words cramming my throat, I tightened my lips so Jamie wouldn't have to hear them. As Stephen went back to the front room, I set Jamie's bowl on his tray. After blowing on it to make sure it was cool enough, I stomped after Stephen.

"Maybe Will's just being affectionate," I flung at him. "Which is more than I can say for you!"

"You know I'm plenty affectionate—"

"Well, you never say 'I love you.'"

"I like to think I show you, instead," Stephen's face was rigid.

I knew it was true but I didn't care. "Whether Will was busy tonight or not, you drove him away!"

"Bad enough I have to think of that other guy who had his hands on you." Stephen clenched his fists. "But Jaysus, *Will*! The nerve of him—"

"Other guy?" I said faintly.

"Jamie's father! You didn't forget he was first, did you? I haven't!"

"Stephen!" I felt blindsided. He'd never mentioned Mike McElligott. "Most girls—" I burst into tears. "Most girls have tons of boyfriends before they get married! And I only had one!"

"Don't you think I know that?" Stephen said bitterly. "Don't you think I know I'm being impossible? But to have Will try a snog right in front of my face—it was a bloody insult!"

"What are you? Lost in the 1950s or something?" Hot anger grew in my chest. "Why throw Jamie's father in my face? Will's little holiday kiss was noth—"

"Don't try and say it's nothing," Stephen's hands worked. "I saw the look on your face."

Defending Will would get me nowhere. "Okay, fine! So he gave me a kiss and drank most of the wine and I can hardly bring a near-empty bottle to Mam's. Now, can we just let it go?"

"Right," said Stephen, as stiff as the angel on the tree. He looked just like his mother. "Consider it gone."

"And here's a plus," I said, resenting his calmness when it

was obvious he was seething. "Since Will didn't stay to supper, we'll have plenty of leftovers—just think of the money we'll save. That'll make you happy, won't it?"

"Not particularly," was all he said.

I wanted to get a bigger reaction out of him. I *wanted* to see him to lose his temper. "You know what else?" I said before I could stop myself. "It's obvious if you begrudge a bottle of wine, you've turned out as mean as your mam!"

Stephen's face lost color. "If...if Mam's miserly, if saving a penny here or there is the world to her, it's because her family was poor."

"Oh, come on—in her day, a lot of people didn't have two pennies to rub together."

Stephen pressed his lips together for a moment, then the words seemed to burst from him. "My mother's family had nothing—nothing! So yeah, if I try and save every euro I can, what harm? But d'you think I wouldn't give you and Jamie the shirt off my back? That I think money is everything?" Stephen's eyes blazed. "I don't give a feck about it! I only care about being able to take care of people—you, Jamie, my parents, when they'll need it. And money's the way I can do it. So I'm not the tight-fisted bastard you want to think!"

He strode to the door and slammed out.

Shock nearly knocking the breath out of me, I stared at the door, my eyesight blurry from tears. We'd never, ever argued like this—and to do it on New Year's Eve! I plodded back to Jamie in his chair, grabbing the kitchen roll to wipe my face. As he watched me, his eyes wide, I smoothed his brown curls then picked up his spoon with a shaking hand. "You'll take a few more bites for Mammy?"

After he'd eaten most of his stew, I put him on the floor again to play, then stared at our still-dark Christmas tree. There was my glittering new angel, presiding over our ruined evening. Taking the angel down, I set it back in its box, then stuffed it into the back of the front closet.

Stephen came in a couple of hours later, after I'd tucked up

Jamie. "Where...were you?" I asked, my voice tremulous. "You left without your coat."

He was shivering. "I've been sitting in the car."

I rose from the couch slowly, without a clue how to act after the ugly things we'd said to each other. "You'll have some supper now?" I plugged in the tree on my way to the kitchen.

After I dished up two bowls of stew, Stephen pulled out my chair for me, like he used to do before we were married. But I couldn't seem to pick up my spoon. "I...shouldn't have criticized your mam. Spoiling our holiday."

"I was...out of line too." Stephen still wore a wounded expression. "As for Will...I only regret I have to see him tomorrow at your mother's."

I could've said *I'm sorry I asked him*, but I was already looking forward to the next day.

"He's been floating in and out of work for months now," Stephen said. "The whole crew has been on edge, forced to cover for him. And turns out this week, after the company has been short of manpower, Will's uncle had to delay a big project. But he won't sack Will because he's family. If I...overreacted, that's part of it."

I could see Will got by on his charm—surely, though, he was meant for better things. "I suppose his heart's just not in the job," I said carefully. Stephen only stared at his plate. "I suppose that's no excuse," I went on, feeling another spark of resentment. "You're doing the same job—not mad about it but you do it." *Sometimes it's hard, being married to someone who always does the right thing.*

He shrugged, then finally took a bite, chewing it slowly. "And just so you know, I'll never mention that other guy—your first boyfriend—again."

38

*A*nd he hadn't.

The next day, New Year's, Will had showed up at Mam's, Jennifer in tow. Our wistful, longing goodbye had only cemented my misty-eyed romantic notion of him as the one who'd got away.

Now, on the back stoop of the farmhouse, I held a tatty black umbrella over my head that I'd found next to the door. As the rain dripped around me, enclosing me like a curtain, I was still shaken at learning our marriage was hopeless—and how ruthless Stephen could be, the way he'd frozen me out.

Tears crowded my throat, but I didn't dare cry. Once I started I knew I wouldn't be able to stop, and I couldn't face my son or husband with a tear-streaked face. What was most ironic about this complete disaster of a holiday was that I'd forgotten all about Mike McElligott. And that I was meant to tell Stephen about Jamie asking after him. Imagine, that I'd felt guilty for not bringing it up! My omission seemed insignificant, though, compared to everything Stephen had been keeping from me.

Yet the ache of his rejection hurt less as I looked round the farm—even though all the possibilities I'd envisioned just days ago—raising food, even selling some for a small cash crop—had vanished like mist.

I stepped under the eaves and closed the umbrella. Giving it a shake, I went back inside. The thing was, Stephen and myself owning this house, this farm…well, it didn't seem real. Actually, it wouldn't be. If Will didn't back out of our deal, and didn't try on a lawsuit or anything else and we had the deed in our hands, I knew what would need to happen. We'd sell the place. Stephen and I would replenish our savings—and get on with our lives. Separately.

"Just so you know, there's a spare key under the mat on the stoop," said Jennifer.

She'd buttonholed me in the kitchen as Stephen and Jamie were bringing down our cases. For the first time I saw her face bare of makeup, her hair uncombed. "Will told me you'll be taking over the farm." She didn't quite meet my eyes.

Had he told her about the rest of the loans? "I know you pinned lots of hopes on the place," I said. "For that, I'm sorry."

"Yeah—I got pretty carried away, thinking we could make a killing on it." Jennifer gazed out the kitchen window. "But to be honest, Will's incredibly relieved. And I don't know how we could have gotten the farm fixed up long-distance." She sighed. "This hasn't been the happy holiday we would've all liked, but you and Stephen and Jamie...well..." Turning suddenly, she gave me a quick hug. "You made it a lot better than if we'd been alone."

Moments later, the family walked us to the Toyota, Will holding the tatty black umbrella over Jennifer and the girls. With the rain, our goodbyes were quick. Stephen and I kissed the little girls—and to my complete astonishment, Jamie did too. Then he fist-bumped Mackenzie and said, "See you." I was pretty certain he knew he wouldn't.

With the umbrella in the way, I'd an excuse for not giving Will a goodbye kiss. Not that I could stand to touch him anyway. Stephen shook Will's hand, and I could tell he was making the contact as brief as possible. Then Stephen and I said, "Goodbye, God bless," at the same time. A few months ago we'd have grinned at each other, and one of us would say, "Great minds think alike!" But like so many others, those days were gone. We piled into the car, and he took the wheel, his face set.

I gazed back at the farm as we drove away, imprinting the house, the orchard, and the lovely firs on my memory. I never knew it was possible to love a place so intensely, yet never want to see it again.

As we drove through Ballydara village, which looked entirely cheery despite the pouring rain, I gazed wistfully at Mrs. Murphy's shop. It would've been lovely to say goodbye to her, and to Fiona Whelan, if she'd been there. And to Mr. Twinkly Bernard-The-Construction-Guy too. But sitting next to Stephen and trying to act halfway normal for Jamie was already making my face crack.

"What do you think of all three of us driving to Shannon instead?" I asked Stephen as he turned onto the N59. "You'd have to change your ticket but you wouldn't have to bother hiring a car in Galway City. Jamie and I wouldn't mind the longer trip home."

Out of the corner of my eye I saw Jamie look up. "Let's do that, Dad. That way, I could see your plane take off."

"I appreciate the offer," Stephen said, his voice formal. "But I think the hire car will be easiest."

For you and me, maybe, I thought. Not for our son.

All the rest of the way to Galway City, Stephen and I didn't say anything. Nor did Jamie, staring at his tablet in the back seat. Not that I blamed him. You could be deaf and blind and still detect the narky atmosphere between Stephen and me.

He stopped at the first hire car place we came to, that he'd rung earlier. Inside the utilitarian lobby with its gray-painted walls and plastic chairs, I stood with him as he did the paperwork. Jamie roamed around looking at hire car posters.

It was then I noticed that Stephen wasn't wearing his wedding ring. It was another stab, even after our devastating arguments—the unmistakable sign that he wasn't all in anymore. In our marriage, that is. He was all out.

I looked at my new wedding band, the gems sparkling even under the dim fluorescent lights. This moment might be my last-ditch opportunity to clear the air. As Stephen started scribbling on another page, I said, low, "You told me you didn't buy my ring here in Galway City. So...when did you get it?"

Scratching out his signature, Stephen paused, just as Jamie wandered back. "How soon do you have to leave, Dad?"

"Right away, son." Stephen's voice shook. "So this is it." He returned the forms to the clerk and we three stepped a little way from the counter, the clerk tactfully rustling the papers.

Stephen pulled Jamie tight into his arms, kissing the top of his head. "Be good." As he slowly loosened his embrace, I could see the effort it took.

Then he faced me. "Well...keep in touch." He picked up his carryon.

"Dad, aren't you..." Jamie caught Stephen's sleeve, like he'd done when he was small. "Aren't you going to kiss Mam goodbye?"

I could see the reluctance in Stephen's eyes. But he couldn't hurt Jamie. As he leaned toward me, I forced myself to keep my arms to my sides, else I'd clutch him, unable to let go. He quickly kissed my cheek. Then almost violently, he dropped his bag, and pulled me close. So close, I was sure I could feel his heart beating against mine. He whispered, "I bought the ring the day after we lost the baby."

Before I could react, he broke the embrace and strode away.

I stood dumbly. Yesterday, Jennifer had said it never hurts to ask. But just now, as waves of pain and regret crashed over me, I learned it actually did.

I watched Stephen through the window as he stepped into a car and drove away. *Stephen, you finally mention the baby, just when there's no hope of having another?* I reached toward Jamie to put my arm round him, but he pulled away to stare determinedly at a wall.

"I still wish he would've let us go to the airport, and see his plane leave." His voice cracked. "Then I could have pretended I was on it."

On the long journey to Dublin, the silence between my son and myself was deafening. But I was too frozen to talk. And just when I thought I couldn't feel worse, after we'd arrived home and I was unpacking my case, I found a folded up sheet of paper.

A letter. From Stephen.

Dublin

39

I couldn't bring myself to touch the letter. I'd too many memories of the sweet little notes Stephen had once left for me. And no one had to hit me over the head for me to know this one would be as bitter as turmeric. And as long as I left Stephen's letter alone, I could keep pretending we still had a chance.

The next day I removed my new ring, staring at it as if to decipher why Stephen had gotten it for me. It was then I'd seen the inscription inside the ring. *Kerry, Forever.*

I didn't cry. I didn't feel any tightness in my throat, or stinging in my eyes. No shuddering in my chest. Maybe weepers like me had an allotment of tears, and I must've used mine all up. And on things that didn't really matter, crying at the least little upset. Now, in mourning for having truly mucked up my life, I was dry-eyed.

I felt like someone had died. Will, maybe—the Will I'd known, or the one I'd made up, no longer existed. If he ever had. Or maybe Stephen—the loving, understanding husband he'd been all these years had changed into someone I didn't recognize. Someone I'd treated so badly he could leave me.

But it was myself I was mourning most of all—for the girl I'd been. Taken in not just once, by Mike, but again by Will. The two men I'd made into romantic heroes, despite the fact neither of them had truly cared for me. And after I'd finally seen them for what they were, I was mortified by my stupidity. And my reluctance to deal with reality. Until I had to.

Anyway, that girl was as good as dead. Gone forever.

Settling back into our house without Stephen—especially with the unread letter sitting in my case like a ticking time-bomb—I felt a post-holiday letdown times ten. Christmas was only weeks away, and the last thing I wanted to do was finish decorating the place. The one string of lights in the front window seemed lonely and pathetic now, and served only to remind me that this coming Christmas would be the worst ever. I'd be back to work in two days—which, on the plus side meant I could be away from this lonely house. Yet the thought of being back at the office was making my stomach churn.

Jamie was in bad form too—staying in his room with the door closed. If he was downstairs, he seemed agitated, hovering by the phone, or watching out the front window when the post was expected. He wasn't eating much either, which really concerned me.

I'd the sudden thought—what if Stephen's letter is not about me, but our son? Maybe there's something in it that might make Jamie feel better. So the night before Mam and Dad were expected home from their cruise, I went to my bedroom, opened my case and pulled out the letter.

After I read it, I curled up on our bed, my arms curled round my middle, remembering. And hurting so much I could hardly breathe. When I finally forced myself to get up, make tea for Jamie, I went downstairs and found him at the laptop. "Dad still hasn't emailed me," he said, red round his eyes.

I didn't dare try and hug him, because if he pulled away I wouldn't be able to bear it. I said, "I'm sure your dad needs a bit more time to settle in before he writes, love." *And you might not want the sort of letter he's writing these days.*

Kerry,
   It's only fair I should tell you why there's no future for us.

That night at the farm, when I saw you with Will in the front garden, I stayed at the window long enough to watch you push him away. But I couldn't get back to sleep.

I felt sick, knowing I'd have to tell you what I'd seen. And there was the decision about Canada hanging over my head. After you came to bed, I could tell you were awake for a long time. I knew I wouldn't sleep the rest of the night. But after you finally fell asleep, I got out of bed and went downstairs.

With the proposal for my new position on the table, I had to pull myself together, sort out some figures for the Vancouver team straightaway. Then my laptop crashed again. I didn't have time to troubleshoot it, and I thought it would be no bother if I borrowed your laptop. So I fetched it out of Jamie's clobber and went back down.

I wrote the email, put it in the drafts folder to send off as soon as I could get on the 'net. Then I remembered another detail I needed to include in the proposal. I went to retrieve it and opened the drafts folder. That's when I saw them—your emails. To Will.

I should have closed the folder, the emails were private, but I couldn't. I had to read them. It was then I understood you really were in love with Will. Right, the emails were from years ago, and it was clear you'd never sent them. But that doesn't matter. You, both of us, had been—and still were—living a lie.

It was bad enough, reading about all my faults, my imperfections laid bare. And the parts where you'd mocked me. I could see you'd never been happy with me, not like I'd been with you. That wasn't the worst, though. What I couldn't get past— what I'll never get past—was discovering that you hadn't really wanted a baby with me. All these years I couldn't wait for us to have a child together, but for the first time I was glad we hadn't.

So don't ask me again, why I had to leave.
Stephen

After tea, Jamie left the kitchen to watch telly. With pain and regret like a stone in my chest, I settled in front of my laptop. Without hesitation, I ruthlessly deleted all my pretend emails.

Imaginary up to a point, I suppose. They'd been real enough to break up my marriage. Then I emptied the Trash folder and stared at the screen. Losing our baby last summer had only been a prelude for the greatest loss of my life.

40

$\mathcal{P}$ulling up to my parents' house the next evening, I made sure Jamie wasn't looking and took my new ring off. Then I stuffed it into my jeans pocket before we went inside.

Mam and Dad looked wonderful—not tired despite the transatlantic flight. They were relaxed and smiling, even a bit tanned. I forced myself to act normally. "You've a new hairstyle too?" I asked Mam as we exchanged hello kisses.

"You like it?" She ran her hand over the layers curving round her neck. "There was a stylist on board, and I told your dad it would cost a packet just for a trim, but he insisted."

From what I could tell, Dad could hardly take his eyes off her. "I told her, 'we're on holiday, the sky's the limit.'"

"The cruise ship was all decorated for the holidays too," Mam said, and as she nattered on about the elegance of the dining rooms, the lovely people they met, and the unbelievable meals. Jamie, sneaking looks at his handheld, didn't join in the conversation.

I tried to be happy for them but all I could do was compare their newlywed-like bliss with Stephen's and my estrangement.

"The food the entire cruise was *heavenly*," Mam said, her eyes dreamy. "I'd never realized how lovely it is to just sashay up to a buffet, eat as much as you please, and no washing up or shopping for groceries. I told your dad, 'I could get used to this.'"

"Good job I brought a treat," I said, unwrapping the jam cake I'd baked earlier. I'd been at such loose ends all day, I started cooking properly in my shiny, empty kitchen. Though my rhythm had definitely been off—a recipe that should've taken me ten minutes took over an hour.

Dad patted his stomach as he gathered up the newspaper to take to the front room. "Thanks love, but I think I'll pass. Who knows how many kilos I put on during the cruise."

"I don't want any either," Jamie said.

I looked at him. He really *had* lost his appetite. "Come on, you can eat my homemade cake in your sleep," I coaxed. "Won't you slice it for us? You always do a great job—"

"Really, Mam, I'm not hungry." He followed his granddad down the hall. "What's on telly?" he asked, but his voice was toneless.

Mam watched him leave with a thoughtful look. "I nearly forgot," she said as I fetched a knife from the drawer. "How was your holiday?"

I applied myself to cutting the bread. "It was...all right."

"Just...all right? What of your friend Will? He's been keeping well?"

I could hardly tell Mam the truth. "He's...great. He and Jennifer have a lovely family—three little girls. I was tempted to bring them home with me."

"And Stephen? Don't tell me he's back to work already?"

"He's...out of town," I said.

Mam got out two plates. "I thought since you talked him into going all the way to Galway, he'd finally take a proper holiday, relax a bit."

I could no longer delay telling her at least part of the truth. "Stephen's actually been posted abroad." I focused on my cutting. "Vancouver, Canada. It's a great career move."

I heard the plates rattle on the table, then felt Mam's hand on my back. "A temporary posting?"

"I don't know." I bowed my head, then dropped the knife. "Six months, maybe a year."

"You'll be joining him, you and Jamie?" Mam's tone was careful.

"No." Putting on a good face was beyond me. I turned round, burrowing into her arms. "He and I—we're separating." Finally. I'd said it aloud. "And it's my fault."

"Oh, Kerry..." There were tears in her voice. "I thought the lights had gone out of your eyes." She tightened her embrace.

I pressed my face into her shoulder. *How could I have not known it was Stephen who'd put them there?*

Mam held me for a long time. I expected her to comfort me with the sort of things she'd always said, like, *it'll be all right, it's not as bad as you think,* and her reliable, *that's it, have a good cry, it'll do you good.* But she was silent. Maybe my lack of tears told her Stephen's leaving was real.

She finally gave my back a brisk pat, then pressed me into a chair. Sitting across from me, she gave me a long look. "You seemed a bit unhappy these last months. I was thinking the pair of you were growing apart."

I nodded wearily.

"I wanted to talk to you, but with this cancer business..." She touched her breast. "I just didn't have it in me. Not that it's necessarily a good thing, to discuss your marriage with your mother—but...did something happen? On your holiday?"

I shook my head. Here I was, lying to her again. But I couldn't tell her about Will, and the vast mistake—make that *mistakes*—I'd made. "You're right, Stephen and I haven't been communicating." After the miscarriage, he and I had forgotten the language of wordless looks and touches that make a marriage.

I swiped at my eyes like a reflex, then stupidly looked at my dry fingers. Searching for some excuse to tell her, I came up with something close to the truth. "I've been so unhappy with my job, and I rather took it out on him." I didn't meet her eyes, sure she wouldn't believe such a flimsy excuse for a marriage to shatter, especially to a steady bloke like Stephen.

"Why have you stayed so long at that office, if you were miserable?" she asked.

I shrugged. "You know—the economy. I was lucky to have the job." Now I was parroting my mother-in-law. I added hastily, "If I left, I probably wouldn't have been able to get on somewhere else."

"Maybe that's true," Mam said, "But it seems to me, that Stephen could have supported the three of you, if you were out of work for a while."

"To do what?" *Keep house, putter in the nonexistent garden? Grieve even more over the baby we'd lost?* "It wouldn't be right, not to contribute to the family income. Not with Jamie being fathered by—" I broke off and looked away.

Mam took my hand. "That boy is more Stephen's son than any biological father's child I've ever seen," she said. "So no more talk of that sort." She looked at me for a long moment. "You've said you've saved up a lot of your salary. Could you take a leave from your job? With Stephen away, maybe you'll take the time to sort out what you truly want to do. Who you want to be."

What I really wanted was beyond the realms of possibility. "But there still aren't a lot of jobs—" I broke off. Now I sounded like Stephen *and* his mother. Always going the safe route.

"Just because the entire country's been on hold for years, doesn't mean you need to be," Mam said, just as my mobile rang.

On the display was the McCormack's number. "It's my in-laws," I told Mam. "I'd better take it."

I connected, stepping away from the kitchen. "Mary?"

"What's happened?"

I'd never, ever expected Mary to confront me over Stephen's leaving. "You must mean…Stephen going to Canada."

"Of course that's what I mean. And no need to tell me about his promotion, all the new opportunities, the rise in pay, because Stephen already did."

"I…I…" I wasn't accustomed to Mary being this direct. "I'm not sure what to say…"

"His leaving just doesn't make sense," said Mary.

There was a long pause. "Mary, are you there?"

"I'm here all right. I'm ringing because it's clear to me there's been a mistake."

"A mistake," I parroted.

"Last time you visited he showed me the ring he'd bought you," said Mary. Her voice seemed to soften. "I'm sure he was warning me ahead of time, to keep me from having a conniption fit when I saw it on your finger."

Surely that wasn't a trace of humor I was hearing? "I never asked for—"

"Of course you wouldn't," Mary said impatiently. "When I recovered from the shock, I told him, 'you've spent a packet for nothing.'"

"I wouldn't exactly call the ring *nothing*," I said in Stephen's defense.

"I said, 'your wife's a sensible girl—what would she do with that big glittery yoke?'"

I blinked. My first compliment from my mother-in-law. "Th...thank you."

"And my Stephen wouldn't have given you a ring like that if he...if he—" She broke off.

Didn't love you, I was sure she was trying to say, but then, I didn't think *love* was in my mother-in-law's lexicon. "So I have to ask again," said Mary. "What's happened between the pair of you?"

Racking my brain for some explanation, I came up with, "Really...we're just trying what a lot of married people are doing this these days."

"Doing what, exactly?"

"You know..." I floundered. "Living apart because of their careers—it's called a commuter marriage—"

"Stephen didn't mention either of you doing any commuting," said Mary. Her voice seemed to catch. "I know he's flying in for Christmas, but when will he be coming back home to stay?"

So Mam wouldn't overhear, I climbed the stairs, then sat heavily on the top step. I couldn't tell her, *I honestly haven't a clue.* Mary seemed so approachable—for her, anyway—I was afraid if I opened up to her, before I could stop myself I'd be confessing what happened with Will and then she'd know what a terrible wife I'd been.

"Stephen and I haven't quite sorted out...the particulars," I tried on.

"That's exactly what my son said to me," said Mary. "But if...when you do," and there was a new vulnerability in her voice, "you'll...let me know?"

"Of...course." What else could I say? "I'm...glad you rang me." It was true, although after we disconnected I was reeling a bit. I'd had my first real conversation with my mother-in-law.

I clutched the mobile with both hands, I'd made Mary into a complete gorgon since the day I'd met her. Okay. She was stern, humorless, and mean about money to a fault. But had she really been so awful? Perhaps it was another one of the stories I'd told myself years ago—that my marriage, that Stephen *and* his family were lacking. To give myself excuses for fancying another man.

Mam appeared at the bottom of the stairs. "Everything all right?"

I nodded. Descending the stairs, I took my ring from my pocket and slipped it on my finger, despite the questions it would raise. "I didn't get a chance to..." I held out my hand. "To show this to you."

"Stephen gave it to you?"

I bit my lip. Would Mam see the ring as proof of his love, like Mary had?

Mam only touched my cheek. "You know, love, cancer has a way of getting your attention."

"Yours got all of our attention," I said wistfully. "Must you really go away for Christmas? Liam will be all right on his own."

"Your brother deserves family too, love," she said gently. "He doesn't mention it much, but he's been as concerned about this cancer as you and Suz and Dad." She was quiet for a moment. "When it happened to me, I saw that I'd two choices. I could wallow in my illness or my misery or what have you. Or I could really start living. Guess which one I chose?"

I wrapped my arms round Mam. "Is that a hint?"

Mam hugged me back, then released me. "With Stephen away, maybe you'll find something new in your life. Have yourself an adventure, for the love of God!"

I almost smiled. Maybe I could fill Mam in on our holiday—without having to give her the *entire* lowdown. "Speaking of news," I said, "I seem to have acquired a farm..."

Just as I finished telling Mam about how Will's farm had sort of fallen into my lap—keeping out the sordid details, of course— Suz and Anthony came round with Ailish. I took Suz aside, telling her what I'd told Mam, about Stephen and me. She only hugged me wordlessly—maybe she'd already guessed my marriage had been heading for trouble.

Holding Ailish was still as bittersweet as ever, but I tried hard to concentrate on the pleasure of it, and not the pain. As I drove home that evening, it came to me that I might not be able to fix my marriage, but I could at least *start* sorting myself.

Turning into our crescent, I approached our house only to see an unfamiliar car parked out front, a small, older sedan. "Did you invite Con over?" I asked Jamie, and pulled into our drive. "But that's not his mam's car—"

"No," said Jamie. Before I shut off the engine he was out the door, scurrying over to the visitors. I quickly clambered out, to see the passenger side window come down. A woman a bit older than Mam said something to Jamie.

I was ready to call a sharp, *Who are you? What do you want?* as I strode over to the car. Then the woman and a man about Dad's age climbed out. "I'm called Shirley and this is Mike Senior," she said, her voice tremulous. "We're the McElligotts."

41

I sat across from Mike's mother and father in our front room moments later, my head still in a whirl. For a moment outside, I'd been ready to grab Jamie and tear into him right in front of a pair of strangers. *You contacted your grandparents, without telling me? Without telling your dad? And you didn't warn me that they were coming? How could you?*

Somehow I managed to bite back my rash words, and invite them inside. After an uncomfortable silence, Mr. McElligott smiled uncertainly. "Your son Jamie there," and he nodded at Jamie, "wrote us a letter."

"A letter," I repeated. *Why do we have to be the last family in modern Ireland to write letters?*

"We considered writing back," said Mrs. McElligott, "but I told my husband, 'I can't wait that long.' And Lord forgive us, but I thought, what if Jamie's parents say no, we can't see him? So I said to Mike, 'Let's just call round and take our chances.' We came by a few times when the house was empty, but tonight, we saw the lights on upstairs, and thought maybe you were home from wherever you'd gone. We were just about to leave when you drove up."

A granny stalker! Any other time, I'd have found it funny. Or scary. Only I sensed how badly she'd wanted to see her grandson.

Jamie was utterly silent. I gave him a stern look. "Jamie, do you have something to tell me? You might as well say it right now—your...grandparents seem to know more than I do."

He slumped in his chair, hands clasped on his knees. "It's true," he began, talking to his hands in a hoarse whisper. "I

232

wanted to meet my other dad. Con told me, 'Google him, you can track down anyone,' but I couldn't go through with it. I mean, he could've been anywhere. Or dead even."

"He's not dead, love," said Shirley.

Her familiarity both touched and grated on me. "Jamie?" I prompted.

"So I decided to…well, that maybe I could find his parents instead." Jamie's voice grew stronger. "So I looked up all the McElligotts in the phone book. When I saw a Michael Senior and the street address, I took a chance. I wrote a letter and posted it. Then I…I felt awful."

He suddenly sat up straight, and looked at his grandparents. "I remembered the look on my mam's face when I first talked about my other father. So I asked my dad if we could go somewhere, the pair of us, where my mam wouldn't hear us. We went to Phoenix Park, and I told him about writing to you."

As Jamie took a deep breath, I felt mine knocked out of me.

"Dad wasn't angry, but he said I had to come clean with my mam. I told him I would, only I wanted him to be there with me when I did tell her. He said of course he would, and the three of us would sort out what to do next. But then he…couldn't."

My husband's abroad on business, I tried to say, but I couldn't get the words past my stiff lips. Stephen had known all this, days before we'd left for Galway. And had kept it to himself. *Probably because you'd picked a fight with him over Will's invitation, and you were all a-twirl about seeing Will and the farm…*

But after our Galway disaster, and our marriage going belly up, maybe Stephen felt some guy from the past was the least of our problems. Like I had.

"My dad's in Canada now," Jamie finished. "So if I wanted to see my other grandparents it was up to me."

Mike Senior and Shirley had listened in silence. But after Jamie ran out of steam, they exchanged a glance. "Jamie's our only grandchild," Mike said heavily.

"Mike Junior's been in London all this time," Shirley added. "He's married, but they don't have any children. We haven't a clue if…" She looked at Jamie uneasily. "Well, if it's because he and his wife don't want…aren't planning to have a family or if they…can't." Give her credit, she was being open with Jamie…and in a way a boy his age would understand. "You can see, can't you, that we'd want to meet Jamie?"

"You'll have to give me a bit of time," I managed. "To get used to all this."

Jamie stood up, looking down at me. "I'm thirteen years of age, Mam. It's time my other dad knew about me. And if he doesn't want to see me, I'm old enough to face that."

It was at that moment I realized, *my son is becoming a man.* He'd never reminded me so much of Stephen. "I can see that," I said round the ache in my throat. "But—"

"Mike Junior will be very keen to meet you," Shirley broke in. She didn't look so sure though. "Until then, we'd like to see you again. Perhaps we can call round in a few days, Kerry? Or meet someplace? We'll have loads to talk about, won't we?"

"Maybe you'll want to look at some snaps, of when I was little," said Jamie, sounding young and eager again.

"I'm sure they will, Jamie," I said in a dampening tone. "But let's hold off on anything solid for the moment." This earnest couple could never be my enemy, especially now that we'd already progressed to a first name basis. All the same, I'd had all the shocks I could take the last few days.

We ended up exchanging phone numbers, Mike and Shirley promising to contact their son as soon as they could and tell him about Jamie. Then they'd ring me, and let me know how it went. "And if Mike Junior is…all right," Shirley said, "I mean, if he takes it…" Her voice trailed away.

If his reaction isn't a complete disaster, you're saying? "I suppose you'll want to…move forward." I twisted my hands together.

"That's it," said Mike. "Then we can set up another get-together."

"Right," I said, but I knew I needed to take this one step at a time. As I ushered them to the door, Jamie alongside me like a proper host, I suddenly felt protective—of Stephen. "You'll want to know—and Jamie, this includes you, that my son actually meeting his biological father face-to-face won't be happening for some time," I said, my voice firm. "Not until Jamie's dad is back from Canada."

After they left, I didn't give out at Jamie. Now that I knew what he'd done, and when he'd done it, I realized reproaching him would only create more distance between us. "Time for bed," I said, watching him as he turned to go upstairs. I felt like I was looking at him through a telescope as he traveled further and further away from me.

He met my eyes for the first time in hours. "You're not angry? I was telling the truth when I said Dad wasn't."

I couldn't answer for a moment. I wasn't sure exactly what I felt, except bereft. Mourning the loss of yet another person— Jamie, my little son. It didn't seem all that long ago that I was holding him, soft and warm in my arms, breathing in the sweet milky smell of him.

But then, you'll have a new Jamie in your life, a voice said inside me. *Your grown son. The man you'll depend on.* "No, I'm not," I said. I couldn't share my emotional maelstrom. I was still the adult here—just barely, maybe, but still. "We'll talk more tomorrow."

"I'll...I'll email Dad first thing? Tell him about the McElligotts?"

"Yes—he'd want to hear it from you." I kissed him quickly, not offering to come into his room to tuck him up. This wouldn't be the first time he'd have to work out this growing up thing on his own.

I felt completely wrung out. But at the strange time, I was oddly alert, and knew I wouldn't be able to sleep. My brain was buzzing with thoughts of Stephen—what generosity of spirit he'd had, to face Jamie's interest in his biological father so calmly and sensibly. And to not make Jamie feel guilty for having that interest. Not like I had.

I went downstairs, to my office. But not to turn on my

laptop—my office nook was too emotionally loaded with my eejit travels down memory lane with Will to spend any time there, at least tonight. I grabbed a piece of paper from the printer and a pen, and sat at the kitchen table.

42

Dear Stephen,

Mam always said you'd taken to Jamie from the first moment you'd seen him. Actually, it was Jamie who'd taken to you.

Do you remember that day? After my meltdown at work and you gave me a ride home?

Why I invited you in...I wasn't sure I wanted to see you again after the state you'd found me in, with my wet dress and tear-streaked face. But it would've been terribly impolite not to give you cup of tea or something. So after I'd been thinking I'd had the worst day of my life, we walked in to find Jamie shrieking, in the middle of a colic attack. "He's been this way for hours," Mam said, looking at her wit's end, and she wasted no time handing him over.

So there I was, stuck in my breastmilk-soaked dress. I slung Jamie on my shoulder, saying something to you about his tummy troubles, and started patting his back. "Mam, this is Stephen," I said, so distracted from Jamie screaming right in my ear I was hardly thinking straight. "A friend from work."

Mam smiled, then disappeared into the kitchen. Baby burnout, I thought, then I forgot you were there. I tried bouncing Jamie, the usual "there, there, it's all right," walking him up and down the hall, but I think his little baby brain knew he was dealing with a rank amateur. His crying seemed to go up an octave, and I was ready to weep with frustration myself.

But I've never forgotten what happened next. You sort of appeared in my line of sight, holding out your arms. "I saw my granddad do something a few times."

Although you were a perfect stranger, I handed Jamie, red-

*faced and screaming, right over to you. I was that relieved. Even
as upset as I was, I couldn't help noticing how nice you smelled,
the scent of a clean shirt and soap and a hint of aftershave...
Murmuring something in Irish, you rocked him vigorously, in a
side-to-side motion, like a big swing.*

*I looked on anxiously, thinking, Much more of this and Jamie
will puke for sure. But within a minute or two, Jamie's cries
dwindled. Then stopped entirely. He stared up into your face and
smiled beatifically, the kind of smile that makes you instantly
forget your baby had been a screaming devil-child only moments
before. Then reached up his little hand and batted your nose.*

*The sight of you and Jamie was so...so tender I got teary
again. "Your granddad obviously had a way with babies," I told
you.*

*"Not human babies, though," you said, and your serious look
vanished. In fact, I could swear your eyes twinkled. "He did this
for sick lambs."*

*So there it happened. I'd brought home a perfect stranger,
who'd turned out to be as near-perfect a father as I could have
wished for. I know you'll never read this—just like I knew Will
would never read my eejit emails. But now that Mike McElligott
will be entering the picture, I wanted to remind myself who
Jamie's real father has been.*

Love, Kerry

I stuffed the letter into my jewelry box, beneath my former
wedding ring. It soothed my heartache, to have written to
Stephen. Even if I was pretending I was talking to him, and that
he was listening, not shutting me out.

I could pretend only so long, though. Especially since the
reality of my job would start back in the morning. To put off
thinking about Mr. Smythe and my narky workspace, I slipped
back downstairs, into my office and turned on the laptop.
Haunted by all those emails to Will lost somewhere inside the
wiring and microchips and all the other electronic innards of the
machine, I recalled Mam's advice. Sort out what you really
want...

Back I went to my favorite farm sites. Now that Stephen and I owned Will's farm, however informally *and* temporarily, I'd take another look at the competition. Scrolling through photos, I leisurely examined each cozy farmhouse, each old barn, each green, rolling pasture. They were all lovely, but none made my heart sing like it had with my first glimpse of the little farm in Ballydara. When my eyes grew scratchy, I turned off the laptop. I shouldn't have gotten back into this farm surfing, I thought. While reading my old emails and fantasizing about Will—or fantasizing about the fantasy Will—had been childish and escapist and just plain wrong, dreaming about farms was simply...ridiculous.

Returning to work, I found Sharon and Veronica weren't exactly in the best form either. "I've put on three kilos lately," moaned Sharon during our morning tea break, "eating sweets at home instead of spending time at the shops."

"Ed's been reorganizing the house as his pre-New Year's resolution." Veronica sounded grumpy too. "Though why he had to start it before Christmas is beyond me." She sipped her coffee. "Kerry, didn't you go up to the West last weekend? Way out in the sticks?" She gave me a look that said, *give over, tell us what a rotten holiday you had.*

Sure, I really had a good story, but I just couldn't bring myself to share: *You think a compulsive husband is bad? Stephen unloaded years of secrets, then up and left me! Top that, will you?* "I..." I tucked a stray tendril of hair behind my ear. "Stephen has actually been—"

"Holy Jaysus, Kerry!" Sharon suddenly screeched. "What's that on your finger?"

I looked at my left hand. "Oh, that." I wished I'd taken off the ring for work, but I hadn't, still feeling sentimental after writing my letter to Stephen. "An early...Christmas present. From Stephen."

Protocol demanded that I hold my hand out so the girls could admire the ring. All I could think was, *don't envy me, because I don't like my new ring, and I don't deserve it anyway.* Then Veronica gave me a sharp look. "Stephen hasn't—" she broke off. I read it in her face—she thought Stephen had been up to something. Like Will had. That this ring was a guilt-gift.

"Actually," I forced a laugh, "I think it was a bit of a bribe. Stephen got a temporary posting to Canada on short notice."

"I'd send my husband away six days out of seven, if I got a consolation prize like that," Sharon said enviously. "My wedding ring was bought on the sales, but I'd always—"

"I've a stack of work miles high," I broke in, and drained my teacup. "I'd better get to it."

As soon as I was back in my office, I slumped into my chair, looking round the gray walls and steel filing cabinets surrounding me. I forced my hand to my computer mouse, and opened a file.

After seeing the loveliness of Will's farm—my farm, I corrected myself—and the hills, the picturesque village, and meeting some Ballydara folk, being here seemed more unbearable than before. My workload had somehow increased while I was away too. Instead of only having to catch up on what I'd missed while I was away, my tasks seemed to have increased three fold, as if some wicked office fairies had it out for me. If that wasn't bad enough, they'd also cast evil spells on my spreadsheet files, switching out the cell contents and scrambling the numbers. With each day at work, I felt my mood spiral downward, felt the walls closing in on me.

When I was home, Jamie was often on my laptop—emailing his dad a lot more than doing school work, I was sure—and hadn't much to say to me. Perhaps we were both on edge, waiting to hear back from Mike and Shirley McElligott. Stephen had emailed me once, a formal note letting me know he'd arrived safely, and asking how Jamie was. I'd replied that Jamie was well, had done well on his school project, and nothing more. Whatever our son had told him about the McElligotts could stay between the pair of them.

In between worrying about Jamie, after our tea most evenings I began walking round the neighborhood in the old coat of

Stephen's that had helped save his life. In the cold and damp, I couldn't help thinking of my transcendent ramble that afternoon in Galway, around the farm, then taking the bike down to Ballydara. Then I'd replay all the mistakes I'd made with Stephen and collapse in my lonely bed.

One night, after another long walk of regrets, I couldn't sleep. Crawling out of bed, I pulled on my dressing gown and went down to the kitchen. I had to write to Stephen again.

Dear Stephen,

The way things are between us, it helps me to think of the past. Not my made-up past I created in all those emails to Will, but my life as it really was.

I have to admit I wasn't really attracted to you that first day, when you brought me home. You see, I didn't quite know what to make of a live guy (not the hero of a love story) who didn't need to do all the talking, like Mike McElligott. But to be entirely honest, once you got Jamie settled down and you mentioned your country roots I looked at you with new interest. Now that Jamie had stopped crying, I noticed all the things about you that I'd missed before—your long eyelashes, for one thing. And although you weren't tall, you'd nice muscles under your shirt, and you moved confidently, like you could easily toss a bale of hay, or wrangle a cow if you needed to. It's funny, I'd forgotten all about changing out of my wet dress. With any other guy I'd have been mortified, but with you, I was no longer embarrassed. Like I'd known you forever.

Maybe Jamie felt the same way. After he'd smiled and gave you that thump on your nose, he was perfectly mellow. I didn't want to think I wasn't a proper mother, so I took him from your arms, my hands brushing against your chest. Which I didn't mind at all! As I settled Jamie onto my hip, he stuck his thumb in his mouth and just looked at you with the most contented baby face I'd ever seen. Do you remember what we talked about then? I've never forgotten it.

I asked you if you'd been on your granddad's farm much, and if so, if you'd liked it.

You took your time answering. "I liked being with my granddad, but farms?" I could hear the humor in your voice. "They're not for me."

Somehow, it seemed important just then to talk you into liking farms. I sort of swished my curls over on my shoulders with my free hand, and looked at you through my lashes, like the heroines in romantic novels did. Of course, I'd no business flirting with a guy—since I'd gotten pregnant I'd told myself a hundred times I was meant to keep my mind on supporting my baby, making a life for us.

But the amused look in your eyes made me want to unsettle you, even though having most of my experience only with book boyfriends hadn't prepared me for dealing with a live, breathing guy. Still, I could hardly believe what came out of my mouth. "What a shame," I said airily. "Because I'm going to have a farm someday."

Your smile widened. I waited for you to make sport with me, but you didn't. And it was at that moment that you became someone I could say anything to. "And if I can't have a proper farm," I said, "one I could make a living from, I mean, I'm going to at least have a country place. I'll have a big vegetable bed and some chickens. Maybe even a cow."

"Will you, now." Your eyes twinkled even more.

"You can laugh at me all you like," I said, "but yes, I will. And I'll have all my friends round for big country dinners."

You didn't laugh at all—in fact, you got this look in your eyes, the nice gray eyes I liked already. "You told your mam I was your friend," you said. "Does that mean you'll invite me?"

I flushed crimson. I had called you a friend, hadn't I? Trying to recover, I said, "Oh, it would be all right if you came. But then, maybe you won't. You said you didn't really like farms."

Suddenly, there was a light in your eyes. "For you, I'll make an exception."

There was something in your look that had me asking myself: What am I doing? You weren't my sort at all. But there was something about you, so capable and unflappable, that I was drawn to. My office meltdown, breastfeeding leaks, crying baby, nothing fazed you. "Then it's a date," I told you. And I hadn't been flirting.

So all this time, I've held out a hope that someday, you and I would have a country place. I shouldn't have counted on an offhand remark—from a guy who was attracted to me—for making a life plan or anything. But I guess that's how much I wanted us to have a farm together.

Love, Kerry

The next day, so disheartened by the tension between Jamie and me, and growing intolerance for my job, by the time I trudged up our footpath and opened the door, I could barely muster the energy for my usual call-out to Jamie. To my surprise, he met me in the entryway, taking my bag from my hands. "Hurry up, Mam."

"What's the rush? Are we meant to be somewhere?" Then I smelled chicken cooking, and slipped off my coat. "Did you fix our tea? That was terribly sweet."

"Yeah, sure," said Jamie, leading the way into the kitchen, my bag in his hand. Following him, all I could think was, what freakish occurrence could compel a teenage boy to carry his mam's handbag? I found the table laid, sandwiches set out, and a pan of soup simmering on the cooker. "Come on!" He slung my handbag over the back of my chair, so eager I thought he was actually going to push me into it.

"Let me wash my hands first," I said, bemused. Was this bouncing off the walls bit a new form of teenager energy? "Jamie, maybe it's time you took up a sport—" The house phone rang.

"It's Dad!" Jamie practically dived into my office nook. "Mam! Get on your mobile!"

"How do you know it's your dad?" I just stood there, thinking, *your father won't want to talk to me.*

Jamie nearly shouted, "Because he's fixed up a conference call!" and grabbed the phone.

I reached for my bag and pulled out my mobile. It was Stephen all right—though ringing with all this ceremony was even freakier than Jamie holding my handbag.

"Mam, you're on the line?" Jamie asked, as Stephen said, "Kerry, can you hear me?"

"Y-yes, it's me," I stammered, standing near the table "I mean, I'm here."

"Right, then," said Stephen briskly. "Let's jump right in, shall we?"

43

"Jump into what?" I clutched my mobile tighter. "What are you talk—"

"Jamie. You've something to tell your mother."

Jamie shifted his feet and switched the handset to his other ear. "Um...Mam." His Adam's apple bobbed. "Do you remember that night we met my new granny and granddad?"

Like I'd ever forget finding the McElligott's at our house. "Of course I do," I said, aiming for a reassuring tone.

"And I said," Jamie swallowed again, "I was old enough to like, deal with it if my other dad didn't want to see me?" He went silent.

"Jamie, it's all right, go on," said Stephen.

"What's all right?" My encouraging mam attitude was running out fast.

"Turns out, I was wrong." Jamie's voice cracked. "I can't take it, if my other father blows me off."

My shoulders slumped in relief. McElligott problem solved. "Of course I understand," I said. "I'll ring the McElligotts—tell them we'll put the whole thing on hold."

Silence.

Feeling uneasy, I babbled, "What I'm saying is, you don't have to see them, you don't ever have to meet your biological father, we can just forget about all of it, go on as we've always done..."

As my voice trailed away, neither Stephen nor Jamie spoke. Then Stephen said, "Jamie, tell your mam what you've got in mind."

"I want to leave," said Jamie, looking past me.

"Leave...where?" Was I missing something. "Take a trip? I suppose there's your Christmas break—"

"I want to live in Vancouver," Jamie said baldly. "With Dad."

I dropped my mobile onto the floor and slumped into the nearest chair.

"Mam, your mobile!" Jamie dived to pick it up with his free hand. "Okay, it's not broken." He held it out to me. "Here—we've a great plan. Dad and me."

I only stared at the phone. Bringer of horrible things.

"Mam?" said Jamie. Apparently I was meant to just carry on. I reached out, my hand shaking, and wrapped my fingers round my mobile. "Dad, you're there?"

Stephen's voice floated from the speaker. "Son, I'm here."

I put the phone to my ear slowly, as if it was radioactive. Jamie said hesitantly, "Mam, I didn't mean to—I don't want you to think I went behind your back. But...but see, I worked out that you and Dad are...are separated." His voice cracked again.

Oh, God. Stephen and I must've been mad, to think we could get away with lying to our boy. Good job I hadn't touched Jamie's supper, or I'd be tossing it all back up. "I'm just so sorry, love." My own voice broke. "We should've told you—"

"I just have to get away," Jamie interrupted. "And I needed...needed..."

I realized how ludicrous that was, for Jamie and me to be right next to each other, on the phone—me hearing Jamie's real voice in one ear and his phone voice in the other, telling me how he was going to break my heart. "What, love?"

"I needed Dad with me when I told you what I wanted to do."

It took every ounce of strength I had not to say to Stephen, *How could you go for this? Haven't I been punished enough?* "How will this...w-work, Jamie?" I stammered. "Your dad's schedule isn't set up for a...a single parent." Rubbing my eyes, I realized I could still keep this from happening. "Stephen," I said, trying to sound less helpless, "you work till midnight half the time—Jamie would be alone in your flat all evening! I'm sorry, this whole thing is just not on."

"It is too!" said Jamie. "I told you—"

"Son, let me talk," said Stephen. "Here's the thing, Kerry. I've cut back my hours. And my office is a ten minute walk from the flat. Jamie can come up to my office after school."

"School! How will you get that organized? There's all the forms to fill out, and—"

"It'll be no bother," Jamie said. "I've looked it all up, I can leave right after Christmas, and go to online school until I can get to a regular one."

"I can't believe this is workable," I said, starting to pull myself together. "No way. Absolutely not."

"But Mam, I've never been *anywhere*," Jamie said, his mouth turning down. "I'm grown up enough, you've got to let me—"

"Son, no complaining," Stephen interrupted. "Kerry, it *is* doable. Kids can do this homeschooling thing." His voice grew more animated. "Parents can find a curriculum online. It'll work for a few days until Jamie's in school. In the meantime, he can do his online schoolwork at my office. We've a crew of interns who're young and enthusiastic, who could teach him coding, all sorts of interesting stuff."

"Great," I said. "Our son being educated by a bunch of kids. Jamie's school administrators will think you and I are the flakiest parents ever born."

"It's only temporary," Stephen said. "Jamie's disciplined, he won't slack, will you, son? If you do, it's off. And remember, you're coming to Vancouver just for the one term."

"Dad, I can't wait!"

I simply could *not* get my head around Stephen being a part of this mad, unorthodox plan... But to fight it? Mam's words came back to me. *Have an adventure, for the love of God!* Even if I couldn't have one, did that mean my son couldn't either?

I pulled myself together. "All right, Jamie," I said dully. Then realized acting all depressed and mammy-clingy was no way to help him start a new life. I forced some warmth into my voice. "It's on. Make your plans."

"Dad!" Jamie shouted. "Did you hear that? I'll be in Vancouver soon!"

"I can't wait to see you," said Stephen. He actually sounded a bit choked up. Why shouldn't he be? A father would miss his son, his only child… "But son, time for me to speak to your mam."

Jamie set down the phone, his face jubilant, and threw his arms round me with such force he nearly knocked me over. "Thanks, Mam!" He released me and ran toward the stairs. "I've got to pack my things!"

Well, as a mam I'd made my share of mistakes, but maybe this wouldn't be one of them. I'd made him happy. "Kerry." Startled, I'd nearly forgotten the phone in my hand. Or that Stephen was still on the line. "I appreciate this." He'd his businesslike tone back. Like I'd done a great job on a work project. "I can email Jamie's school too, if you like."

I wouldn't spoil his moment. "That's all right—I'll do it." I took a deep breath for courage. "So then…what's next?"

"As you know, I'll be flying into Dublin late December twenty-third."

I was afraid to hope that he'd still come to visit for Christmas. Now I could see he'd planned it for our son. "And Jamie will go back with you straight after Christmas," I said.

"I'll make a reservation for him as soon as we ring off. I…well, Jamie coming to live with me must seem very last minute, but—"

"It's all sorted then," I broke in. I couldn't wait to end this phone call. I'd a lot to work out. Like how my life would go without Jamie in it for the next few months. "I've got to go. Cheers—"

"You aren't going to ask about the farm?"

The Ballydara farm had completely slipped my mind. "What about it?" Trying to get my head around Jamie living abroad for several months, I couldn't care about much else.

"I've been going back and forth with the pair of solicitors I retained—I've one on our end and an American solicitor too, to sort out the farm ownership. The paperwork should be coming through within a few weeks. There will be more waiting, but it won't be much longer before the farm will be officially yours."

Yours jolted me. "You mean, 'ours,'" I said tonelessly. "I'll be lining up an estate agent, get it on the market so we can pay ourselves back for all the mon—"

"Sell it, keep it, do what you like," Stephen said, his voice cool. "It's up to you."

Was the new wedding ring he'd given me last month just a warm up for my *real* consolation gift? Trading my son for a farm? I didn't have it in me to keep talking. "Thanks," I said politely. "But I'll be selling it. To pay us back. And put this entire episode with Will behind us." And to find closure, but I couldn't tell Stephen that. "I'll keep in touch." I rang off, not knowing what to think.

I couldn't believe my husband could be that underhanded—to give me the country place I'd longed for, but well aware that with all of its narky associations, I could never take possession. On the other hand, surely it couldn't be that Stephen, knowing I'd always wanted a farm, had found a way to make sure I had one?

But I could hardly worry about all that, when I had to cope with losing Jamie. Not that I could blame him for wanting to be with the father who loved him like Stephen did. At the kitchen table, I cradled my head in my hands as an ache spread through me.

Finally I made myself rise. It would hurt less, I decided, if I could have another heart-to-heart with my husband. I grabbed a piece of paper and began to write.

44

Dear Stephen,

Before I move on to more important things, we need to get Will out of the way. For good.

Maybe you've already realized why I allowed myself to have a fancy for him—to make up for all the flirting and going out with boys I didn't do when I was a teenager. When we got married I was still a kid, a romantic eejit who'd had a baby too soon. And writing those emails after Will left Ireland were my way to have a little fantasy life.

I'd needed an outlet, what with my worries about Jamie when he was small. He's grown into such a fantastic kid, I often forget that he had a bit of rough going at the beginning. I'm sure you haven't forgotten the way he didn't start talking for the longest time. I'd fret, but you were the one to sit him down, your face close to his, and try to sound out words to him. He wouldn't have it though—I can laugh now, to think about how he'd put his hand over your mouth and nestle his head on your shoulder. Just wanting a cuddle.

My worries grew when he entered playschool. He seemed a bit...well, odd, compared to the other children. The teacher was concerned that he didn't interact much with anyone. We were so proud when he'd learned his ABCs twice as fast as the other kids, but he'd promptly lost interest in the pre-reading activities.

When I'd go to pick him up, I'd watch him from the doorway, such a quirky little boy, and feel my heart sink to my toes. One day, Jamie and I were at Mam's and we were watching him play. He was talking to himself, repeating the dialogue from a cartoon he'd seen on telly. I said to her low, "I hate to even think it, but I have to wonder, is Jamie all right in the head? Not mad or anything, but...some compulsive thing?"

"You know you've another option," Mam said briskly. "Besides wondering."

"Tracking down Jamie's biological father?" My stomach rolled over. "Tell him about Jamie, and ask if there's some dodgy brain thing that runs in his family?" I shuddered. "Just thinking of it puts me in the horrors."

"Well, they've lots of tests these days," Mam said. "Then you wouldn't have to speak to his father. What does Stephen say?"

I told her we hadn't really discussed it. I felt the strain of...I don't know, disappointing you, for bringing a son into your life that mightn't be all right. Mam said in a chiding voice, "What are you waiting for, love?"

That night I found the courage to sit you down and talk about it. "Should we get Jamie tested? You know, for..." I swallowed hard. "Autism?"

I'll never forget how you took me in your arms, so gently. "We could," you said, and you kissed the top of my head. "Or we could just accept him the way he is, not put a label on him. I mean, maybe he's on the autism spectrum, or maybe he isn't. But does it matter?"

I lifted my head to look up at you. "You researched autism, yourself? You were that concerned?"

You'd said that if I wanted, we could do the tests straightaway, get Jamie whatever therapies they recommended. Then you told me, "Whatever happens, we'll just love him and do whatever it takes to help him."

I'd pressed my face into your shoulder, more grateful than I could ever express. I know you'll recall what happened next. I couldn't go on, not knowing if Jamie might really need whatever therapies were available. So we took him in, got him tested, got the report. I can still hear exactly what the psychologist said: "Your son has a few behaviors that could be consistent with a diagnosis of an autism spectrum disorder." Of course my heart sank. Like a rock. Then she said something about Jamie being quite bright. Not in the gifted range, but very intelligent. And that when all was said and done, the tests had been inconclusive. She said we could do further testing, she'd a colleague who specialized in this inconclusive test range, but I met your eyes and knew what you were thinking. Suddenly the pair of us couldn't get out of there fast enough.

So we'll never really know, but does it matter? It seemed like as soon as I stopped worrying, Jamie began talking almost overnight. And pestered you to listen to him read all those books you got him. And I knew that no one—maybe not even I—loved him more than you did.

Love, Kerry

I stuffed this letter in my jewelry box, under the others. All weekend, I tried to enjoy Jamie's excitement at living in Vancouver, and putting up Christmas decorations with him on St. Nicholas Day. But Jamie and Stephen and the farm I'd soon own fled my mind when I walked into work Monday morning.

MEMO:

Monday, 9 am, 7 December
To: Kerry McCormack

We are delaying the office re-organization at this time. Due to the press of new projects, my attention will naturally be devoted to them. I won't be initiating the workspace process until the spring. Please note that you will be working in the file room until further notice.

Theodore Smythe, CEng

I stared at the page for a moment. But my decision was already made. I strode into Mr. Smythe's office without so much as a rap on the door, and slapped the piece of paper onto his desk. "Kerry," he began, his voice stern. "I'll not have—"

"I would have prepared a memo in response to yours," I said, suddenly feeling quite pleased that Mr. Smythe had forced my hand. "Especially as it seems appropriate to remind you that a proper office was meant to be ready for me before Christmas.

And if it wasn't, I'll further remind you that I indicated my future here would be up in the air."

His frown deepened. "I told you tha—"

"But who's got time to write memos?" I said cheerily. "My attention is going to be devoted to trying...some new things. So I've decided I'll be taking a sabbatical for several weeks."

"A sabba—" he sputtered. "You realize you're risking being sacked! And I can hardly provide a reference for an employee who exhibits such erratic, unprofessional beha—"

"That's a shame," I said airily. "I'll be in touch. Maybe after the holidays." I grinned. "*Whatever.*"

He opened his mouth, and his jaw just sort of hung there, as limp as wet laundry. I turned on my heel, and with a spring to my step, returned to the file room for my bag. I stopped at Sharon's desk, to apologize for doing a runner on such short notice. "I don't know how all the work will get done," I said, "but I just *had* to get out of here."

She looked envious for a moment, then grinned. "Fair play to you—if I could, I'd do the same. Now go on!" After quick goodbyes all round, I left the building, feeling lighter than air.

Once home, I knew I'd have to email Stephen, and confess that I'd blown off Smythe's—and that I couldn't be happier. (Unless he would come home and love me again.) But that could wait. I flew into my office nook to get a sheet of paper and a pen. There was one more thing Stephen needed to know.

Dear Stephen, I began, but I couldn't bring myself to write any more. Telling him what I'd kept inside since last August was far harder than I thought it would be.

45

A few days before Christmas, I was sitting on my old bed at Mam and Dad's, Ailish on my lap. I was reading *Little House in the Big Woods* to her while Suz helped Mam choose outfits for her Christmas trip. The sound of the programme Jamie was watching with Dad drifted up the stairs, and every so often I'd hear Suz say, "You'll look great in that," or "Sorry, Mam, no way. That top's ready for the rag pile."

In the last fortnight, now that I wasn't working, I'd spent as much time at Mam and Dad's as I could. Unfortunately, with all my free time, it was too easy to dwell on Jamie's departure. To take my mind off it, I'd often think about the Ballydara farm.

I resettled Ailish in my arms, and glanced at Stephen's jacket that I'd slung over the chair in the corner, covering my old baby doll. I was still puzzling over why he'd signed the farm over to me.

"What do you think he's about?" I asked Ailish, wiping the baby drool off my red wool jumper. She only grabbed my book. "I mean, not even your Uncle Stephen could be that generous, after I ruined everything between us."

As the doorbell rang downstairs, Ailish began chewing on a corner of the book.

I gently wrested it from her grasp. "Anyway, how I'm meant to face him in four days I've no cl—"

"Kerry, you've a visitor," Dad called from downstairs. "No—two visitors!"

I frowned at Ailish. "You don't think the Persistent McElligotts wouldn't have tracked me down here—"

"Mary, this won't do—" My father-in-law's voice.

I heard a flurry of steps on the stairs and Mary burst into the room, looking like the wrath of God. "I had to—oh."

She broke off as Ailish dropped the book and clutched my shirt. "Mary," I said calmly, as if she came barging into people's houses every day of her life. I curved a reassuring hand round Ailish's head. "How...lovely to—"

"Hallo, Mary." Suz appeared suddenly, obviously having sussed out what was happening. Or going to happen. "I'll just take the baby..." Before I could move she whisked Ailish from my arms and was gone, closing the door behind her.

Mary was breathing hard, her face red. "I heard from Stephen this morning—Jamie's leaving Ireland after Christmas, you've taken a leave from your job, and...and..." She took a big gulp of air. "And my son won't tell me what in the world the pair of you are about!"

I spread my hands in a helpless gesture. "Will you...sit down?"

"Who can sit? It was all I could do to ride in the car on the drive here!"

I sighed. Stephen had always been our go-between. And my rather freaky phone conversation with Mary weeks ago hadn't prepared me for dealing with her in a full-on strop. "I'm sure it seems like the world's gone mad, but Jamie and Stephen made this plan. As for my job, it's—"

"We'll leave your job out of it," said Mary, as if she hadn't been the one to bring it up. Despite her agitation, she pulled up the chair. Shoving Stephen's jacket onto the floor, she grabbed the doll and sat down.

Any other time, I'd have had a proper giggle at the sight of Mary clutching a baby doll. But now she looked ready to burst an artery.

"I told Stephen, this...this dodgy situation started with that blasted ring he bought you—"

"I'm sure that's not really the case," I said. "Our troubles actually started...em...when—"

Mary waved her hand. "Oh, I know my son can be rather...bull-headed. Which was why I didn't press him to take that silly yoke back where it came from." Mary looked at the ring on my finger, her hands tightening on the doll. "Or…why, years ago, when he fell for—" She broke off, her face flushing even redder. "I have to say it—that when he told us he was going to marry you, I said to myself, No! He mustn't do it, she's all wrong for him."

Ouch. I could hardly say, *Right, like I couldn't tell you didn't like me.* Trying to keep my voice neutral, I said, "Most mothers would react the same way, if their only son brought home a girl with a baby."

A relieved expression crossed her face. "I was tempted to go all out, try and put a stop to your engagement. But I held my tongue. I knew he was set on you. I was near sick with worry, though, about…" Her voice trailed away.

My stomach tightened. I'd have rather been chained to my desk at Smythe's for a week than face Mary getting personal. "The expense of a child?" I asked. "Since you knew I hadn't pursued child support?"

"Not exactly." She set the doll on the floor. "I was worried that Jamie's father was someone you'd see around Dublin—that you still…carried a torch for him."

That *was* personal. "No," I said faintly. "He'd left for London before Stephen came into my li—"

"Then I discovered that…you were a level-headed sort of girl."

I thought of the years I'd had my head in the clouds over Will. "Not…always," I admitted. "I'm a real expert, sometimes, at building castles in the air."

"Well, you had a good job. You were a good mother. And…you've been a good wife to our Stephen."

But I haven't… Feeling my way toward this new side of Stephen's mother, I was struck by tenderness for her, not wanting to disillusion her with the truth. *I've not been a proper wife at all, married to one man, thinking of another…* "He's been a good husband," I finally got out.

"If he has," Mary said, her voice strained, "Why…why did you send him away?"

Poor Mary. I sensed what this was costing her. "Shouldn't you...ask Stephen that?"

"What would he say? He's never had a word against you. So please tell me, why'd you break up your marriage to my boy?"

Her beseeching look tore at my heart. "I didn't mean to..."

"It's not too late," Mary said urgently. "When Stephen gets here for Christmas, will you...will you tell him you've changed your mind? Ask him to come home?"

*But your son left me...*Only I couldn't tell her that. I would sound like I was blaming Stephen, and then I'd have to admit how I'd ruined every chance we could ever be happy. I stared at my lap, unable to bear her vulnerable look any longer.

"I see." Hearing the chill in Mary's voice, I looked up to find her tight-lipped expression was back. "I've been presumptuous." She stood up. "Forget I mentioned it."

Mary had reached out to me—maybe more than she ever had to anyone, except her son. "Wait—don't go!" It was all I could do not to grab for her hand. "It...it wasn't presumptuous at all—you've a right to know what's happening with your only child."

Only child. That I'd likely have only one myself gripped me with sadness. "If it were Jamie we were talking about I'd feel the same. I wish..." I couldn't say, *I wish we'd had a houseful of siblings for him, I wish Stephen and I had tried again, I wish we'd just tried...*

"Only child," Mary repeated. She sat on the end of the bed, hard, as if her knees had given way, her head bowed. "I came to regret that Stephen was the only one."

Roused from my sense of loss, I stared at Mary. Confiding in me? "I thought perhaps you and Brian couldn't...have any more."

She clasped her hands. "I took...measures."

"Oh," was the best I could come up with. "Most women do."

"Brian wanted more babies, but all I could think of was the cost of them." She looked up at me then, and the grief in her face made it hard for me to meet her eyes.

"Children are expensive." Suddenly I'd do anything, say

anything to take that look from her eyes. "These days, lots of people are making that choice—"

"I grew up in a family of ten," she said. "You might think I'd had my fill of kids but that wasn't why."

Her face seemed to age before my eyes. "Then…"

"Dad was out of work more often than not. And my mam having a baby every year…well, there was never enough food on the table." She seemed to swallow hard. "There was hunger." Now she was the one to look away. "And the shame of it."

Oh, everyone was poor then, I'd said callously to Stephen years ago, when he'd said his mother's family was poor. *Mary, why did I never try to understand you?*

"Once, after Dad had just found a new job, it was my birthday. We could never afford to celebrate birthdays, but that year, Dad brought home a tin of shop biscuits for me. I thought it was the greatest present on the face of the earth. I knew I was meant to share them with my brothers and sisters, and I did. But here's the real shame—I begrudged every single biscuit I didn't get to eat."

And so Mary had given us the same present each visit—a gift that had meant the world to her. I had to clear my throat twice, before I could speak. "That's understandable, I'm sure—"

"I thought, if we only had one child, Stephen would never know what it was like to have an empty tummy. We could give him the best we could. I didn't realize the best would be a brother or sister. And now I'll wish I did things differently to my dying day."

I wanted to comfort her, but the chances of Mary accepting an embrace were…remote. Forcing the words out, I said, "I've done…something myself I'll always regret. You said I've been a good wife, but that's not true. It's my fault that Stephen left."

Before I lost my courage I told her the lot, about Will and the emails. I made myself look at her, as a kind of penance. And with each damning word I spoke I watched her mouth tighten, then tighten even more, until her lips had almost disappeared. I knew it was the end of the friendship we'd begun only moments before. "I hurt Stephen terribly," I finished bleakly. "I can't blame him if he never forgives me."

She didn't say anything for a long time. Finally she shifted on the bed. "You've been very foolish."

I nodded wearily, bracing myself. *Now you'll stand up, maybe box my ears for good measure, and slam out of the house.*

"But then," she said slowly, "You were very young. And perhaps Stephen's been an eejit too."

My mouth dropped open. "What…what do you mean?"

"My son has always tried to be perfect," said Mary.

"Oh…right," I said. "Stephen does like to do his best at everything." Slicing bread, creating emails, always surpassing his boss' expectations.

"No, I mean, *perfect*. When he was a boy, and he made a mistake on his schoolwork, instead of erasing the error he'd rip the paper in pieces and start over."

"Oh, Mary." I felt tender, picturing an intent look on Stephen's young face.

"I wouldn't stop him. I'd say, 'try it again, until you get it right.' I was proud, you see, that he wanted to get top marks. So I always told him, 'you can always do better.' I came to wonder if I'd made a mistake, though—if he'd began to set his standards too high."

"I don't know," I said, to lighten the atmosphere. "Stephen took me on, after all."

Mary only shook her head. "Brian tried to get him interested in cabinetry. The first time Stephen pounded a nail in wrong, he gave it up entirely. And when he got older," Mary went on, "when he didn't go out with girls much, I got a bit worried. 'He's not a nancy boy, is he?' I asked his dad. I don't know if Brian spoke to him, but one day I heard Stephen tell his father, 'I'm just waiting for the perfect girl.'"

"The perfect girl," I repeated. I felt sick, knowing how badly I'd let my husband down. "I'm hardly that."

"What woman is? If you ask me," said Mary in a crisp voice, "He was doomed to disappointment. So you turned out not to be perfect. My guess is, he didn't know what to do."

Mary and Brian didn't stay long after that. I'm sure it had something to do with my mother-in-law feeling uneasy, after being so...vulnerable with me. But Mam, after telling them about the upcoming trip to see my brother Liam, was able to coax them to stay for a cup of tea. As Jamie and Suz munched on some crisps—Dad looking longingly at them but resolutely not taking one—Mam passed filled cups to my in-laws. "With Stephen home over Christmas, you'll join our crew? Suz will be putting on Christmas dinner."

"That'd be grand, just grand," said Brian. "We'll want to see as much of this young man as we can before he leaves." He reached out and tousled Jamie's hair.

Mary was silent. She seemed far away. "Jamie," she said after a pause, "Will you show me that fancy little computer thingummy your dad gave you? I'm thinking I might get one of those myself."

Jamie nearly choked on a crisp. Clearing his throat, he said, "No kidding, Granny? A tablet? I could teach you all sorts of things."

"Right," said Mary. "I thought, why not take a chance? Have a bit of an adventure."

I stared at Mary as she nearly...dare I say it? *Beamed*. Struck by an impulse, I said, "Jamie, I just had a thought..." My voice drifted away as I looked through the front window. It was pouring rain. Dusk was coming on. It would be altogether daft to do what I'd in mind.

"Mam?" Jamie prompted.

Okay, why not be a nutter, take a chance? "Son, since you're on break, how would you like to go back to Wicklow with your granny and granddad? For a day or two? Plenty of time to show your granny what she needs to know."

"Yeah...okay." Jamie crammed one last crisp into his mouth, then looked at his grandmother. "I mean, if it's all right with you."

"Oh—sorry!" Feeling a flush crawl up my neck, I glanced at Mary and Brian. "I should have asked you first."

For a moment, Mary looked taken aback. Then suddenly, she broke out in a smile, such as I'd never seen on her. "Go on then, Jamie, get your things! Do you think your granddad and I would pass up a chance to have you?"

Jamie jumped up and ran up the stairs. Mam, Dad and Suz said their goodbyes, then moments later, Jamie met Mary, Brian and me at the front door. His carryall looked flabby—if he'd packed more than a clean pair of underpants I'd have been surprised—but he actually seemed excited about going.

I kissed him quickly. "I'll be down to Wicklow to fetch you before your dad arrives, okay?"

"Or we can bring Jamie to Dublin when we come for Christmas," said Brian. Opening the front door, he leaned in to give me a peck on the cheek. As he and Jamie went down the footpath, Mary took a tiny step toward me, an oddly expectant look on her face.

Was she actually waiting for me to kiss her? I hesitated, then took a chance and embraced her, brushing her cheek with my lips. For a moment, she clasped my forearm, then nearly dove through the door headfirst.

Utterly bemused, I watched their little car pull away from the curb. I'd lost a son—temporarily—but apparently, had gained a new ally.

Then I ran up the stairs. "Mam, might I borrow a nightie?" I called to her. "I'm leaving for the weekend. Right now."

County Galway

46

I awakened at midday, in the bed Maddie Power had slept in.

Turning onto my back, I stared at the ceiling with bleary eyes. Last night, I'd wound my way up the dark road above Ballydara village, turned in the now-familiar drive and put my little Ford into park. With the windscreen wipers still swish-swashing away, I peered at the farmhouse, barely visible through the wet glass.

Alone in the middle of the night, I had to wonder what had possessed me to take off from Dublin on the spur of the moment. And motor across Ireland in the driving rain, sustained only by a cheese sandwich and my own determination.

What was even more ill-advised, every time I switched on the radio to help myself stay alert, I'd hear some broadcaster say something about the West being in for a bit of weather. I'd promptly turned the radio back off—if the region was in for a gale, or just a massive downpour, it couldn't rain much harder than it already was.

Last month, when I'd first seen the Power farmhouse, it had been lit up by autumn sunshine, and all I'd felt was incandescent joy. After this brutal drive, I'd found the farm all but invisible in the storm. Having passed exhaustion while I was still in the Midlands, I was almost drunk with fatigue. *I had to come,* I told myself the last few kilometers. *I need closure.* But at the same time I was asking myself, *had I gone completely round the bend?*

After staggering into the house, I knew I couldn't fall asleep in the room Stephen and I had shared. Even as tired as I was. And I certainly wouldn't go near Jennifer and Will's. So after I'd let myself in with the key under the mat, I'd gone upstairs, straight to the girls' bedroom. Pulling off my jeans and jumper, I climbed into Maddie's bed. It still smelled of baby shampoo and sweaty kid. I buried my face in her pillow, too tired to think about how my life had fallen apart in this house only weeks ago.

Now, with late morning light slanting across the bed, I felt a thrum of something inside me, a small spurt of vigor. I would have two days to tidy up this house, and line up an estate agent. Then I'd leave for Dublin late afternoon on the twenty-third. When I saw Stephen Christmas Eve, I could tell him it wouldn't be long and we could pay back all that money he'd loaned to Will. I'd no idea how we'd split our savings and other finances, but that could be organized later. However misguided Stephen had been, I could understand why he'd made the loans. And even if he no longer...loved me, I had to make things right.

A burst of energy made me throw the covers aside. The weather folk, happily, hadn't known what they were talking about. Almost skipping to the window, I pulled the curtain aside, blinking at the sun breaking through the clouds. I looked down into the wet, weed-choked back garden. I'll want an industrial-sized tiller to get those weeds out, I caught myself thinking. The apple trees would need the pruning of their lives too. And the chicken coop? One wall had collapsed—it would require total redo!

Then I quickly remembered. *Wait just one minute—you're only going to fix up the place. Get it ready to sell. And put this entire episode—Will, those loopy emails, your shattered marriage, the whole caboodle of mistakes and memories—behind you.*

I turned away, and pulled on my clothes from yesterday. I'd left all my things in the car last night—not that most of what I'd brought would be terribly useful. After splashing water on my face and drying it with a mildewy-smelling towel, I resolved to buy new linens before the estate agent started showing the house. Padding downstairs, I got as far as the bottom step and sat down, gazing around me.

I was determined to have changed my mind about Will's

farm—to have gone off it entirely. I was ready to look at the dusty furniture and worn kitchen with distaste, smell the mustiness all over the house, and think, Jaysus, get me out of here! Same for the neglected outdoors, full of rusty tools and bits of farm equipment. And how could I possibly want that moldering old barn—even if I'd once found it so charming—that was probably swarming with every rodent under the sun?

And I *wanted* to see Will everywhere I turned, to be reminded of what a fool I'd been. Like...like aversion therapy, so I wouldn't want to stick around here any longer than I had to.

Only I...didn't.

I didn't see Will at all. I looked through a front-facing window, at the swing hanging from the big oak. Instead of seeing the eejit moonlit flirt-at-thon I'd had with her father, I imagined Maddie belly-surfing on it in the pale winter sunshine, shouting, *I'm flying*!

And there was Jamie too, in my mind's eye, practicing football on the grass. As I looked away from the window, into the front room, I pictured Stephen, his face relaxed as he'd played tea party with the little girls. I sat on the worn step feeling a stream of joy running through me like a river, wishing my arms were big enough to hug the entire place.

Enough of this romanticizing, I told myself, smiling. So much to do...where to begin? The enormous Christmas tree was still standing in the corner, ornaments dangling from its dried yellow foliage, a circle of needles beneath it littering the old carpet. Whether Jennifer had been too overwhelmed to take the tree down before they left or had thought, *I'll just leave it—serve those grasping McCormacks right*! I preferred to believe the former.

I immediately started a mental list. #1: Haul out Christmas tree. Then ideas for the home makeover started flying at me: new furnishings, flooring and fixtures, kitchen units and appliances. Suddenly overwhelmed, I said aloud, "Enough! You haven't even had breakfast yet!"

I went into the kitchen, trying *not* to envision the remodel the farmhouse would surely need. Opening the fridge, I discovered

Jennifer hadn't packed out the food from our holiday. There was butter, eggs and cheese, and some apples left over from the pie I'd made. The freezer was full of the bread and frozen vegetables Jennifer had bought, as well as the leftover ham. As I rustled up a meal, I'd a sudden urge to cook properly again, and bake the puddings I'd always loved. Turning a knob on the old, unreliable cooker, I thought, wouldn't an Aga be great? Now that would really give the place the farmhouse vibe I wanted...

"Stop!" I said, trying to laugh. An Aga wouldn't be for *me*. The buyer would get it.

With sprucing up the house in mind, after eating I took the ornaments off the massive tree and hauled it outside. I had to admit the house looked rather bleak, inside and out. I could spruce up the place before I rang up any estate agents and invited them to come round. I would fetch a fresh tree, string up a few lights, give the place a bit of holiday spirit.

I shrugged on Stephen's coat. Stepping outside, I shivered and looked at the sky. The sky had clouded over again, tiny needles of ice stinging my face. A frigid wind cut through the jacket. I pulled up the hood, then trod to the barn. Finding the saw Stephen and Will had used just inside the doors, I headed through the pasture, down the slope to the grove of firs.

It was easy enough to find the stump of the big tree they'd cut. I stared at it, remembering how Will had returned alone, telling us Stephen was traipsing round the countryside trying to zero in on a stray mobile signal—only reinforcing my conclusion that my husband had no interest in me. Or our holiday. Although Stephen had redeemed himself a bit, shaping the tree so it could fit in the house, everything had gone downhill from there.

Deciding I'd dwelled long enough on that miserable holiday, I looked round for a right-sized candidate. There were only a few dozen firs to choose from, and as I'd feared, almost all of them were too big for me to manage. The rest were little more than a meter high. The one just next to the stump was hardly that, but seemed to be the bushiest of the lot. I knelt down next to the little tree, tamped down the grass surrounding it, and brushed the dried fir needles away from the base of the trunk.

In the dead needles, a piece of metal gleamed. I reached for it, and picked up a circlet of gold. A man's wedding band.

Oh, Stephen.

When I'd seen his bare ring finger at the hire car place last month, I just *knew* what he was about—he'd removed his wedding band as his way of telling he was done and we were over.

I clutched the wet ring in my fist. Years ago, he'd never worn his wedding band to the construction job. He'd told me his dad always said was safer not to wear a ring when you're using sharp tools. That day that he and Will had cut the tree, and he'd been away from the farmhouse until dark, maybe he hadn't been thinking about his job—hadn't been trying to sneak in another phone call to the boss. Had Stephen slipped his ring into his pocket to cut the tree, then lost it?

And spent the afternoon in the rain and the cold, searching for his wedding ring?

47

It wasn't the first time I'd thought the worst of Stephen, then realized I'd been terribly wrong. The memory was painful—yet I knew, as I knelt on the wet grass in the middle of the firs, I could no longer put off facing it.

One night last August, six weeks after Mam's surgery, Stephen and I had just climbed into bed. He turned to me, gently brushing stray curls off my cheek. "What do you think?" He trailed his hand down my side to curve it round my hip. "Are you feeling any better these days?"

Not thinking, I jerked away. "I...can't. Not yet."

He yanked his hand back as if he'd gotten a burn. "Right. Not tonight."

Again, I could just hear him thinking. "You know I've been worried sick about Mam," I said defensively. "I can't think about lovemaking."

"I do know," he said stiffly. "But you don't even want to be touched." He rolled onto his side away from me and thumped his pillow.

"Oh, don't be like that." He didn't answer. "I know her recovery is going well, but still..."

"I won't trouble you again," was all he said.

I was too tired to reply. And too tired to tell him I'd hardly felt like myself the last few weeks. I was exhausted and eating too much, lots of chips and cookies. The stress had even given me spots, which I hadn't had since I was the age of fifteen.

Stephen had already left for work by the time I awakened. And as I lay in bed, trying to force myself out of it, my body felt heavier and stranger than ever. At work all day, I'd moved like I was wearing concrete blocks on my feet. PMS, I told myself.

That night, he and I had been getting ready for bed, stiff and formal with each other. Maybe even more than we would've been otherwise, since Jamie was at Con's house, and it was clear we weren't going to take advantage of having the house to ourselves. Alone in our ensuite bathroom, I was cleaning my teeth, and glanced at Stephen through the open door. He sat silently on our bed. "You're free to have a go," I said through a mouthful of foam, and gestured to the second sink.

"I'll wait until you're done," he said.

Okay, have it your way. Be alone, keep yourself to yourself. I closed the door to give my teeth a second once over, hoping I'd be able to resist going back downstairs to polish off the packet of biscuits I'd started after tea. Suddenly, I felt a hot, sharp pain in my abdomen. Gasping, I spit out the foam. Banging down the seat of the loo, I collapsed on it as the stabbing pains grew worse.

"Stephen," I could only whisper, my head swimming. When I felt a dampness spreading between my thighs, I mustered up every bit of strength I had to scream, "Stephen!"

The only way I could stop from sobbing, from shrieking in pain and the knowledge of what was happening to me—to us— was to shut myself down. From that moment of that dreadful night, I pretended I was somewhere else.

I pretended too, that I didn't see the blood. All the hours at hospital, I did what they told me, but I let Stephen answer all the questions. Because of *course* I wasn't really there.

All through the exams, the pokes and prodding, the tests and scans, I imagined myself at Aunt Rose's farm. I imagined she was holding me though the final horrible procedure. And I imagined the sweet scent of the roses on her front stoop during the long wait afterward, before they allowed me to go home.

Through it all, Stephen had only spoken when necessary.

Once we arrived home, he helped me upstairs and into bed, his face impassive. After fetching me hot tea and tissues, he spoke the first words to me in hours. "If you don't need anything else," he said, as polite as the night-duty nurse, "I'll leave you now." He turned away.

It was at that moment I woke up. Woke up and saw his expression, so stiff and cold. I began to cry as a wave of grief and fury struck me. "I do need something, Stephen!" I sobbed, grabbing a wad of tissues to mop my eyes. "I need you to say something—anything, for God's sake! Tell me you wanted the baby! Tell me you feel sad—that you feel anything!"

His expression was so frozen it could have been a block of ice. Suddenly, his face contorted. "I did—I am—" Then an odd sound, a low moan like I'd never heard from anyone tore from his throat. He bolted from the room and seconds later, the slam of a door made the entire house shake. Stephen had left me. Left me to bear this pain by myself.

Now, in the fir grove, I shivered at the memory. And at the secret I'd kept from him...

The icy mist turning to flurries was a welcome distraction. I lifted my face, feeling the tiny wet stings against my cheek. Relieved to think about, to *feel* something else, I opened my fist to look at Stephen's ring again, then slipped it into my pocket. I shifted my knees and began sawing the small trunk. Hearing a snort, I looked up to see a skinny brown cow with a hardly-there udder standing in the road, watching me.

"Are you the one Stephen almost ran down last month?" I asked her. "You should get out of the road. Go away home."

She switched her tail.

"I get it," I told her. "You want to watch me make a fool of myself—putting up a Christmas tree when I'll be leaving soon. But it'll make the house look cozier." She only blinked. "You see, I'm having to sell the place. To sort of redeem myself."

She began walking away. "You don't have to go," I called to her. "I'm sure I must seem like a right nutter, but there's no one else to talk to..." My voice trailed away as she trotted down the road. She was soon out of earshot.

"I *am* mad," I said aloud as it began snowing properly. "Talking to a cow." I sawed through the last of the small trunk, then dragged the tree back to the house. Even before I took off my coat, I placed Stephen's ring in the saucer next to my fancy one. Somehow, leaving his ring there didn't feel right—like I was discarding it. What else could I do? I rummaged in the jumble drawer of Will's granddad, and found a shoelace. Stringing it through the ring, I tied the shoelace round my neck.

Feeling the gold against my skin, I felt my spirits rise a bit. I'd see Stephen two days from now. Maybe, at least for Jamie's sake, we could make peace with what had happened between us.

I set up the tree, strung the lights and set on the ornaments. Plugging in the lights, I stepped back. Now the house looked cheery, and with a bit more cleaning, it would be fit for a viewing.

I really should drive down to the village, find a phone and ring up an agent. Instead, I found myself going to the kitchen and pulling out flour, sugar and butter. It was lonesome here, with no phone. It would've been great to have a quick chat with Mam before she and Dad left. Or confirm Christmas plans with Jamie and my in-laws. Still, an apple cake would lift my spirits, and I could bring it with me to Dublin tomorrow. Standing at the window stirring the batter, I watched the snowflakes hit the glass. In another, happier universe, Stephen and Jamie could have joined me here for Christmas. Wouldn't we have enjoyed the village, looking so festive with a dusting of snow...

As the snow began blanketing the farm, I went to bed. Of *course* it would turn to rain by morning, I thought sleepily. Like most snow did in Ireland.

48

$\mathcal{I}$ awakened with a jolt, to my mobile alarm buzzing.

I'd set the alarm for nine, but the room was so dim I must have set the time wrong. The cold in the room made it hard to even contemplate getting out of bed, but finally I tossed the covers aside and shut off the alarm. As I noticed the odd light, shivering, I peered out the window.

Last night's fat snowflakes had turned into a wall of blinding white. Like the heavens were dumping buckets of snow. The wind rattled the window casements. I checked my mobile to discover that it really was nine in the morning, yet the sky was a strange amber-gray, like twilight, the clouds so low they seemed to be hovering near ground level. Feeling a stab of anxiety about my trip later today, I thought, *If only I'd driven Stephen's Toyota here!* But surely conditions couldn't be like this everywhere, even if getting into Galway City would be dicey.

My trip here the night before last started looking even more ill-advised by the minute. If I'd been thinking straight when we left the farm last month, when it appeared we'd be the new owners, I'd have gotten phone service in here. Without it, I was completely cut off from the outside world. And because I'd procrastinated about going down to the village yesterday, to ring an agent, no one in Ballydara knew I was here. The drifts were too high for me to venture out on foot, to make it even one kilometer down the road to the Whelan farm.

I stared outside again at the waterfall of white. As the wind gusted, the snow swirled in little cyclones. How would I even get to Galway City in this?

"Come on," I said into the silence. "Don't catastrophize! The snow could turn to slush anytime…" I hurried downstairs to put the kettle on, and remembered the ancient, dusty radio in the front room.

I went to turn the switch, and was rewarded by a buzz. At least the article worked! I fiddled with the knobs, and finally tuned in a voice, barely audible above the static.

"…The entire West of Ireland is starting to…down," a female newscaster said, with more relish than I thought appropriate. "It's looking like the blizzard of the century!" I could barely make out some scratchy details on several smashups on the N6 between Galway City and Athlone. "If you haven't stocked your house with holiday food or…" more static "…Christmas shopping, officials say, it's too late now—"

As the kettle boiled, I turned off her cheery voice and returned to the kitchen. "The weather people are reporting on the worst situations," I said into the quiet. "Folk love that stuff." Pouring hot water into a cup, I kept speaking aloud, although a melodramatic voice inside my head was saying, *But getting to Dublin is your only chance! To make anything right with Stephen!* "I'll sit tight for today. Tomorrow, the roads should be hugely better, and I'll leave first thing."

I was starting to get why people who lived alone talked to themselves.

I spent the afternoon cleaning the house, to take my mind off being stranded. Would Stephen even worry about me, here alone? Probably no more than he'd feel pity for anyone who was snowed in on their own. In fact, it was probably all the same to him whether he saw me at Christmas or not.

By lunchtime, I'd abandoned all hope of getting to Dublin. I had to be realistic. Which was *so* not my strong suit.

Didn't I specialize in pretending? Wishful thinking? Wishing the snow would go away? Wishing Stephen and I had a chance of repairing our marriage? Maybe these last difficult months had gotten my head so far in the clouds I didn't know what I was about.

Once again, I'd romanticized a situation. I'd come here, thinking I could find closure. Instead, I was missing out on Jamie's last few days in Ireland. And what if I didn't get to Dublin before he and Stephen had to leave for Canada? I would not only be missing saying goodbye to Jamie, but lose any chance for Stephen and me to sort out our lives from here on out.

I was too blue to eat the tinned soup I'd heated. I put the kettle back on, plugged in the lights on my wee tree, and hunkered on the couch with a blanket and Aunt Rose's little coverlet that I'd brought from Mam's house. I couldn't help thinking of Christmases past. How Stephen, Jamie and I used to cuddle in front of the Christmas tree...Jamie's wide-eyed anticipation of Santa on his way. And after we'd tucked him up, Stephen would enfold me in his arms, and tease me that I believed in Santa even more than Jamie did. "But there's a holiness in believing," I'd told him once. "After all, isn't the story of the Christ Child magical?" Stephen would only chuckle and hug me closer.

Missing my husband and the closeness we'd had, I couldn't wait any longer to tell Stephen what I'd kept from him. I struggled out of my little nest of covers, fetched the yellowed tablet from the kitchen drawer and a pen from my bag. Settling back on the couch, I began to write.

When I was finished, I set down the pen and folded the sheet of paper neatly. And on the eve of Christmas Eve, I spent the dark hours jagged up on tea and what-could-have-beens, wishing for a Christmas miracle that would let me see my husband and son tomorrow. And knowing that was the most magical thinking of all.

49

Christmas Eve

$\mathcal{I}$ stared at the winter fairyland outside my windows, setting the pan of shortbread I'd just made on the table. The snow had finally stopped, the clouds breaking up, pure whiteness glittering in the sunbreaks. After feeling terribly sorry for myself for the last twenty-four hours, though, I'd finally had my fill of self-pity. Along with a case of cabin fever.

"For the love of God," I said aloud, "go outside and make yourself useful!"

I shrugged Stephen's coat over my red wool cardigan, trying to nerve myself up to face the cold. I couldn't help thinking of the family. Of Stephen and Jamie. By now, they would probably be at Suz's for Christmas Eve, maybe helping her get ready for the big dinner tomorrow. Now that it was mid-afternoon, she was likely setting out appetizers. Jamie would be digging in, Stephen watching our son fondly. But then his cool voice when we'd last talked on the phone came back to me—like he didn't care what I did.

I rubbed my forehead, feeling spacey with too much caffeine and too little sleep. Assuring myself that everything would work itself out had been yet one more of my little fairy stories.

It was time I made a clean break. Weeks ago, over the ruined holiday with Will, Stephen had accused me of never being truly invested in our marriage. That I'd never been all in. And I saw it now—I couldn't sort myself until I let go of Stephen and any hopes for our marriage. For a short while, I could just stop worrying myself sick about it.

And maybe, one of these days, it might be a nice change to get angry with him for leaving me.

Desperate for some fresh air, I stumbled to the mud room and donned the wellies Jamie had left indoors last month. Spying a moth-eaten woolen scarf hanging from a hook on the wall, I wrapped it round my neck, and lumbered out to the barn. It was exhausting to wade even that short distance.

Opening the barn doors to let in the light, I looked round at all the farm detritus that would need to be cleared out for selling. The amount of rusty tools, metal scraps, cardboard and old petrol cans seemed overwhelming, but I set to, sifting through old straw to create a pile of throw-aways in the middle of the barn, and a second pile of possible keepers. As I worked, I dimly remembered Aunt Rose saying to me when I was small, "My Seamus always said the worst day in the country—as long as you've your family round you—is still better than the best day in town."

I swallowed the lump in my throat. Aunt Rose had been onto something, but then, she'd been my uncle's *anam cara*—his soul friend. At that thought, I felt sorrier for myself than ever.

The light was waning by the time I took a break. Warmed by the activity, I discarded my scarf, and was unzipping Stephen's coat when I heard a faint rumbling. I put a hand on my middle. My gnawing stomach, maybe? My sleep-deprived imagination? The rumbling grew louder, turning into a *chug-a-chug* punctuated by coughs—an old car? I went outside, craning my neck to peer down the hill, toward the village. You'd have to be completely cracked to drive in these conditions.

I swiped at my streaming nose, and saw the source of the rumble: a tractor slowly coming up the road. An old one, ancient, even, by the looks of it. The machine looked familiar...the Whelan's, perhaps? But who would be operating it? Perched upright, the driver maneuvered confidently through the drifts like he'd been driving tractors all his life.

The rust-spotted tractor turned into the drive. I could see the driver now. Hatless, he wasn't in the usual work gear you'd expect from a farmer. I stood rooted to the spot, unable to move. Was I dreaming? The man was wearing a posh overcoat. Like a city bloke would wear...

Before reaching the oak tree, the driver pulled the machine to a stop. With a huge, clanking sputter, the chugging ceased. Swinging off the seat, the man gazed round the place, then I saw him spot me. He began wading through the snow toward me, slipping and sliding, his dark trousers and coat covered with snow. I couldn't seem to move as a rush of joy and confusion and trepidation swirled through me.

He stopped a short distance away. "I guess it's like riding a bike," said Stephen with a tired smile. "Driving a tractor—you never forget how."

I gazed at his face. He looked exhausted, circles under his eyes, his face drooping in fatigue. "How...w-what are you...?" Stephen. Driving a tractor. To see me on Christmas Eve.

"I thought I'd give a country holiday another go." Was Stephen making a *joke*?

I swiped at my runny nose again. I must've looked positively desperate—dirty coat and Wellies, no make-up. But then, Stephen looked nothing like his usual polished self. His face was pinched with cold, his nose was bright red and his hair stood on end.

It came to me, the effort Stephen must have made to get here. "How on earth...?"

"How I got here?" His smile was crooked. "The roads were fairly open until I hit the Midlands, but traffic was at a crawl on the motorway to Galway City. West of there, the N59 was impassable. I waved down a bloke from a motorway crew and caught a ride into Ballydara. I made it part way up the road on foot, then I found the Whelan's at home."

"The Whelan's," I repeated. Stephen had walked nearly two kilometers in this deep snow? "And you borrowed their tractor?"

"Mr. Whelan seemed delighted to let me give it a go. I was

surprised when the engine started up—the tractor looked like it would have given up the ghost long ago—but here I am."

"Your trip—it must've taken…hours." Feeling the chill again, I zipped my coat back up.

"I left around dawn." He rubbed his forehead. "This morning. I think."

I stared fixedly at him. Stephen had come straight off a transcontinental, then transatlantic red-eye flight? Then had set out on what had to be the most bizarre journey of his life. And true to form, he was giving no hint of why he'd come. "I…I can't quite take in, your being here."

"I can't either," said Stephen, "but…you'll invite me in?" He shifted his feet and slipped again. "I've turned into a block of ice."

Realizing how long we'd been standing in knee-high snow, I led him to the back door into the mud room. It was awkward, the pair of us trying to take off our outdoor gear in the small space. Stamping his feet on the mat, he brushed the snow from his trousers, then he looked at me curiously. "Is that my old coat you're wearing?"

I nodded self-consciously. My jeans were on the grimy side from working in the barn but they were all I had. "Go on into the kitchen and get warm."

After I brushed off the worst of the dirt, I joined Stephen. He still looked chilled to the bone.

"Where's Jamie?" I asked as he filled the kettle.

"I left him with my parents at our house." Stephen pulled in the kettle. "They'll all three be at Suz's tomorrow. If I got stranded, I didn't want Jamie's Christmas spoiled too."

"So," I said, "you're here." The sting of his rejection last month—and the humiliation of begging him to listen to me, of all my apologies that he'd thrown in my face—was sharp and fresh. Suddenly, my temper flared. "Why'd you come all this way, anyway?"

"It's…Christmas," he said. "It wouldn't have been right, to have you alone here."

It felt good to be angry. Like a relief, and I yanked the kettle lead from the socket. Tea could wait. "Yet you've taken a job abroad. You must really want to get away from me. And given that Jamie will be living in Vancouver with you, I'll be alone plenty. So—what are you really doing here?"

Stephen took a deep breath, his gaze steady on mine. "Did you hear the one about the Irishman who loved his wife so much he almost told her?" I blinked. "Well, I'm telling you now."

50

My legs began to shake. Not wanting to blubber in front of him after all he'd put me through, I rushed out of the kitchen, to my sad little tree. Plugging in the lights with a shaking hand, I saw darkness was falling, the last of the light coloring the snow grey-blue.

I heard Stephen's footsteps behind me. "You say you...you love me," I said without turning around. "I can't remember the last time you told me—why now?"

A long silence. "Last weekend, Jamie rang me."

"He talks to you every weekend, doesn't he?" I said. "But I can't believe he'd say, 'By the way, Dad, will you tell Mam you love her?'"

"No," said Stephen. "There's another reason. Or reasons."

Turning to face him, I felt another flash of anger. "If you've come here because he asked you to, then you can go back to where you came from."

"He only told me you and his Granny McCormack had talked up in your room. All afternoon."

I didn't know what to say to that.

"Then," Stephen went on, "Jamie sent me an email the next day."

"He emails you all the time," I pointed out, determined not to make this easy for him.

"He hadn't written the email, though." He took a step closer, his face vulnerable. "It was very short, one line. Not Jamie's usual. It said, 'This is from your mother. Here's what I have to say. Nobody's perfect.'"

Shocked, I couldn't speak. So that was why she'd asked

Jamie to show her his tablet. "You've come then, on your mother's behalf? Now that's romantic."

He crossed his arms over his wool sweater, tucking his hands in his armpits. "I did a lot of thinking on my way here."

"Sometimes I think you do nothing but think," I said, unwilling to back down.

"Well..." Stephen hesitated. "I realized that trying to be perfect has done nothing but make trouble for me. Starting with...Will."

"I thought you never wanted to speak of him again," I said. "Or let me. Why do you get to change the rules?"

He didn't speak for a moment. "Because I've been wrong. You'll...hear me out?" When I nodded, he said, "All the years I knew Will, I felt in his shadow." His voice was halting. "Only there was one way I could top him, and that was with my career. So last month, when I found the emails, I told myself all the success in the world didn't matter if your wife fancied someone else."

"I told you I don't—"

"I thought I was in the right. Dead right, and the way a man deals with a straying wife is to leave—"

"How many times do I have to tell you! I would *never* have had an affair with—" I stopped, clenching my fists. "Listen— I'm done pleading. I won't lie to you, I did have some feelings for Will when I was younger. He made me feel pretty and fun, not a tired mammy with a dead-end job. But for God's sake, it was years ago!"

"I...I realize that. But I still felt like I'd every right to go over-the-top self-righteous," Stephen said doggedly. "Isn't that bloody despicable? Reading those emails, I actually saw a bright spot—I could be the perfect one in this relationship."

Mary really *had* been on to something. Stephen and perfection. "Maybe you were."

"But I didn't know how to...to reach out to you. To talk to you anymore." He tightened his arms across his chest. "After I got to Vancouver, I got a taste of life without you. It wasn't the life I wanted."

"So you travel across the country in the worst weather in decades, to tell me it's not all my fault we separated, give me this grand speech like you rehearsed it—"

"I did rehearse it. Like I've always done for my work presentations, so it could be perf—"

"If you blather on about trying to be perfect one more second I'll give you a clout!" Fury and hurt were like a lump in my chest. "That awful letter you wrote me—well, as cold, as *horrible* as it was, at least you were finally sharing your feelings." I clutched my jumper over my chest, feeling his ring through the wool. "You hadn't the decency to tell me to my face, so we could hash it out together."

"Decency had nothing to do with it," said Stephen. "I hadn't had the courage to confront you. So there was nothing for me but to leave."

"All right, so you're here now, and you make your little speech. Fair play to you. But I don't know if we can get past...past all the ways we've hurt each other."

Stephen uncrossed his arms, reaching for me, but I stepped back. As the silence stretched out, I refused to soften what I'd just said. If he wanted to get right back to his safe little life, keeping himself to himself, well, let him.

"With all the pain between us," Stephen said, "I didn't know if I really could face you. It was like I needed...proof. If you were wearing your new ring, that would mean you loved me. If you'd left it behind at our house, then I'd know for sure I'd killed your feelings for me. So before I left Dublin I checked your jewelry box. That's when I found...everything I needed to know."

I colored. The three letters I'd written him. That I thought he'd never see.

"For a moment I couldn't bring myself to touch the paper—we both know the Pandora's box I'd unleashed when I read the emails to Will. But I couldn't help myself. I unfolded the letters, my hands shaking and fair sick to my stomach, wondering what I'd find."

His voice caught. "And it was all there—everything I'd

always felt for you, would always feel for you, you felt too. I'm not too proud to say my eyesight was so blurred I could hardly walk downstairs. Within seconds, I was in the car, heading for the motorway to see you. And not caring if you'd decided since writing the letters that you'd changed your mind. That you'd no use for me anymore."

I felt the hard lumps of my anger melting. "I...I wrote you something else." I stepped toward the end table, to retrieve the paper I'd left there, but before I could give it to Stephen, he reached for me.

"Please," he said low. He brushed my hair from my cheek, then trailed his hand down my neck. "What's this?" He touched the shoelace I wore, following it round the curve of my neck, stopping at my collarbone.

His expression, as vulnerable as it was the night we'd first made love, made it easy for me to pull on the shoelace with my free hand, to show him his lost ring. "We seem to..." I laughed shakily, "have a *lot* of misunderstandings with wedding rings."

He stared at the ring in wonderment. "The day we were out getting the tree, I'd put my ring into my pocket to crawl under the big yoke, to get the best cut. The ring must have worked itself out somehow—I thought it was gone forever."

So I'd been right. "You could have told me," I tipped my head to meet his eyes. "Jamie and I would've helped you look for it."

He set the ring against my heart, on the jumper. "And let Will have the laugh at me? What sort of husband loses his wedding ring?"

"The imperfect sort," I said tenderly. Stephen reached out his arms and slid them around me slowly, carefully as if I were made of glass, and buried his face against my neck. I dropped my letter to return his embrace, the familiar contours of his body feeling like I'd come *home*. I kissed his hair, then leaned back just enough to see his face. "Why did you get me this farm? Really?"

His face was serious. "Last month, when we drove up here to the farmhouse, I saw your face glowing—a look I hadn't seen in a long time. I thought it was the prospect of reuniting with—"

"Stephen, don't." I touched his cheek. "Not now."

"It's all right," he said. "You see, afterward, I realized it was the farm that had put the light in your eyes. That's what you'd come for—what you really wanted. So I…I never lost hope."

I put my finger against his mouth. "Life's not perfect. Marriages aren't perfect. And I'm not either."

"And I'll stop trying to be," said Stephen. "I don't know what the next few months will bring. There's the Vancouver position—I've made promises, signed a contract. Will you at least come back with me? Have a holiday, relax a bit. For a fortnight or so?" He flushed. "No…pressure."

I'm sure my husband, in his usual Stephen-like way, was delicately referring to how we'd have to get used to being together again, before leaping into bed. "Stephen," I said, my voice quaking with nerves, "Before we decide anything, I'll have you read this." I broke our embrace to pick up the letter. "There's something we've never…talked about."

A sheen came to his eyes and he nodded. He pulled me to the squishy couch, and as we sank onto the cushions, he unfolded the letter….

Epilogue

Dear Stephen,

That terrible night last August still haunts me. You see, losing the baby wasn't the worst of it.

After we got home from hospital and you helped me to bed, your face completely expressionless, I can hardly bear to remember how I shouted at you. Even if the painkillers had made me not quite myself. I wanted to mourn our loss together but you were shutting me out. Then, as you began to...I don't know, lose control, you left me sobbing there. You slammed out of the house!

I was altogether shattered, until I remembered something. The only other time you'd been overcome by emotion. I climbed out of bed, and staggered down the stairs. Creeping to the door to the garage, I opened it carefully, looking into your car. And there you were.

You had your head in your hands, your face covered. But through the car I could hear you. Weeping. Your muffled, unearthly groans tore at me in ways the miscarriage had not. Thirteen years we'd been married, and you'd never wept in front of me. Somehow, my sadness paled next to the grief I saw in you, and I guessed that these were the first tears you'd shed in your adult life.

I ached to go to you, for us to go back to bed and for you to let me hold you, let your tears wet my nightgown, but I hadn't the nerve. Watching you cry seemed like the rudest intrusion, after all the times you'd kept your feelings to yourself. And it came to me that you'd wanted a baby in ways I never had, to the depths of your soul.

Certain that you wouldn't want me to see you like this, I closed the door and crept back upstairs. As I lay down the sounds of your weeping rang in my ears—the last sound I heard before I fell asleep.

When you never spoke of the miscarriage again, or reached for me in bed, I felt some part of us, of our marriage, died with the baby. But I've come to see that in endings there are beginnings.

In one of my eejit emails I wrote something that was such rubbish it still makes me shudder—that if I was to have another baby I'd need to hook up with a soulmate first. After the miscarriage, I began to realize how overjoyed I would have been to have your child, and how deliriously happy we would have made each other. Which tells me who my real soulmate has always been.

Stephen, you've got to know that you've been the one thing in my life I've never romanticized, and it's worked out the best.

Love, Kerry

As he read, he took my hand, his own shaking. A long moment later, Stephen cleared his throat twice and set the letter aside. "Hands down, it's the most perfect letter I've ever received," he said, and kissed the top of my head. "And I can say that, after getting three very brilliant letters lately."

I leaned against his shoulder and gazed at my—our—little Christmas tree, joy filling me. As soon as the road was passable, we'd want to get back to Jamie. Stephen and I could drive the tractor down to Ballydara, perched on it like a pair of madzers and the village folk would be sure to say, "Sure those McCormacks are a pair of odd ducks."

Wherever Stephen and I ended up, whether it was a Vancouver flat or the Dublin house, he and I had a lot to sort out between us. To talk about all we'd nearly lost...and grieve over what we *had* lost. To put our marriage back together when the future—and our son's future—was up in the air.

But one thing we had plenty of...was hope.

– The End –

Dear Reader,

Thanks so much for your interest in The Hopeful Romantic. Kerry and Stephen's story really isn't over! Please watch for the sequel to The Hopeful Romantic in late 2015 or early 2016.

I'm always grateful for insights and comments from readers about my characters, storylines and books! If you are so inclined, I would deeply appreciate your sharing your thoughts, good or bad, in a review of this book. In any event, I'm grateful for your support, and would love to hear from you at www.susancolleenbrowne.com or www.littlefarminthefoothills.blogspot.com.

Best regards,

Susan Colleen Browne

Acknowledgments

I'm grateful to the first readers of *The Hopeful Romantic*, Lish Jamtaas, Lori Nelson-Clonts, Becky Burns and Pam Beason, for their friendship, critical eyes, and insightful suggestions. Many thanks as well to Patricia Davis, for her meticulous editing and proofreading job. Big kudos to the Formatting Fairies for the absolutely wonderful cover.

Boundless hugs go to my wonderful family for their support and inspiration—you make my writing life possible! Finally, I dedicate this book to my husband John—and to him goes my deepest appreciation for his ideas, wordsmithing talents, and artistic eye, and especially, his love and encouragement.

About the Author

Susan Colleen Browne is the creator of the Village of Ballydara series, Irish romantic women's fiction set in the Irish countryside, as well as the Morgan Carey adventure series for tweens. She's also the author of a memoir, *Little Farm in the Foothills: A Boomer Couple's Search for the Slow Life*, a Washington State Library "Summer Reads" book selection. Susan is a community college creative writing instructor and lives with her husband John in the foothills of the Pacific Northwest, USA.

When Susan isn't in the garden, she's working on her next Village of Ballydara book or Morgan Carey story!

You can contact Susan at www.susancolleenbrowne.com. You'll also find recipes, book excerpts and tales from Berryridge Farm at www.littlefarminthefoothills.blogspot.com

Books by Susan Colleen Browne

The Village of Ballydara Series

It Only Takes Once
A Village of Ballydara Novel, Book 1 (print and ebook)

Mother Love
A Village of Ballydara Novel, Book 2 (print and ebook)

The Hopeful Romantic
A Village of Ballydara Novel Book 3 (print and ebook)

The Secret Well
short story ebook

A Christmas Visitor
short story ebook and the sequel to *The Secret Well*

The Morgan Carey Series for Kids

Morgan Carey and The Curse of the Corpse Bride
Book 1, a lighthearted Halloween story for middle-grade readers
(print and ebook)

Morgan Carey and The Mystery of the Christmas Fairies
Book 2, a fantasy adventure for middle-grade readers
(print and ebook)

The Secret Astoria Scavenger Hunt
Book 3, a haunted house adventure for tweens (print and ebook)

Memoir

*Little Farm in the Foothills: A Boomer Couple's Search for the
Slow Life*
(print and ebook)

www.ingramcontent.com/pod-product-compliance
Lightning Source LLC
Chambersburg PA
CBHW030031180626
46810CB00001B/308